THE BELVEDERE AC

THE BELVEDERE ACCORDS

Dale Jenkins

HEADLINE

First Published in 1994
by HEADLINE BOOK PUBLISHING

10 9 8 7 6 5 4 3 2 1

British Library Cataloguing in Publication Data

Jenkins, Dale
Belvedere Accords
I. Title
823 [F]

ISBN 0 7472 0986 3

Typeset by Avon Dataset Ltd., Bidford-on-Avon

Printed and bound in Great Britain by
Mackays of Chatham PLC, Chatham, Kent

HEADLINE BOOK PUBLISHING
A division of Hodder Headline PLC
338 Euston Road
London NW1 3BH

For my parents

THE BELVEDERE ACCORDS

1

Ciccio Buonolini walked into his bank and knew at once that something had happened. Normally the clerks never paid him much attention; he was only a bookshop assistant, after all. But now everyone who recognised him gave him a nod of acknowledgement and their faces expressed respect, deference and burning curiosity. Signor Rossini, the branch manager, came out personally to beam and usher him into his office.

'A bank transfer has been made in your favour,' he said. 'Taxes pre-paid.'

'Are you sure? How much?'

'Quite a lot of money,' replied the manager, pushing the telex across his desk towards him.

Ciccio gaped. He could hardly believe his eyes but there it was in black and white – 384,508,800 lire from a Palermo branch of the Banco di Sicilia, and made payable to him personally. The equivalent of just over three hundred thousand dollars!

'I don't understand. I . . . I think there must be some kind of mistake,' he stammered, immediately wondering why he didn't just shut up about it, withdraw the money and make a quick getaway before anybody realised their mistake.

'No mistake, Signor Buonolini. As you see here it's confirmed. The money has been transferred irrevocably. If an error of some kind has been made, there is nothing they can do about it now. The Banco di Sicilia is bound, in honour and in law, not to claim the money back.'

Ciccio stared at him. 'But who could have sent it?'

'I could try and find out, if you wish.'

'Would you, please?'

'Happy to oblige.' The manager picked up the phone and rang his opposite number at the Banco di Sicilia, who promised to make inquiries and ring him back. A few minutes later he was informed that the order had come from their main Rome branch and thither from somewhere else. But the ultimate remitter wished to remain anonymous. Rome could divulge this information only under a court order and, since the Italian currency laws had not been infringed, no court would issue one. It was all perfectly legal and the donor's anonymity had to be respected. But, of course, if Signor Buonolini wasn't happy about it, he was perfectly at liberty to return the money.

Ciccio walked out of the bank in a daze. So dumbfounded was he that he hadn't even remembered to draw out any cash, which was why he'd gone there in the first place. After wandering, mystified, around the streets for a while, he eventually pulled himself together and walked into a car salesroom.

A few days later, after Ciccio had tired of driving around the streets of Palermo in his Lamborghini, trying to look like somebody important, he decided it was time to go and show off his newly acquired wealth to his home town of Enna. His family lived on a small farm just outside it.

He arrived expecting his mother Margherita to be wide-eyed with astonishment, but to his surprise she merely nodded her head in tired resignation and said, 'I knew you'd do something foolish with the money.'

'How did you know I'd got it?'

'The whole family did. Your brother, both your sisters, plus Aunt Claudia and Carlo and all *their* children, too.'

Ciccio blinked at her.

'Park that stupid thing out of sight,' she told him. 'If people find out we've now got money, every scrounger in the province will be around here on the cadge.' She turned and went indoors again. Ciccio hurriedly put the car away and rushed into the kitchen after her. While she pottered around, preparing the evening meal, he fired a barrage of questions. But, beyond giving him a summary of what had been said at the family gathering two evenings previously, she wasn't able to tell him anything new. Eventually tiring of his interrogation, she sent him out to feed the chickens.

Ciccio approached the coop along the side of the barn, so the birds couldn't see him coming. Keeping himself hidden, he threw handfuls of feed high into the air so that it came raining down on the abruptly hysterical creatures as if cast by the hand of God. Or by the claw of the god of chickens, anyway. After figuring out that what they were being pelted with was food, they stopped panicking and settled down to a furious pecking competition.

Ciccio sat down on a log to watch them, suddenly seeing the analogy. What he'd just done to the chickens some other, invisible hand had done to the Buonolinis.

Sixteen people – and three hundred thousand dollars each! It was like a fairy tale. Their family had always been relatively poor: smallholders who had been landless peasants only a few generations before.

According to his mother, the sixteen recipients had two things in

2

common: they were over twenty-one years of age, and they were all *direct* descendants of Giancarlo Buonolini, Ciccio's great-grandfather, who had died thirty years before. Thus Ciccio's mother, widowed early by the death of her husband Giuseppe through cancer, was not herself a beneficiary, because her connection to the Buonolini family was by marriage not blood. Occupation didn't seem to matter either; the sixteen held a wide variety of jobs. One of them was even a priest. And there was no upper age limit, as Great-Aunt Claudia was eighty-two.

The big mystery was how Giancarlo should be the cause of their good fortune. There hadn't been anything special about him. He had been a bit of a roughneck in his youth, so the stories said, but when he inherited the smallholding from a distant cousin he'd settled down and worked it as best he knew how. He had managed to get along with most people – which was important in a town of less than thirty thousand – but he'd apparently been neither more nor less popular than any other resident.

Giancarlo had fathered six children, four boys and two girls, but three of them hadn't lived to marrying age. In order of seniority the survivors had been Great-Aunt Claudia, Giacomo and Benito, who was Ciccio's grandfather. Claudia would probably not live for very much longer, but Giacomo had died the year before and Grandfather Benito just eight months later. Since the donations had come only four months after Benito's death, Ciccio's elder brother Luigi had wondered whether there might be some connection with him. But it was a bit difficult to see how: the only thing of any value he had possessed in his life was the smallholding which – after Claudia's marriage to a grocer's son, and upon great-grandfather Giancarlo's death – had become Benito's and Giacomo's joint property. Giacomo had taken a job as the caretaker of a house near Corleone for the last twenty years of his life, so it was left to Benito to run the farm. Having not only his own children and grandchildren to help him but also Giacomo's, he'd done so pretty competently. But otherwise he'd been an ordinary man.

Ciccio pursed his lips and frowned. The invisible hand had scattered the equivalent of four million eight hundred thousand dollars on a family of smallholders distinguished only by their lack of distinction. What on earth could be behind it?

One of the chickens was eying him suspiciously, perhaps wondering if he was responsible for the recent peculiar weather. Edible hail. What will they think of next?

Ciccio stood up and went back to the house.

That night at dinner their windfall inevitably dominated the conversation. By this time Ciccio had evolved a theory which at once found a supporter in his brother Luigi: that Giancarlo had once performed some service for somebody very rich, who now wanted to repay the favour.

'And he waited thirty years to do it?' protested his mother incredulously.

'Perhaps he's only just got rich,' replied Ciccio.

'Or perhaps he's dying, and wants to get in God's good books before he goes,' suggested Luigi.

'But why do it anonymously?' she wanted to know.

'So that people won't know who he is.'

'Thank you, Luigi,' replied his mother ironically. 'I *know* what anonymous means.'

Maria, the younger sister, intoned, 'It is easier for a camel to pass through the eye of a needle than for a rich man to enter the kingdom of heaven. Maybe he's just decided to slim down a bit before he dies.'

'A crash diet, if that's the case,' grunted Luigi.

'You're all talking rubbish,' said their mother, Margherita. 'But that's nothing new. If anybody wanted to buy his way into heaven, he'd give his money to the Church, not to us.'

'Then where do *you* think it's come from?'

'I don't know, Luigi, and I never said I did. But I can tell you all one thing for sure: there's nothing good behind this. It smells to high heaven.'

'What do you suggest we do? Give the money back?'

Margherita looked slightly uncomfortable. 'No,' she said. 'Now we have it, we may as well keep it. After all, *we* haven't done anything wrong. But you mark my words: there's something bad involved in all this. Because nobody gives away six billion lire to the likes of us. But now we've got it, we don't want people coming round here on the scrounge. The best thing is keep quiet about it. And our bank manager here,' she added looking reproachfully at Ciccio, 'was sensible enough not to tell his clerks.'

Two days later Ciccio returned to Palermo and switched banks.

He also changed apartments.

Despite the family's acceptance of Margherita Buonolini's wise counsel, their newly acquired wealth couldn't be hidden unless it wasn't spent at all, and since occasional purchases were too tempting to avoid, their improved circumstances were soon plain to all. But the Buonolinis knew how to keep a secret, and the story that eventually got around was that they'd had a big win on the National Lottery.

Theirs was not a prize to be squandered, however. They husbanded their wealth, founding modest and moderately successful little businesses, or investing in land to expand the farm, and as the years went by they inched their way up the economic scale.

4

But not Ciccio. He was a born loser.

True, he had a number of positive qualities. He was fairly intelligent, certainly imaginative, and over the years he'd read a great deal – his tastes being eclectic, although tending towards the mysterious and arcane. But, on the negative side, he was basically lazy, unrealistic and a spendthrift. His biggest weakness, however, was that he never really got to understand how people operated on the inside, so his judgement was consistently poor.

His first business venture was glamorous. Of course. It comprised a small film company but, aside from managing to bed a few would-be starlets, the only thing he got out of it was a headache. In just six months he lost two-thirds of his fortune, and was forced to sell the Lamborghini. Then he tried a series of less ambitious projects, some of which even managed to make a bit of money for a while. But, time and time again, some crucial operation depended on his accurate assessment of a situation or a personality, and his invariably fallible judgement then wrecked it.

Gradually Ciccio's bank account dwindled, though all the while he tried to give his friends the impression of being a playboy with millions stashed away. One had to maintain one's image, he told himself: otherwise it would be much harder getting girls into bed. By lashing out on dinners and drinks and presents, however, his money had dwindled even faster.

So, eight years after the mysterious donation, Ciccio found himself down to less than five hundred dollars in his bank account, and with no assets worth mentioning. He also had a couple of sizable debts to people whose patience was starting to wear thin.

Before the windfall he'd been young, and his good looks and a certain charm had gained him entry to social circles without too much scrutiny. But that was when he had first moved to Palermo nine years ago, when he had been an unknown quantity there and the page was still fresh. Now it was scribbled all over, and people were not overly impressed. Ciccio had no job, no qualifications beyond his secondary-school education, and he was twenty-nine years old. Whenever he thought of how much money he'd blown, he broke into a cold sweat.

The alarm went off; it was nine o'clock. Ciccio had to let it ring itself out, because otherwise his landlady would know he was in and she would come looking for the rent money owing from the week before. The shrill sound jangled his nerves, and even when it finally died he was left with a feeling that some awful Cassandra had just spoken to him of doom. The inexorability of time is more keenly sensed by those who have wasted too much of it.

Ciccio reached for a cigarette and lay back against the pillows, wondering again what he could do to save himself.

5

He realised now that it was the windfall itself which had ruined him. It had led him into fatally expensive habits, and away from the people of his own kind. He'd turned his back on them – not obviously perhaps, but they'd noticed it. And Sicilians never forgot slights like that.

For the ten-thousandth time he wondered about that windfall, the strangeness of it and where it might have come from. At the beginning the whole family had assumed that sooner or later there would be *some* kind of follow-up – an explanation, or a request for some corresponding favour, or, at worst a demand for the return of the money because the whole thing had been a mistake after all. Even as much as six months afterwards, they were still half-expecting someone to turn up and demand the quid pro quo. It seemed simply impossible to be given so much money for nothing. But as the months became years, they had been forced to accept it as an absolute gift with no strings attached. No further reference, no explanation. It was theirs. End of story.

And now Ciccio's share was gone.

Five hundred dollars, he brooded. All that was left out of three hundred thousand. And he owed six hundred. Plus the rent for this month, he reminded himself, getting out of bed and switching on the coffee-maker. He stared out of the window at Palermo harbour, at the sea and the blue sky beyond. In that moment it came home to him that on the following morning he would be looking out on a very different view. He had to go home. There was nowhere else to go. If he signed on for welfare benefit here, he'd become the laughing stock of the whole city.

An hour later he'd packed his bags and was ready to leave. He waited until his landlady had gone out shopping, then sneaked down the stairs to his little second-hand Ford Fiesta. He'd told everybody that he needed it to carry dirty canvases around, his latest project being art dealing. That sounded glamorous, but in fact he hadn't sold a picture in two months.

He stopped by the bank to empty his account; keeping up pretences to the last, he explained to the teller that he was moving to Rome. He climbed back into his car and edged out into the dogfights. For a short while he followed standard *Palermitano* driving habits: ignoring traffic signals, aggressively nosing into the available spaces, frequently blaring his horn to tell people to get out of the way, even when they obviously couldn't. It was the Sicilian system to cope with chaos by adding to it. But after a while it occurred to him that he wasn't in any hurry – not today. So he let patience take over from the horn, and resigned himself to the crawling pace of the traffic.

Three-quarters of an hour later he at last reached the Viale della Regione, the dual carriageway which skirted the bulk of Palermo,

6

and was soon driving out of the city. He wondered when he'd see it again.

Normally, on his rare visits home, he would take the A19 Autostrada which followed the coast as far as Buonfornello, and then ran inland directly to Enna. It made a total of a hundred and twenty kilometres of fast driving. The trip never took much more than an hour, so his usual departure time was late afternoon, allowing him to reach his mother's house in time for an *aperitivo* before they had dinner.

But today was different. He had set out unusually early so as to be gone before his landlady returned, but he certainly was not looking forward to admitting his colossal failure to his mother. He had been forced to tell her about *some* of his mistakes, otherwise she would have expected him to make a regular contribution to the running of the family home, as his siblings did, but he'd always let her believe he was still keeping himself afloat. Now he was going to have to confess that his finances had fallen through the floor. He was going to have to grovel in front of his whole family, and they'd be laughing at him for the rest of his life.

No, he was definitely in no hurry to reach Enna – when his purgatory would begin. But he could at least postpone that unpleasant moment, because he now had most of the day to get there. So at Villabate he left the autostrada, turning south and taking the route into the mountains – the *old* road to Enna.

Away from the breezes of the sea, the landscape looked and felt hot, but the pollution of Palermo had also been left behind, so the air shimmered cleanly. Ciccio had previously never much cared for the Sicilian interior: it had always seemed primitive to him. But now, as he drove slowly through the rugged scenery, he felt as if he was going into hiding, being swallowed up by the natural fastnesses all around him. In a way it felt like being forgiven. He was going home. There they would punish him because they loved him. In the big city they had punished him because they loved it.

He passed Misilmeri, and shortly afterwards a church he had completely forgotten about. It made him realise that he hadn't come this way since they had built the autostrada. He was approaching Bolognetta when he began to think about lunch. On the road to Enna there would be dozens of transport cafés. The idea of eating with a bunch of lorry drivers didn't appeal to him very much. He felt that, since he was now facing a fate which he morally equated with execution, then surely the condemned man was entitled to something a little more stylish. But where? As far as he could remember, he had never been to a good restaurant anywhere along this route.

He was searching his memory when a signpost indicating the turn-off for the town of Corleone came into view, and he suddenly remembered that many years previously, in his mid-teens, he and his family had stopped for coffee at a restaurant there. His father had come out of the place irritated by the prices, Ciccio recalled. Going to Corleone would mean making a detour, but he had the whole afternoon ahead of him. So he took the turn-off.

The little town had been made internationally famous by the *Godfather* films, which to a Sicilian was something of a joke because almost all of the sequences portraying the town had been shot in places close to Taormina, near Etna on the east coast: Forza d'Agrò, Savoca and Franca Villa. The shooting which went on in Corleone was of a different kind. It was a violent highspot in a generally violent land, and one of the consequences had been a Corleonese takeover of the leadership of the Sicilian Mafia from the Palermitano families.

But Ciccio wasn't dissuaded by this fact. To a Sicilian the Mafia was just another government, and entering an area in which its presence was stronger than elsewhere made as little impression on him as would going into a pub in Westminster to an Englishman. The violence of Cosa Nostra was usually part of the perpetual struggles for power, and seldom directed at outsiders.

The road twisted along the southern side of a steep gorge through which ran the river Eleutero, and the traffic was light. Soon he came to the town of Marimeo with its dramatic sugarloaf rock, surmounted by a cross – a reminder of yet another omnipresent government in Sicily: the Church.

The valley widened now, rolling green fields finding room among the spreading hills, while the abrupt mountains containing it retreated. Here and there tractors worked the noonday heat in lazy solitude. It was a peaceful scene, typical of the land, and hard for foreigners to reconcile with Sicily's famous violence.

Soon a roadsign tersely announced *Corleone,* and Ciccio found himself in a street lined with modern blocks of flats, four or five storeys tall. He didn't know very much about the place except the population was about eleven or twelve thousand. It had no heavy industry, but there were several food-processing plants.

Independently of the *Godfather* movies, Ciccio always associated Corleone with the Yanks because his father Giuseppe, then eleven years old, had happened to be here with Grandfather Benito in July 1943 when a unit of Patton's Seventh Army arrived to liberate the town. His father had often recalled that event, the last time being the night of Ciccio's nineteenth birthday, when Giuseppe was already popping pills by the hour to keep the pain of his cancer at bay. A month later he was dead.

Ciccio misguessed the road and came into a large piazza in the centre of the town, where the newer buildings gave way to the old. The focal point seemed to be a little filling station in front of a bar. There a cluster of old men chatted quietly among themselves, lazily observing the passing cars, while nearby a gang of teenagers demonstrated their prowess in kickboxing. But these groups were beginning to break up as people went home for the midday meal.

Corleone was built on the side of a low mountain, cleft by precipitous ravines. The main road ran up its side to a tunnel excavated through the top of it. Ciccio found the restaurant a few hundred yards before that. The Leon D'Oro was set back from the road and enjoyed a spectacular view over the whole plain, hazy in the noonday heat. He parked his car and got out to look at the menu prices. They were not excessive and he reminded himself he had five hundred dollars in his wallet, so he went in.

The building was relatively modern and several tables were already occupied with local businessmen engaged in relaxed conversation. Most of them glanced at him, but with little curiosity. He was shown to a free table and, after a careful perusal of the menu, he decided on *tagliatelle alla cardinale*, followed by *pesce al cartoccio*. A chilled bottle of white Regaleale was brought, and the waiter withdrew.

Ciccio lit a cigarette, then sat back to gaze out over the valley. This was his favourite moment of any meal. Olives and bread to take the edge off the hunger, the anticipation of the food itself, the luxury of being waited on, and a glass of wine and a cigarette. Blowing out a satisfied plume of smoke, he pushed the forthcoming encounter with his mother from his mind.

Discreetly he observed the other patrons, and noticed one man being treated with particular deference by his three luncheon companions. In a town like Corleone this suggested he was a member of Cosa Nostra, but that was by no means conclusive. Identifying the Friends was no easy task. Giovanni Falcone – the judge assassinated in May 1992 – had estimated Cosa Nostra membership for the whole island as slightly over five thousand. That was out of Sicily's total population of five million, so, even discounting women and children, and other unsuitable candidates, the ratio was still only one in a hundred.

It had not always been so. There had been a time when *mafiosi* could allow their behaviour and demeanour to say what their code forbade their tongues to express. But that age was long gone. The state had been forced by public opinion to declare open war on the organisation – the effect being simply to drive it underground.

Ciccio tried to remember the day when he had first visited this restaurant. They had been invited to lunch by Great-Uncle Giacomo, who lived nearby, and the family had set out from Enna very early that day. Once they had reached Corleone, his father realised they had time in hand before they were due at the old man's, so they had stopped here for refreshment.

Memory was a funny thing, Ciccio reflected. Since that day,

9

fourteen or fifteen years before, he hadn't returned to Corleone or given this restaurant another thought, yet somehow his brain had stored the information for future use. Now other memories of that day came back to him: like his trying to make friends with a scruffy little stray dog which looked as if it had been kicked more days than not throughout its life. It had orbited him for a while, intrigued by his attention and dying for love, then thought better of it and had finally beaten a sad retreat.

Afterwards they'd driven down into the valley, and along an interminable country lane to the solitary house where Giacomo was caretaker. A table had been set up out front, Sicilian-fashion, and young Ciccio had been most impressed with his surroundings. It was as if they had been the visiting relatives of the house's owner, rather than just those of the caretaker. He began to wonder who the real owners were. Perhaps they would need another caretaker, and what better reference could he offer than having a granduncle who had worked there for twenty years?

But he doubted he could even manage to *find* the place again. He'd only seen it that once, and it had taken ages to get there, as he remembered. A really long, slow drive along a dusty road. He gazed expansively over the wide valley. Giacomo's house was down there somewhere – but then so were dozens of others. It would be pointless trying to describe it to the locals, because he couldn't remember it very clearly himself.

On the other hand, he thought, I did find my way up *here*. My subconscious mind knows how to get there, even if my conscious one doesn't. It would be an interesting experiment. And it was only lunchtime. He had the whole afternoon ahead of him before he'd have to face his mother – and the music.

It was a challenge, and he'd take it up.

When Ciccio later left the restaurant, the streets were deserted. Everyone else was indoors sleeping. He climbed back into his car and restarted the engine. He felt certain his father had not taken the main road, but had headed down through the town. From the glove compartment he took a map and consulted it. In the area to the west of Corleone lay a maze of minor roads, though these were connected to the town itself by only two routes.

'Let's go and have a look then,' he murmured, putting the car into gear. He drove slowly down through steeply-angled streets, lonely in the beating siesta sunshine, till he came to the divide. He stared at the signs with a frown, but there was nothing to indicate which way they had gone all those years ago. Giving a shrug, he chose the left fork; there was a fifty per cent chance this was the right one. But he hadn't gone far before the odds became a hundred per cent, for he

had come to a rocky outcrop of distinctive shape and was certain he
had seen this before. Shortly afterwards he passed a country house
whose driveway was lined with cypress trees. Giacomo's house had a
similar arrangement, though this wasn't it, because it was too near
the town.

Soon he came to another fork, and again went left, but nothing
else looked familiar. After a mile he stopped, turned around, and
went back to the fork. This was the first of several wrong turnings,
but each time he patiently retraced his route. Then he came to a
reservoir, crossed at its shallow end by a bridge, and this too he had
seen before. Immediately beyond was a wood of eucalyptus trees,
which struck a chord also. He remembered now that they had driven
through woodland, and the road had been very bad, so he was
interested to come to a narrow, dusty lane leading off from the road
and into the wood itself. He braked sharply and stopped to look
along it. The lane veered into a bend just fifty yards away, so all he
could see ahead was the trees.

Was it or wasn't it?

Unsure, he turned into the lane with some reluctance. Just past
the bend it narrowed even further, and two homemade signposts
advised 'No Through Road' and 'Beware! Poor Road Surface'. How
considerate, he thought. The lane had now become badly potholed,
and at times the overhanging branches seemed to form a tunnel. As
the track emerged from the wood, he noticed a clump of trees enclosed
by a long, high wall still half a mile away. Amongst them ran the tops
of two parallel lines of cypress trees marking a driveway down to the
gate. The lane passed in front of the gate, and continued to a cluster
of farm buildings a short way beyond. The estate was surrounded by
vineyards extending in all directions.

He had found Giacomo's house but, bumping along at ten miles
an hour, the drive towards it seemed interminable, without actually
bringing it any closer. Ciccio's parents had been invited there two or
three times a year, he remembered, but Giacomo's own children had
made the trip much more frequently, Uncle Carlo had said. Talk
about filial devotion, thought Ciccio. Jesus! He must have had to
bring a spare axle with him!

At last Ciccio reached the wall. It stood twelve feet high –
considerably more than it had seemed when he'd first emerged from
the woods. The gates were shut but not locked. Only a part of the
house could be seen from there, because the cypresses hid most of it.
He parked the car on the grass verge, and stepped through the gate.
It had a thick coil spring so it would close automatically behind him.
As he walked up the drive he saw someone come to a ground-floor
window and look out. He wondered whether his opening of the gate
had triggered an alarm inside the house. The front door opened as

he reached it, and a woman in her early sixties looked at him inquiringly, and not without a certain wariness. It took him a moment to realise she was someone he knew from Enna. She, too, was frowning as she searched her memory, and then suddenly her face lit up and she exclaimed, 'You're Giuseppe Buonolini's boy!'

He smiled pleasantly, but she could see he hadn't put a name to her face, so she introduced herself. 'I'm Angelina Lupillo. I went to school with your father. But come in, come in! You must let me get you something.' She led him into the house, calling out to her husband, 'Adriano! We have a visitor!'

She opened the door to the sitting room and revealed Adriano standing by the fireplace. Ciccio had seen the man around Enna once or twice, but he'd never known his name.

'Now, who do you think this is?' announced Angelina gaily. It took him only a second to identify Ciccio as Benito's grandson and he too came forward with a friendly smile to shake hands.

Angelina asked what she could fetch him to drink. He decided on coffee and she went out to make a fresh pot. Meanwhile Adriano waved him into an armchair and offered him a glass of local brandy to accompany the coffee.

He was a stocky, thickset man in his early sixties, with heavy jowls but humorous, if somewhat suspicious, dark brown eyes. Angelina was probably five years his junior. She'd obviously been pretty as a young girl and was still wearing her years with some grace, refusing to dye her hair or lard her face with make-up. The couple's clothes were sensible and testified to a frugal use of meagre resources.

While his host busied himself at the drinks cabinet, Ciccio glanced around. There was a modern television set with a VCR attached, but both were low-price makes. All the furniture was cheap-looking and dull, the ugliest item being a badly-proportioned and scruffy old grandfather clock which looked far too heavy to be lifted by a single man, but which was screwed to the floor in case anyone tried. It didn't even seem to work. Ciccio tried to imagine a burglar's reaction on casing *this* joint and decided he'd feel sorry for him.

Several newspapers were strewn across the coffee table, national and Sicilian, and even a copy of the local Enna weekly. There was also a bookcase, but it was full of tatty paperbacks – apart from a set of Russian classics, elaborately bound in gilt-tooled imitation leather, of the type usually offered at knock-down prices in colour supplements, bought as Christmas gifts and then never read, taking on a solely decorative function. These ones, however, did look as if someone had finally got around to reading them. Still, in a lonely place like this there wouldn't be much else to do, he thought.

'So what brings you so far off the beaten track?' asked Adriano handing him the brandy.

'No particular reason. I was on my way home and thought I'd take a look at this place again. I came here once before, you see, when I was about fifteen.'

'Bit of a detour, I'd have thought,' Adriano replied, frowning slightly.

'It is, really. But I stopped off for lunch in Corleone and remembered this house. We came here to visit my Granduncle Giacomo. He used to be the caretaker here, you see. Did you know him?'

'By sight.' He offered Ciccio a small cigar, then lit it for him. 'It's still a long way out of your way,' he repeated, sitting down opposite.

Ciccio gave him a wry grin. The man was obviously no fool. *Nobody* would undergo the purgatorial drive to get here without a good reason.

'The truth is I need a job. And it occurred to me that maybe this place might need another caretaker, and since Giacomo was my great-uncle . . .' He let the sentence hang.

Adriano nodded in understanding. 'I see. But I thought your family was rich now. I'm sure someone told me you'd won the Lottery.'

Ciccio smiled ruefully. 'I'm afraid I haven't managed my share of it very successfully. In fact I've had a lot of bad luck.' Suddenly he felt embarrassed about revealing all this to a complete stranger and decided to change the subject. 'If I'd known how long it was going to take me, I don't think I'd have come at all. The road out here is really bad.'

'Yes, I know. I've been trying to get the owners to do something about it for years, but they say it would cost too much.'

'Who are they?'

'A family called Tognazzi. They live somewhere on the mainland. I've never met any of them. Everything's done through a lawyer in Messina.'

'How did you get the job, if you don't mind me asking?'

'Same way as Giacomo, I suppose. I answered an ad in a newspaper.'

'He was here for twenty years, so I should think he must have liked it. How long have you been here?'

'Nine years now.'

'I don't suppose you're thinking of retiring,' said Ciccio with a sly grin.

Adriano laughed. 'No, I'm afraid not.'

Angelina returned, carrying the coffee. 'So what's been happening in Enna?' she wanted to know.

But there wasn't a lot he could tell her because he hadn't been home for six months, so they asked him all about Palermo. Having only the men who worked the estate to talk to, they were obviously news-starved and a bit lonely. In turn, he asked them politely about their lives, their families, their grapes, their little library of video tapes.

13

Angelina was a great film buff, it turned out. Adriano's tastes were more to current affairs, sport, and documentaries on animal wildlife. They were a pleasant, if somewhat boring, pair of souls, but he was still in no hurry to go home so in the end his visit lasted more than two hours.

Eventually, however, he began to feel restless and he was looking for a graceful way of terminating the conversation, when a loud bell suddenly rang. Ciccio glanced out of the window and saw that someone carrying a box had just opened the gate.

'It's one of the estate workers bringing us a few supplies,' explained Angelina, and she went out to attend to him.

Ciccio decided to take this as his cue and stood up. 'I must be going, I'm afraid. It'll be getting dark in a few hours and I want to get home before nightfall.'

Adriano accompanied him out into the hall. There was a letter lying on the side table, already stamped. As they were passing it, Ciccio glanced down and saw it was addressed to Riccardo Lupillo, Adriano's son, at Via Nicosia in Enna. Ciccio knew the street.

'Do you want me to deliver this for you?'

'No, that's okay. I wouldn't want to put you out.'

'You wouldn't. It's on my way.'

'It's nice of you to offer, but I'll probably be going to Enna myself next weekend.'

'Bit of a waste of a stamp, then,' replied Ciccio grinning. 'What are you going to do? Read it out to him?' Adriano coloured and Ciccio's grin vanished. 'I'm sorry. I didn't intend that to sound cheeky. It's just that I realised there must be something private in the letter and, to show you I wasn't blaming you for not trusting it to a total stranger, I was just trying to make a joke. That's all,' he added lamely. It was Ciccio's crowning defect to be intelligent enough to make sound logical deductions, but not enough to ensure other people had kept up with him. He frequently had trouble keeping his jokes within acceptable social limits, too.

Adriano smiled. 'No secrets, I promise you,' he said, picking up the letter and handing it to him. 'The house is next door to Grisoldi's chemist's shop. You can't miss it.'

Ciccio nodded. He knew where Grisoldi's was. He'd been there dozens of times in his youth.

Something bothered him about the exchange, however, but, before he could identify it, Angelina returned.

'Going so soon?' she asked with a look of dismay.

'I'm afraid so.'

'You're sure you wouldn't like something to eat before you go?'

'That's very kind of you but it's getting late. I really must be getting home.'

14

'Well, if you must, you must,' she replied ruefully. 'Don't forget, if you're ever in the area you must drop by and see us again.'

Ciccio promised to do so. They accompanied him part of the way down the drive, before shaking hands and saying goodbye. Four men were now at work among the vines in the middle distance. Ciccio climbed into his car and – with a final glance up at the high walls – drove away. It had been a pleasant if dull conversation.

In marked contrast to the one he would shortly be having with his mother, he thought ominously.

He was so preoccupied with the disagreeable evening ahead that it took him a while to remember that something about their parting exchange in the hall had bothered him. Adriano had said something which sounded wrong.

A moment later Ciccio realised what it was.

Grisoldi had moved.

Six years previously Ciccio had paid his mother a surprise visit and found her lying ill in bed. The doctor called soon afterwards and handed him a prescription. Ciccio had driven into Enna, made a beeline for Grisoldi's in the Via Nicosia and found the shop was now a fruiterer's. The new owner told him that Grisoldi had moved the year before to larger premises around the corner in the Viale Diaz.

Nothing to it. Adriano had just forgotten. That was all.

He was on the point of dismissing the thought, when it dawned on him that it was a very strange mistake to make. Enna was only sixty miles away, so presumably Adriano would make frequent trips there to see his family and friends. Once a month or something; certainly several times a year. Yet Grisoldi had moved *seven* years ago. The house where Riccardo lived was the Lupillo family home and it presumably still belonged to Adriano himself. He must have visited it dozens of times during the last seven years, so obviously he couldn't have failed to notice that the shop next door was now a fruiterer's and that Grisoldi had gone elsewhere. How on earth could he have forgotten that?

By now Ciccio had reached the woods again. He drove a little way into their shady tunnel, pulled over and switched off the engine, frowning. It just wasn't a normal mistake to make.

So what? Adriano had just made an *abnormal* one. Big deal!

Ciccio shook his head and was reaching for the key to restart the car and drive on, when he stopped. An image of the sitting room came into his mind and for some reason something seemed odd about it. Abnormal.

And that was the second abnormality, he reminded himself, although he couldn't put his finger on exactly why it was so.

Abruptly he got out of the car and walked back to the edge of the trees to look at the house. This was where his granduncle had lived

15

for twenty years. Ciccio had only met him the once, but during his childhood he'd seen plenty of photos of him, so he'd seemed very familiar. Giacomo had a limp, Ciccio remembered – from some accident in his younger days. They said he'd fallen down a cliff somewhere and the bone hadn't healed properly, so he'd had to use a walking stick for the rest of his life. His wife, Leonora, had predeceased him by eight or nine years.

That was all Ciccio could remember about him.

After the windfall it wasn't only Grandfather Benito whom Luigi had investigated. He'd taken a close look at Giacomo too, thinking that perhaps the old man had been a lot richer than anyone had realised. But he'd soon dismissed that idea. Uncle Carlo, Giacomo's eldest son, had informed him that he'd left an estate of only seven hundred dollars in the bank and a few shares worth about sixteen thousand. Nothing to be sneezed at, considering his humble origins, but typical for a man who had lived carefully and frugally all his life. Besides, Giacomo had died a whole year before the donations had been made. That seemed too much time for there to be any connection.

Since then Ciccio had barely given Giacomo another thought.

And there was no reason to do so now, except that there, in the distance, was the house where Giacomo had spent the last twenty years of his life; and the current occupant had just voiced a peculiar ignorance which had then provoked Ciccio into realising that there was also something odd about the sitting room – although he couldn't work out what.

How ridiculous!

He shook his head in self-disgust, took one final glance at the walled estate, which he never expected to see again, and, thinking how peaceful it looked under the afternoon sun, returned to his car. He lit a cigarette and drove away, wondering what it was about the sitting room that seemed peculiar.

By the time he finished the cigarette, he was approaching the main road. He needed to pee so he stopped just past the two homemade signposts and got out. After relieving himself he happened to glance at one of the signposts again – the one which said '*Beware! Poor Road Surface*'. There was a black, felt-tipped marker in the car, which he'd used to number the backs of the paintings he'd bought for his failed art business. He retrieved it and went up to the sign. There was no one in sight, so he inserted the word '*Very*' in its message. The other sign said '*No Through Road*', but he couldn't think of any way of improving on this, so he headed back towards the car.

He was just about to climb in when he stopped, turned to look at the signs again, and frowned. What a funny place to put them. The main road was seventy yards away, around a bend. Why not put them right back at the beginning of the track?

But this thought was at once overtaken by another. How amazingly discouraging those two signs were. Aloud he murmured to himself, 'You can't get anywhere this way, and you'll probably have a puncture if you even try.'

It was funny, he mused. If you looked at the whole setup one way, you saw nothing but dullness, ordinariness and a probable waste of time and effort; but if you looked at it another way, it was as if somebody was trying very hard to *make* everything seem dull, ordinary and a waste of time and effort. Everything deterred. The track to the house couldn't be worse without being deliberately converted into an obstacle course. The furniture inside defied resale. The occupants obviously possessed little or nothing that was worth stealing.

Ciccio climbed back into his car and drove off.

The lane itself was obviously a private road, which was why those signposts were home-made. In Sicily it wasn't exactly unheard of for people to put up signs around their property, but few people bothered. Any burglar reconnoitring the countryside was likely to consider a notice saying '*Private Road*' worth investigating, and if those two signposts had been set up at the beginning of the track, he might well assume that they'd been placed there not out of courtesy but as a deterrent. By placing them seventy yards back from the main road, intentionally or not, the Tognazzis had managed to avoid provoking curiosity in casual passers-by, while discouraging the casual Sunday driver who still happened to venture onto their property.

It was all inconsequential, but it was something else that nagged at him.

When he reached the road he turned right, back towards Corleone. The letter to Riccardo lay on the seat beside him. No secrets? he wondered. He lit another cigarette and asked himself aloud, 'If Adriano didn't make a simple mistake, then what's the logical explanation?' There was only one answer. He didn't *know* that Grisoldi had moved – which meant he hadn't visited his family home in seven years.

That was really very odd.

What was more, Ciccio recalled that he himself had met his granduncle only once. He'd been less than one year old when Giacomo had gone to work at the Tognazzi house, but the first and last time he had ever seen him in the flesh was that day the family had been invited there to lunch. He couldn't be certain, but he strongly suspected that all the time while Giacomo had been living at that house, *he* hadn't visited his home town either.

'Perhaps they're not *allowed* out,' he murmured to himself jokingly. But into his mind came an image of the house with its formidable walls. Prison walls.

17

2

The sun was half an hour from setting when Ciccio reached the town of Enna, perched atop its plateau rising sheer from the surrounding plain. The family farm lay beneath the southwesterly cliff. No one was home when he arrived, so he made himself some coffee and used the boiling water to steam open Adriano's letter. It was full of junk: gossip picked up from the estate workers, comments on items in the Enna weekly paper – plus a few suggestions to Riccardo on an appropriate name for his next child, due in three months' time.

'Looks like he was telling the truth,' muttered Ciccio. No secrets here. But then why be so against him delivering it? And he *had* been, Ciccio was sure. Adriano had stupidly backed himself into a corner as a consequence. Answer: it wasn't the letter he didn't want Ciccio to see, but the addressee.

What intrigued Ciccio was that he could see a reason for this. The Donor wanted to keep his motives secret. But if those motives had something to do with the Tognazzi house, and if Adriano – like Giacomo before him – was earning money for his family, which they would receive upon his death, the Donor wouldn't want anyone to realise the connection between the two men, so any situation in which members of their families might meet and compare notes would need to be avoided. In offering to deliver his letter for him, Ciccio had put Adriano on the spot, because the one thing he would not want was that a Buonolini should become intimate with his son Riccardo.

Ciccio left the house and walked up the hill to call on Uncle Carlo. Although twenty-seven years older than Ciccio, Carlo was actually a cousin but, as Giancarlo's oldest surviving male grandchild, he was regarded as the family's patriarch.

He seemed delighted to see Ciccio and invited him in for a drink. His wife was out shopping, he explained. 'Spending the money I earn,' he added humorously. Carlo was a dapper man with an easy smile, and a successful wholesale business which accounted for most of it. While he was pouring two glasses of beer, Ciccio wandered around the sitting room, looking at photographs. He picked up one of Giacomo. 'I only met your father once. How come I didn't meet him more often? Didn't he come to Enna to visit?'

'Not very often. When the family had grown up, he went off to work as the caretaker of a house near Corleone. He didn't feel happy leaving it. He was always worried he might lose his job if anything happened while he was away.'

'So he did come here sometimes, then?'

Carlo nodded. 'Just for weddings and funerals, I think. And for not very many of those. He came for Marco's and Roberta's weddings. You would have been too young to remember. A bit of a palaver he made of it, too. He always insisted on driving himself, and he only had two speeds: slow and very slow.'

So Giacomo *had* come to visit, after all, thought Ciccio – and the edifice of his early suspicions began to crumble.

'My mother's was the only funeral he came for. You were sick at the time, I remember. Everyone was very worried about you.'

'Who looked after the house whenever he was away?'

'One of the men who worked the estate.'

'How often did you visit him?'

'Pretty frequently, considering what a pain it was to get there. Once every six weeks on average. He used to pay for our petrol. There wasn't much else he could spend his money on.'

'How did he get the job, do you know?'

'Through an ad in some newspaper.'

Ciccio nodded. Same as Adriano, he thought. He took a sip of his drink. 'By the way, does the name Adriano Lupillo mean anything to you?'

Carlo frowned. 'Lupillo . . . Lupillo. There's a *Riccardo* Lupillo who works at my local garage. He's one of their mechanics.'

'Adriano's his father.'

'Oh yes. Now I know who he is. What about him?'

'Oh, nothing. It's just that I ran into him recently and he seemed to know us quite well.'

'Everybody in Enna knows us now. There's nothing like a bit of money to get you noticed. How's *your* business coming along?'

'So-so.'

Carlo looked at him suspiciously. 'What's that mean? Bad?'

Ciccio deflected the question with a smile. 'By your standards I suppose it would be.' Then, before his uncle could probe further, he went on hurriedly, 'Coming back to what I was asking, this guy Adriano wasn't a friend of your father's, was he?'

'I shouldn't think so. Dad didn't have a lot of time for people outside the family. He *knew* lots of people, of course, but he never got close to them. Almost never, anyhow. There was *one* special friend he had. Someone from Lercara Friddi. I think Papa got to know him during the war.'

'What was his name?'

19

Carlo shook his head. 'I can't remember. But I've got a feeling it began with *D*.'

Ciccio couldn't think of anything else, so he changed the subject. He asked if Carlo happened to know where his mother was.

'At Aunt Claudia's, I expect. She hasn't been very well lately. The doctor thinks she might have suffered a mild stroke.'

This gave Ciccio an excuse to take his leave. 'Perhaps I'd better go over there then, in case Mamma needs any help.'

Carlo nodded approvingly.

Ciccio walked back down the hill to his car, then drove up the steep, winding road into Enna.

Great-Aunt Claudia lived in a little house on the Viale Caterina Savoca, very close to the Lombardia castle, which occupied the eastern apex of the roughly triangular plateau. The view from her house was spectacular and – in Ciccio's view, at least – was enhanced by the autostrada which swept through the valley below the Enna plateau. Built on thick, concrete stilts, it looked futuristic and made the area seem less primitive.

Claudia was ninety years old, and the only survivor of Giancarlo's six children. She had been the eldest. Giacomo, the fifth child, had been eleven years her junior.

Ciccio found his mother in the kitchen, preparing a light supper for her aunt by marriage. He waved at her through the window. She gave an upward jerk of her head, as if to say, 'What do *you* want?' But she couldn't quite hide her pleasure at seeing him. He was her younger son, after all, though sometimes she wondered why she couldn't have been blessed with chronic diabetes instead. At least there might be a treatment for that.

'What are *you* doing here?' she asked, as she opened the door for him, managing a note of peevishness in her voice.

'What a way to greet your son,' he replied cheerfully, then gave her a kiss on the cheek. 'How is she?'

Margherita shrugged. 'She comes and goes. Yesterday the doctor said he didn't think she'd last a month, but this afternoon I've been playing cards with her, so I think she's going to outlive *me*.'

'Isn't there anybody else here who can look after her?'

'A nurse comes in during the day and we'll be getting someone to live in soon. For the time being we've arranged a rota to spend time with her. I'm on till ten o'clock.'

'I think I'll go and cheer her up.'

'All right. But, for heaven's sake, don't smoke.'

Ciccio went into the sitting room, where a bed had been set up. The human being lying on it was not the person he remembered. Her body was shrunken and somehow distorted. He was looking at a

20

body preparing itself to be a corpse. He didn't like this reminder of what would one day happen to him.

The television was on, although Claudia seemed to be dozing. But as soon as he walked in, her eyes opened and she smiled. 'Haven't seen *you* for a while,' she said conspiratorially. He wondered if she could actually remember his name.

But seeing her had abruptly depressed him. Here he was, already sentenced to talking politely to a dying old crone. This was the result of having pawned his life, and long dreary days stretched ahead of him with similar mind-mortgaging interviews. Either with her or with someone else. The dreamed-of logical progression of Enna-Palermo-Rome-New York had become Enna-Palermo-Enna. He felt like a guard at some frontier post in the Sahara Desert, and it felt as claustrophobic as being in a coffin.

He longed for a cigarette, partly because he needed the relief, and partly because he wanted to exhale a lungful of death all over her so that she could get her disgusting dying over with.

He made the effort to ask her how she was feeling.

'I don't think I'll be making the Olympic team *this* year,' she replied, cackling drily – and he burst out laughing.

She asked him about his life in Palermo, so at least she knew who he was, even if she still hadn't put a name to his face. He gave her the sort of answer he thought she might like to hear, and then she asked him about his girlfriends and whether any of them stood a chance of becoming permanent. He fed her a tempting line in romantic possibles to keep her happy. The truth was that distress in others produced distress in himself. His innate selfishness and moral ambivalence made him incapable of supplying real comfort, and the result was a general irritability at his own inadequacy.

Soon she started to reminisce and he remembered that he wanted to question her about her brother Giacomo. He asked her first if she'd ever heard the name Adriano Lupillo. Claudia squinted up at the ceiling and for a moment he thought she was trying to defecate in bed. But that was just an effort to sort through her ninety-year-old memory. 'It rings a bell,' she pronounced at last. 'Who is he?'

'He lives over on the other side of town. On the Via Nicosia. Next to Grisoldi the chemist.'

'Grisoldi isn't *on* Nicosia any more. He moved round the corner to Diaz.'

So there really wasn't much wrong with the old bat's brain, he decided. But she didn't seem to know much about Adriano, so he got her talking about Giacomo, instead. Most of the photographs around the room were pictures of her own children and their families, but amongst them there were two of Giacomo. In one shot he was all dressed up in his Sunday best and looking about fifteen. It had probably been taken at somebody's wedding, Ciccio guessed. In the other picture he was looking much older, probably about forty, and was clasping the walking stick he would need for the rest of his life.

'How old was Great-Uncle Giacomo when he broke his leg?' Ciccio asked.

The old woman had to think hard. 'It was in 1949, early winter. So he'd have been thirty-two, then.'

'What happened exactly?'

'He fell down a ravine. The one up on Monte Cannarella. He'd gone out hunting on his own.'

'So how did he get home afterwards?'

'Somebody heard him calling for help and carried him home piggyback.'

'But that's three kilometres, at least.'

She nodded. 'About that, I should think.'

'Who was he?'

She shrugged. 'Some boy. I didn't know anything about the accident till the next time I saw Giacomo about five or six weeks later. His leg was still in plaster, I remember.'

'But was it a boy or a man?'

'A boy. Sixteen years old.'

'How do you know?'

'Because Giacomo told me, of course,' she replied, eying him as if he was a mental defective.

'He told you his age, but he didn't mention his name?' asked Ciccio incredulously.

'I don't remember if he told me his name or not, but he certainly told me his age. He was amazed that someone so young had been able to carry him so far. Giacomo wasn't fat, but he was a stocky, muscular type. Heavy.'

'The boy's name couldn't have been Adriano, could it?'

She frowned in concentration, but eventually shook her head. 'I really can't remember. It was a very long time ago. But I'm positive about his age. Giacomo definitely said sixteen.'

If a young man of thirty-two could fall down a ravine and break his leg and be left so helpless, he thought, just how easy it would be for an old woman like her to suffer a mishap. He glanced around at all the ornate, angular furniture and decided she'd been asking for trouble for years. This place was a deathtrap.

It was then that he finally realised what was peculiar about Adriano's sitting room. It was the furniture. It had no angles or sharp corners. Everything was smoothly rounded. He remembered too what Carlo had said earlier about Giacomo being such a slow driver.

Giacomo and Adriano. Two careful men.

It was Riccardo he needed to talk to now, but it was too late to call on him today. The one thing Ciccio did *not* want to do, however, was go home with his mother. She'd be bound to start prying, and he wasn't ready to answer her questions yet. So he told her that he'd arranged to meet a friend and would get home late.

Disco 21, Enna's single discotheque, was open only on Saturdays. The best alternative was a bar called Terzo Cerchio. In comparison with the terrific places he knew in Palermo, it was as depressing as hell. His enforced visit had its compensation, however, because he spotted someone he recognised – Pietro Grisoldi, the chemist's son.

Ciccio went over to speak to him, but it didn't prove easy to bring Adriano into the conversation casually, and the last thing he wanted was to provoke curiosity. Then he hit on the ruse of asking if Pietro could recommend a good mechanic, and Riccardo Lupillo was the first name mentioned.

'I don't think I know him. Who's his father?'

'Adriano Lupillo.'

Pretending to search his memory he asked, 'What's he do?'

'He used to be a mechanic, too. Then he got a job as an estate manager near Roccamena. About ten years ago now. Come to think of it, I haven't seen him since.'

'Good people are they?'

'Oh, sure. Best kind. Hard up, but they'd go hungry rather than not pay a bill. Adriano's one of the old breed. He'd go to hell for his family.'

Then, unfortunately, a woman friend of Pietro's joined them, and it would have been far too suspicious to press the subject again. Ciccio had noted the job description, though – why not 'a caretaker near Corleone'? – and decided to consider this another abnormality.

That night, in bed, he lit a cigarette and stared up at the ceiling. If someone had said, 'Adriano's an old barnacle. He hasn't been home for seven years,' he wouldn't have thought anything if it. But seeing it as a puzzle, he'd stopped to wonder about it, and then, one by one, odd little details and coincidences had started to appear in a different light. He knew the reasons behind it all could still be completely innocent, and then he'd be forced back on confessing to his family the mess he'd made of his life and persuading one of them to give him a job. But the truth was that he hated Enna to the depths of his soul, and was ready to grab at anything which might promise him a way out of the place again, so he decided to hold off for a while. He would explain his homecoming as simply a need to be with his family for a few days. Sicilians didn't question feelings like that.

The following evening he called on the Lupillos and was invited in for a glass of wine. Riccardo was in his late thirties, with the same build as his father, but without either his humour or intelligence.

'I must say, I thought your father was looking very well,' said Ciccio. 'How old is he now?'

'Sixty-three.'

'Really? He looks a lot younger. Must be all that fresh air. What does he actually do there? I forgot to ask him.'

'He's the estate manager.'

'Sounds like a big job. He must be a busy man. Does he manage to get over here to see you much?'

Riccardo grunted. 'He doesn't get over to see us at all. I sometimes think he's anchored to that place. The last time he came was for my sister's wedding, and that was eight years ago.'

As they continued talking, Ciccio was invited to stay for supper and accepted. Their conversation was all about local and family matters, but he picked up a lot of interesting information. It was eleven o'clock when he emerged from the Lupillo house. He went for a walk around the quiet streets, thinking about what he'd gleaned.

Adriano had been sixteen years old in 1949. His birthday fell in mid-December, so in early winter of that year he would have been close to seventeen. Riccardo confirmed that, even as a youth, his father had always been physically strong, mentioning instances which left little doubt in Ciccio's mind that even at sixteen he would have been able to carry a man for three kilometres.

That wasn't proof, but Ciccio would have accepted bets that the boy who had heard Giacomo's call for help that day was Adriano Lupillo. And that was the sort of deed to create a lifelong friendship because, if nobody knew where he had gone, Giacomo might easily have died of exposure on the mountainside. Such a debt would never have been forgotten, and Giacomo would have found some way to express his gratitude: such as recommending the younger man as a replacement after his death.

Ciccio was beginning to see how it all worked. Same house and same job, but one was described as 'caretaker near Corleone' and the other as 'estate manager near Roccamena'. So long as only their kinfolk ever visited them, no one would be any the wiser. And who but kinfolk would want to make that long, tortuous journey along more than a mile of potholed cart track?

Only Ciccio, by chance, because of the peculiar circumstances of his wasted life.

In his thoughtful stroll he had come now to the famous bronze statue of Euno, the leader of the slaves' revolt in AD 137. It stood in a recess in the rock just under the Lombardia castle. Ciccio walked on to the end of the promenade and heaved himself up to sit on a wall overlooking the valley. On the autostrada far below, the lights of a solitary car flew silently towards Catania.

24

He lit a cigarette and stared up at the black vault of sky overhead with its arching carpet of stars.

The reason for their deception was obvious. The Lupillos would one day be wealthy, too, but the Donor didn't want anybody to make the connection with a similar windfall once received by the Buonolinis. This also explained why Adriano had claimed he'd only known Giacomo by sight. The same desire for obfuscation would explain why the donations had been made to all the descendants of Giacomo's father, not just those of Giacomo himself. Supposition had thus focused on great-grandfather Giancarlo, and not on his fifth child who had worked as an obscure caretaker and died leaving an unremarkable estate – especially since those donations had come a full year later.

Ciccio saw now that, when he'd found out that Giacomo had visited Enna from time to time after all, he'd been wrong to assume this disproved his earlier suspicions. The system, whatever it was, required these caretakers to behave as normally as possible, and for them not to attend weddings and funerals of their close family would attract inevitable comment.

So ordinariness and obscurity were the mysterious Donor's watchwords.

But it wasn't so much all these tiny coincidences and deceptions that impressed Ciccio; by themselves they meant little. It was the one extraordinary fact that eight years ago someone had donated nearly five million dollars to a family of smallholders, and nothing could even remotely account for it.

The secret lay in that house and he knew it in his bones.

But why should anyone pay a man such a huge sum merely to stay at home for twenty years?

Logic told him there could be only one reason. The caretakers were guarding not the house itself, but something else. Something *in* the house. Something of very great value.

3

A half-moon leered at him from somewhere above Libya as he walked stealthily through the vines towards the house. He didn't think there'd be tripwires – not outside the wall, anyway – because they would be set off by rabbits and foxes and even the occasional wolf.

The grounds were walled all the way round and there was only one gateway. He'd spent the day observing the house through binoculars, and at dusk he'd watched Adriano stroll down the drive and lock the gates. The key he'd used was as long as his hand and probably just as old. It was almost pure theatre. Anyone casing the joint would see a house with its gates open during the day and locked at night with a rusty old key to keep tramps out. But four point eight million dollars told him there had to be another locking device on that gate, one operated electronically from the house itself.

He reached the wall and looked up at it. It rose sheer. It would be a very difficult climb, and he suspected there'd be surprises on the top – tripwires and probably tiny spikes or shards of glass. The typical method of defending a wall with chunks of broken bottles on top was designed to dissuade any casual thief from even trying to enter, but it wouldn't deter the determined professional who knew how to deal with the challenge. Chunks of broken glass were merely an advertisement: an announcement to the world that the wall enclosed something of value.

But this wall was different. Its top appeared innocuously unprotected. The gates stood unlocked during the day. There were no guards around. So the message to any observer was that there could be nothing of any value inside and the wall itself was high enough to deter him from making the effort to check and make sure.

No, any dissuasion here lay not in the security measures that were visible, but in the likely waste of time in overcoming the few obstacles there were. Which was precisely why there had to be some hidden surprises on that wall, because anyone who persisted in the effort of climbing it would be no ordinary thief and the occupants needed to know if any attempt was being made.

Ciccio laid the pole he was carrying on the ground. From his sports bag he pulled out a block of plasticine and worked it with his fingers until it was warm and soft. He flattened this into an approximate

26

rectangle, twelve inches by six, and stuck it on to the underside of the plywood board he had attached to the bracket at the end of the pole. He then raised the pole above him and very slowly and very carefully fed it downwards through his hands till it met the top of the wall. When it came to a stop, he raised it again, then lowered it to the ground. He took out his lighter and struck up a flame to see by. The impressions in the plasticine resembled two rows of regular-shaped teeth, thin as razor blades, positioned at intervals of an inch. He couldn't tell how high they projected because he hadn't dared apply too much pressure in case there was a weight-activated tripwire underneath the teeth, but they were at least half a centimetre in height. Very nasty if you weren't prepared for them, even when wearing gloves.

It seemed to shout confirmation of all his previous deductions.

Ciccio walked away feeling very clever.

Giancarlo Buonolini had been the apex of the family pyramid, chosen to distract attention from the real source of their unexpected wealth – the fifth figure from the left in the second rung of the family tree. So, say Adriano Lupillo were to die tonight, then to distract attention away from *him*, presumably the next lot of donations would be dished out on the same basis. Adriano's father would form the apex of a new pyramid of beneficiaries. This reasoning led Ciccio to wonder exactly who those beneficiaries might be.

Adriano was sixty-three and could easily last another twenty years. Maybe not all of them would be prepared to wait that long, once they knew what was coming their way.

The next day Ciccio was driving up into Enna with the intention of finding out who they all were, when it suddenly dawned on him that Adriano was Giacomo's *replacement*. Had Giacomo replaced somebody too? And if there had been a string of guardians and he could manage to identify the first one, might not this give him a clue as to what it was they were all guarding?

So he turned about and headed instead towards Corleone.

The estate workers knocked off for lunch at twelve-thirty and went home together in a Land-Rover. He followed it into Corleone, and waited as the labourers were deposited at their homes one by one. Only one of them was old enough to have been working the Toganazzi land for as long as twenty-eight years – a weatherbeaten man in his early sixties; the third of them to be dropped off. Ciccio parked the car, made himself comfortable, and prepared for a long wait.

When the old man emerged an hour later, Ciccio followed him to a nearby bar. There he was greeted by two other aging men who addressed him as Aldo. Ciccio sat at the table next to theirs, sipping

27

a beer as he listened to their conversation. They glanced at him from time to time, obviously curious, but Ciccio bided his time. After fifteen minutes he pulled out a cigarette and leaned across to ask one of Aldo's friends for a light. As it was supplied, he inquired, 'You don't happen to know Maria Leggio, do you?'

'Where does she live?'

'She didn't give me her address, but it's somewhere on the road to Prizzi. She's twenty-five, her hair's dark brown and long, and she's got blue eyes.'

The men looked at each other. It was pretty obvious what this young pup was after, but none of them could identify this non-existent girl.

Then Aldo said, 'Where did you meet her?'

'Palermo – where I live.' The ice now broken, he let them take the conversation where they wanted. Ten minutes later he decided it was time for his main gambit. 'This is my first visit to Corleone, but a friend of my grandfather's was estate manager of a vineyard near here, on the road to Roccamena.'

Aldo looked up. 'What was his name?'

'I don't remember. But my grandfather took me there once. Must be about thirty years ago now. I was six or seven,' he said, adding eight years to his age. 'I remember the house, though.' He proceeded to describe it.

Aldo nodded. 'Dionisio Bompietri?'

Ciccio frowned. 'I think it was. Where did he come from?'

'Lercara Friddi.'

Of course, thought Ciccio. The friend Uncle Carlo had mentioned; the one Giacomo had got to know during the war. Dionisio must have recommended Giacomo for the job, just as Giacomo himself had later recommended Adriano.

'That's it,' he nodded. 'Lercara Friddi. I remember now. How long did he work there?'

'Since the Tognazzis bought the place. Not long after the Americans came – 1943.'

4

Adriano's father, Calogero Lupillo, had died in 1962. He had nineteen descendants over twenty-one years of age. His eldest daughter, Paola, was now sixty-eight. She'd married Luigi Donatella and had six children by him. Her grandson Giorgio Donatella had been in a juvenile remand centre for grievous bodily harm and had later spent six months in prison for burglary. He was twenty-three and lived in Palermo.

It was a busy time of year for him. All the tourists were here, waiting to be fleeced or fucked – Giorgio didn't mind which. Now he was walking along the Via Schiavuzzo, a dark street near the harbour, towards the bar where his gang hung out. As he passed an alley a voice said, 'Congratulations, Giorgio.'

He stopped and peered into the gloom. 'What do you mean?'

Ciccio stepped out and smiled. 'Because you're going to be a very rich man.'

'Is this a joke? Who the fuck are you?'

'I'll tell you over a drink, if you want. You pick the bar. Some place quiet.'

Giorgio looked at him suspiciously. Was he a queer? He didn't look like one, but you never could tell. What the hell. The bastard was offering to buy him a drink, so it couldn't hurt to listen to him for five minutes.

Giorgio chose the bar, but Ciccio picked the table. Then Giorgio picked the most expensive scotch.

Ciccio smiled. 'Two,' he said to the waiter. When the man had gone, Ciccio dropped his identity card on the table. Giorgio examined it and gave a shrug, as if to say *So what?*

Ciccio retrieved the card and took out a bank statement from his jacket pocket. 'Eight years ago this was what I had in my bank account.' Giorgio looked at the figure and was unimpressed. 'A month later I had this.' Ciccio took out another statement and placed it face up on the table. Giorgio stared at the nine-digit number. As the waiter came back with the drinks, Ciccio casually picked up both statements and put them away.

'Every adult descendant of my great-grandfather received the same amount. Anonymously. We never knew who gave it, or why.'

Ciccio lit a cigarette, partly to give the other man time to absorb this information and partly to hide his own nervousness. Alongside the other man he felt very inexperienced in criminal activities, but if he was to retain the upper hand in their relationship, it was important Giorgio didn't detect this.

Making a casual gesture with his cigarette, Ciccio continued, 'Twenty years before that, another family received similar remuneration. Every adult descendant of a certain man received a packet anonymously. The money was a lot less in actual lire but, as near as I can make out, its value at the time would have been about the same.' He waited for this to sink in, then said, 'I know what the common denominator is.'

When he didn't elaborate, Giorgio prompted, 'What?'

'I'll tell you if we're partners.'

Giorgio looked at him. 'What will I get out of it?'

Ciccio's reply was breezy. 'To tell you the truth, I'm not sure exactly. At the very least we ought to pick up something like half a million dollars and we'd go fifty-fifty. But there's a chance we might get more.' He looked the other man straight in the eyes. 'A *lot* more.'

Giorgio considered. All this was really interesting. Maybe the guy was a nut, but Giorgio didn't think so. And if he wasn't, then this was the opportunity of a lifetime. Things hadn't been going too well for him up to now. Since his early teens, like most other Sicilians with a criminal bent, he'd been on the fringes of Cosa Nostra – under its general supervision, receiving a nod for some illegal activities and an unappealable shake of the head for others. Defiance, of course, was out of the question. He lived in a neighbourhood controlled by a *cosca* which might not be wealthy enough to support many soldiers, but its word was law, and CN did not deal with infractions leniently.

The plain fact was that the families who controlled the Mafia always gave preference to their own kinsmen, and Giorgio's family had rarely had anything to do with it. It was galling to think that there were some villages in Sicily where the taps in every house were made of gold, because the families living there had shown the good sense to smuggle drugs for the big *cosche*, while his own kinfolk, stupidly following the path of righteousness, were lucky to have taps at all!

So, wanting to be *in*, but not having the right family connections to open the door for him, Giorgio seemed doomed to wait forever on the threshold. He had, however, performed the occasional service for associates of Don Fabrizio La Barbera – who was widely believed to be a member of the Palermo Provincial *Cupola* – and had received appropriate remuneration. Answering his doorbell a few days later he had found a colour television set waiting in the corridor outside. A handsome gift, yes, but a far cry from being on the permanent payroll.

But, in any case, Giorgio wasn't altogether sure that he wanted closer involvement with someone like La Barbera. He was too public. After the maxi-trials of the 1980s and the assassinations of judges Falcone and Borsellino, Cosa Nostra had gone underground again. Those people still in the public eye were most likely small potatoes. Don Fabrizio might be a figure of importance in Palermo-Central, but Giorgio doubted he pulled much weight in Sicily as a whole, much less in the world. The men in the public eye were the ones who usually got arrested and went to prison. The guys that Giorgio was interested in were the untouchables, the unidentifiables, the ones who had cabinet ministers in their pockets. And they might as well be living on another planet. If you didn't know who they were, you couldn't talk to them.

So Giorgio was condemned to scrimp along, hoping somebody *somewhere* would take an interest in him, and, while he waited for something to happen, he fucked around with dickheads and prostitutes and gigolos. What a life!

Yet now here was this guy who had suddenly dropped out of nowhere with an offer from the stars! Maybe this was something worth looking into.

'What would I have to do?' he asked cautiously, doing a good job of sounding indifferent.

Ciccio shrugged. 'Maybe steal something. Maybe kill someone. Ever killed anyone, Giorgio?'

There was no reply. Which, in Sicilian, meant yes.

Giorgio leaned back from the table, feeling replete. He lit a cigarette and blew a plume of smoke up towards the clear blue sky. As expected, it had been a good meal. Angelina and Adriano were lonely, so the best way of enticing relatives to visit them was to make damn sure they got fed properly. It had been a simple matter to find out when his cousin Riccardo was next due to visit Adriano, and then wangle himself an invitation. Today it was a larger group then usual: twelve adults and six children. Most of the other adults were lighting up, too – which the kids took as permission to go off and play. Giorgio stood up, and wandered towards Adriano's end of the table.

'Mind if I have a look around the house, Uncle?'

'No, sure. I'll come with you.'

He had expected as much, but what happened next did surprise him. Although his great-uncle showed him all around the ground floor, he declined to come upstairs with him, merely telling Giorgio to go ahead. The old man then rejoined the others outside. As there was no one else in the house now, this was Giorgio's chance. He climbed the stairs and went from room to room. The smell in each was the same: age and disuse. They all needed airing and clearly hadn't been used in a long time. Adriano and his wife obviously lived entirely on the ground floor.

All the upper rooms were bare. There wasn't even a carpet to be seen. So it didn't look as if any of the Tognazzis ever came to visit. In many Sicilian country houses, the ground floor was used for stores, and even stables, while the family lived upstairs, but there was nothing sacrosanct in the arrangement. Besides, Adriano was getting on, so not having to climb the stairs every day he was likely to regard as a blessing.

Even so, it did not escape Giorgio's attention that the ground-floor living accommodation had been specifically created out of what had once been storerooms and stables. And this had been done a long time ago, too – before Adriano had come to live here. That struck Giorgio as peculiar.

He went right up into the attic and then down to the cellar – both were completely empty, too. The wine and olive oil and other provisions for daily use, which might normally have been stored in the cellar, were kept in a large pantry next to the kitchen. It seemed that Adriano had a phobia about using stairs.

The ground floor formed a complete apartment: hall, sitting room, dining room, bedroom, bathroom and kitchen. The most logical place to hide something valuable would be in the bedroom, but after opening all the cupboards and drawers Giorgio came to the conclusion that the treasure, whatever it was, had to be concealed behind some secret panel somewhere . . . or maybe not in the house at all. He went out for a walk around the immediate grounds, making sure his granduncle spotted him, to see what the old man's reaction would be. But Adriano merely glanced at him and carried on talking to his other guests.

It's in the house then, Giorgio decided. In the house and bloody well hidden. So well hidden that Adriano could let an army of us tramp in there, and he would still carry on chatting unconcernedly about the bloody family.

Eventually Giorgio returned to the table, sat down on one of the kids' abandoned chairs nearer to Adriano, and spent the rest of the afternoon trying to behave like an exemplary grandnephew.

That evening he took a walk down to the ruined house close to the railway, just before the line disappeared into a tunnel, below the western cliff of the Enna plateau.

Ciccio was waiting for him in the ruin. He listened carefully to Giorgio's description of the house, then began asking questions.

'What about electronic gadgets?'

'Nothing. Everything there is old and cheap. The furniture looks funny, though.'

Ciccio nodded. 'Rounded edges on everything.'

'Yes, that's right. But why?'

'For the same reason they live on the ground floor – to cut down the risk of accidents. I think the amount of money your family will eventually receive depends on how long he manages to live. The longer he works there, the more you all get. And if he commits suicide, or dies in an accident which might have been suicide, the amount will probably be heavily reduced as a penalty.'

'But why?'

'Because the system depends on nobody noticing. If the successive caretakers died off too quickly, a hell of a lot of people would be getting anonymous donations. And if that was the case, somebody would have smelled a rat years ago.'

Giorgio was impressed. He pulled out a packet of Marlboro and offered one to Ciccio. It was a kind of homage.

'But if suicide will be penalised, so will murder.'

Ciccio nodded.

'So if we kill him, we'd probably get a lot less than half a million dollars.'

'Maybe nothing at all.'

'Jesus! We could have to wait twenty or thirty years for him to die naturally! I'd be an old man by then!'

'Not if we could make it look like a natural death.'

Giorgio considered this, but then shook his head. 'Look, I don't know about that. They're getting pretty good at forensics and things like that. You see it in the movies all the time.'

'You're right. I don't think there are many ways of killing someone which can't be detected these days. But there are some autopsy procedures which aren't normally used, and if they were demanded for an ordinary old caretaker, the police pathologist might smell a rat. That's the sort of thing the Donor would want to avoid.'

'Suppose he brings in his own pathologist.'

Ciccio shook his head. 'That would look suspicious, too. This is Sicily, Giorgio. Adriano's going to be lying in an open coffin for everyone to take a last gander at. What do you think a corpse looks like after a full-scale autopsy? It wouldn't look as if he'd died of a heart attack at all. It'd look as if he'd trodden on a mine.'

Giorgio shook his head. 'Look, I still think we'd be better off forgetting about the bloody donations, and going for the treasure itself. You said yourself the amount of money's probably linked to the time served. It took Giacomo twenty years to earn you lot four hundred million lire each, but Adriano's only clocked up nine years. Suppose the amount isn't stepped up regularly. Suppose it's . . . what's the word?'

'Exponential. It could very well be.'

'So why don't we just grab Adriano and beat the shit out of him

33

until he tells us where it is? This treasure or whatever.'

Ciccio smiled and gave him a mock scolding. 'Shame on you. Fancy suggesting we treat your poor old granduncle like that.'

But then he became serious again. 'You're not thinking straight, Giorgio. It isn't a question of one *or* the other. We knock off Adriano first and *then* we go for the treasure. That way the man you beat the shit out of won't be of your own blood, so you'll go to hell for only two eternities instead of three.'

Giorgio grinned broadly at him. Yes, definitely, this was a partner worth having. Then a thought struck him. 'But suppose old Angelina's a guardian, too. It would look like a hell of a coincidence if they both snuffed it through natural causes, one after the other.'

Ciccio shook his head. 'No, I don't think she's involved. Dionisio Bompietri was the first caretaker and his wife outlived him by fifteen years. She went back to live with her family in Lercara Friddi. Towards the end of her life she went gaga and started rambling, but whatever she said didn't make anyone suspicious, so I don't think she knew what her husband was really up to. It stands to reason, anyhow, if you want security, then the fewer people that know, the better.'

'How would you make it look like a natural death?'

'There are some poisons which are almost impossible to detect.'

'Do you know how to get hold of them?'

'No, but I know somebody you could frighten the life out of to tell us.'

Giorgio grinned, then turned serious. 'The problem is that it's easy to get into that house as a visitor, but nearly impossible to get in without being seen. So we couldn't get rid of Adriano without his wife knowing we were there.'

Now it was Ciccio's turn to smile. 'Think, Giorgio. If your great-aunt Angelina isn't an essential part of the deal, and if she doesn't know exactly what's going on, do you think she'd agree to stay cooped up in that place for nine years?'

'So she does come out after all?'

Ciccio nodded.

'To go shopping?'

'No. The groceries and things are delivered.'

'To go to the doctor?'

'I'd like to bet it's the doctor who has to do the visiting. But a dentist would be a different matter. I bet that's like funerals and weddings: he's allowed to go to the dentist. But we can scarcely hang around for six months waiting for Angelina to get toothache. No, there's somewhere else she goes regularly, and its not to have her hair done.'

'Where?'

'When you went into the bedroom, did you see anything hanging on the wall above the bed?'

Giorgio's eyes lit up. 'Church!'

Ciccio went up several more notches in Giorgio's estimation when his insistence on observing the house closely for a couple of weeks was rewarded. Adriano played a regular game of liar dice with some of the estate workers every Sunday morning, while Angelina went off to church, but the couple spent the rest of the week mostly on their own together. This knowledge was going to prove useful.

To show his appreciation, Giorgio mugged a tourist and on the proceeds took Ciccio out for a slap-up dinner at the Trattoria Al Buco in Palermo. Later they picked up a couple of hookers and went back to Giorgio's apartment. The girls liked them; their firm, strong bodies made a pleasant change from the fat middle-aged men they usually had to service. So afterwards they hung around, dawdling over their drinks as if hoping there might be some regular contract in the offing. But as Ciccio lay silently smoking a cigarette and staring at the ceiling, Giorgio realised he was deep in thought, so he paid the girls off and threw them out.

When he put a mug of coffee on the bedside table, Ciccio looked up and said, 'Tell me about that time you killed somebody.'

'Some*bodies*,' replied Giorgio casually. 'Once was in prison. A nark. The shithead was overheard talking to the screws, so we drew straws to decide who should take care of him – and I won. I tried to drown him by shoving his head down the bog, but he must have had a heart attack or something, because they found no water in his lungs. The screws didn't twig, even though I'd twisted his arm so hard they wondered about the torn ligaments. Anyhow, he snuffed it. The second time was just last year. This big kid from Messina fancied himself becoming boss of my gang, so I had to fight him for it. The idiot chose knives and that's my speciality. Curtains for fuckface.' He frowned. 'I can't remember his name.' Then he shrugged. 'Not that it matters.'

Ciccio grinned. 'How do you feel about killing a woman?'

Giorgio lay down on the other bed, lit a cigarette and glanced his way. 'What, you mean one of those two?' he asked, nodding towards the door. 'No good, huh?'

Ciccio cracked up.

Angelina's place of worship was the Church of Sant'Andrea in Corleone. After Sunday morning mass it was her custom to go to a café with friends, where they would sit and gossip. Today the main topic was the arrest the night before of some young ruffian who had been on the run for eleven days after knifing a policeman. He was suspected of being one of the Friends, although Angelina and her companions were more interested in his possible relationship with the policeman's wife.

After an intriguing hour she emerged from the café, said goodbye to her friends, and headed back down a steep alley towards the piazza where she'd parked her car. Few people were about now; just the stragglers on their way home late to Sunday lunch. It was a beautiful day and she hummed an old folk-tune as she walked. Suddenly, from behind her, there came a cry of warning. She turned to look back; her eyes widened in terror, and she made a desperate move to get out of the way. But the driver-less fruiterer's van hit her head-on, knocked her to the ground and jolted over her body. She died a quarter of an hour later, on her way to hospital.

Angelina was buried in the Lupillo family sepulchre in the cemetery at Enna two days after the tragic accident. Giorgio attended the funeral, naturally, so it was Ciccio who kept watch on the house that day. At eight o'clock in the morning Riccardo arrived to drive his father to Enna. Angelina herself had been taken away for preparation by the undertaker the day before. In Adriano's absence four estate workers, including Aldo, looked after the house. They spent the day playing liar dice at the table outside.

Riccardo brought his father home at seven thirty. The workers tactfully put their dice away and waited. The two Lupillos went into the house alone. Some ten minutes later they emerged. Riccardo was carrying a tray with a bottle of brandy, and he poured out six equal measures. Everyone took a glass and waited on Adriano. He spoke some words, everyone else nodding and muttering agreement, then all six raised their glasses and drank to the memory of Angelino Lupillo.

Eventually the four estate workers took their leave. For a few minutes Riccardo stayed talking to his father. The two men suddenly hugged each other; after which they both took out handkerchiefs to wipe their eyes. Finally Riccardo kissed his father on both cheeks, returned to his car and drove away.

For a long while Adriano stood on the same spot, staring around him as if he was lost. Then he sat down at the table and poured himself another glass of brandy, which he sipped intermittently for more than half an hour. Finally he broke down again, hiding his face in his hands and heaving with the immense sobs of an ignorant man who must make sense of the pain of death within the context of an all-loving faith.

Quietening again, he wiped his eyes and stood up. It was now dusk, so he headed down the drive with the long key to lock the gates, then walked around the enclosed grounds for a while before going inside.

That was all. No unusual security precautions and no other visitors.

Ciccio crept back to his hidden car and returned to Enna. Giorgio had kept a careful watch on Adriano throughout the funeral, but his granduncle had done nothing out of the ordinary. Everyone agreed that Adriano's behaviour had been properly dignified and manly. He'd broken down only once, which everybody had considered appropriate. And since he was five years older than Angelina, it probably wouldn't be too long before he rejoined her.

'No, probably not,' agreed Ciccio, and Giorgio burst out laughing.

5

They let ten days go by before they went to tackle Adriano, waiting until just after the estate workers had gone home for their lunch and siesta. He was still so grief-stricken that it wasn't for several minutes after they had arrived that he began to wonder why they were both together. He had already poured them glasses of brandy and was sitting down when he remembered that Ciccio was one of his predecessor Giacomo's heirs. He was the one who had come to visit them out of the blue – and that soon after that the wayward Giorgio had turned into a prodigal son.

And then his wife had been killed!

He was on the point of tying it all together when they acted.

Their plan to use an undetectable poison had been abandoned after a talk with a pharmacist. Although a great many poisons could not be easily traced, their operation was either too slow or would leave Adriano with all the wrong symptoms – most of them indicating death from asphyxia, rather than from a heart attack. Aside from this, the poisons could not be easily administered without the victim being aware of it, which meant rendering him unconscious. The standard cinematic method of doing so without causing him a visible injury – a wad of cotton wool soaked with chloroform or ethyl ether – was an example of literary licence. Both substances required several minutes to take effect, during which time the victim's struggles would leave several telltale bruises which even the most inexperienced doctor would have little difficulty in recognising.

But Ciccio's pharmacist acquaintance had given them an alternative method.

Giorgio pulled from his pocket a small canister of anti-attack CS gas and sprayed the vapour directly into Adriano's face. The old man was temporarily blinded, and almost paralysed. In no state now to offer any serious resistance, Lupillo allowed the young men to straighten his arm. Giorgio had no difficulty in inserting the needle of a large syringe into a vein in Adriano's forearm. He began to press down the plunger. The syringe contained a hundred millilitres of air.

Adriano's eyes half-opened. Seeing what was happening, he began to struggle ineffectually and gasped, 'Wait! Giorgio! You don't . . . understand! The fire . . . place.'

His body gave a sudden jerk. Adriano Lupillo was dead.

'What was he saying?' asked Giorgio.

'Something about a fireplace.'

'What did he mean?'

'I don't know. We'll have a look in a minute.'

Ciccio put on a rubber glove, then picked up Adriano's glass and, in order to break it, let it fall from head height onto the hard compacted surface of the drive. Now he and Giorgio laid Adriano's body down on the ground beside it. Ciccio carefully cut the skin surface of the old man's forearm right on top of the puncture mark made by the syringe. To the police it would look as if Lupillo had fallen on the broken glass after suffering a heart attack.

Satisfied with their handiwork, the two young men went into the house to examine all the fireplaces. The one in the sitting room drew their attention at once because it had been installed when the downstairs storerooms had been converted into living accommodation. Its surround was crafted of wood, with heavily ornate carvings of serpents battling with Herculean figures and with damsels in improbable distress. They spent ten minutes examining it meticulously, but although it was assembled from more than a dozen separate sections and many of the panels were slightly loose, there didn't seem to be any moving parts. The hearth itself was bare, and the lever controlling the chimney flue was rather stiff but seemed to work normally.

Ciccio stepped back, and examined the wall behind and the nearby furniture. The grandfather clock still wasn't working, he noted absently.

He was bothered by the way Adriano had died. When a man realises he's about to be killed, there are not many things worth the trouble of saying. Only weak men usually bothered to plead. No, the old man hadn't screamed or begged. He hadn't tried to bargain for his life. He'd said, '*Wait! You don't understand!*' The manner of dying is the clearest indication of the man who dies. How one dies shows how one has lived. Adriano's words indicated that in those last moments he'd understood exactly what was happening, and why. It was as if he hadn't been protesting against the *fact* of his murder but the *methodology* of it. Or the *timing*. His protest was as if to indicate that they weren't going about things the right way. As if they'd failed to fix something beforehand, and that failure was now going to spoil everything. Everything Adriano had striven for: the wealth and security of his own family after his death.

Behind him Giorgio was cursing. He just couldn't see why the fireplace was so important. Perhaps Adriano's dying words had been just as trivial as Citizen Kane's, he thought. He turned around. 'Come on, Ciccio!' he hissed. 'We've got to get away! It was you who insisted we shouldn't waste time looking for any treasure now. Never mind the Donor, think of the police!'

But Ciccio was hypnotised by the scene. He thought of all those years in which a lonely, determined man had been prepared to sit in this quiet room waiting for death. Comfortable, yes, but it truly *was* a prison. And much more so before the days of television and video recorders. In 1943, Dionisio had been obliged to make do with books.

Looked at from the points of view of Sicilian peasants such as Dionisio, Giacomo and Adriano, to give up nine-tenths of their freedom for the sake of the families they loved made a lot of sense. But looked at from the point of view of the Donor, nothing made any sense at all. What treasure could possibly be so valuable that it had to be hidden away for more than fifty years – and at such cost? If it was hidden behind some secret panel here, it couldn't be very sizable. So why not store it in a bank vault somewhere, which would be much cheaper? Then, at least, you could look at it from time to time.

No, this wasn't a treasure that anyone ever wished to look at. So what kind of treasure had to be so expensively guarded, yet no one wanted to see?

And the answer came back with dread finality: *nothing*.

Abruptly it came home to Ciccio that there wasn't any treasure here at all.

Not now.

Because they'd just killed it.

The treasure wasn't in the house. It was in the man.

For it was not Adriano who had guarded the treasure house, but the treasure house which had guarded Adriano. That was why he had so seldom gone away from it, yet still been able to go sometimes; it was why the Donor could not have employed *two* guardians with a rota system, nor have simply buried his treasure and done without any guardian at all; and it was why Adriano, not fearing death, had spent his last seconds of life trying to warn them that they were making a mistake – that they did not understand.

Ciccio realised now that they were up against something far bigger than he'd previously thought. He also knew they were trying to penetrate a protective system so well thought out that they stood no chance of beating it. His paltry observations and investigations now seemed laughable. His reasoning – so impressive to Giorgio – had been a miserable failure. Yet another in a life of miserable failures.

What they had just done might fool the police and the doctors.

But it wouldn't fool the Donor.

And then he would come after them.

Ciccio turned around to find Giorgio glaring at him in exasperation. He laid a hand on his shoulder. 'Giorgio,' he said quietly, 'we've just made a terrible mistake.'

The other's exasperation evaporated instantly. He stared at Ciccio for a long moment. He didn't know what Ciccio had come to understand, but the tone of voice said it all. He ranged his friend's ominous words alongside this whole strange setup – the house, the guardians, the voluntary incarceration and the donations of millions of dollars – and suddenly Giorgio knew he was a dead man.

He leaned forward, hugged Ciccio and kissed him lightly on the cheek. 'Then, brother mine, we've just made a mistake. Now we must run – and survive as long as we can.'

6

Giuseppe Rampone, a member of the Illustrious College of Notaries Public of Palermo, returned to his office in the Via Maqueda at ten to four, mumbled 'Good afternoon' to his clerks and assistants, went into the private office and sat down at his desk to read the *Corriere della Sera*. Just after four o'clock his secretary walked in with a telephone-message slip. On it were the words *No message*. Rampone pulled a pad towards him and jotted down some words.

'Send this telegram immediately. Then call the operator and check if the telephone lines are down anywhere in western Sicily. And I want a seismological report, too.'

It was 4.18 when she informed him that the Sicilian telephone network was working perfectly, and there had been no earth tremors recorded for the last two weeks. Even Etna – in the far east of the island – was behaving itself. The news slightly surprised Rampone. Twice before there had been an absence of message, but on both occasions that had been due to a brief failure in the telephone network.

Abruptly businesslike, Rampone replied, 'Then cancel my engagements for the afternoon.' He went over to his safe and withdrew a sealed envelope which had lain there undisturbed for nine years. He took it to his desk, sat down and, using an elegant, sword-shaped paper knife, slit open the envelope. Inside were three keys and a sheet of paper containing his instructions. He read them through carefully. They did not seem unduly complicated, but they were certainly detailed. The first step, however, was very easy: he was to make a simple telephone call. He dialled the given number and a secretary replied. He told her who he was and said he had an urgent message for Michele Diriazzi. When he was put through, he said, 'I have a priority patient for you, Doctor.'

There was a moment's silence at the other end, then Diriazzi asked him where they should meet.

'Where's your consultancy?'

Diriazzi gave him an address in the Via Cavour, just a few streets away. Rampone said he'd pick him up from there in ten minutes. He left his office at once.

Diriazzi and his assistant were waiting in the street outside his surgery. Rampone realised he knew him by sight; they were both supporters of the Teatro Massimo.

'Where are we going?' asked Diriazzi, climbing in alongside the notary, while his assistant got into the back.

Interesting, thought Rampone; he doesn't know. 'Some private estate near Roccamena.'

'Big?'

'I don't know. I've never been there.' Being a lawyer, Rampone erred on the side of caution, so omitted to mention that he'd learned of the house's location only fifteen minutes ago.

Rampone's car was a Mercedes and he took the road to San Cipirello, which had recently been improved, so they reached the house in under an hour. He saw several men working the nearby fields as if nothing had happened, so presumably none of them had yet ventured inside the enclosed grounds that day.

Adriano Lupillo was still lying on the ground next to the outside table. His forearm lay among the broken pieces of a brandy glass. Diriazzi began his examination at once, while Rampone went inside.

Entering the sitting room, he immediately inserted one of the three keys in the right-hand aperture in the face of the grandfather clock and began to wind. Both minute and hour hands moved forwards together, their motion looking completely unnatural. They stopped at the eighth minute, and the winding mechanism was now blocked. He made a note of the time shown, then inserted the same key in the left-hand aperture. A panel in the base of the clock swung open. Inside this there was a simple bin containing several papers, which he removed. The bottom one was a yellowing inventory of the household goods; the remainder were invoices for items bought over the last nine years.

Rampone wrote out a full new inventory to include the recent purchases, with a carbon copy, then walked around the whole house to check if anything was missing. After that he placed the new inventory back in the clock's recess and closed the panel. The original inventory, the carbon copy and invoices he placed in an envelope, which he consigned to his briefcase.

All this was a bit intriguing, he thought. Still, sometimes his clients liked to generate a bit of mystery to make themselves feel important and romantic. He wondered who the Tognazzis were. One didn't need to be clairvoyant to realise they were using the place as a tax fiddle, although exactly how it worked he wasn't sure. Anyhow, good luck to them; Rampone sympathised. He paid too much in taxes himself. And he was happy with any client who paid his fees each month on the dot.

Evidently the absentee Tognazzis did more than just grow grapes on their estate, because a lot of the messages were to do with buying and selling other items, and in every communication there was a list of six prices. Rampone had sometimes taken down the messages himself, although more usually his secretary had done so. The essence of his involvement as a notary was to pass on the messages by telex to the Tognazzis' bankers in Rome, and every month send off by post a notarised declaration that no irregularities had occurred. Rampone was virtually certain that some of these messages were in code, probably to warn the client that some tax inspector had come nosing around. But that was nothing to do with him; his involvement had always been strictly legitimate. As it should be for a notary public.

Rampone left the sitting room. By now Diriazzi had finished his preliminary examination and the corpse had been carried on a makeshift stretcher into the dining room. Through the open door Rampone caught a glimpse of the doctor unbuttoning Adriano's trousers. He went outside to take a walk around the grounds.

Diriazzi came out to join him nearly an hour later. 'Heart attack,' he announced. 'Who was he anyway?'

'Don't *you* know?'

'No. I was retained by a representative of a bank.'

'The Banco di Sicilia in Rome? Nine years ago?'

'That's right. I was paid a fee in advance and instructed that if a notary ever rang to say "I have a priority patient for you", I was to accompany him straight away to examine a corpse. I was then to ascertain the cause of death and inform the notary. That was the end of it, and I'd be paid a further fee within a few days.'

'May I ask how much?'

Diriazzi grinned. 'You may, but I'm not sure I ought to tell you.' He shrugged. 'If you must know, it was originally five thousand dollars, but that amount would increase each year to keep pace with inflation – so now it'll be about nine, I imagine. Now, you tell me what you're getting.'

'I've been paid regular fees for a different matter,' replied Rampone. His tone made it clear he wasn't going to reveal anything else.

Diriazzi smiled wryly. Notaries were notaries. 'Hadn't we better inform the authorities?'

Rampone nodded and re-entered the house. There was just one last thing he had to do. He went into the dining room, put his hand in the corpse's trouser pocket and removed a small key. This he put in an envelope, which he stowed in his briefcase. Then he went looking for the phone to ring the police.

They arrived a quarter of an hour later. A sergeant was conducted into the house to take a look at the body.

'Adriano Lupillo's his name,' he verified. 'Originally from Enna.' The officer accepted the death certificate from Diriazzi and said, 'Okay. We'll handle it from here.' He watched the three other men return to their vehicle. The same thing had happened the last time, he recalled. *Good people, the Tognazzis: they look after their employees.*

It was dark by the time Rampone reached his office. There he wrote out the text of a telegram: YOUR EMPLOYEE DIED OF HEART FAILURE THIS AFTERNOON BETWEEN TWELVE AND ONE STOP BODY WAS NOT DISCOVERED MEANWHILE STOP INVENTORY CORRECT AND COMPLETE STOP EIGHT EIGHT STOP. Next he rang the telegram operator and passed it on. The addressee was the main branch in Rome of the Banco di Sicilia.

Then Rampone went home.

Georg Zaunmacher stepped briskly through the Paradeplatz and a few yards along the Bahnhofstrasse to the Bessmer Schweizerische Handelsbank. As he approached, the doorman saluted him.

'*Guten Morgen, Herr Direktor.*'

'*Guten Morgen.*'

Zaunmacher glanced at his watch – a reflex action, to check his arrival time. It was 7.44. Exactly one minute later, he walked into his office, sat down at his desk, and opened his copy of the *Züricher Tagesblatt*.

At eight o'clock sharp, his assistant came in carrying a file, placed it beside him and walked out. On its cover were the words: ACCOUNT NUMBER 38141. Zaunmacher opened it quickly. Inside was a telex from the Rome branch of the Banco di Sicilia. He got up from his desk and went over to the safe. Among the papers inside was an ancient leather-bound notebook. He flicked through the pages till he found the words '*Natural, Undiscovered, Inventory Complete*'. Underneath was a list of figures. Opposite the number 88 was the instruction: ENVELOPE NO 6.

He replaced the book in the safe, took out a key and went downstairs to the safe-deposit boxes. The one corresponding to Account 38141 was number 49. He gestured for the guard to carry it to a private cubicle. There he shut himself in, opened the box, and flipped through the six envelopes till he reached the last one.

Upstairs in his office again, Zaunmacher opened the same envelope and took out two sheets of paper. He read through them carefully and then buzzed for his assistant.

'Send Bohle to me, please.' A few minutes later a fair-haired young man came in. 'Good morning, Hans. I have something for you to do.' He handed him one of the sheets. 'As you can see, all these are American business firms, but each one has a special contact listed. It's the contact man who's important. I expect many of them will be dead by now, so it's their immediate heirs I need to get in touch with. According to the instructions, although the addresses and phone

45

numbers of the firms may have changed, their basic names won't have, so you shouldn't have any difficulty in finding them in the international telephone directories in the Commercial Library. The surname of the contact man won't have changed, either, but his heir's first name will probably be different. You should find, after the name of each firm, some cross-reference in brackets to some other firm, such as 'John Smith & Company', or 'Paul Johnson Enterprises'. That will give you the first name of the current contact. I shouldn't think there'll be any telephone listed against the bracketed entry, but even if there is, it doesn't matter. Under the name of each firm, you'll find several entries – accounts department, mail order, sales, stores, whatever. Probably these will all vary, but whichever is the last telephone number listed for each firm, that's the one I want. Understood?'

Bohle nodded and went out.

At quarter past ten he returned to Zaunmacher's office and placed a neatly typewritten sheet of paper on his desk, and withdrew. It listed twenty-four names along with their present telephone numbers. Zaunmacher looked at his watch and calculated the present time in the various American time zones. It was still night even in the most easterly of them. This was going to be a long and boring job. He preferred delegating disagreeable work, but this client was very important, so the task had to be handled properly. He dialled the number at the top of the list.

Seconds later, in New York City, the phone rang in a penthouse apartment on Park Avenue. A girl's hand reached out for it, but from behind her a man leaned over, gave her a playful smack and murmured, 'Naughty.' He picked up the phone. 'Yes, who is it?'

Zaunmacher was to the point. 'Who I am doesn't matter. I have an important message for Mr Robert Ferrandini, person to person. Will you please tell him it concerns Belvedere. I'll wait.'

'Look, chum. It's quarter-past four in the morning. You can't . . .'

'I am aware of that. I repeat, this is important. It is also very urgent.'

Ned sighed. 'Okay. Hang on.' He touched a button to transfer the call to his sitting room, went out to pick up the other phone, and touched a second button. Eighty yards away, in a different part of the same palatial apartment, another telephone rang. A man was awakened by the sound and picked up the receiver.

'Sorry to disturb you, Robert. I've got some bird on the line with a foreign accent who says he's got an urgent message for you. Won't say who he is, but says it's something to do with Belvedere.'

Ferrandini became fully awake instantly. 'Put him through.'

There was a click.

'Mr Robert Ferrandini?'

'Speaking.'

'Please give me your password.'

'Long Island.'

'Thank you. The message is as follows: the trigger has been pulled. Shall I repeat it?'

Ferrandini's breathing became harsh. No. Thank you. I understand.' He started to say something else, but the caller had already hung up. For a moment he could only stare up at the ceiling in wonder.

They'd done it! They'd finally done it!

Then he jabbed a button on the phone. 'Ned, get us out of here. Now!' He slammed down the phone and turned to his wife who was sleeping beside him. He shook her awake. 'Get dressed, Barbara. We're leaving.'

'Uh . . . ? What? What's happened?'

But Ferrandini had already left the room and was striding down the corridor, putting on a dressing gown. He had three sons and a daughter to save.

7

Ned Moreno didn't waste any time. He picked up the phone again, dialled a number and said, 'Black Car. Twenty minutes.' He replaced the receiver and checked his pistol.

His clothes were still lying in a heap on the floor next to Sandra's. She was already asleep. He dressed quickly, slipped quietly out of the room and hurried along to his boss's office. Then he opened a wall panel behind Ferrandini's desk, using his own key. He took out four handguns, made sure they were loaded, then left the office through a side door, leading to the family's private suites.

Robin, twenty years old and the eldest son, was already dressed and was throwing personal items into an overnight bag. Ned handed him one of the guns and said, 'Stick close to your sister.' Robin gave him a single nod in reply, checked the gun himself, to Ned's approval, pocketed it and continued with his packing.

Moreno moved on to the rooms of the two younger sons, Tom and Matthew, and handed guns to them, too. To Tom he said, 'I'll have my hands full looking after your father, so you keep an eye on Matt for me, okay?'

'Sure. But do you think it's a good idea to give him a gun? He's only fifteen.'

'I want all of you able to defend yourselves if you have to. He can handle it.'

Ned strode along the corridor to the master bedroom and knocked on the door. Bidden to enter, he found his boss already fully dressed. He was taking papers out of the wall safe and putting them in a briefcase. Together they went back to the office, where Ferrandini opened another safe and took out several wads of banknotes and a large bag of diamonds. When they stepped out into the front hall, the three boys were already waiting for them. Diana, the daughter, twenty-two years old, fear showing in her dark eyes, joined them a moment later. Their mother Barbara took another five minutes to arrive.

The red light on the phone next to the private elevator began to flash and Ned picked it up. A voice said, 'Basement's clear. Elevator's okay.'

'Right. We're coming down now.'

After the family had crowded into the elevator, Ned jabbed the button for the bottom basement.

Two minutes later the doors reopened to reveal six men holding machine-pistols deployed around five ordinary-looking Ford saloons, all with drivers at the ready and their engines running. The cars were of an identical dark blue.

Ned Moreno herded the young people into the fourth vehicle while Robert and Barbara climbed into the third. Then he signalled to his men, who split into pairs, each pair getting into one of the other three saloons. Ned climbed in alongside the driver in Ferrandini's car, and the convoy moved off, winding its way up through three levels. At each floor another dark blue Ford saloon joined the queue in first place. There were now eight identical cars, their registration numbers differing by a single digit in ascending order.

When they reached street level, a man standing at the entrance gave them a nod and the first four cars drove out fast, grouped close together. These were decoys and the remaining four held back to wait for another signal from the lookout, before they too emerged but at a more sedate speed – the first and last acting as escorts.

'Perhaps we should have rehearsed this,' remarked Barbara to Ned. But he was busy watching the thin pre-dawn traffic that shared the streets with them.

Robert murmured, 'He has done. Several times.'

The convoy took a zigzag route through the West Fifties. As they crossed Ninth Avenue, Robin, watching out of the rear window, saw the fourth car deliberately stall at the lights, thus preventing a solitary taxi from following them. It rejoined its companions several zigzags further into West Side.

Finally the four saloons pulled into a warehouse adjoining the Hudson River, its tall doors opening smoothly to let them through just as they reached it, then closing neatly behind them.

Shortly afterwards another convoy, this time four ordinary-looking cars of various makes and colours, emerged from the warehouse and headed out of the city towards the Bronx. They joined the New York State Thruway at Van Cortlandt Park, crossed the Hudson by the Tappan Zee bridge, and an hour later reached a rambling nineteenth-century mansion in the Catskill mountains. Ned Moreno was feeling pleased with himself. Operation *Black Car* had gone very smoothly indeed.

Back in the penthouse apartment, Ned's latest girlfriend Sandra Walsh got fed up waiting for him to come back to bed and went looking for him. When she opened the door leading from his private sitting room, she found Fredo, the butler, busy polishing the magnificent antique furniture in the corridor outside. Sandra looked at her watch: it was six o'clock. Polishing furniture at six in the morning?

'Good morning, miss. I'm afraid Mr Moreno has been called away unexpectedly. He asked me to offer you his apologies. Would you like breakfast now, or shall I serve it later?'

Hm. Pretty obviously this old bird was hanging around to make sure she didn't walk off with the family silver. 'No. Later, I think.' And she went back to bed. It had taken her weeks of patient work to get this close to the Ferrandinis and she was going to get her pound of flesh. She had to admit that Ned was pretty good in the sack and she wondered why he'd gone off so suddenly. It must have had something to do with that phone call. Well, she'd think about that later. First, it was time to screw up Fredo's morning and get some more shuteye until ten or eleven. She turned onto her side and went back to sleep.

In the Catskills retreat, Robert Ferrandini was busy on the telephone, while in another room Moreno was explaining the security arrangements to his boss's family.

'Nobody knows about this house except the men who drove us here. Although you probably don't know them, they and their fathers before them have been part of the Family for decades. Robert trusts them completely.'

'Does Dad own this place?' inquired Diana.

'Yes, but not in his own name. That's why it's safe. In fact your grandfather bought it.'

Robin asked, 'What's happening, Ned?'

'I don't know. Your father's trying to find out. For the moment I don't want any of you to go outside. Is that clear?'

Ferrandini's wife and children nodded meekly. You didn't argue with Ned. Not when it came to security. If you were one of the boys you were likely to get a punch in the mouth for any infraction. And Diana had once been picked up bodily and locked in her room. When he let her out again three hours later, she'd made a beeline for her father to complain. 'I hope you had something good to read,' was his only response.

Orphaned early in life, Ned Moreno had developed his hard fighting skills on the New York streets. But he wasn't only tough; he had a keen intelligence which his boss had begun to channel into business management. He had an aptitude for picking up foreign languages too, which made him particularly useful to Ferrandini, who had eventually appointed him his personal assistant.

But all the while this tough young man from the streets was gradually becoming emotionally involved with the wealthy family which had adopted him, although only Robert himself had spotted this. He had come to love them, though his guarded nature would

50

allow him to show it only through an unwavering concern for their safety.

His lecture over, the family went upstairs to choose their rooms, and soon Ferrandini called Ned into the study. He invited him to sit down and offered him a cigarette.

'It's time I told you about Belvedere,' he continued, reaching across to offer him a light. 'But before I do, there's one thing you must understand. There's nothing I've ever said to you which contradicts what I'm about to tell you now. More to the point, there's nothing I've ever done which hasn't been in accordance with what I believe to be right, in spite of Belvedere. When you know everything, you may find that hard to believe.'

Ned gave him a half smile. 'What say you let me be the judge of that?'

Robert looked at the other man, who was almost like another son to him, mentally contrasting his dark-eyed, black-haired, Italianate good looks with the fair hair and blue eyes of his real sons, and raised an eyebrow in something like admonition.

'You will be anyway, Ned.'

In that instant Ned realised that Ferrandini was going to tell him everything. He suddenly knew that whatever it was that Robert was going to say would change their relationship irrevocably. He studied the older man's suave bearing. He was like an advertising agency's idea of power made elegant: the cocktail mix of gymnasium-prepared trimness of figure and the prematurely whitening hair kept youthful and sexy by being so carefully cut and groomed atop the smooth, elegant tan of the still clean-cut face. But now, for the first time, he saw aging and apprehension akin to fear. Whatever debts had been run up in the past were about to be called in.

Robert got up and went over to the window. The sun had been up for two hours; it was going to be a glorious morning. Ferrandini pulled out a cigarette and lit it. This action was the final reprieve. Afterwards he had no alternative but to tell the tale.

He spoke for half an hour and Ned listened spellbound – soon realising that he was hearing the explanation of why much of the world was as it was.

They spent the rest of the morning on the telephone, partly in making inquiries to find out what had prompted the crisis, and partly in trying to get in touch with the other Codeholders. This second task wasn't easy, because they too had gone to ground. But their lieutenants remained accessible and one by one the messages were passed on.

Eventually, after much discussion, it was agreed to hold an extraordinary meeting of the Curia that night in a building belonging to one of Ferrandini's untraceable companies.

51

In the meantime Sandra Walsh had got tired of screwing up the butler's schedule, and she finally emerged from Ned's private rooms at half past eleven. She then stretched Fredo's patience to breaking point by ignoring his offer of breakfast in Ned's private sitting room, sweeping along instead to the main dining room, where she sat herself down at the head of the huge table – in Ferrandini's own chair! Ten minutes later he began serving her a spectacularly awful breakfast as punishment. Sandra ignored the burnt bacon and the fried eggs almost raw. She smiled sweetly at him. He smiled back.

'Is Mr Ferrandini at home?' she inquired.

'Not at the moment, miss,' he replied, pouring her a cup of stale coffee.

'Perhaps he'll be back for lunch?'

'I've had no instructions to that effect, miss.'

She doubted she'd get anything more out of him so she picked up her bag and moved towards the main door. Fredo hurried ahead of her, ever the polite servant. Probably wants to slam it behind me, she thought. Just before reaching the door, however, Sandra turned abruptly along the short side corridor to Ferrandini's office.

A female secretary and a male assistant were busy in the anteroom. They both looked up startled at her abrupt entrance and regarded her warily when she asked, 'When will Mr Ferrandini be back?'

The woman replied, 'We don't know. May I help you?'

'What about Mr Moreno?'

'I believe he's had to go out of town for the day.'

Just then Fredo appeared behind her and, in a voice which brooked no misinterpretation, said, 'The way out is this way, miss,' laying unusual stress on the word 'out'.

The secretary had no difficulty in understanding his tone. 'I'm so sorry we aren't able to assist you,' she added coldly.

'So am I,' replied Sandra winsomely and left.

Down in the street she went into a nearby bar and rang Bill Jackson, editor of the newspaper she regularly sold her stories to.

'I think something's up with Ferrandini: get some people to phone the apartment, pretending to be friends of his kids and asking to speak to them. You'd better space the calls out a bit, or they'll smell a rat. Maybe they can find out where he's gone.' She hung up and left the bar, swinging her handbag in a small circle.

A few yards away a man who was looking in a store window broke off his examination and began following twenty yards behind her.

Ned Moreno did the driving as far as Kingston on the Hudson River. Ferrandini rode in the back with Amadeo, his fifty-year-old Filipino bodyguard, rescued by Robert's father Salvatore from a white slavery racket nearly forty years before and who now lived in semi-retirement, looking after the Catskills mansion with his Cuban wife. In Kingston they all transferred to a black-windowed bullet-proof Lincoln driven by Stelio's right-hand man.

Stelio Mascagni, known to everybody by his first name, was the head of a large detective agency and security service, with several enforcers on the payroll who handled bad debts – or more usually bad debtors – and was one of Ferrandini's most reliable collaborators. Although there was no written contract between them, he was counted as part of the wider Ferrandini 'Family'. This was yet another element in Robert's broad-spectrum inheritance from his father Salvatore.

As the Lincoln joined the New York State Thruway, two downmarket-looking but souped-up vehicles promptly sandwiched it fore and aft in escort. Each had a first-class driver at the wheel and an armed marksman sitting alongside him. None of them would know who they were escorting but each, being one of Stelio's men, understood perfectly well what he would do to them if any misfortune befell their charge.

As they entered the city suburbs a Mercedes C Class began to overtake them and the lead car accelerated enough to allow it to slip in between. The driver gave a brief wave as he passed. It was Stelio himself. His almost excessive good looks didn't quite hide the ruthlessness and chained savagery that could be glimpsed in his eyes.

The convoy took the Roosevelt Drive and then the South Street Viaduct to the Brooklyn Bridge and crossed the East River into Downtown Brooklyn. On Court Street it swung into an underground garage beneath an office building, owned by one of Ferrandini's front companies. The Lincoln halted next to a door leading through to the stairwell.

Stelio surrendered his Mercedes to one of his men and came over to open the doors for them. He herded his charges through the exit door, saying, 'Sorry, Robert. You'll have to go up on foot. We haven't had time to check the elevators properly. We've tested them and they look okay, but I'm not a hundred per cent sure. They might still be booby-trapped, and somebody's waiting to bag a few members of the Curia.'

'Jesus Christ! It's thirty floors! *I'd* have difficulty enough and I'm only fifty-four, but what about men like Cattagna? He's eighty-five!'

Stelio could only shrug. 'I've set up chairs on every tenth floor. We can take the older men up in carry-chairs. Anybody else who wants it, if it comes to that.'

Ferrandini shook his head firmly. 'No, Stelio. I'm not having Cattagna subjected to such an indignity. Check the goddamn elevators again. We'll wait. If you still can't find anything, we'll take the goddamn risk!'

Stelio puffed out his cheeks in exasperation. 'Be reasonable, Robert. I'm doing this entire job with only nineteen men.'

'Why so few?'

'Because half the guys I can trust are already doing a job in Vegas. I've called 'em all home, but they won't get here till later tonight. I can get you all out again, safely, but getting everybody in now, with only nineteen heads, is a hell of a business. You haven't exactly given me much time,' he added pointedly.

'How many men are you covering?'

'Aside from you, fourteen. They'll be brought in in three groups of four, and one pair: four operations in all, at intervals of half an hour each. The other nine are making their own arrangements.'

'I hope none of those nine know the final address.'

Stelio looked offended. 'Of course not. We've picked a rendezvous near Kennedy and we'll guide them in from there. The agreement is that each man is allowed two of their own bodyguards inside the building and two men down in the street, while the meeting's in progress, but they stay in sight of my people at all times. So there'll be eighteen of them, but I can handle that. I can swell out the numbers with casuals who won't know anything. I'll make it look like a low-level parley on jurisdictions.'

'Shame about this building, though. We'll never be able to use it again.'

Stelio's reply was pointed. 'It may not even be secure now. If the balloon's going up, who knows what preparations they've already made. They might have had moles tunnelling through your setup for years. And, as I say, I've only got nineteen men.'

'Any of them know much about booby traps?'

'Half a dozen have got notions, but none of them's an expert. My technical people are all in Vegas.'

'So there's no alternative. We'll go up one at a time, but we'll use the elevators.'

Stelio gave a shrug of resignation, 'Okay. You're the boss.' He went out to organise a final check.

Ned murmured to Robert, 'If anything does happen to somebody, what about his part of the Code?'

'Hm.' Ferrandini thought for a moment. 'Tell Stelio to find me twenty-four envelopes and a pad of notepaper.'

Twenty minutes later the first guests arrived. Robert explained to them the problem with the elevators. 'Personally I'm prepared to take the risk. Stelio says they look okay, but he's not completely sure. I'll put my money where my mouth is and go first, but if anyone does get hit, we'd lose his code.'

'What's the point in worrying about that? The Code's useless now,' said Lovegni, the look of tension seeming out of place on his plump, down-to-earth, good-natured face.

'Maybe. Maybe not. It might contain a second message – one directed specifically at us.'

'So what do you propose?'

'That each of us write down his own code on a separate piece of paper and seal it in an envelope with his signature over the flap. Stelio will hold on to the envelopes until we're all safely upstairs. But first we agree upon our honour that if anything happens to any individual, whatever value there may still be left in the Code will benefit his Family to the same extent as it benefits everyone else.'

Lovegni nodded. 'Seems reasonable. I accept. Since you're going to be the trailblazer, I'll stay down and explain it to the other guys when they get here.'

Ferrandini nodded and moved away. Stelio accompanied him to the elevator and wished him *bon voyage*. Robert went inside and, without a qualm, pressed the button for the penthouse floor. He simply didn't believe they'd come after them with bombs.

Moments later he stepped out unscathed, and shook hands with Dino, Stelio's second son and his own godson, who was there to act as bartender.

'Scotch and soda, Don Roberto?'

Ferrandini grinned. The boy had spoken in jest. The title *Don* was hardly ever used in America these days, although this evening everybody was going to be 'donning' everybody else a lot. It was the custom at 'meets'. Some people could be very sensitive and it wouldn't do to show the wrong kind of familiarity.

'Mainly soda. Just let me taste the scotch.'

The boy served him, then Ferrandini took a walk around the elegant suite of offices – the headquarters of a toy manufacturing company. It had been several years since he had last been here. He wandered into the library with its large picture windows, which faced west and afforded a spectacular view of Brooklyn Heights and the towers of Manhattan beyond, now framed against a horizon reddened by the setting sun.

After a few moments of appreciation of the scene, he returned to the bar, just as the next Codeholder arrived. This was Lorenzo Brunetti, who Ferrandini didn't particularly like, but they greeted each other with scrupulous courtesy.

Brunetti was followed by Antonio Patellini. He was not a close friend of Robert's, but their two Families had always cooperated closely. After greeting Ferrandini with worried cordiality, Patellini took him to one side.

'Robert, Rule Three forbids me to ask you if you know who set up Belvedere, but it doesn't say anything about volunteering information.

55

When my father was on his deathbed, I couldn't resist asking him if he was the Designer. He swore to me he wasn't.' Prohibited from prying, he now waited for Ferrandini to reciprocate.

Robert shook his head. 'Antonio, I know a lot of the Codeholders think my father worked some fiddle with the lottery to make sure he'd be the Designer, but I promise you I never asked him, and he never told me.'

Patellini nodded. 'If he had done, I wouldn't have blamed him. In fact, I don't think many of us would.' He changed the subject.

The fifth arrival was Vincenzo Cattagna from Chicago. He and Ferrandini embraced each other warmly; it had been nearly a year since their last meeting. Cattagna and Robert's father Salvatore had been close friends and allies, and, as a boy, Robert had looked upon Don Vincenzo as almost an uncle.

As they separated, Ferrandini now said, 'I don't suppose it was you who set up Belvedere, was it?' It was a forlorn hope, born of the fact that, since the death of Michael Gabrielli four months previously, the old man was now the only survivor of the original Curia.

'You've just broken Rule Three, Robert,' replied Cattagna with mock severity.

'To hell with the rules, Vincenzo,' muttered Ferrandini. 'This is no time to worry about formality.'

Vincenzo nodded grimly. 'I suppose not. The answer is no, Robert. I was not the Designer. Unfortunately. If I had been, I might know how to stop the damn thing.'

Ferrandini was obliged to cut short this conversation, in order to greet the next Codeholder, but soon afterwards he spotted Cattagna in a corner of the room, keeping very much to himself. He seemed to be preoccupied about something.

One by one the Codeholders appeared. The mood was generally tense, and Ferrandini noticed that several were eying each other suspiciously. Obviously Ned wasn't alone in suspecting that, if the balloon was about to go up, pressure might have been brought on one of the Codeholders to betray his confrères.

It was nearly ten o'clock when the last man joined them, and the meeting could begin. The twenty-four men drifted into a large boardroom. There was no particular seating arrangement, but the head of the table was reserved for Ferrandini, who was acting host. All their bodyguards and assistants were excluded because, however much a man might trust his own employee, the others could scarcely be expected to do likewise. Since any one of them might have been forced to betrayal, many did not now even trust each other.

8

'Miss Walsh?'

'Yes. Who are you?'

'FBI.' The caller flashed his ID. 'May we come in?'

'Sure. What's up?'

'We understand you're a friend of Mr Robert Ferrandini's.'

'Then you understand wrong. I've never met him. But I'm a friend of his assistant, Ned Moreno.'

'You spent last night in his apartment.'

'Is that a question?'

'No.'

'Then I won't answer it.'

'Could you tell us why Mr Ferrandini and his family suddenly left home this morning?'

'I've no idea. I only know that someone called up at four o'clock this morning and Ned answered the phone. Then he left the room for a while and when I woke up this morning all of the family had gone.'

'Did you hear any of the conversation?'

'Not really. I was half asleep. But I'm pretty sure it was someone Ned didn't know. That's all I can tell you.'

'I see. Thank you very much, Miss Walsh. We won't detain you any further, for the moment.'

The agents left her apartment building and one of them went straight to a public phone. He rang his boss. 'Same story. A call at about the same hour of the morning, and then they scattered.'

'Hm. Okay, now try and find out about Patellini and Lovegni.'

Meanwhile Sandra Walsh was phoning Bill Jackson at his home. 'Guess who I've just had a visit from.'

'Give up.'

She could almost hear his eyelids blink as she gave him a brief account of the interview. 'Sounds very interesting, I agree, but I can't publish it. What's there to say? That a rich man went off with his family for a surprise vacation? We'd be laughed out of court. And that's where Ferrandini would put us, because any story's bound to look as if we're making innuendoes.'

57

'Come on, Bill. Just one little paragraph about the FBI's surge of interest in him.'

Jackson sighed. 'I've told you before, Sandy. I'll consider anything you write about Ferrandini, but I'm not going to publish a word unless there's cast-iron proof. This isn't some soda jerk we're talking about, for Christ's sake. He's one of the richest men in the country. You just don't mess with people as powerful as that. He's got a regiment of lawyers on his payroll, and we'd get a writ from every one of them.'

'I suppose that'd be better than a bullet, anyhow,' replied Sandra absently.

Jackson grunted. 'It's *your* contention that he's a member of the Mafia – not mine.'

'I thought I'd won you over on that point.'

The editor sighed, then replied patiently, 'Sandy, I only conceded that it was *possible*. Just because people like Ferrandini and Cattagna are so rich and *happen* to be Italian-Americans, that doesn't mean they're inevitably members of Cosa Nostra. You haven't met any of them yet, remember, and I have. For God's sake, they're so damn courteous and educated, you wouldn't think they were Americans, let alone Sicilian-American Mafiosi. When I first met Cattagna, he was so courteous and charming, I thought he was a British lord.'

Sandra snorted. 'How they behave in public doesn't mean anything.'

'No, of course not,' replied Jackson irritably, 'but nor does how much money they have in the bank, either.'

'What about Ferrandini's father? You're not telling me *he* wasn't a member?'

'There were rumours, yes,' conceded the editor. 'But there've also been rumours about every other rich Italian in this country.'

'He was a known friend of Lucky Luciano's, for God's sake!'

'So what? Charlie Luciano was a popular guy. He made friends all over the place. That's not only not proof; it's not anything even remotely like proof. Besides, even if Ferrandini's father did have something to do with the Mafia, he's been dead for something like twenty years, and it's the son I thought you were investigating.'

'If the father was a member, you can bet your last dollar the son is too.'

Jackson replied in incredulous tones, 'Sandra, I wouldn't bet my last dollar or any other dollar on it. Even as a hunch, it stinks. Don't forget that a lot of the Mafia's dirty laundry came out during the Sal Gotti trial, and it became pretty clear then who all the members of the Commission were. There wasn't a whiff to suggest that Ferrandini and his pals had anything to do with it.'

'But, Bill, the whole point is just what *did* come out of the Gotti trial. When Jack Ayala gave evidence, he said there was something higher up than the Commission. He said the Commission was the board of managers – not the board of directors.'

'Ayala was a two-bit punk with a big mouth and a brain the size of a wart. He was just trying to divert the jury's attention away from Gotti to some fictitious higher-ups.'

'Then it's funny that Gotti went to so much trouble to distance himself from him.'

'Just tactics, I'd have thought.'

'Bill, we've had this argument before. I told you when I started this assignment that, if you read between the lines, it's obvious Ayala hated Gotti. He wouldn't have gone out on a limb for him even if they'd paid him. He didn't have the intelligence to realise he was helping Gotti unintentionally, and he didn't have the imagination to invent something like a Mafia supreme court.'

'If his evidence was even half accurate, how come nobody paid any attention to him?'

'*Somebody* did, Bill. Why else did he end up in the East River?'

'But that could have been for almost anything, Sandra. When it came to rubbing people up the wrong way, he was a professional.'

'But it might also have been because there really *is* a Mafia supreme court.'

Jackson sighed. 'Yes, that's true. But look, Sandra, the people you think are sitting up there on the bench – Ferrandini, Lovegni, Cattagna, Patellini and so on – they're super-rich businessmen with interests in dozens of legitimate enterprises. What possible motive could they have for involving themselves with petty thugs and drug-pushers?'

'That's the whole point, Bill! That's what I need to get to the bottom of. They clearly can't be doing it for the money.'

'Fine. That's what investigative journalism is all about. But you've got to have something more to go on, Sandra. Not just the testimony of a pathetic loser like Jack Ayala.'

'I do have other things to go on. I've spoken to half a dozen Mafia-watchers and at least three of them believe the Commission doesn't have the last word – that there's somebody else higher up, pulling the strings. Mario Fanucci is one of my sources. He's even got a name for it – the Curia – and *he* got it from a contact in the FBI.'

Jackson gave a heavy sigh. 'All right. I'm not convinced, but I'll read anything you send me. Just remember one thing: conspiracies may sell newspapers, but conspiracy theories don't.'

'Okay, Bill. If I send you anything, it'll be gospel.'

'It'd better be.' He hung up.

Sandra put down the receiver, and stared into space, wondering what the latest developments might mean. She knew a lot about organised crime now. It was Mario Fanucci who had opened her eyes to how things really worked. Factor number one, he had explained, was that, if one's business activity was illegal, then the courts would not enforce one's business agreements, so the bottom line was power – straightforward, raw power. This meant that the barons of the underworld were those who could draw on the most firepower and the most effective firepower – meaning the toughest soldiers organised into the best-equipped battalions, with spies, police contacts, and the essential paraphernalia of good communications, sophisticated technology, reliable hardware in terms of guns, transport and so on. All this required a lot of money, so the richest groups were best placed to hold the centre stage.

But this was not the deciding factor. Far from it. Because, as Fanucci had further explained, factor number two was the importance of prison in the scheme of things. Few people realised how integrated were the two worlds of gaol and the street. That wouldn't be so if, once a man was sent to prison, he never came out again. But the fact that so many low-level criminals were constantly in and out of gaols meant that debts incurred and promises made inside could be called in on the outside, and vice versa. Criminal organisations in the streets had counterpart structures inside the prisons. The effect of this on the individual criminal was considerable. His loyalty to any particular group was increased or diminished according to the weight it pulled on the other side of the prison walls. Thus, drugs and other creature comforts inside were powerful inducements for him to lend his allegiance to the group on the outside capable of supplying them. Additionally, if he knew that, while he was inside, he would have friends on the outside able to protect his family and take care of their problems, he would have a powerful incentive to keep well in with them. The net result was that whoever controlled the inside also controlled the outside, and however much money a group might be able to deploy in the street, its power was seriously weakened if it had no influence inside the prisons.

The importance of having money *outside* gaol and power *inside* helped to explain why the various races held their particular positions in the underworld pecking order. The Chinese, for example, were rich, but they were not demographically numerous enough within the United States to provide a large prison population, so they were forced to operate through alliances of one kind or another. The Jews were in much the same position. The blacks on the other hand, had a large inmate population but they had no real money on the outside, so they were obliged to work as hired hands for other groups. The Hispanics, regarded by many Anglos as a single grouping, were in fact factionalised, firstly according to country of origin – mainly Mexico, Cuba and Colombia – and secondly by their internecine wars.

60

So, on the surface, it seemed easy to understand why the Italians should be ruling the roost. They had both money and a powerful presence inside the prisons, either directly or through one of their client groups. Also they had been at the game longer than most of the other sections. They had been the best organised when Prohibition had enabled crime to turn into big business and, thanks to the success of Lucky Luciano in sinking differences between the Families and forging them into a national crime syndicate, they had emerged from the violent 1920s as the most powerful ethnic group engaged in illegitimate enterprises.

But Sandra now had enough of the picture to realise that nobody could see all of it.

To begin with, the Italians had their internal divisions too. There were Sicilians, Calabrians, Neapolitans, from the south; and northerners from Turin and Milan. Also there was a major difference between long-settled Sicilian-Americans and native-born Sicilians now operating in the USA, who were considered much tougher than their Americanised cousins.

As an extra complication, many of the Hispanic groups far outnumbered the Italians and, although they might not be so rich, they were certainly rich enough to buy whatever equipment was needed to mount a challenge. Moreover, since Latin America was separated from the States only by a notoriously leaky frontier, reinforcements were speedily available to the Hispanics, whereas the Italians were obliged to fetch theirs across an ocean.

But the greatest puzzle arose from the fact that the Italians were only distributors – not manufacturers – of the raw materials. The Colombians, for example, were the sole suppliers of cocaine, the yuppie drug, therefore they were in a position to call the shots. So why did they let the Italians control world cocaine distribution instead of taking it over themselves?

Something Mario Fanucci said had stuck in Sandra's mind: 'If there's a niche in the environment, pretty soon something will evolve to fill it. In pre-Industrial Revolution England the grey moth was king because its colour against the bark of birch trees made it hard for the birds to see. The black moth was a mutant which stood out so much it had a pretty hard time of it. But when the Industrial Revolution came along, with it came factories and chimneys pouring out black smoke. The trees changed colour and the grey moth could be seen easily. In the space of just a few years the position of the two moths was reversed. That's how natural selection works. That's what Darwinism is all about. The best is chosen by circumstances, not by intrinsic quality. And it doesn't matter whether you're talking about the best boxer, or the most successful religion, or the car manufacturer who sells most cars. Somebody is *always* the best, no matter how

61

poor the best is in objective terms. And *somebody* was going to control world crime. But why should it be the Italians? It made sense in the 1940s and '50s. But when cocaine became the big kicker, starting in the 1960s, the social environment changed and the Italians should have begun to give way to other groups more suited to it. They didn't. They're still calling the shots. It's as if Social Darwinism doesn't work any longer.'

Fanucci had then given her a series of explanatory theories, but he clearly wasn't impressed by any of them. He'd mentioned the Curia theory in a completely different context. It was Sandra herself who had wondered whether there might be some connection with the 'Social Darwinism' puzzle. What prompted her was that Fanucci made a throwaway remark about the more powerful people being those more able to concentrate on dealing with their opponents, i.e. being less distracted by worries about their own vulnerability to the police or legal process. In general, he said, the criminal tries to secure some kind of protection from the legal authorities – police, city hall, judges and so on – and the bigger the fish, the higher up the protection he can afford for himself. Sandra had wondered just how far up that protection might be available, and when Fanucci had mentioned the Curia theory, she realised that the corresponding protection at that level would be provided by the highest echelons of government. Could that be why the Italians still controlled world crime? Was there an alliance between some invisible group of them and a powerful faction within the US administration itself?

From this speculation it was an easy step to look around for likely members of such a Curia, and men like Ferrandini, Lovegni and Cattagna were obvious candidates. For Sandra the idea had a hypnotic appeal, but she'd had conspicuous lack of success in spreading her enthusiasm for it. Even imaginative people like Bill Jackson simply dismissed the Mafia as mere criminals. And what exactly *was* a criminal? A man engaged at some level in punishable and, hence, *risky* activity. Therefore it didn't make any sense for a man like Ferrandini, vastly wealthy from his legitimate enterprises, to involve himself with them. Unless he had protection from on high.

But now here was the FBI *investigating* him, for Christ's sake! What the hell was going on?

9

Ferrandini closed the double doors and went to his seat at the head of the table. The small talk died and everyone waited on their host.

'Gentlemen, it looks as if we're about to be run over by a steamroller. The question is: who released the brake?'

He glanced around the table, and Antonio Patellini said, '*My* sources tell me everything's pretty quiet. Asians, Colombians, Jews, Irish – everybody seems happy.'

Ferrandini nodded. 'I've already sounded out all of you privately and nobody's heard anything. Besides the groups just mentioned, we've probed our contacts in the White House, Justice and FBI, State and CIA, the police. Everybody except the Boy Scouts. But there is another factor to consider. We're all still here. No move has been made against us.'

He was about to go on, but Brunetti interrupted. 'What's stopping them making their move tomorrow?'

'Nothing, Don Lorenzo. But if anyone *has* launched an attack against Belvedere, at least it wasn't a coordinated plan to knock out both the system and us at the same time, and we've always agreed that any serious attack would do so, otherwise we'd have time to launch the Code.'

Brunetti shook his head impatiently. 'So what if we have? Maybe we were just wrong.'

Ferrandini glanced at Cattagna, who was sitting on his right. The old man had seemed lost in thought all evening, as if he was trying to make up his mind about something. But now he stirred, evidently having decided to answer Brunetti. Elegantly flicking a flake of ash from his jacket sleeve, he said, 'If we were wrong, then Belvedere would have ceased to be a deterrent. It's true the world has changed, and many attitudes have changed with it, but do any of us believe the US government thinks they've changed enough for it to ignore the damage Belvedere could do?'

'We discussed that as a serious possibility in 1989, when the Soviet Union collapsed,' Brunetti reminded him.

'Indeed we did, Don Lorenzo. And we decided two things: *one*, the continued existence of communist regimes in countries like China and Cuba was in any case a sufficient guarantee of the status quo;

two, that even if these countries too changed their political systems, the *international* dimension of Belvedere's deterrent value might be reduced, but its *domestic* impact would be unaffected. We mustn't forget, Salvatore always warned us that, as time went by, the deterrent value would shift from the international element to the domestic issue.'

'So what are you saying?'

'Simply that I don't think the government is behind it.'

'Then who is? The Chinese?'

Patellini put in, 'They're our clearest rivals. They have the best organisation to take over, and they've been champing at the bit for years. And they wouldn't worry about the damage Belvedere could do because they don't know it protects them as well as us.'

Ferrandini countered, 'They know *some* kind of defence mechanism exists, even if they don't know exactly what it is.'

'Why couldn't the government have simply told them?' suggested Brunetti.

'Why should they do that?'

'They might be employing them.'

Ferrandini shot a sideways glance at Cattagna, who started to make a tactful rebuttal, but he was silenced by Lovegni's down-to-earth bluntness. 'What for? To get rid of a threat to reveal a secret by letting the Chinese in on it?'

Brunetti looked as if he was about to organise another excursion into surrealism, so Ferrandini hurriedly put in, 'Besides, the old guard is still very much in control. Lee Kwan was hospitalised last month, but he's out again now and, from what I hear, firmly back in the saddle.'

Cattagna nodded. 'And he's always counselled moderation. Under his influence the Chinese Council has consistently favoured an accommodation with us.'

Ferrandini decided to hammer the point home so that they could get on. 'The plain fact is that Belvedere protects the Chinese too, because we decided it should. Which, in effect, puts them in the position of being licensees. They may not know the details, but they do know *some* kind of protection system exists, and that while it does, it covers them too.'

Lovegni grunted, 'For them it's a stand-off. Their younger people don't like it, but the alternative would be a full-scale war between us and we'd be back in the Twenties all over again.'

'In any case,' added Ferrandini, giving the nail one final bang on the head, 'they now have too many legitimate interests, to risk any confrontation in the illegitimate sphere – which is why they've always resisted the Young Turks' demands for staking out a bigger share of the pie.'

Brunetti's ears pricked up. 'Turks? Since when have the Chinese been allied with the Turks?'

There was a moment of tense silence. Several men successfully covered their smiles, but Brunetti was saved from embarrassment by a suave intervention by Cattagna. 'You must forgive my young friend, Don Lorenzo. He sometimes gets carried away with his own erudition. I remember coming across the expression in my youth. I think it means "hotheads". Isn't that right, Robert?'

Ferrandini shot the old man a look of gratitude.

Brunetti, missing everything, replied, 'Well, if it's not the Chinese, who else *is* there? The Japs and Koreans have always kept to their patch and they've got no base here. The Irish and the Jews are happy with the arrangements they've already got. The Hispanics are too busy knocking each other off. And it's certainly not the blacks. So who else is left?'

'Nobody,' replied Cattagna inscrutably, and someone burst out laughing. That gave them all an excuse to release tension and the accumulated debit of laughter owed to Brunetti's ridiculous remark about the Turks could now be paid off in safety.

When it died, Patellini said, 'Let's take a vote. Who believes the Accords are being violated?'

Not a single hand was raised.

'So, unless this is the quietest operation since the Manhattan Project, we don't think Belvedere is under attack. So who's pulled the trigger?'

A silence of several seconds was broken by Cattagna, who remarked reflectively, 'It would seem to be the general opinion that Belvedere has been set off . . . by accident.' Robert noted he seemed more troubled by something than ever.

But Brunetti's response was predictable and angry. Looking at Ferrandini accusingly, he said, 'Whoever set up Belvedere gave us assurances that it couldn't happen.'

'When did he do that?' asked one of the younger men.

'In the anonymous notes which he sent to our fathers, when the system was set up. You must have read yours, because it gives you your part of the Code.'

'I know, and I memorised it. But I don't remember reading that accidents were impossible.'

'The Designer said a mishap was out of the question.'

'That's not true,' countered Ferrandini, in a defensive voice because he too suspected that the Designer of the Belvedere system had been his own father. 'He said it was *virtually* impossible.'

Cattagna took out a sheet of aged paper and interposed, 'This is the anonymous note that *I* received. I imagine some people will have re-read theirs today, but it might be useful to refresh the memories of those who haven't, so I'll read it out. *"Friend and brother, the Belvedere system has been set up, in line with the general suggestions made by Don Salvatore Ferrandini. Hence, we have a considerable degree of protection. The scheme will certainly last for decades, and possibly even for centuries. I am satisfied that all realistic eventualities have been anticipated. The system will come into operation automatically if there is a unilateral cancellation of the Accords, accompanied by a direct attack on us – providing every future member of the Curia bears the surname of the current member from whom he inherited his seat. Therefore, whoever succeeds to your position in the Curia, Don Vincenzo, even if he is not a direct male descendant, should legally bear the surname 'Cattagna'.*

' *"Belvedere will also be triggered if an attack is made on the system itself, like a burglar alarm going off when a thief tries to deactivate it prior to committing his burglary.*

' *"The Curia itself, in joint session, may activate Belvedere voluntarily, by issuing a coded instruction. The part of the Code corresponding to you, Don Vincenzo, is: T-A-2. Your position in the Code is number 21. The segments of the Code held by each Codeholder have been arranged so that, even if some segments are lost – through some accident, or even by the simultaneous abduction of several Codeholders – the complete Code will still be deducible, or at least guessable, by the rest of the Curia, although in the case of numerical portions, permutations will be required.*

' *"If Belvedere is ever activated, for whatever reason, each Codeholder will receive an anonymous phone call notifying him of the fact. But to ensure that the caller is able to contact you, always retain the legal ownership of your firm 'Chicago Entertainments, Ltd' and list it in the telephone directory. Whoever holds the Cattagna code must also set up a separate company (the name to consist of his own first name and an alias surname), with some legal link with Chicago Entertainments, so that it can appear in brackets in the directory listing underneath the heading. This will enable the caller to ask for the current Codeholder by name. However many telephone numbers may be listed, the last should be the number at which you wish to receive notification. The entry alongside the number can be a fictitious department of your company, such as 'Maintenance' or 'Archives', which nobody would normally ring. The caller will say he has a message concerning 'Belvedere'. To verify your identity, he will ask for your password. The Cattagna password is: 'Manhattan'. Then the caller will notify you of the activation of the Belvedere system, with the message:* The trigger has been pulled.

' *"As regards some kind of accidental triggering of the system, a clerical error is virtually out of the question, and the only other kind of mishap possible would be if Belvedere was attacked by somebody who did not realise what he was doing, and the control system failed to distinguish this from a deliberate assault by someone who knows what Belvedere is for. This could only occur in extremely unlikely circumstances."* '

'Not so unlikely, if that's what's happened,' said Brunetti.

It was a stupid observation, but Ferrandini decided to treat it as intelligent and concede the point. 'Maybe not. But with due respect, Don Lorenzo, I think what matters now is not who is to blame, but how to stop it.'

Cattagna nodded to show his support for this sensible advice, but almost everyone else wore expressions of varying degrees of confusion. '*Is* there any way to stop it?' asked Lovegni.

'I don't know. If it was my father who set it up, he never told me how it works. But what we've all *always* known is how to trigger it ourselves.'

'What good will that do us now?' snorted Brunetti.

'Perhaps none at all,' replied Ferrandini patiently. 'But if we could follow it through in its early stages, maybe we could see how it eventually works. I propose we look at the Code.'

Cattagna raised an elegantly manicured finger to speak. 'I support the proposal, though I don't think the Code itself will tell us very much.' He glanced around the table and decided it would be useful to remind them all of his authority. 'I am now the only survivor of the original Curia. I was present at our first meeting when Salvatore outlined his basic idea to set up a burglar alarm system, and to decide by secret lottery who should actually design and construct it.'

He paused, as if reluctant to say something. Once again, Ferrandini noted, he seemed to be wrestling with some problem.

Now, giving a small sigh, Cattagna went on, 'Gentlemen, I once gave Salvatore my word that I would never reveal something to you. I have never in my life broken a vow, and I never thought the day would dawn when I would need to – least of all, a vow made to Salvatore. But, because of the crisis in which we now find ourselves, and because – in common with you – I believe that crisis has arisen through some accident, I think Salvatore, were he alive to do so, would release me from that vow.' He threw Robert – as stand-in for his father – an apologetic look. 'So I have a confession to make you. As many of you already suspect, Salvatore arranged matters to take charge of the Accords himself. I was his accomplice.'

Most greeted this announcement by merely nodding at the confirmation of what they already suspected, but some wanted to register a protest. Brunetti – predictably – was one of them.

'He swore the lottery would be fair!'

Cattagna replied suavely, 'No, Don Lorenzo. He spent some time considering the precise phrasing of the promise he intended to make, and we discussed the matter together at some length. So I can assure you that his exact words were: "*Since it is in the interests of all of us that nobody should be able to deduce the identity of the man who designs the Belvedere system, I give you all my word that the lottery will be fairly*

67

conducted, so that no one can infer who is the Designer." A careful analysis of the construction of that sentence will show that he did not commit himself to making the lottery itself fair.'

'But he still broke his word, because *you* knew who the Designer was!'

'Because he told me. Therefore I did not infer it.'

Several men laughed at this.

'How did he fool our fathers?' asked Patellini. 'They all saw the Accords going into one of the envelopes, and blank sheets of paper into the other twenty-three. Once the envelopes were sealed, they were identical.'

'*Visibly* identical, yes. But there was another part of the procedure, which perhaps your father didn't mention to you. No one ever questioned it, because it seemed absolutely essential to the construction of the alarm system. And how Salvatore used it to trick everybody is an interesting illustration of his mind.

'You see, whoever was to have custody of the Accords would also take the twenty-five million dollars which we had earmarked to set up the system. Obviously, if we could see who walked off with the money, we'd know who had the Accords. Therefore a way had to be found for the winner of the lottery to take the money anonymously. Salvatore privately told me beforehand what to say, and, at the meeting to discuss how we were going to organise the tombola, I suggested we use twenty-four identical suitcases and pack the money in one of them. The key to it would go into the same envelope as the Accords. The other keys would be allotted to the remaining envelopes at random. The suitcases would be placed in an adjoining room, then a few men would go out to select some young lad passing by, and offer him a dollar to go into that room, on his own, and move the suitcases around, so that subsequently none of us would know which of them held the money. Then, after the tombola, each man would take out the key from the envelope he had selected, go into the room with the suitcases, alone, and take away whichever one his key fitted. My suggestion was accepted. In fact it was Don Lorenzo's father who undertook to buy the suitcases.

'Just before the tombola itself, Salvatore came into the room where the suitcases were waiting and put the money on the table. Four of us began to count it. Then Philip Lovegni's father, Don Arturo, returned to say the young lad they'd picked was waiting outside. Salvatore covered the money with a tablecloth, then the boy was brought in and asked to pick out one of the suitcases. We packed the money into it and I locked it. I took out the key and looked around for a suitable place to put it down, at which point Salvatore came forward with two empty shoeboxes. I placed the key in one of them and put it down on the floor, in full view of everybody, beside my left shoe; the other I put next to my right one. Then we rapidly filled the other suitcases with newspapers. I locked them and dropped each key into the second shoebox after every operation.

'Then, while the boy was earning his dollar, the tombola was carried out. The key from the first shoebox went into the same envelope as the Accords; the keys from the second shoebox were put into the other envelopes at random. The packages were churned, then Don Arturo and I took them out and arranged them in a row along the table. Salvatore had claimed first choice for himself and, since the entire scheme was his, nobody objected. When we had finished arranging the envelopes, Salvatore walked straight up to the table, snatched an envelope and walked away with the Belvedere Accords.

'He needed a completely transparent procedure, because he knew everyone would be watching him like a hawk. So, of course they were all so busy watching *him*, that it didn't occur to anyone to watch *me*, and nobody noticed the wristwatch I was wearing. It had a tiny compass in its face. Salvatore and I had worked out beforehand a simple system of gestures for me to indicate the right envelope.'

'The key was magnetic!' exclaimed Brunetti, as if he had just discovered gravity.

Patellini frowned. 'I don't understand. Did you switch keys?'

'No, Don Antonio. With so many people around, all watching like hawks, any sleight of hand of that sort would have been practically impossible. The metal used in keys is very easily magnetised. In fact, if a key is left undisturbed for a few weeks, the atoms in the metal will align themselves with the earth's own magnetic field. That was why I dropped all the others from table height into the second shoebox, because a sharp jolt knocks the atoms out of alignment. Needless to say, we couldn't rely on the critical key *not* having been jolted by someone recently, so in the heel of my left shoe we had fitted a small magnet. Our only worry was that when the envelopes were churned, the key might lose its magnetism. We tested this beforehand, and found that since it was cushioned by the paper the key could be churned for several minutes before it lost its magnetism.'

Philip Lovegni was smiling in admiration. 'Ingenious.'

'Salvatore got away with it, because none of your fathers was very scientifically minded. But there was no way he could fool everybody without an accomplice, which was why he had to involve me. By the way, no one ever doubted that the Accords really had been raffled, but many of *you* – their sons or grandsons who didn't witness the tombola – have always suspected Salvatore of somehow fixing the race. It's an interesting confirmation of the old saw "*Seeing is Believing*".'

' "Fixing" is right. It was dishonest,' grumbled Brunetti.

Cattagna replied patiently, 'You should remember, Don Lorenzo, that the object of the exercise was to build a secure system for the preservation of the Accords, so the lives of all the Codeholders – Salvatore's included – depended on the inability of any opponent to move against us without risking a triggering of the alarm system. That implied two conditions: *one*, the burglar alarm itself had to be well designed: *two*, the opponent must not be able to identify its designer, with any certainty of extracting from him the method of operation, before the alarm went off. Salvatore could have let someone else set up the system, and himself remained ignorant of how it worked, but perhaps there was a chance that this other Designer might not have been so meticulous as he knew himself to be. So he did what I think many of us would have done – he tricked the whole Curia, with the aim of tricking the Curia's opponents. He did it to survive – and so that all your fathers could also survive.'

Patellini nodded. 'Yes, Don Vincenzo. I don't think there's any need for further justifications. Don Salvatore may have deceived our fathers, but he did not betray them.'

Wanting to take the discussion back to the immediate crisis, the ever-practical Lovegni asked, 'Did Salvatore explain to you anything about the system he set up?'

Cattagna shook his head. 'No. In fact, I asked him how it worked, and he said, "If I tell you anything about it, I weaken it. As it is, the fact that you know I'm the Designer already weakens it slightly, and it's just as well for you that we're such close friends, because if we weren't, then logically – for the sake of my family – I ought to be thinking about arranging an accident for you. The system is practically foolproof, and it will keep us ninety-nine per cent safe while I'm alive, and ninety-nine-point-nine per cent safe after I'm dead, when nobody at all will know how to dismantle it." '

'But didn't he give you *any* hint?' persisted Brunetti.

'Not really. The only other time we discussed the matter was when I got the "anonymous" note. Actually, he handed it to me over dinner together in the Pierre. After reading it through, I asked him why he'd chosen the phrase *"The trigger has been pulled"*. He replied, "A burglar alarm is simply a type of booby trap, and all booby traps have some sort of trigger or tripwire, and something which is then released. Belvedere will be activated if one of three things happens: if we launch the Code, if we're attacked as a group, or if somebody tries to dismantle the system. The exact mechanical analogy is a bit different in each case, but what they've all got in common is a trigger." I then said, "And the very last thing we want it to do is just ring a bell. It's a booby trap with a bomb. In fact, since the explosion can't be instantaneous, it's a time bomb. How long would we have, if someone triggered it?" He looked at me thoughtfully for a moment, then replied, "If you knew how long it takes to operate, you might be able to deduce something about *how* it works." '

This provoked several murmured discussions. When they died away, Ferrandini asked, 'Vincenzo, why do you think the Code itself won't tell us very much?'

'Because over the years I've thought a great deal about how *I* would have set up a foolproof scheme, and I'm quite certain that, whatever the Code is, it can only allow us to pull the trigger. It can't lead us to find its location, however much we might want to, because obviously, in that case, we could also find it . . .' He paused, glanced around the table and finished meaningfully ' . . . however much we might *not* want to.'

There was a silence.

Then Cattagna continued, 'However, knowing how a man responds when his threat is ignored is usually a good indication of how he intends to follow it through.'

Ferrandini said, 'I think Don Vincenzo has made a good point. We have to look at this thing in the same way my father did. Even if Belvedere *has* been set off by accident, it was still something which his system misinterpreted as an attack. Since the system itself was a product of his mind, then in a sense *its* response is a reflection of how he would have reacted himself. So we've got to get into his mind and follow his thought processes.'

Lovegni, down-to-earth as always, said, 'Sounds impressive, but where do we start following them *from*?'

Cattagna replied, 'The Code would be one point of departure.'

'I thought you said we weren't going to get anywhere with it,' objected Brunetti.

Cattagna turned a patient gaze on him, and wondered whether his stupidity increased or lessened when he wasn't thinking. Deciding it was important to maintain the unity of the group, he chose to take the fool's remark seriously.

'My apologies, Don Lorenzo. I think I explained myself badly. What I was trying to say was this: for Belvedere to protect us properly, then we could never, any of us, be in a position to be physically forced to cooperate with anyone who wanted to deactivate it. Salvatore's solution was, in the first place, to conceal the fact that it was he who devised the system, and then to set it up without telling us where it was located. Our own ignorance was part of the deterrent, because, however much torture was applied to us, we couldn't reveal what we didn't know, and the system would come into operation as soon as it detected that any move had been made against us. So my earlier point was to say that Salvatore could not possibly have given us the means to locate the trigger without putting his whole system at risk. That's why I'm pretty sure the Code itself won't tell us where it is.

'But I think what Robert was trying to say a moment ago was that we should examine as much of the system as we can actually see, and attempt to deduce how the rest of it is structured. By trying to get inside Salvatore's mind, there's a chance we'll have some idea of how we might have been able to deactivate Belvedere if we'd built it ourselves.'

There were murmurs of agreement from around the table, and Ferrandini took charge again. 'In the anonymous notes which my father sent to everybody – himself included – each Codeholder was given a number corresponding to his segment of the Code. He didn't leave instructions about how to use it, but I think the simplest and most obvious system would be to rearrange ourselves according to that number. Mine's twenty-two.'

A few men were surprised because, now they knew for sure that the system had been set up by Salvatore, it seemed logical to suppose he would have made his own son number one.

Cattagna sitting on his right said, 'Then stay where you are, because I'm twenty-one.'

But everyone else had to move.

When they were reseated, Ferrandini slid a pad of paper across to number one, a man called Brazzi. He wrote down the letter *P* and passed the pad to his left. There were no spaces between letters, so the fifth man along was faced with the Spanish word for 'whore' – *PUTA*. He blinked at this, then remembered that Ferrandini's father and his own had disliked each other strongly. It was a barb from beyond the grave to beyond the grave. He gave a short bark of laughter, then wrote down *D*.

The seventh man added an *N* and said, 'Looks like it's in English. I always imagined it would be in Italian.'

Ferrandini shook his head. 'English takes up less space.'

The pad travelled around the table twice and almost completed a third trip. Inevitably, the final symbol was written down by number twenty-two. Cattagna smiled. He liked the neatness of it. That was Salvatore's style. He'd left his own son with the option to complete the Code or not.

Ferrandini put in strokes to divide up the words and announced, 'The Code reads as follows: "Put ad in all Palermo and three top national Italian papers: Cane perduto, Vincenzo 23".' He leaned towards Cattagna and murmured, 'You were Dad's closest friend. Why do you think he included your name in the Code?'

'It's a private joke. Your father used to say I was his lost dog. I was twenty-three when I first met him. "Vincenzo twenty-three" was a term of affection he used whenever I said anything stupid. It meant I hadn't learned anything from him. I'd almost forgotten it.'

'So it's not significant?'

72

'No, Robert. It's just a joke. But it's a pleasant surprise for me to hear it again nineteen years after his death.'

A kiss from the Unknown Region, thought Ferrandini, who was a devotee of Walt Whitman. 'Did you guess this was what the Code would say?'

'Not this exact instruction, of course, but I did expect newspapers to be involved.'

Robert nodded thoughtfully, and listened to the further comments around the table.

'I bet there's no Vincenzo street in Palermo,' someone said.

'Yes, that would be too obvious,' agreed his neighbour.

'So what does it tell us?' asked a third.

Brunetti replied, 'I'll tell you what it tells us: that somewhere in Sicily there's a man looking through the newspapers every day, waiting for this ad to appear. When it does, he pulls the trigger.'

'Then why the national papers too?'

'In case the Palermo newspapers are on strike – or being deliberately interfered with. The guy doesn't need to see all the papers. One's enough. Salvatore was just making sure.'

Cattagna replied, 'I think it's more likely he wanted to guard against errors or misprints, as there often are in newspapers. That's why it was to appear in several – they couldn't *all* get it wrong. Salvatore must have told the man with his finger on the trigger not to react unless the Code was exactly correct.'

Obviously, thought Ferrandini, grateful for the old man's good sense.

Philip Lovegni, who could always be relied on to be practical, suggested, 'Perhaps we ought to make sure this ad hasn't appeared somewhere recently.'

Ferrandini stood up, went out of the room and beckoned to Ned Moreno. 'I want photocopies sent over by fax of the small ads sections of all the Palermo local newspapers and of all the top Italian nationals for the last ten days. It's urgent.'

As Ferrandini returned to his seat, Brunetti was saying, ' . . . and we can't search the whole of Sicily for one man who happens to read a lot of newspapers.' Brunetti had a reputation for stating either the obvious or the absurd.

The table broke up into small groups as men discussed with their neighbours the magnitude of the problem. Ferrandini glanced at Cattagna, who sat back quietly biding his time, letting the others have their say until they were satisfied their own ideas wouldn't get them anywhere, and then they would be more prepared to listen to him. Ferrandini recognised this as a sound tactic normally, but with time being so short he wasn't sure it was the right strategy now. Still, fifteen minutes was unlikely to make much difference, so he let Cattagna play it his own way.

But he noticed that Peter Gabrielli had been silently staring up at the ceiling. At thirty-five he was the youngest man present, and Ferrandini privately considered him the most intelligent. But he was also rather bookish and intellectual, which sometimes made him seem cold and distant. He had been a member of the Curia only four months, since the death of his grandfather Michael Gabrielli. His father had died in a car accident eight years previously, so the inheritance of the Gabrielli seat in the Curia had skipped a generation. Eventually he cleared his throat and spoke up.

'Vincenzo Cattagna has the advantage over me, because over the years he's spent a lot of time thinking about how Belvedere might work, whereas I've never given it much thought until today. But, as we've just heard Don Vincenzo remind us, there was no time limit. Belvedere was supposed to work for decades, but it was theoretically possible it might go on functioning for centuries. Since a human agency must be involved, the man guarding the trigger must die at some time. So how is his successor chosen?'

Brunetti replied, 'If we knew that, we might know how to choose the successor ourselves.' It was such a stupid remark that Gabrielli could only blink at him.

Pazzo! thought Ferrandini irritably.

'The most likely method would be for him to choose his own successor,' said Cattagna quietly. Several heads swung in his direction, but he made no attempt to explain.

'Why should that be the most likely?' prompted Gabrielli.

'Can you think of a viable alternative?'

'Yes. A firm of lawyers might select him.'

Cattagna smiled slightly. 'If so, then they'd be choosing someone without knowing what he was being selected to do.'

'Obviously.'

Brunetti frowned. 'Why obviously?'

'Because otherwise they could do the job just as easily themselves, and it would be an unnecessary complication if they therefore didn't,' replied Gabrielli without taking his eyes from Cattagna's face.

'More important, the lawyers would then have us at their mercy,' Cattagna pointed out. 'But if they don't know what the guardian is supposed to do, how is he briefed?'

Gabrielli slowly nodded in understanding. 'They'd have to show him secret instructions, which they might be tempted to read themselves. That would be too risky.'

'Yes, far too risky. But I think you're right to focus on the question of the succession. If you think about it for a moment, you'll see what the real problem is.'

The younger man lit a cigarette, the pause gaining him time to

74

think. 'As I see it, the main difficulty is that whatever loyalty the original guardian owed to Salvatore, that wouldn't necessarily apply a generation later.' Cattagna nodded. 'So he has to have other incentives.' Again the old man gave a brief nod. 'Money, obviously.'

Cattagna gave him a penetrating look. 'Exactly,' he breathed significantly.

Gabrielli frowned at him. 'Why is that so important?'

Knowing he had everyone's attention, the old man stared down at the table and his reply was leisurely. 'I must admit it took me a very long time to get there. Many years, in fact. As usual, it's the human element that matters.' He looked up at Gabrielli. 'Only a fool makes a threat he cannot carry out, and Salvatore Ferrandini was the least foolish man I ever knew. For him to be certain he could carry out his threat, then whoever he chose as the guardian must get to know about anything that harms us. How? Because he reads the newspapers regularly, and because news of anything happening to us will get back to Sicily as sure as night follows day. In which case, he must know who we are.'

'So?'

'So the guardian is someone whose motivation is money, yet who doesn't realise he controls something which could bring him *billions* of dollars if he handled it right.'

Gabrielli blinked. And then he got it. 'My God, he's the *whole* of the system, and he thinks he's only a *part*!'

The assembly remained hushed for a moment, then disintegrated into an excited babble. Imperturbably Cattagna lit a cigarette and gave Gabrielli a nod of his head in compliment.

Robert murmured to him, 'He's bright, this Gabrielli.'

'I agree. I think he'll be very useful to us.'

'What else have you deduced about Belvedere?'

Cattagna threw him a sly, sidelong glance. 'Do you want me to have to say it all twice?'

Robert smiled. 'All right, I'll wait. Just don't die on us in the next ten minutes.'

Cattagna laughed. He glanced across at Brunetti, who was talking into the glazed eyes of the man on his left. Poor Brunetti, he thought. So different from his father. If it wasn't for him, the average IQ of the assembly would be quite respectable. But under the rules of the Curia he was his father's chosen heir and hence a life member.

Gradually the table fell quiet again and everyone's eyes returned to Cattagna. When he had their full attention once more, he continued, 'The conclusion which Peter Gabrielli has just reached so rapidly cost me many years of idle speculation. Before I got there, I'd experimented in my mind with all sorts of setups, using everything from lawyers and landowners to mafiosi, and even blackmailees. The reason I came to reject them all was because I was in a privileged position: although hardly anybody was aware of it, I was Salvatore's closest friend. I knew him – as much as anyone can ever know a man of his genius – and over many years I had the opportunity to observe his mind in operation. He always preferred the simple to the elaborate, so whenever I dreamt up something complicated, if I could see some way of simplifying it, I was pretty sure that's the version Salvatore would have chosen.

'But there was one aspect of him which was very hard to imitate: he was a man of great faith. I'm not talking about religion. I mean that once he'd made up his mind about something, he believed in it on a continuous basis. Most people aren't like that. Most people are ditherers. You see it all the time in drivers who sometimes put their seatbelts on and sometimes don't. Salvatore's attitude was, "If something stands a one-in-ten chance of happening, then it's going to happen to me once every ten times." He was forever calculating probabilities. He was a born actuary. He believed in insurance and we mustn't forget that's basically all Belvedere is – an insurance policy. He was constantly thinking about risk and how to cover himself against it. Suppose, for example, something had gone wrong during the tombola, so the Accords ended up in someone else's hands. Salvatore had a failsafe device. By prior agreement, he included with them a page outlining a few general ideas to help the Designer set up a system. For reasons of security, the rest of us weren't allowed to see it. In fact, the note said he had a foolproof scheme ready to be set up, and asked the winner of the lottery to contact him in private, so they could organise it jointly. The measure was hardly necessary, because almost nothing could go wrong. But Salvatore *still* wanted to improve the odds.

'Cost was always secondary to him. What mattered was *need*. If he decided he really *needed* something, then somehow he'd find the money to pay for it. The original Belvedere setup fund was twenty-five million dollars in 1943 money – though we can be sure he invested it as cleverly as he did his own money, so it will now be worth many hundreds of times as much. But if Salvatore had needed an elastic band to make sure Belvedere worked properly, he'd have spent that twenty-five million on it without a qualm.'

For some reason Brunetti thought this was funny, and laughed. The rest of the assembly glanced at him in irritation. Cattagna ignored him.

'The picture I'm drawing is of a careful man, not an overcautious one. Someone who calculated the odds but wasn't afraid to play them. But there's one other vital aspect which mustn't be forgotten – his attitude towards people. It was in people that his faith was strongest. He believed in them; in their strengths and their weaknesses. When

76

Ben Siegel was building Las Vegas and running way over budget, Luciano was ready to boil him in oil. It was Salvatore who calmed him down. When Siegel was shot, it looked like the Las Vegas project was finished, but Salvatore persuaded four new investors to come in. Not many people shared Siegel's vision in those early days. Who could believe that gamblers would come in droves out to the middle of a desert? But Salvatore understood people, and how they operated. He believed in their conforming to their own behaviour patterns.' The old man paused and surveyed the faces around the table. 'That's how he was still able to control the guardian for nineteen years after his death.'

There was a moment's silence, broken by Gabrielli, who asked, 'What do you mean by "control"?'

'The guardian has to think he's part of a larger network, as you've just pointed out. To persuade him of that, you have to do two things. You must put him in a chain in which he has to regularly pass on bits of information which he thinks are important, but which are actually completely worthless. And you have to put him under surveillance. He must be aware of that surveillance, and think it's part of a more elaborate system. Obviously the people who are observing him will also know virtually nothing, but the guardian won't know that.'

'Who's doing the observing?' Lovegni wanted to know.

Cattagna shrugged. 'I don't think it matters. A bank perhaps, a security firm – even that firm of lawyers we were talking about. In fact, I think the best system would involve several different observers who the guardian would think were each controlling different things. So long as he sees activity beyond the little tasks he has to carry out, he'll perfectly happily assume he's part of a larger organisation and has a responsible role in it.

'Please note,' he emphasised, 'a man who is presented with an opportunity for theft and takes it will now behave like a thief. But if no opportunity is offered in the first place, he'll behave like a trusted employee – a model citizen. We can expect the guardian to be very ordinary. Very ordinary indeed.'

'And have an ordinary, fairly menial job,' returned Gabrielli. 'If he was a lawyer or a businessman or something, he'd have resources to explore the system from the inside.'

Cattagna nodded. 'I agree. And I'll go further. The ideal candidate would be someone who respected us but feared us. In the same way that he's likely to be God-fearing – an uneducated type. But he wouldn't be stupid, because he has to choose his own successor, remember. So it's someone whose position in life hasn't enabled him to *use* his intelligence to the full.'

'A peasant?' suggested Lovegni.

Cattagna nodded. 'Somebody poor and underprivileged, anyhow.'

Abruptly Gabrielli snapped his fingers and froze like a statue. His eyes had gone wide. 'Jesus Christ! He's paid the reward after he's dead!' he exploded at last.

'Of course,' replied Cattagna blandly. 'Otherwise he wouldn't remain poor.'

The table once again broke up into huddles of discussion.

Brunetti exclaimed, 'He does it for the money!'

The hubbub ceased and everyone turned to look at him. He was staring into space and had evidently made several associations of ideas, because he was stuttering to backtrack.

But Gabrielli had had enough of his nonsense. 'No,' he said, quietly but with force. 'He does it for love.'

Cattagna sighed softly, even sadly, and nodded. 'Yes, Peter. You're right.' The use of the first name escaped no one; Cattagna had decided to ally himself publicly. 'His family's poor and he thinks they always will be. So he does it for them. If he knew he could steal for them, he would; but since he doesn't, he plays it by the book. The key to the success of Belvedere is that the key figure in it doesn't understand his own role.'

The table fell silent.

Ferrandini decided it was time to make a contribution of his own. 'The guardian may be poor, but he won't be doing this for peanuts. So when he dies, his family will be receiving a sizable amount of money. If he picked a successor of the same sort of age, it wouldn't be long before another poor family received a surprise packet. Pretty soon, people would start looking for common denominators. My father would therefore have wanted each guardian to live as long as possible, and each to pick someone a good deal younger as his successor. The only practical way to ensure that would be to make the financial reward dependent on the length of time served.'

Cattagna nodded. 'Exactly right, Robert. And probably on the fulfilment of a series of conditions as well. Salvatore would want him to live carefully; to avoid dangerous activities, keep out of quarrels, make minimum journeys, and so on.'

'Okay. But a few minutes ago, Vincenzo, you pointed out why a firm of lawyers couldn't safely be involved in the process for selecting a new guardian, as they could only brief him if they had access to his instructions. So the guardian has to brief his own successor. Right?'

'Go on.'

'Once the successor knows that the amount of money his family will receive is proportionate to the amount of time he serves, he'll have a hell of a motive to step into the current guardian's shoes as soon as he can. That would be an open invitation to murder him.'

Several heads nodded, and Cattagna replied, 'Very astute, Robert. And there's another difficulty. What happens if it's the designated successor who dies first?'

'Right. The guardian would have brought someone else in on the secret needlessly. And Belvedere's bound to depend upon the fewest possible people knowing about it.'

'So what solution do you see?'

Ferrandini pursed his lips. 'That firm of lawyers, maybe. The guardian draws up a list of two or three possible successors from suitable people he's met over the years: men he knows and trusts. He gives the lawyers the list and when he dies they pick one of them. The new guardian then receives his instructions via a private letter from his predecessor.'

'Well done, Robert. That's exactly the system *I* came up with.'

Brunetti interrupted impatiently, 'All this is very interesting, but shouldn't we be thinking of *where* Belvedere is, instead of how it works?'

Ignoring him, Ferrandini looked at Cattagna thoughtfully. 'That aspect of it is important, isn't it?' he murmured.

'Yes, Robert, it is,' replied the old man with an enigmatic smile. 'Why do you think so?'

Ferrandini's eyes went out of focus. Perhaps because he carried his father's genes, or perhaps because, having been trained by him, he had absorbed some of his mindset, he was now starting to get a feel for Salvatore's system from the inside – a feel for the mechanics of a scheme to threaten the unthinkable.

The ingredients were varied. There was method. There was security. There was faith – in human nature. The good side of it and the bad. There was also the implacability of a threat which said: *If you harm my family, I will wreck the world.*

But above all, there was *safety*. That was the main ingredient. Salvatore would not have taken any risk – not with the safety of his own family. Robert thought about that letter containing the instructions. Flashing through his mind went a series of images – the scenarios in which it could be *safely* passed to the guardian's successor – and none of them was convincing.

Except one.

He saw a little farmhouse in the country. A peasant's cottage. The letter was hidden somewhere inside.

Robert's eyes refocused on Cattagna. 'We're looking for a house, aren't we, Vincenzo?' It was a statement.

The old man nodded. 'And I think a big one.'

'Why?'

'Because he must be surrounded by plenty of physical security: warning systems, and so on. If it were me, I'd have put him in a fortress. Harmless-looking from the outside, but a fortress.'

'Why couldn't it be a *small* fortress?'

'Because he's not supposed to stand out. He's poor, remember? So what's a poor man doing with warning systems in his little house, if he hasn't got anything to steal?'

'If it comes to that, what's he doing with them in his *big* house if he hasn't got anything to steal?'

'Obviously, because it's not *his* house.'

Ferrandini could have kicked himself for asking the question. The answer had been evident.

'You mean he's a caretaker?' asked Lovegni.

'Something like that,' agreed Cattagna. 'He'll have some job that goes *with* the house, anyhow.'

'Have you formed any notions about where this house might be?'

The old man's face creased. 'Only very tentative ones, I'm afraid, but anything which might help us to stop Belvedere has to be considered. Point one: the house won't be in or even near a city; the main reason being the risk from burglars and casual intruders as one gets nearer to a built-up area. Point two: it will be sturdily built, but Sicily is subject to earthquakes, especially in the vicinity of Etna, so we can rule out any area prone to violent quakes. Point three: we must remember our origins – western Sicily. That's where respect for us is at its greatest. We don't know how many guardians there have been, but we know the *first* must have been a personal acquaintance of Salvatore's. He was born in Lercara Friddi. I'd say that we should limit ourselves to western Sicily – no further east than the Monti Erei.'

Lovegni turned to Ferrandini. 'Would you have a map brought in, please?' Ferrandini went out to fetch an atlas from the library. Lovegni studied it for no more than ten seconds, then shook his head. 'Vincenzo, we've got so little time, and the area to be searched is huge. To find one man in a population of more than five million . . .' He pursed his lips. 'It's hopeless.'

Ferrandini sat down again. 'Perhaps Vincenzo hasn't finished,' he suggested.

Again all eyes turned to Cattagna, who now looked distinctly unhappy. 'Gentlemen, we must obviously do *something* – and quickly. But I'm wary of making any suggestion which might put us on the wrong track. However, you've asked me, so I'll tell you my opinion: Belvedere has been triggered by accident. We don't know what set of circumstances conspired against Salvatore's scheme, but we do know that the dangerous moments – in this as in any other system – occur when changes are made.' He glanced rapidly around the table. 'I remind you of what the anonymous note says: a clerical error was

80

practically out of the question, so the only other kind of mishap would occur if somebody attacked Belvedere without knowing what he was doing, and the control system failed to distinguish this from a deliberate attempt to penetrate it. That's what I think has happened. I think the guardian has just died. In fact, I suspect somebody has killed him. So, instead of looking for the house itself, I think we ought to examine the police and civil registry records over the last few days.'

Stelio looked up from the computer monitor. 'How far do you want to go back?'

Robert shrugged. 'A week?' he suggested, and Cattagna nodded.

Stelio typed an instruction, and a moment later reported, 'A thousand and twenty-eight.'

'Can you eliminate the cities and towns?'

'Sure. This is an actuarial programme. It can list people by just about every category you could think of.' He selected *rural deaths* and found the number had shrunk to one hundred and forty-four. Pulling out people of obviously the wrong age brought the figure down to one hundred and ten.

'The guardian must be relatively poor, remember,' said Cattagna.

After Stelio had eliminated the landowners and professional classes, he announced that there were eighty-eight possible candidates left.

'Would my father have used a woman?' asked Robert.

Lovegni shook his head. 'What matters is what sex the last guardian chose, and we're talking about Sicilians here, so let's leave out women for the moment.'

'And eliminate the eastern half of the island,' reminded Cattagna.

'We're down to twenty-two,' reported Stelio, after making the adjustments.

'That's not bad,' remarked Robert.

'We can do better than that,' said Gabrielli thoughtfully. 'If you're right about him being a caretaker or some such, then he wouldn't have been the owner of the house.'

Stelio gave him an apologetic look. 'This programme does list home-owners, but it doesn't make clear whether those homes and their residential addresses are the same.'

Ferrandini frowned. 'Can you bring up each file on that machine?'

'Sure.'

'Then eliminate all the addresses which mention a street, or sound as if they're located in villages. We're only interested in villas or farmhouses.'

Twenty minutes later their options had been reduced to just four. One of these was a self-employed furniture remover. The second was a bus driver. The third was a gardener living and working at a country house on the coast, near Marsala. It was the fourth man who interested everybody: the estate manager at a house near Corleone, a half-hour's drive from Lercara Friddi, Salvatore's birthplace.

10

Robert Ferrandini stared at the house and felt he'd wandered into somebody else's dream. It looked so ordinary. So peaceful and innocent. So utterly Sicilian, rustic and tranquil. But here, for more than fifty years, had been located the switch to hurl the world into chaos.

And now somebody had thrown that switch.

What was even worse was not knowing how much time they had left before whatever was due to happen *would* happen. He felt a tremendous sense of futility, and it was hard to avoid thinking that, since he did not know how much time he had, it would be better to spend the little there was in converting as much as he could of his wealth into hard cash, and sending his family to some secret island in the Pacific.

Ferrandini glanced at his watch. Allowing for the time difference, it was exactly fifty hours since he had received the anonymous phone call. The trigger had been pulled. But it was not the trigger of a gun; it was the armer of a time bomb. How long was the fuse? Hours? Days? Or even weeks?

Had his father Salvatore foreseen some situation in which his successor might want to halt the timer before it detonated the bomb? And had he made provision for it? Robert was inclined to think not, since they'd only been able to reconstruct the system at all because Vincenzo Cattagna had been his father's closest friend and had filled in the idle moments of half a century in second-guessing him. Cattagna was an old man; he might have died ages ago. In which case we'd be up shit creek, Robert thought. They were up shit creek anyway, he reminded himself. Adriano Lupillo was dead. The trigger had been pulled. This house had no further function. So their presence here was more in the nature of an archaeological dig.

Or an autopsy.

Peter Gabrielli walked up to him and said, 'If I hear Vincenzo warn us again about booby traps, I'm going to scream.'

Ferrandini glanced across the lawn at the elegant figure supervising one of the excavation works, and shrugged. 'He's been right about everything so far.'

'Yes, but if there's a bomb anywhere, how long has it been here?

Wires can corrode. It would be too dangerous. It would have put Adriano himself at risk.'

'Suppose it's something mechanical.'

Gabrielli sighed. 'Yes, okay. Maybe you're right. I'm just nervous.'

'So is Vincenzo. So are we all.'

A Mercedes pulled up outside the gates. Tommaso Vitellini, the local don, and two of his men got out. The men went to the boot and took out folding tables and chairs, which they set up on a patch of grass close by. 'We will eat *al fresco*,' announced Vitellini, a smile warming his chubby, rubicund features. 'We may all be dead tomorrow, but let us at least eat, drink and be merry today.'

Ferrandini smiled. 'You're right, Don Masino. And I hear your wines are the best in the region.'

'Then your sources are good,' he replied, beaming.

Lovegni came up to join them. He glanced back worriedly at the men slowly walking their way around the grounds with electric current detectors. 'I hate putting my men at risk when I can't tell them what the risk is,' he said and pursed his lips.

Ferrandini went off to fetch Cattagna, and soon the four American dons and their Sicilian host were at lunch. For a while the conversation dealt with the condition of this season's grapes, which only served to increase Robert's impression of the surrealistic. Of Cattagna he might have expected it; of Gabrielli too, at a pinch. But that Philip Lovegni, basically unimaginative and down-to-earth, should join in the debate so enthusiastically – as if his livelihood depended on the harvest whereas in fact he was one of the richest men in America and stood to lose at least as much as anybody when the Belvedere bomb exploded – seemed simply *unreal*.

When this topic was eventually exhausted, the five men fell silent apart from murmured comments about the excellence of the food. Vitellini poured everybody more wine, by scrupulous order of seniority.

'It would be a good idea if those estate workers were to keep their mouths shut,' said Lovegni to no one in particular.

'Don't worry, my friend,' replied Vitellini, languidly. 'This is Sicily, not America.' Then realising how his words might be interpreted, he added hurriedly, 'Here people need to be earning three thousand dollars a month before they realise they're worth it.' It was a winsome recovery and the four Americans showed their appreciation in deliberately loud guffaws.

Half an hour later Ned Moreno came up with a preliminary report. 'The only tripwires are on the top of the boundary wall. Under the drive we found five cables. One of them is a regular electricity cable, although the house has an emergency generator of its own. The second

84

is the telephone line. The third enables the gates to be locked from the house. The fourth and fifth are connected to two weighing machines buried under the drive, just inside the gate. We're going to start on the house now.'

'How much weight can the machines detect?'

'We're not sure yet, but at least half a ton.'

Ferrandini nodded and Ned went away.

'What do you make of that, Vincenzo?'

'Simple. A car comes in. As it passes over the machines, its weight is registered somewhere inside the house. When it leaves, it should weigh approximately the same. If it doesn't, Lupillo would know someone had been hidden in the boot.'

A short while later, one of Vitellini's men drove up and informed them, 'The civil registrar in Corleone confirms that this estate was bought in 1943 by a certain Bruno Tognazzi. He listed his place of residence as Cuma, a small town near Naples; but there's no record of anyone of that name living there either in 1943 or ever since.'

Cattagna had expected this. 'I'd be surprised if Tognazzi ever existed. It was Salvatore who bought this place, and with a fake identity card.'

'I wonder where the title deeds would be,' mused Gabrielli.

'In a safe-deposit box in some bank, I expect.'

'What about things like taxes and wages?'

'No problem. It's a vineyard: financially self-sufficient. Lupillo pays both himself and the estate workers out of the profits and sends the excess off to some lawyer or accountant somewhere. You can bet the shirt off your back that he was scrupulousness personified when it came to filling in the returns, too.'

'Because he thought he was under observation, you mean?'

'No. Because any irregularity might have been spotted by the tax authorities, and you can be sure that any trouble of *that* sort would be heavily penalised in the postmortem financial settlement to his next of kin. Adriano was a man who kept his nose clean and his head down. Of that you can be sure.'

'Fat lot of good it did him,' grunted Lovegni.

They contemplated this observation in silence. It was a kind of mourning for a good man who had kept his word to them.

'I'll see his family's well taken care of,' murmured Ferrandini after a while.

Ned Moreno kept bringing regular reports, but it wasn't until late afternoon that the booby trap was finally discovered. It was a bomb, after all. When it was deactivated, the dons could finally enter the building in safety.

The explosives expert was Jim Toomey, one of Stelio's men. He led them into the bedroom, and made his report in a puzzled voice.

'I've seen some queer setups in my time, but this beats the lot. The bomb is underneath the floor. It's a blast bomb of German manufacture. If it had gone off, its power would have been directed upwards through the floor, and killed anyone in this room, but it's unlikely to have done much damage anywhere else. The weirdness lies in the method of activation. You notice how springy these floorboards are? Well, believe it or not, we're standing on a weighing machine – a larger version of those old-fashioned machines you find in funfairs. With one small difference: instead of a single pointer, there are two. The ends of those pointers are connected by several wires.'

He walked across to the telephone on the bedside table. Its cable ran into a little box attached to the wall. On top of the box was a lever pointing vertically.

'Everything is controlled by this,' he continued. 'Under normal circumstances, when this lever is vertical, the weighing machine doesn't register the weight, because a ratchet stops the pointers from moving. If you move the lever to the right it releases the ratchet entirely, and both the pointers move together. If you move the lever to the left, only one of the pointers moves. You need a key before you can move the lever at all.'

The five dons wore identical expressions of puzzlement.

'The thing is,' went on Toomey, 'this lever does something else too. If it's in vertical position the phone works normally. If you move it either to the left or to the right, it acts as a scrambler relay. In other words, the numbers you dial won't be the numbers you get. Move it to the left, it scrambles them one way; move it to the right, it scrambles them differently.'

'Where's the key?' asked Vitellini.

'We don't know. We haven't been able to find it.'

'It wasn't on Lupillo's body. I had it searched.'

Toomey shrugged. 'I've dismantled the lock anyhow.'

On the bedside table was a telephone pad. The top page was blank, but Ferrandini could just make out the impression of writing. He asked Toomey for a pencil, and coated the surface with a layer of graphite. Three lines of numbers emerged. The top was: 102 32 77 401 203 89. The line underneath was 11 11 11 11 10 11. The third consisted of the sums of the upper two lines. He studied them for a moment, and then eyed the control box thoughtfully. Moving the lever to and fro, he asked, 'Am I right in thinking that if those wires connecting the two pointers break, the bomb explodes?'

Toomey nodded vigorously. 'Yep. When the lever is pressed to the left or right, electricity is diverted into the pointers, forming a circuit which activates a tiny magnet. This draws a little metal flap towards it. If the circuit is broken, the flap flicks back to a contact, and the current is directed into it. Boom.'

'How long are the wires?'

'About nine inches.'

'What weight difference would that mean if they were stretched taut?'

'About a hundred and ten pounds.'

Ferrandini nodded. 'How would an earthquake affect things?'

'Hardly at all. The part we're standing on is the movable part of the weighing machine, so *that's* able to withstand a terrific shock. The bomb itself is free-swinging in a hammock, and it's connected to the rest of the apparatus by a long wire with plenty of give. The bit in the middle which connects the two – the metal flap arrangement – is resting on a bed of mercury. This thing could stand up to at least a force six.'

'How long could it all last?'

Toomey stroked his chin. 'Everything, apart from the bomb, halfway to forever. The bomb itself is in good nick *now*, but in two or three decades' time . . . Well, I wouldn't like to commit myself.'

'Could it last for centuries?'

'Well it *could*, of course, and we're a long way from the sea, so there can't be much corrosive salt in the air, but sooner or later corrosion would put paid to it.'

'What would happen then? Could it explode by accident?'

Toomey shook his head. 'Not unless somebody started tinkering with it. You see, the electric current is fed into a small quantity of gelignite, which explodes, sending a percussive shock into the detonator of the main explosive. If anything is going to seize up, it will be the detonator. When it did, the bomb just wouldn't work any more.'

'I see. Thank you very much.'

Toomey nodded and went out of the room.

Cattagna turned to Ferrandini. 'Well, Robert? You look as if you've figured it all out. Tell us how it works.'

Ferrandini gazed around at the little bedroom, where the guardians had slept for more than half a century – Dionisio Bompietri, Giacomo Buonolini and Adriano Lupillo. 'This is it,' he said quietly in a respectful voice, as if he was in church. 'The centrepiece of Belvedere.' He moved the lever from side to side again. 'Here's your chain, Vincenzo. Left, one link; right, the other. Neither of them knew who was calling them, but Adriano didn't know that.'

'Who are the people he was calling?' asked Lovegni.

'Just observers. The guy on the left gave him the top numbers, he added on all his elevens and passed them on to the guy on the right.'

'But why?'

'At a guess, I should think the elevens correspond to aspects of his job and the estate. In fact, they might not be elevens at all. Just a series of ones. Anyhow, I think they meant everything was normal. By the looks of that ten, something must have been a bit below par.'

'Then what do the top numbers mean?'

'I'd be very surprised if they mean anything at all. Lupillo probably thought they were a message in code. Maybe he even whiled away his long winter evenings trying to crack it.'

'But maybe it *is* a code. Why couldn't he have been right about that?'

'Because we already know that he was the sole operator of the alarm system. If the numbers were significant, then other people would be feeding him important data – so they'd be *involved*. What matters is that, because of these numbers, he *believed* other people were involved. All he was actually doing was passing an empty box from A to B, believing there were some goodies inside.'

Lovegni shook his head. 'I don't understand this at all. A and B were still sending and receiving the damn things. What the hell did *they* think they were doing?'

Ferrandini gave a little shrug. 'The sender can be anybody you like: a stockbroker giving him share prices, a bookie giving him odds, a winemaker giving him the prices of grapes. It doesn't matter. As for the receiver, he was probably monitoring the day-to-day functioning of the estate.'

Gabrielli was in like a shot, 'To do that he'd need to know the top line, in order to subtract it from the figures Lupillo had given him.'

'I expect he did. What's wrong with him just picking up the phone and calling the sender himself?'

'It would look bloody peculiar,' grunted Lovegni. '*That's* what's wrong with it.'

'All right. I concede the point. In which case, what about *this* for an idea? It's not A and B, with Adriano playing pig-in-the-middle. There are *four* people, not three. Let's call them North, South, East and West. Adriano is South. All the others are lawyers. North sends out the numbers to West and gets them back again from East with all the elevens added on.'

'Now *that's* an interesting idea, Robert,' said Cattagna nodding his approval. 'Though I think it would make better sense if North wasn't a lawyer but a bank.'

'Why a bank?' asked Gabrielli.

'Because the postmortem payments are being made out of the interest on the original Belvedere setup fund; so somebody's managing a small fortune in our name.'

'But why on earth send numbers?' complained Lovegni. 'What's wrong with words?'

'Because banks deal with numbers routinely,' replied Gabrielli. 'People would be less likely to pay attention to them.'

'They deal with words too,' Lovegni reminded him, annoyed.

'Maybe Adriano wasn't very good with words. Most uneducated people aren't.'

'It might even be a foreign bank, for all we know,' put in Cattagna.

'Then why not just send the elevens?' demanded Lovegni almost angrily. 'Why all the complication? Won't the bank staff think it's peculiar that they're subtracting outgoing numbers from incoming ones?'

'It's a very effective way of preventing industrial espionage,' Gabrielli pointed out. 'And that's what the bank would think it's helping to avoid.'

Ferrandini put in thoughtfully, 'It's not really important what the bank thinks about it, anyway. They'll follow their instructions whatever happens, because they're already holding the money. If they didn't, they might lose the client. And since they won't have the slightest idea of what's at the back of it all, they couldn't prejudice Belvedere. But Adriano's different. He was the crux of the whole scheme. By all accounts, he was a good man and a reliable type, but there's not the slightest doubt in my mind that if he'd understood what he was *really* controlling, he'd have looked for ways to make it benefit his *own* family without worrying too much about the effect it would have on *ours*. Since he *had* to know we were involved, it was essential to present him with a distorted view of what he was actually doing. By making him fiddle around with numbers and codes, my father was distracting him. He was making him *believe* that was the most important part of his job.'

'Whereas the *really* important job was to read the newspapers,' murmured Gabrielli, amazed by the simplicity of the deception.

'Exactly. He reads that we've been arrested, or he finds the Code in the announcements column, then he adds the information in coded form to the string of numbers he passes on to East.'

Lovegni looked doubtful. 'Wouldn't it be a bit risky if he knew our names?'

Cattagna shook his head emphatically. 'He won't have been looking out for news just about *us*. Salvatore will have given him a list of names as long as your arm. Ours will be buried somewhere in the middle.' He turned back to Ferrandini. 'But what *I* don't see is how the bomb fits in with all this.'

'Don't you? Actually it's incredibly simple.' Gabrielli nodded; he'd figured it out already. Ferrandini looked at Cattagna. 'You realise, Vincenzo, that without you we'd never have found this place?'

'Yes. The thought had occurred to me that you might have been in difficulties if I'd died last week,' replied the old man drily.

'Do you think the US government could ever have found this place?'

Cattagna considered, and then shook his head. 'No. Even *with* me it was still essential to *know* that Belvedere had been activated and then to *guess* that Adriano had just died. The government didn't have enough information to go on.'

'But suppose they'd found it anyway. Suppose that, by some miracle or incredible coincidence, a CIA agent stumbled on this place and somehow or other realised that this was where Belvedere was located. What would he do now?'

'If he limited himself to observing Adriano, he'd never get anywhere. Even if he tapped the phone, he'd just hear a string of meaningless numbers. He'd have to force the issue somehow.'

'Right. But Adriano was on *our* side, remember – not the CIA's. He wouldn't have cooperated. Not voluntarily. The agent would have had to blackmail him: "Tell us how Belvedere works or we'll kill your family." Something drastic like that. And what's Adriano's answer? I'll tell you. And it knocks them for six. He says, "What's Belvedere?" He's never heard of it, you see. He knows practically nothing about how the system he's controlling really works. So the agent realises he's going to have to spend a little time studying it.

'Adriano doesn't want to betray us, but now he has no option. He tells him about the weighing machines at the bottom of the drive, and also about the one in the sitting room, but he doesn't tell him about this one in the bedroom, because he never knew it was here. *This* was the failsafe device.

'Adriano's always done everything by the book. He's been told he'll be financially penalised if he doesn't. One prohibition is that no one else must be present when he calls West and East, so he always locks the door. He's never realised that whenever he moved the lever to the right, he was reweighing the floor. It was necessary, of course, because as he gained or lost weight over the years, the weighing machine had to keep up with him. So whenever he rang East, he was resetting the machine, bringing the pointers together and establishing a new normal weight for the whole room with himself inside it.

'While our hypothetical CIA agent's studying Belvedere, he obviously wants Adriano to follow his normal routine, including making those regular calls to West and East. Naturally, he'll stick with him to watch everything he does and to make sure he doesn't try to double-cross him. Neither of them gives a thought to the fact that the room, with both of them inside, is now at least a hundred and twenty pounds heavier than normal. Adriano pushes the lever to the left, and one of the pointers swings violently away from the other, breaking the wires. A second or two later . . .'

He let the sentence hang in the air.

His four listeners remained silent, contemplating the elegance of

90

the system and the diabolical ingenuity of Salvatore's mind.

Eventually Cattagna commented, 'The beauty of it is that when the bomb goes off, it will destroy the scrambler relay, so even if the agent has friends waiting outside, and Adriano has told them the numbers he dials, they'd know only the scrambled sequence and have no way of working out what the unscrambled version was. The phone calls are probably supposed to be made between fixed times, so East is alerted to the fact that something is wrong when the call period expires a few minutes later. By setting off the bomb, Salvatore has given East time to relay the news to North, who then takes the appropriate action. I must admit, Robert, I'd always suspected your father had devised something clever to prevent a forced betrayal, but this really takes my breath away.'

Gabrielli was shaking his head in something like awe. 'Weights and measures. The weight of a man measures his reliability. Who would ever have thought it? What a pity I never knew your father.'

'Let's go and see how the rest of his system worked,' replied Ferrandini. The others walked out ahead of him. He took a last glance around the bedroom, noting the crucifix above the bed and the cheaply framed photograph of Pope Pius XII on the wall. How appropriate, he thought. He looked down at the bed and thought of Adriano, the sacrificial lamb lying on the Belvedere altar.

Robert shook his head regretfully, and followed the others out.

In the sitting room Ned Moreno was supervising two technicians who, after dismantling the grandfather clock with its built-in barometer, were now reconstructing it. In front of the fireplace the floorboards had been torn up, exposing another weighing machine.

Ferrandini came up to his assistant and laid a hand on his shoulder. 'How does this fireplace arrangement work, Ned?'

'Pretty ingeniously. Especially when you remember it was all constructed with SecondWorldWar technology. Toomey says it would be difficult to manage it today, but in 1943 . . .'

'Manage what?' put in Ferrandini with a touch of impatience.

'Okay. What your father wanted to do was to monitor everything coming in and going out through the gates. If the house had *two* driveways, the incoming traffic always using one and the outgoing traffic using the other, there'd be no problem. You'd merely stick a weighing machine at the bottom of each drive, and one would record weights as positive and the other as negative. The problem is you've only got one drive.'

'So how did he solve it?'

'Well, he didn't solve it *absolutely*. At the bottom of the drive, there are two underground weighing machines, each connected to a separate wire. The wires come up below the drive, pass through this control mechanism here – the fireplace – and then go into the

91

grandfather clock. The order of activation of those weighing machines determines whether the reading is incoming or outgoing. The system isn't foolproof, because somebody might change direction while on one of the machines, so there's a manual override here in one of the fireplace panels.

'The panels only work when someone of the guardian's exact weight is standing on this other weighing machine in front of it, and he could adjust it to remain sensitive to him personally, regardless of how much he gained or lost in weight.'

'Okay. What does the grandfather clock do?'

'Both the clock and the barometer *register* the weights, but there's an important difference in how they do it. The barometer has two pointers: each connected to a spring and a solenoid. The electricity makes the solenoids spin, which winds up the springs. In other words, weights are accumulated for registration later on. After his visitors had gone, Adriano could release the springs, and the pointers would move. Incoming weights are recorded on one, outgoing ones on the other, so obviously he could tell the weight *difference* between incoming and outgoing items by comparing the position of the two pointers. If they didn't coincide, he knew that something or somebody was still inside the grounds.'

'Okay. That's pretty clear. The barometer enabled him to monitor his own safety. What does the clock do?'

'The minute hand records the incoming weights, and the hour hand the outgoing ones. The reset position is twelve o'clock, and the weight of a man corresponds to four minutes, more or less. When the minute hand moves past the third minute, it trips a tiny lever which connects this hand to the electricity supply. If the hour hand now catches up with it, two metal contacts on the insides of the hands come together, and an electric timer is activated. Five minutes later, unless the barometer springs are released, the system disconnects, and the clock hands freeze. If Adriano exceeded the time limit, he could still reset the clock by resetting the barometer to its zero position.'

Ferrandini nodded. 'So if Adriano received visitors, he had five minutes after they left to tell the system he was okay. If he didn't do so, the system would assume they'd done something to him, and freeze the position of the hands so that an investigator would subsequently be able to deduce their total weight.'

'Exactly. And since the system was now disconnected, the body weight of the investigator himself, or anyone else who'd entered in the meantime, wouldn't mess things up.'

'My God,' breathed Gabrielli. 'It's brilliant!'

Cattagna put in, 'And, presumably, some investigator has already been here, which is why Belvedere has been activated.'

Lovegni replied, 'The investigator is obviously East, who drops by to find out why he hasn't received his latest dose of elevens.'

Ferrandini looked down at the pieces of the grandfather clock. 'What's the reading now?'

'Two men.'

'I see. Is that everything?'

'I think so. We've hunted high and low for that letter of instructions you mentioned, but we can't find it.'

'Keep looking. It's here somewhere, I'm sure.'

'What we did find was an inventory of all the stuff in the house: anything sizable or of value. It was hidden in a panel in the base of the grandfather clock. Nothing seems to have been taken.'

Ferrandini gave a slow nod. 'So, just two weeks after his wife was killed in a strange accident, and while the estate workers were conveniently home at lunch, Adriano had two visitors and died while they were here. They didn't panic, otherwise they'd have left the premises before the five minutes were up. Yet they didn't report his death, either. They didn't even help him, as ordinary Sicilians would. On the contrary, they left a scenario looking for all the world as if he'd died alone. They didn't take anything away with them, therefore they weren't common thieves.'

'And the death certificate says "natural causes",' Vitellini reminded him. 'So they were cleaver enough to fool the doctor.'

'Murder,' said Cattagna. 'And a killing with a motive. They wanted to kill Adriano because he was Adriano.'

Ferrandini nodded. 'A man living quietly, who hardly ever goes out. Voluntarily incarcerating himself for the sake of his family. He wants to live as long as he can anyway . . .'

' . . . And penalised financially if he doesn't die naturally,' interjected Gabrielli.

'Right. So he avoids involving himself in quarrels with other people, yet he's murdered by two men who specifically wanted to kill him.' He sighed. 'The one thing my father couldn't guard against. The system can't distinguish between a professional assassin hired to destroy Belvedere and a murderer, with some motive other than theft, who commits a deceptive murder.'

He gave a helpless shrug. Destiny had ultimately defeated Salvatore.

One of Vitellini's men came in to announce, 'We've found Diriazzi, the guy who signed the death certificate. He says he was informed of Lupillo's death by a notary called Giuseppe Rampone. Rampone's still at his office, though he'll be going home shortly. My people in Palermo want to know what to do, Don Masino.'

Vitellini turned to Ferrandini and raised a questioning eyebrow.

'There's no time for anything subtle,' said Lovegni.

'No, but let's not cause a scene,' replied Cattagna.

Gabrielli's face registered distaste.

Ferrandini sighed. He disliked thug tactics at the best of times, but using them against a man whose involvement was so obviously innocent went very much against the grain. Still, this was no time for niceties. He gave a brief nod and Vitellini's man went out.

A little over an hour later, Rampone himself was brought into the sitting room, looking frightened. He stared down at the holes in the floor then up into the taut faces of the grim men watching him – made grimmer still by the fading light of the sun which had sunk behind the mountains. He wondered why they didn't turn on a light.

Ferrandini indicated a chair. 'Ned, give him a brandy.' He sat down opposite. 'The offer is this,' he said quietly. 'You will tell us everything about your involvement with Adriano Lupillo and this house. Then you will be driven back to Palermo and paid well for your time. You will then forget all about this meeting.' He didn't stoop to outlining the alternatives.

Rampone talked rapidly, though he had very little to say. In a few minutes the notary had confirmed what they had already been able to piece together. The only item of real interest was the name of his client – the main Rome branch of the Banco di Sicilia.

When he'd gone, Cattagna said, 'That's not the real client. It has to be a front.'

'Why do you say that?' asked Lovegni.

'Because Salvatore set up Belvedere in late summer of 1943. Rome and most of Italy were still occupied by the Germans.'

'Then where's the real client?'

'Some place that wasn't occupied by the Germans in 1943. Either Britain or one of the neutrals.'

'My bet's Switzerland,' said Ferrandini, switching on a table lamp. Everyone looked at him quizzically. He explained, 'The guy who rang up to warn us the trigger had been pulled had a German accent. Switzerland was the only German-speaking neutral in 1943.'

Cattagna frowned thoughtfully. 'Yes, Robert. That's a good point. So we think North is a bank in the German-speaking part of Switzerland. But perhaps I can narrow things down a bit further.' He turned to Moreno. 'Let me have your mobile phone for a minute.' Ned handed it to him. Cattagna consulted a pocket diary, then tapped out a lot of numbers. After a moment he said, 'Eddie? It's Cenzo. A small favour. See if your computer can dig out the national and international flights for Switzerland during World War II, would you?'

'I can only give you the regular flights.'

'Yes, those are the ones I want.'

'Okay. I'll call you back.'

94

'No, I'm not at home. I'll hold.' Covering the phone, he explained, 'He's an old pilot friend of mine – an airplane freak. He's writing a history of air travel.'

Several minutes later Eddie came back. 'Okay. Got a pencil? Regular domestic flights in Switzerland during the war – none. Regular international flights were operated by Swissair with DC-2 and DC-3 aircraft as follows. Daily flights were flown on the following routes: Zurich-Munich, from 30 September 1940 to 14 November 1941; Zurich-Stuttgart-Berlin, from 19 November 1941 to 29 January 1943; Zurich-Stuttgart, from 30 January 1943 to 16 August 1944. Thrice-weekly flights were: Locarno-Rome, from 18 March 1940 to 25 June 1940; Locarno-Rome, from 2 January 1941 to 15 January 1941; Locarno-Barcelona, from 1 April 1940 to 11 June 1940. That's all.'

'I'm very grateful, Eddie. I'll be talking to you.' Cattagna hung up. He turned to the others. 'The bank's in Zurich.'

Lovegni had come to stand over him, to read the information he had jotted down. Now frowning, he said, 'Forgive me, Vincenzo, but I don't understand. How does this information show where the bank is? Couldn't Salvatore have travelled by some means other than an airplane?'

Cattagna shook his head. 'Salvatore had to act very fast in setting up Belvedere, but in 1943 Switzerland was surrounded by Nazi-occupied territory. There was only one fast way to get in: to fly from Lisbon to Germany, on a false passport, and then take a flight on to Switzerland. The only available route in the summer of 1943 was Stuttgart-Zurich.'

'Yes, okay. He flew *into* Zurich, but he didn't need to stay there.'

'Eddie said there were no domestic flights. So, travelling overland to any other main banking centre would have added another day and a half to his journey time, there and back.'

'But why would it have to be an important banking centre?'

Cattagna smiled. 'Philip, where's the best place to hide a pebble?'

Lovegni blinked at him, but Ferrandini, grinning broadly, supplied the answer. 'On a beach.'

Cattagna nodded. He pursed his lips. 'Even so, there'll still be scores of banks in Zurich to choose from.'

Ferrandini was practical. 'But this bank in Rome will know which one. The Swiss bank must use it as a clearing house to monitor this estate. My father simply put up another barrier. To find out the name of the Swiss bank would cost the government that much more time.'

Gabrielli grimaced. 'Us too.'

'We can do it by tomorrow lunchtime,' said Moreno. 'Robert, send Stelio to Zurich. I'll go to Rome tonight.'

Ferrandini nodded. 'All right. Take my plane.'

Vitellini said, 'I know a couple of good men in Rome. Very able and most discreet. I'm sure you'd find them very useful.' He went towards the door. 'In the meantime, I shall make it my business to find the two men responsible for this murder.'

Cattagna said tactfully, 'Perhaps it would be useful if we had an opportunity to question them after you do.'

'Of course, Don Vincenzo. Revenge does not need to be hurried. Just sure,' he added as he went out.

11

Giorgio walked up the sloping Piazza Vittorio Emanuele through a deep mist, and in deep thought. The mist was actually cloud, which frequently enveloped the top of the Enna plateau. It had moved in shortly after dusk, and brought some chill air with it. Around him the crowds of young people, who always hung around the streets in this part of town in the early evening, were beginning to thin.

At the end of Vittorio Emanuele Giorgio turned left into Francesco Crispi, another little piazza, situated on the very edge of the northern cliff. It was a pedestrian precinct with trees and grass-beds, and much favoured by young couples. It had now become too chilly for most of them, and only a pair of diehards remained. These too got up from their bench and walked away just as Giorgio was passing. He followed the balustrade into the Viale Marconi, a promenade with the cliff on one side. The streetlamps were sparse and few windows were lit, so the promenade was dimly illuminated. Beyond the balustrade the mist created an eerie effect, as if he was walking along the edge of the world. Enna was the highest provincial capital in Italy – nine hundred and fifty metres above sea level.

Giorgio stopped to light a cigarette and stood for a moment staring into the slow swirling veil of cloud, which matched the churning doubt which hid his fate from him.

The danger in which they now found themselves had caused a reversal of roles. Previously Ciccio had been the leader and Giorgio his trusty instrument. But now Ciccio seemed out of his depth, and Giorgio had taken charge to prevent his friend cracking up. He, at least, had experience of living dangerously. To run away now would amount to an admission of guilt, and it wasn't feasible to remain on the run for more than a few days with both the police and the Donor's men looking for them. Their best option was to play the innocents, and as long as they both stuck to the same story, they'd surely be all right. Though Ciccio retained a nagging suspicion that the Tognazzi house itself would somehow tell the Donor who they were.

It didn't quite do that much, but knowing the donations were the likely murder motive, Vitellini had phoned a friend in Enna and asked him to make discreet inquiries about Adriano's family. This friend already knew all about Giorgio's recent performance as the prodigal son – and it was an act which he found very unconvincing because he'd known him all his life. Now learning that a few weeks later Adriano had been murdered – and almost certainly for profit – he would have taken bets that Giorgio was responsible. 'I have a feeling you won't have to wait long for my call,' he said, and hung up.

At that very moment Giorgio walked into La Sala da Giuoco, a bar on the Viale Marconi, and spotted Dino Langella, one of the very few people in Enna he admired. Dino was tough, strong, with the good looks of a film star, and had built up a successful TV and video business, and he wasn't even twenty-five yet. On top of everything else, he had a stunningly beautiful wife. They greeted each other amicably, and Dino produced a sympathetic grimace. 'I was sorry to hear about your great-uncle.'

Giorgio shrugged. 'Yeah, well, he was getting on a bit, and losing his wife was a hell of a blow. The funeral's tomorrow and I'll have to attend.'

'What'll you have to drink?'

'I think I'll have a beer.'

They then turned to more cheerful topics, like the good life in Palermo.

'Dino – for you,' called out Enzo the bartender a few minutes later, laying the telephone receiver down on the counter. 'You ought to close down your office and do *all* your business here.'

Grinning, Dino went to pick it up. The ensuing conversation became quite lengthy, so Giorgio wandered around the café to see who else was there.

The Sala da Giuoco attempted to cater for all tastes and ages. Tables on the promenade out front made it popular with those who wanted to enjoy the spectacular view. The bar inside was small, with space for only two tables, but the counter was clean and well stocked with fresh pastries.

There were two other downstairs rooms: one devoted to computer games, where half a dozen teenagers worked the buttons with a speed that managed to be both frantic and cool; the other a billiards room with four tables. Only one was in use as six youths played bumper pool. For spectators they had three old men sitting on a bench against the wall, making desultory conversation.

It was in the doorway to this room that Giorgio chose to stand, halfheartedly watching the game while he waited.

Dino eventually returned, looking thoughtful. Before Giorgio could inquire what was up, three of Dino's friends came in and joined them rowdily, choosing the billiards table furthest from the door. The game soon became a focus for their high spirits.

The old men looked on gladly and sadly. It seemed only the other day that their own bodies had been strong and firm, full of the juice of life and love. Their only consolation now was that these young princes too would soon know the velocity of time, the brevity of life, and the closeness of death.

The six younger lads, not yet out of their teens, continued to concentrate on their own game. Their reigns as princes lay five or six years in the future. Meanwhile they knew their place . . . and waited their turn.

Enzo poured himself a Coca-Cola and turned over another page in the newspaper. He knew that life and the living had one thing in common: they both stank.

But soon someone else came into the bar. Everyone knew him by sight, and several gave him unsmiling nods. Antonio Leggio was high into his sixties but well, if waxily, preserved. His profession was officially lawyer, but he had fingers in a lot of pies, especially estate management for absentee landlords – which in the postwar years, when peasant living conditions were really hard, had made him less than popular. He was rumoured to be a Friend of the Friends, but then so were a lot of people at one time or another. Leggio ordered a glass of red wine and carried it into the billiards room. He exchanged nods with the three old men, but none of the younger people acknowledged him. He moved over to stand near Dino's table and leant his back against the wall, sipping his wine as he observed the game. He seemed particularly interested in Giorgio.

There was no sudden change of mood but all the men present began to realise that something was going to happen. Dino kept glancing at Leggio apprehensively. Giorgio, ever alert to undercurrents, put two and two together – this new apprehension caused by Leggio, and the telephone conversation which had left Dino thoughtful – and started to brood about what might be waiting for him outside. As his companions picked up his air of foreboding, their lively conversation withered.

The old men, like so many radar dishes aching to blip, also noticed the silence around Dino's table, and their own murmurs ceased. When the youths at the second table sensed the gathering tension, they too fell silent. Now nobody in the billiards room was talking at all. Enzo looked up.

As soon as his game was over, Dino said quickly, 'Well, my wife's waiting and so's my dinner. I'd better go and do justice to both.' He gestured to Enzo to chalk up the round of drinks to his account. 'See you around, boys.'

Giorgio rapidly said his own farewells and hurried out after him, catching up with Dino twenty yards along the street. The promenade was deserted now and the mist seemed thicker, as if closing in to claim the territory which man had abandoned.

Dino turned and demanded, 'What the hell's going on, Giorgio?'

'What was that phone call about?'

'Do you think it's any of your business?'

'I think my name was mentioned.'

Dino hesitated. 'Just someone asking if I'd seen you recently. He seems very interested in you.'

'Who?'

Dino shook his head. 'I can't tell you, Giorgio. But exactly what's going on?'

The other glanced apprehensively around. 'Dino, I'm in trouble. *Real* trouble. I've got to get away, hide somewhere.'

'What have you done?'

Again he shook his head. 'Don't ask, Dino. Please don't ask.'

Dino's face hardened. 'What the fuck do you think I am, Giorgio? You can't expect people to help you blind.'

Giorgio stared at him like a hunted fox. 'I killed a man in Palermo. I think he was one of the Friends. I didn't know that at the time.'

Suddenly there were footsteps in the street. Giorgio glanced back towards the bar and saw Leggio. Jesus!

Giorgio hissed, 'Help me, Dino! For the love of God, help me!'

For a moment Dino looked panicky, then he calmed a little. 'Okay, okay. Let's get out of here.' They hurried to the end of the promenade, where Dino's car was parked. 'Are you sure they know it was you?'

Giorgio considered, hope suddenly thrusting to the surface. They *couldn't* know for sure. There was nothing definite to link him with Adriano's death.

Except Ciccio. And the thought came like a slap in the face, because he knew that Ciccio was fundamentally weak. If *they* so much as looked at him, he'd panic; and Ciccio wouldn't last two minutes in an interrogation by the Friends. He had to get Ciccio to safety – or kill him.

They had now reached Dino's BMW, and a moment later were driving along the Viale Caterina Savoca – where Ciccio's great-aunt Claudia lay on her deathbed – towards the Lombardia castle. It was a one-way street and they were driving the wrong way, but in Sicily only foreigners paid attention to traffic signs.

'I don't know why the fuck I'm doing this,' muttered Dino in irritation. 'I don't even know where I'm supposed to be taking you. And what the hell's Leggio got to do with it?'

Giorgio shrugged. He didn't know, but he had to make a decision *now*! Either to solve the problem of Ciccio, or spend the rest of his life in hiding.

Suddenly the castle, eerily illuminated by orange light, loomed through the mist. Dino swung around through the piazza in front of it, and headed down the Via Cittadella till they came to a fork. Left was the road eastwards out of the town, connecting with the main roads at the foot of the plateau; right was a street which would take them back into the centre.

Dino pulled up. 'Giorgio, I don't know whether I'm more pissed off than frightened or the other way round, but this is a mess! If you're going to play it cool, then I've got to take you home *now*! If you're going into hiding, then your only chance is Palermo. You wouldn't stand an earthly out in the country. Sooner or later someone would spot you, then the Friends would hear about it. If you want, I can drive you to Palermo later on. But, whatever the hell you choose, make up your mind now! I've got to think of myself too.'

'I know, Dino. I know,' replied Giorgio. And then he realised he couldn't possibly leave Ciccio running loose. He had to take him under his wing for the moment, then decide what to do about him later. They'd better accept Dino's offer, too. To be seen alone with Ciccio in his car would give away the alliance, where as in the presence of others it would not be clear that one existed.

'There's a friend involved in this. Can you take the two of us?'

'Who is he?'

'Ciccio Buonolini.'

Dino made a face. 'I don't like that guy. All those airs and graces – he's a creep.'

'Yeah, but if I don't get him under wraps, I'm dead.'

Dino sighed. 'Okay.'

'I'll call him. Can you find me a phone box?'

Dino took the right-hand road and threaded his way through the streets to the Piazza Scarlata, just behind the Duomo. There was no one about as the BMW stopped next to a phone booth.

Giorgio climbed out to ring Ciccio. 'They think it's us, but they can't be sure. You have to get under cover for a few days, till I can straighten things out and put them off the scent.'

'And how the hell are you going to do that?' demanded Ciccio, his voice quavering.

'I know these guys, and you don't. I'll pick you up at the T-junction near your house in an hour. So be ready. This is the *right* move, so don't fuck around.'

'Are you armed?' asked Dino, as Giorgio climbed in again.

'Just a flickknife.'

'You'd better get a gun.'

'There's someone in Palermo who can fix me up.'

'I've got to go home for dinner now, or my wife won't speak to me for a week. Where shall I pick you up?'

Giorgio considered. It would be best for him to stay out of sight meanwhile. 'At the crossroads between the Corso Sicilia and the road to Calascibetta. If you drop me at the castle now, I'll go down through the woods.'

'In the dark? That'll be bloody dangerous.'

'I've done it before.'

Dino shrugged, and drove him back up to the Lombardia castle. Giorgio stepped out, and the BMW took off. He climbed over the wall at the top of the cliff and walked down a narrow footpath into the woods which covered the almost sheer, northern face of the plateau. Soon he didn't have even the dim light of the streetlamps to help him and, as he edged his way along in almost pitch darkness, he realised that the idea of coming this way at night had not been exactly brilliant. If he put one foot wrong, he'd go over the edge. The trees were thick enough to stop his fall, but he would be badly cut up in the process.

After what seemed a significant fraction of eternity, he reached the Panoramica Casina Bianca. He waited behind a tree as two cars drove past, then he jumped down to the road, crossed it quickly and re-entered the woods. The slope was not so steep now and his progress was easier. Soon he got down to the crossroads, but stayed hidden in the woods. He sat down on a stone and lit a cigarette. Jesus, what a mess I'm in, he told himself. That wonderful scheme Ciccio had presented to him had blown up in their faces.

After a quarter of an hour he stubbed out his second cigarette. Dino wouldn't be long now.

Only three cars passed in the next five minutes, and the fourth was Dino's. Giorgio climbed in, and they picked up Ciccio a few minutes later.

'I'm sticking to the back roads,' said Dino. 'If they think Giorgio's doing a bunk, they'll be watching the motorway.'

They all fell silent for a while. Then Dino tried to lighten the mood by telling jokes. Surprisingly this worked, and soon the other two were making their own contributions. For the moment they felt safe.

They were rounding a bend a few miles past Santa Caterina Villarmosa, when Dino was forced to brake sharply. Two cars blocked the road ahead. As he came to a stop, four men with guns jumped down from a bank, yanked open the doors beside Ciccio and Giorgio, and dragged them out. Only Giorgio put up resistance, which was terminated by a sharp kick in the testicles.

When they were both handcuffed, each prisoner was led to a separate car, forced into the back, and made to lie on the floor. Giorgio knew what was coming: *lupara bianca* – 'white shotgun'. No one would ever see either him or Ciccio again.

After a ten-minute drive, the two vehicles turned into a recently asphalted side road. A mile further on stood a grand villa surrounded by cypress trees. The cars pulled up in the forecourt, and the two captives were hauled out.

Giorgio noticed that at one corner of the villa stood a square tower with an overhanging roof above an open loggia at the top, whose archways revealed the flickering of candlelight. Perched on the sill sat two elegant men.

Ferrandini and Gabrielli glanced down idly as the two young men in handcuffs were hustled in, but neither made any comment. At the dinner table behind them, Vincenzo Cattagna made some remark which set them both laughing.

The lights of another car could be seen, and a moment later it pulled into the forecourt. Dino got out of his BMW just as Vitellini emerged from the villa. 'I said you wouldn't have long to wait for my call, Don Masino,' he said, kissing the older man's hand respectfully.

Vitellini clapped him on the shoulder. 'You did well, Dino. I'm proud of you.'

'Leggio handled his part beautifully.'

'Give him my thanks. But come on in. There are some friends I want you to meet.' He put his arm around the young man's shoulders and led him into the villa. Giorgio and Ciccio were standing under guard inside. The former glared at Dino, his hatred blunted by the sure knowledge that he was going to die this very night. Barely glancing at the two captives, Dino followed his don up the stairs.

'A friend of mine's building a new hotel at Taormina,' Vitellini was saying. 'Two hundred rooms. He wants television and video in all of them. Top quality. Think you can handle it?'

'Of course. I'm grateful to you, Don Masino.'

Giorgio heard these words just as he and Ciccio were being pushed into the study. He knew they would be the last he would ever hear his erstwhile friend speak. Dino was on his way to wealth and power; he and Ciccio to unmarked graves.

As they climbed the second flight of steps, Vitellini stopped and put his hand on Dino's shoulder. He murmured, 'The men you are about to meet are the summit. They themselves have asked to meet you, and that's a great privilege. Remember their names, but never mention them to anyone. If ever they ask you to do something, regard it as a direct order from me.'

Dino nodded gravely. Vitellini led the way up into the tower loggia. The four Americans came forward to greet the young man and Vitellini presented him to each in turn. Cattagna was the first.

Looking him in the eye, Dino took his hand, then bowed to kiss it. Straightening, he said, 'An honour, Don Vincenzo.' He then treated the others with identical elegance. Dino came from a humble family, but he had learnt how to behave in the presence of the powerful.

Vitellini smiled with satisfaction as he left the room and went downstairs to his study. His right-hand man was his first cousin, Gaetano. Gaetano's lack of intelligence was something of a handicap for Vitellini – although much more for Gaetano himself – but his loyalty was beyond question, so he would remain his right-hand man for as long as Vitellini needed one. Now Gaetano pushed the two young men to their knees, grasping each by the hair and forcing them to look up into the face of their judge and jury.

'Life is a serious business,' said Vitellini quietly, 'as you two shits are about to find out. There are two ways of getting information. One is quick, the other slow. The quick method is that I ask a question, and you give me a truthful answer. If you hesitate, if you contradict yourselves, if you contradict one another, if you say anything which makes me suspect you are lying, we pass automatically to the slow method. That requires the use of an oxyacetylene torch down in the cellar. Five minutes of that is more than sufficient, but since I have guests upstairs and don't wish our agreeable conversation to be interrupted constantly, the first session will last half an hour. We *know* you did it. Now we want to know exactly why.' He made a gesture and Giorgio's mouth was gagged. 'Better take him away,' he said. 'I'll talk to them separately.'

He turned back to Ciccio. 'Go ahead. I'm listening.'

In the midst of the unreality of the situation, Ciccio saw the sudden reality. To die was one thing, but to die after half an hour under an oxyacetylene torch was something else.

Eleven minutes later it was all over. Vitellini then rejoined his American friends and began to fill in the gaps in their knowledge. Since no one had anything further to ask the two youths, a postponement of execution was unnecessary. He returned to the study and gestured Gaetano to come close, murmuring something which neither captive could hear.

The condemned men were walked back out to the cars, resolved – in the face of the inevitable – to muster what dignity they could. They were driven along a dusty cart track till they reached an abandoned farmhouse. Unusually, it had a cellar, which was soundproof.

'*You're* all right,' said Gaetano to Ciccio, as he tied him up.

For a moment Ciccio thought he would be allowed to live, and that his witnessing of Giorgio's execution was intended as a warning. But Gaetano's real meaning was not long in becoming clear. When Giorgio's trousers and underpants were cut away, his eyes went wide and he struggled frantically against his bindings, screaming uselessly into the gag.

Gaetano waited for his effort to expand itself. 'Orders of Don Masino. You killed you own great-uncle, Giorgio – for gain. That is an *infamia*. You have to pay for it.'

To his men he said, 'Hold him down,' then he produced a large carving knife and performed the act himself, clutching the testicles and penis together in his left hand, and cutting with his right. Afterwards he pulled out his gun, stepped back from the body, aimed squarely at Giorgio's midriff, and fired.

'Remove the gag.'

One of the men obeyed, and Giorgio's agony came into the room with them in slowly expelled, hoarse screams as he tried to reduce the pain by controlling his breathing.

Gaetano washed his hands at the filthy old sink in the corner, then went upstairs to smoke a cigarette. While the fourth stayed behind to keep a watch on Ciccio, three of his men came with him. One of them made a joke, but Gaetano silenced him with a scowl. He didn't think any death was a fit subject for levity, but he suspected the joke had been motivated by fear. The man had never witnessed an execution accompanied by castration before. It didn't happen all that often, and was intended as an expression of extreme contempt. Castration was painful, certainly, but nothing like as agonising as the bullet in the stomach.

Gaetano had his men take turns in standing guard down in the cellar, half an hour at a time. Giorgio lived until just before the end of the fifth watch, and Ciccio spent this time alternately praying for their two souls and trying to beam telepathic messages of sympathy to his friend as he watched him writhe.

Finally Gaetano was summoned to check the pulse. Satisfied, he stuffed the severed testicles into Giorgio's mouth. Then he stood up, turned around, pulled out his gun, and shot Ciccio between the eyes.

The bodies were heaved into large sacks, which were then dumped in the boots of the two cars and driven across several fields to an abandoned vineyard.

Gaetano picked up a torch and walked around to look for a suitable site. 'This'll do,' he called. 'Get a move on. I'd like to get some sleep tonight.'

The men worked in pairs, and in shifts of five minutes. Gaetano judged seven feet to be deep enough, then the bodies were thrown in one on top of the other. It didn't occur to anyone to wonder which would support the other for all eternity.

The refilling of the hole was rapid, but afterwards Gaetano spent several minutes rearranging leaves and broken vines across the site.

Engines were started, and the vehicles bumped away across the fields into the distance, leaving the burial ground in silence and tranquillity.

12

The main Rome branch of the Banco di Sicilia was in the Via del Corso. Five minutes after it opened the following morning, Ned Moreno entered and went up to the Foreign desk, asking to speak to the head of the department. Moreno's dress and general manner left the clerk in little doubt that he ought to transfer this inquiry to someone higher up. A few moments later, Ned was introducing himself to Ernesto Provini – but using the identity James Bakewell from New York City and handing over a business card run off for him a few hours before. Leaning forward to imply the need for discretion, he explained that he represented an American bank which required the services of a financial manager on behalf of a very important customer.

'A friend in Zurich recommended your bank to me,' he continued. 'I understand you've been handling an estate in Sicily for him for many years.'

Provini frowned slightly. 'There are several estates there with which we are involved in one capacity or another.' He allowed himself a small smile. 'We are the Banco di Sicilia, after all.'

Ned smiled back, showing a fine set of white teeth. 'Near Corleone, I think he said. But the local manager lives in Palermo. Rampone is his name.'

'Ah, yes. I know the account you mean. A very old and valued client. But I have to tell you that, in their case, our function is purely intermediary – making payments, arranging bank transfers, passing on messages, that sort of thing.'

Ned treated this admission to a slight frown. 'I must have been misinformed, then.'

'We do supervise the management of some estates, of course,' went on Provini hurriedly. 'But not theirs,' he added lamely.

Ned let his frown deepen. 'I hope I haven't got things muddled.' He paused for a moment as if thinking hard. Then his brow cleared. 'You wouldn't mind if I rang my friend from here?'

'Not at all, Mr Bakewell. Please use this phone.'

'Thank you.' Ned opened his briefcase and hunted through it. 'I seem to have left my address book at the hotel. Never mind, I'll get the number through information.'

'If you'll just wait one moment, Mr Bakewell, I'll find it for you myself. We'll have it on computer.'

He turned to the desktop computer and did some impressively rapid typing. Provini's fingers were fast, but not as fast as Ned's eyes. He now knew the name of the Swiss bank. It only remained to do a little play-acting to keep Provini happily ignorant of the service he had just performed for him.

'Shall I dial it for you?' asked the Italian ingenuously.

'That would be very kind.'

Provini handed him the telephone while the number in Zurich was ringing.

'*Bessmer Schweizerische Handelsbank. Guten Tag.*'

'*James Bakewell am Apparat. Darf ich mit Herrn Dörfling sprechen, bitte?*'

'*Dörfling? Wir haben keinen Herrn Dörfling bei uns, mein Herr. Vielleicht haben Sie falsch verbunden. Hier ist die Bessmer Schweizerische Handelsbank.*'

'*Ach so. Dann werd' ich später anrufen. Wiederhören.*' Ned hung up. 'He was out. Back at twelve, the receptionist said.' He glanced at his watch, looking thoughtful for a moment. Then he said, 'Look, I have an appointment in a few minutes. I'll ring my friend when he gets back, and call in again this afternoon. Thank you very much for your help. *Arrivederla.*'

Ned left the bank, walked around the corner, and took out his cellular phone.

Georg Zaunmacher returned to his office in the afternoon a little earlier than usual. Having spent most of the morning at a meeting of creditors, he had gone for an early lunch. Now he was informed that an American visitor called Collins, who wished to open a large account, was waiting to see him.

Zaunmacher entered his office by a private door, and buzzed for his assistant to show the man in.

'I'm so sorry you've had to wait for me, Mr Collins. It's been a busy morning, I'm afraid.' The banker allowed himself a thin smile as he got up to shake his visitor's hand. 'May I offer you a glass of something?'

'No, thank you.' The American glanced at the assistant who was standing nearby, ready to attend to his master's wishes. 'I would prefer to explain my intentions in private.'

Zaunmacher nodded and the assistant withdrew. 'Now, how may I help you?'

'It's very simple, Mr Zaunmacher. I represent certain powerful interests in the United States who wish to make a transaction with you. I shall be receiving a telephone call here in a few minutes. I shall pass you the receiver and you will hear a voice. I think that voice will probably be enough to persuade you to what extent it would be in your interests to do business with us.'

'Can you perhaps not intimate to me the general nature of this transaction?'

'I can tell you that it concerns an estate in Sicily which your bank has been managing for more than fifty years.'

Zaunmacher pursed his lips. 'I hope we can be of service to you, Mr Collins, but I have to tell you that account has a closed procedure. We are not authorised to make any arrangements outside the specific guidelines originally laid down by the client.'

His phone rang. He picked up the receiver and heard his secretary say. 'There's a gentleman calling who wishes to speak to Mr Collins.'

'Put him through.' He passed his visitor the phone.

Collins took the receiver, listened for a moment and then said, 'Just one moment. I'll pass you over to him.' He handed the receiver back, and Zaunmacher put it to his ear.

'Daddy? Is that you?'

The colour drained from his face. 'Dieter, are you all right?'

'Yes. I'm here with these two men. They came to the school this morning and said you wanted to see me.'

'Hold on a moment, Dieter.' He looked up into Stelio's face and saw some things there that in his innocence he had not detected before. 'What do you want from me?'

'Ask your son to put one of them on, then hand me the phone again.' Zaunmacher did so, and was astonished and relieved beyond measure to hear him say, 'Okay, you can release the boy now. Let him have another word with his father before you take him home.' Stelio covered the mouthpiece and said, 'Mr Zaunmacher, I don't go in for hurting children, but the same doesn't apply to adults. I'm sorry for giving you a scare, but we're very short of time. I had to make you understand as quickly as possible. Tell your son that something's come up, so you can't go and see him now. And then we'll talk.'

'An ad, you say?'

'Yes. In the classified announcements section.'

'Which newspapers?'

'Any top five British national newspapers. Zaunmacher picked the *Times, Independent, Daily Telegraph, Guardian* and *Financial Times.*'

'When did it appear?'

'Yesterday.'

'What's the wording?'

As Stelio told him, Ferrandini noted it down. 'Right. Hang fire till I get back to you.'

'Beautiful,' murmured Cattagna when he heard the news. 'The perfect cutoff.'

Gabrielli looked at him. 'Didn't you deduce this?'

'No.'

'Then what did you think would happen?'

'That the banker would send a copy of the Accords to the nearest newspaper, of course,' replied Cattagna slightly irritated. 'There wouldn't be much point in setting up such a complicated system otherwise. As Salvatore often said: never make a threat which you can't or don't intend to carry out.'

'So now what do you think he's doing?'

Cattagna sighed. 'I don't know, Peter. Perhaps the Accords have always been held by some different bank, and this is the coded instruction to publish them. What do you think, Robert? You're his son.'

Ferrandini shook his head. 'No, Vincenzo. Not another bank. There really wouldn't be any point.'

Lovegni said, 'In that case he hid them somewhere and now he needs an agent to go and fetch them.'

Both Gabrielli and Cattagna nodded at this explanation. Ferrandini felt less sure. 'Why England?' he asked.

'Why not?' replied Gabrielli.

'Yes, but in 1943 it wasn't exactly an easy place to get in or out of.'

Cattagna replied, 'My dear Robert, in 1943 *no* place was very easy to get in or out of.'

Ferrandini fell silent, brooding. The others turned to speculating how they themselves might have got somebody into England in 1943 without the authorities realising it. Ten minutes of this exhausted their imaginations, and they too became quiet.

In the midst of the heavy silence, Ferrandini suddenly said, 'The bombs – that's what I don't like about it.'

The others looked up and stared at him. 'What bombs?'

'The *German* bombs, of course! What else?'

Peter looked blank. 'I'm sorry, Robert, I don't understand what you mean.'

Cattagna intervened. 'I think what Robert is saying is that Salvatore would never have put the Accords somewhere where they might easily have been destroyed by enemy bombing.'

Lovegni grunted. 'He wouldn't have hidden them in a city, perhaps, but what about the countryside? Not even the Germans were bombing that.'

Ferrandini shook his head. 'Not the Accords. I'm not talking about the Accords. I'm talking about this agent who's supposed to go and fetch them.' Seeing everyone's blank expression, he went on, 'Look, if this ad in the newspaper is supposed to instruct somebody to go and fetch the Accords, how old is he now? How old would he have been in 1943? How old would he be thirty years from now, if that was when Adriano got murdered? Don't you see, if your idea about an agent is right, then he can't be too old. In which case somebody has to select him now. A firm of lawyers, perhaps, or some kind of personnel employment agency. A firm that has clients and keeps files. An office. But where do you find firms like that? Not out in the countryside; in cities and towns. And the Germans were bombing them. The risk of this particular firm being hit and its files destroyed was small, of course, but it wasn't negligible. My father would never have taken it.'

Gabrielli nodded slowly. 'All right, Robert. You've made a good point. But where does that leave us?'

Ferrandini shook his head in defeat. 'I don't know.'

But Cattagna was smiling broadly. 'Robert, I congratulate you on an excellent analysis. You're absolutely right. Salvatore would never have employed a company which stood any chance of being bombed in the hostilities. But your objection has just pinpointed its location for us. There were two places in England that were absolutely secure in 1943. They were never bombed because the British and the Germans agreed at the outset of the war that each side could declare two university towns open cities, providing no heavy industry was located there. The Germans picked Heidelberg and Göttingen, if I remember rightly; but I'm quite sure which the British picked – Oxford and Cambridge.'

His three companions responded with excitement, then Robert became thoughtful again. He had suddenly remembered accompanying his father on a business and leisure trip to Britain in 1973. As a surprise, their London host had planned two days of excursions for them: the first to take in Oxford and Stratford-on-Avon, the second Cambridge. On the morning of the first day his father had claimed he was catching a cold so intended staying at home for the day, although he insisted that Robert should go anyway. By the evening he had marvellously recovered, however, so the next day they had all gone to Cambridge.

Now, twenty-three years later, Robert knew why his father had invented that cold: he hadn't wanted to go to Oxford – not then, not ever. Because he'd already been there, thirty years previously, and there was someone there he did not want to risk running into ever again.

Ferrandini turned to the others and said, 'It's in Oxford.'

They turned inquiringly for an explanation, but he was already picking up the phone.

13

On the day he would remember for the rest of his life George Williamson stepped out into a glorious September morning just as a flight of Spitfires passed overhead. It reminded him of the summer of 1940: languid, hot, lazy, with death reigning in the rainless skies. What a low moment that had been, he reflected. Invasion expected at any moment and only Churchill's steel-cast words between the nation and national panic. '*Let us so bear ourselves that if the British Empire and its Commonwealth should last a thousand years, men will say*: This *was their finest hour.*' What a giant to be able to stand behind!

And what a contrast between 1940 and now, he reflected. El Alamein, Stalingrad, Tunisia and now here they were, on the point of conquering Sicily, with an invasion of mainland Italy sure to follow! In just three short years a seemingly inevitable defeat had been turned into a virtually certain final victory!

From a house on the other side of the street Major Truscott, half his face gone in the first lot and probably some of his brain too, strutted out for his morning constitutional, fully clad in his shabby but knife-creased dress uniform of 1914. Punctual as a Swiss clock, thought Williamson. Albeit a cuckoo clock. His abrupt turn when he passed through the garden gate was precisely ninety degrees. He saluted Williamson, who saluted back, and went on his way in the other direction. Truscott always made George feel vaguely embarrassed because of his terrible wounds, while Williamson himself, born in the safe year of 1901, had been too young for the first scrap and too old for the second.

There having been a first one, it was ridiculous that there was now a second, he thought, feeling indignation rise within him. They'd called it 'the war to end all wars', yet here they were in the middle of another one. They'd wasted the peace of 1918.

No, he thought, that's too simplistic. The truth was more complicated. It was the 1917 Bolshevik revolution that was to blame. Fear of communism had produced a backlash bringing into being a succession of right-wing dictatorships of one sort or another in a dozen of the poorer European countries, and Germany had been made poor by having to pay the crushing reparations imposed by the victors of the first war. In effect, it was the Allies themselves who had

111

created the German need for a Hitler.

So here we all are – at it again.

John Tewbury had made an interesting point at the pub the night before. He'd said the Allies would be certain to aim to knock out Germany before Japan, because the Germans had better scientists, and you never knew how some new miracle weapon might swing things around. 'Like the tank might have done in the first lot, if only they'd used it properly.'

Williamson frowned. Tewbury was right. The Allies were obviously winning, but you never knew what surprises might lie around the corner. And there was no getting away from it: the Germans were an inventive bunch of bastards. Williamson quickened his step, suddenly feeling the need to work hard, as if his own job might somehow – miraculously – affect the outcome of the titanic struggle taking place far away to the south and east, and in the Pacific on the other side of the world.

He hadn't gone far before his own foolishness became apparent to him. He wasn't even engaged in a vital war industry. He was only the surviving partner of a silly little business engaged in the placement of people in business, in schools and universities. Thus far, his only contributions to the war effort had been to donate the railings around his house to be melted down for ships, buy a few war bonds and grow vegetables in his flower garden to help the nation become a tiny bit more self-sufficient. His only chance of making some real contribution to victory lay in signing up some new Einstein who walked into his office looking for a job in an armaments factory.

Williamson swept this daydream out of his mind and returned to speculating on the course of the war. On reaching the High, he called in at his regular newsagent's, and Mr Hardy handed him his reserved copy of the *Times*.

'Patton's making better progress than Monty,' he commented, with the same amiable ruefulness as he might have used to report the English cricket team's poor performance at a test-match.

'Yes, but Patton's having an easy time of it. Monty has to fight yard by yard.'

Hardy accepted this analysis with several consoling nods. Sometimes it seemed that their enemy was less the Axis than the Americans, reflected Williamson, and bade him a good morning.

His office was located two doors further along, with the firm of Williamson and Gabbitas on the first floor. His secretary was already at work, moving papers from one place to another; that was almost all there was to do these days. Gabbitas had died many years ago, and it was just as well he was dead, thought Williamson. There wouldn't be any chance of *two* families surviving on so little income.

'Good morning, Edna. Any tea left?'

112

'Enough for one pot. Then that's that till next week.'

'We'd better enjoy it, then.'

'Do you want some *now*?'

'Leave it for an hour. That will give us something to look forward to.'

He went into his private office, glanced at the mail, checked the job vacancies in his newspaper in case there was anything suitable for the people on his books, decided not, and settled down to read the news. The principal story was the capture of Palermo by General Patton's Seventh Army. It was an exciting event. The city was a major regional capital of one of the three big enemies. Williamson pulled out a dog-eared agenda from one of the desk drawers, and made an entry. He called it his 'war diary' and in it had faithfully recorded every event of significance since the British declaration of war on 3 September 1939. Now he turned back and leafed through the book, following the progress of the immense conflict.

Poland, Denmark, Norway, the Low Countries and France. Mussolini had waited until the French army was clearly reeling, and then declared war, too. In ten weeks it was all over. The British Expeditionary Force escaped from Dunkirk by the skin of its teeth – 360,000 men returning to safety out of an original 400,000 – but at the cost of nearly all its equipment. Out of seven hundred and four tanks, only twenty-five were brought back. On top of this, the RAF was outnumbered by the German Luftwaffe by two to one. Yet Hitler delayed fatally before beginning his attack and this respite gave the British time to re-equip and prepare themselves for the onslaught. The ensuing dogfights in the air over southern England took many young men to their deaths, but what became known as the Battle of Britain was a victory which forced the Germans to turn to less costly ways of reducing the island. And while the Luftwaffe had to content itself with painful night attacks on British cities, Hitler tried to starve the island into surrender by sending out his submarines to sink its merchant shipping.

For a year after the fall of France, Hitler's energies had been devoted to subjugating the unruly Balkans and to rescuing his Italian ally from a series of military disasters in Greece and North Africa. Then on 22 June 1941 the Germans invaded Russia and by the end of the year were at the gates of both Moscow and Leningrad. But the predicted collapse of the Red Army had not occurred, despite its vast losses in men.

In the meantime the United States had been moving closer and closer to belligerent status. It was supplying Britain handsomely through Lend-Lease and, after an incident in July 1941 between a US destroyer and a U-boat near Iceland, the defence of which had been taken over by the US from the British, President Roosevelt had given warning that if Axis ships entered the waters around Iceland – the protection of which was deemed essential for the defence of America – they would be sunk. On 7 December Japan attacked Pearl Harbor, and four days later Germany and Italy declared war on the United States.

The year 1942 was mostly black for the Allies. In Russia the Germans continued the same sort of rapid penetration which they had achieved the previous year, although now the direction of their main thrust was towards the Caucasus oilfields. By November they had come almost within reach of their goal.

Meanwhile, the British had suffered a string of disasters all over the globe. In the Far East, calamity followed calamity with astonishing speed – the sinking of two important capital ships, the loss of Hong Kong, Malaya, Singapore, Burma – and then the Japanese were at the gates of India. In North Africa, Rommel pushed the British back to the Egyptian frontier and, when Tobruk fell, 35,000 men were taken prisoner. Worst of all, shipping losses in the Atlantic reached alarming proportions. Britain could not remain a belligerent if she lost her capacity to feed herself.

But, later in the year, events began to move in a different direction. The Japanese expansion was halted, and pressure was taken off Australia. In Russia, Hitler was distracted by an unimportant city on the left flank of his advancing armies because of its name: Stalingrad. And, in North Africa, Rommel was brought up short by Montgomery and the battle of El Alamein was a resounding British victory. But, above all, in November the Anglo-Americans, anxious to take the pressure off the Russians by opening some kind of front elsewhere, but not strong enough yet for a direct assault across the Channel, suddenly, unexpectedly and brilliantly invaded Algeria. The Germans were pushed back on two fronts to Tunisia.

In mid-January 1943, Churchill and Roosevelt met at Casablanca in Morocco, where they issued a call for the unconditional surrender of Germany, Italy and Japan. Nothing could more clearly have indicated the changed situation. The Allies were winning, and had said so.

In February the Germans suffered a colossal defeat at Stalingrad and lost 300,000 men. In May, German resistance in Tunisia ended, the Allies taking more than a quarter of a million prisoners. The entire North African coast was now in Allied hands. What was more important, however, was that fifty-six U-boats were sunk in April and May, so Allied shipping losses were drastically reduced. The rumours were now too numerous to be brushed aside, and they clearly announced that the Allies were winning the Battle of the Atlantic.

On 10 July, Sicily was invaded by the American Seventh Army under General Patton, and by the British Eighth under Field Marshal

114

Montgomery. Patton's progress had been spectacular and on 22 July, yesterday, he'd captured Palermo. Meanwhile, ever greater numbers of American uniforms seen around Britain testified to the inexorable build-up of forces necessary for the coming cross-Channel invasion of Hitler's Fortress Europe – some time in the spring of the following year. The betting was on 1 May.

Williamson closed his war diary with a satisfied sigh. Things were going extremely well and the closer that victory came, the greater the chances that his own two sons would come home alive.

He opened the *Times* again and turned to the domestic news. By the time the cup of tea was brought in, he was deeply engrossed in the crossword. The accompanying homemade biscuits were almost sugarless but at least dry. When Edna had withdrawn he softened them by dunking them in his tea, a solecism he would have never countenanced with a witness present.

Half an hour later Edna came back into the room, visibly excited.

'There's a Major Davis outside to see you. An American,' she added breathlessly, in the same tone she might have used to announce the Archbishop of Canterbury.

Williamson hurriedly pushed the newspaper into a drawer, and asked her to show him in.

Davis was a tall, handsome man in his late thirties, who advanced towards him with a friendly smile and an easy, confident air, his handshake firm and warm. Williamson gestured him to sit down, and asked how he could be of service. But Davis was in no hurry to get down to business and instead glanced around the office, making polite inquiries about the framed paintings lining the walls and admiring the view from the window of the fourteenth-century spire of St Mary the Virgin. His attitude seemed friendly and respectful but there was something about his demeanour which told Williamson that this man was accustomed to command in civilian life.

For a while they chatted about the war, discussing the strategic implications of the recent events in Sicily, and whether Stalin would behave himself when it was all over. Most people in Britain and America thought the Russians were wonderful and Stalin himself was being called 'Uncle Joe'. The fact that both men agreed he could not be trusted gave each a reason to respect the shrewdness of the other.

At last Davis got around to the purpose of his visit and explained that he was here for entirely private reasons, representing a consortium of American businessmen who had decided that postwar Europe was going to be *the* place to invest. Though they had complete faith in each other's word, they felt concerned lest their sons should not possess the same degree of honour. So they'd devised an elaborate system to protect themselves, and part of it would involve the services

115

of a firm such as Williamson and Gabbitas.

Williamson replied, 'Please assure your principals that we would be delighted to serve them. But what exactly would we be required to do?'

'It's a simple job. Your secretary would need to check the announcements column in the top national newspapers every day. In return for this, your company would be paid a monthly stipend. If a certain advert ever appeared, you'd need to go to a specified bank and they would tell you about the next part of the assignment. If you didn't want to continue, there'd be no problem. The bank would simply select another company. Your stipends would cease, of course, but in return for having fulfilled all the conditions of our agreement, you'd be suitably recompensed. If you accepted the further assignment, however, the financial compensation would be very rewarding.'

'And what would this further assignment consist of?'

'The selection of someone suitable to persuade the transgressor to return to the fold.'

'I see.' Williamson frowned. 'I must say, Mr Davis, it's a somewhat unusual way of going about things. Why couldn't they just wait for this development to occur, and select somebody themselves when it did?'

'They want somebody impartial, and since these business enterprises will all be rooted in Europe, rationally he ought to be a native European. Our reason for organising things in advance is really quite simple. If anyone were to renege, this might seriously undermine business confidence in our consortium as a whole. Normally, when anything casts doubt on the credibility of a large business group, the worst thing they can do is panic. Rumours start flying. Reporters begin poking their noses into things, questioning employees: secretaries, chauffeurs and so on. The bosses find their whole lives suddenly being put under a microscope. In such an emergency the best policy is to act perfectly normally, just follow your daily routine, and try and give the impression you can't understand what all the fuss is about. Successful business is all about planning ahead and making provision for the untoward. If anything ever went wrong with our venture, the men I represent would like to be able to send you a single message which would cope with it, and then carry on with their lives routinely, confident that their interests were in competent hands.'

'But surely the best way of dealing with any aberration would be a properly drawn-up contract?'

Davis's reply was surprising. 'There isn't going to be a written contract. It's a totally verbal agreement.'

Williamson frowned. 'Isn't that rather unwise?'

'But necessary, I'm afraid. I assure you that no illegality is involved, either in this country or the States, but there might be technical infringements of the anti-trust laws in one or two European countries.'

'Ah,' replied Williamson, his frown disappearing. He was beginning to see the light. This wasn't a consortium; it was a price-fixing agreement. A cartel. And the Americans were ideally placed for it. When the shooting stopped, all Europe was going to be broke. No one would have any money to invest. So the Americans would step in, build immense multinational companies from scratch, and then clean up. Oh yes, they'd rebuild Europe all right, but they wouldn't do it for love or philanthropy. They'd make the Europeans pay through the nose as punishment for having ruined themselves and half the world.

Davis pursed his lips, regarding the other man speculatively, as if wondering whether he could trust him a notch further. Then, seeming to make up his mind, he went on, 'There is one other reason for the rather complicated arrangements my principals require. The best way to discourage someone from doing something is to make things too costly for him if he does. My principals want just such a deterrent. The person your firm selected would be put in a position to conduct a damaging financial campaign directed against the reneger. He'd have access to certain codes which would shift consortium money sideways, to the detriment of the transgressor – buying and selling shares in his company at awkward moments, and so on. Several alternative moves would be available, preventing him from preparing countermeasures in advance, but it would be essential for our operator to remain anonymous. The idea is that the financial consequences of breaking our agreement would be so daunting that, with any luck, those measures would never need to be implemented.'

Williamson found this explanation entirely satisfactory. But what an arrangement! These Americans were amazing people. Their business methods were getting more and more complicated every day. 'Very well, Mr Davis. I think the basic proposition can be countenanced. Perhaps now you could explain the details.'

'As I said, your precise instructions, and those to be handed on to the person you select, will be in the trust of a certain bank. The name of that bank will be kept in an envelope inside a safe, which your firm would be expected to take charge of, and the safe itself will be fitted with a combination lock. As I've explained, your secretary would need to check the announcements in the newspapers every day, and when a particular advertisement appeared, you'd open the safe. The advert itself will tell you the combination for the safe.' He made a gesture to indicate how simple it all was.

'Exactly how much are you proposing to pay us per month?'

Davis took out of his top pocket a folded slip of paper and passed it across the desk. Williamson opened it and nodded slowly. For the little work seemingly involved it was more than acceptable, without being overgenerous. 'And the final payment?'

Davis shook his head. 'I'm not authorised to say now, but I can assure you that you'd find it satisfactory. Obviously, a great many years might go by before the announcement you're looking for appears – if ever – but, so long as your firm keeps to its side of our agreement, the financial compensation will be respected.'

Williamson nodded. 'Very well, Major. Williamson and Gabbitas are happy to accept you as our client. Will you draw up the contract, or shall we?'

Davis smiled, stood up and offered his hand. '*This* is our contract, Mr Williamson.'

The Englishman smiled back, and they shook hands.

After Davis had gone, Williamson got down to the little work there was. These days, because of the war, nearly all the company's business was concerned with placing not very bright or wealthy people at good Oxbridge colleges. Specifically, he had to write letters of application which made the candidates seem less dull than they really were and to prepare them for interviews. That wasn't much of a problem these days; with so many young men serving in the armed forces, the colleges were empty.

Williamson spent the afternoon shunting papers around, between bouts of trying to finish the *Times* crossword. At six o'clock Edna went home. Almost as if he'd been waiting for her to depart, Davis arrived promptly in a van, together with two beefy-looking companions in American uniforms. The two men carried a safe into the building and when they'd gone, Davis handed Williamson a sheet of paper with a few typewritten lines on it.

'That tells you how to recognise the advertisement, and how to deduce the combination. By the way, the dial itself is locked. Here's the key. Better keep it somewhere safe.'

'Inside, perhaps?' suggested Williamson, nodding towards the safe.

Davis smiled. Then serious, he added. 'You can make copies of it if you wish, but you ought to have at least one within easy reach. Your monthly payments will be sent to you by registered mail. These will be simple money orders made out to the bearer, so they won't need to be declared to the Inland Revenue. I'll arrange for the first payment to be made within a few days from now. There is one small detail I haven't mentioned: what happens if you decide to close up your business. Our agreement is between you and me personally, so you have a choice: you can continue this as a private business matter within your family, or you can find another firm in the same line of work and pass it on to them. I rely on your judgement to choose somebody dependable.'

Williamson nodded. Because of the financial remuneration, they both knew he would choose the first option. 'And if I die?'

Davis smiled at him. 'If?'

Williamson grinned. 'When.'

'The normal rules of executorship apply in the case of either death or incapacity. Of course, that means you'll have to add a codicil to your will. Perhaps it would be a good idea to write one now,' he suggested, and the Englishman concurred. On a sheet of paper Davis wrote down a few lines in clear though legal-sounding terminology. Williamson scanned them and agreed. Under British law, wills did not require notarisation, but to be legally valid the will or codicil had to be signed in the presence of two people, neither of whom could be either executor or beneficiary, who would then add their signatures as witnesses. Davis clearly knew this, and Williamson suggested they deal with the formality over a glass of sherry at his house nearby.

He locked the office and together they walked through the streets to his home in Norham Gardens in north Oxford. He called in at two houses on the way and invited a couple of neighbours, John Talbot and Geoffrey Bray, to come over and witness the codicil. The gathering was a social success. Davis recounted some interesting stories about the Tunisian campaign. The sherry party then turned into a dinner party when Williamson's wife Edith insisted they all stay to eat.

Inevitably the conversation turned to grand strategy and Talbot asked Davis what he thought of the developments on the Russian Front. He was referring to the recent thwarting of Hitler's attempt to nip off the Kursk salient, which had forced yet another German retreat. 'The Germans are obviously going to have to bring in reinforcements from France, which surely ought to make the invasion easier for us.'

But Davis's reply was surprising. 'No, I don't think so. Hitler knows what the Soviet losses are, and how badly they need a second front in the west to take the pressure off them, so he knows our invasion must come soon. I think he'll keep up his strength in France to repel it, and *then* move a lot of his divisions to Russia for an all-out assault. But I think what the events of the last year have shown is that the Germans' main problem is not so much men as fuel. There are only two main sources of oil in Europe: Romania and the Caucasus. When they invaded Russia, they obviously thought it was going to be a doddle and went for Moscow and Leningrad. But last year there was a change in strategy and they made that immense effort to reach the Caucasus, which might have succeeded if Hitler hadn't been distracted by Stalingrad. I think that means that Romania just isn't supplying him with all the oil he needs. If so, then he's in a real fix, because he can't go after the Caucasus again without the reinforcements from France, and he can't move *them* until he's thrown back the invasion.'

This was an intelligent, well-informed analysis which impressed all of them. Williamson decided it was time to make a useful British contribution to the discussion and repeated John Tewbury's remark of the previous evening about some new German secret weapon screwing up the works. Geoffrey Bray was on to it at once.

'Yes, I had dinner with one of the dons at Magdalen a few nights ago and he said that, before the war, a lot of physicists were talking about the possibility of a new kind of radioactive bomb made from uranium. In theory, it was supposed to be extremely powerful. When the war started they all hushed up.'

Everyone looked at Davis in case he had anything to say about it, but the American remained impassive.

It was eleven o'clock when the dinner party came to an end. Davis wanted to catch the 11.45 train to London, and Williamson offered to walk him part of the way to the station. For a while they strolled in silence, breathing in the night air. Suddenly he asked, 'How long do you think it will last?'

'The war?'

Williamson nodded.

Davis pondered for a while, then he said, 'Hitler will never give up. He can't do. He couldn't face the humiliation, let alone the firing squad. So, unless his generals decide to get rid of him, the war will only end when Germany is beaten to its knees. We can't win by going through Italy or the Balkans. It has to be through France, which means we'll have to pull off the biggest amphibious invasion ever mounted, and it's far too late this year to organise a cross-Channel operation of that size before the rough weather sets in. The earliest realistic moment would be May of next year. After that, it'll be in the lap of the gods. I've heard some people say it will all be over by Christmas – but that rings a bell, and a cracked one.'

Williamson frowned. 'So it could drag on for years?'

'Yes, but my guess would be somewhere between six months and a year after the invasion.'

'And if Italy leaves the war? Could that speed things up?'

Davis's response seemed guarded. He paused before replying, 'Possibly.' There was something about the way he'd pronounced the word that told Williamson he knew more than he was saying. And, if so, this man was no ordinary infantry major.

'What's to stop the Germans withdrawing to a really strong defensible position and just letting us all knock our heads against them uselessly – like we did in the first lot? If they did that, the war could last halfway to forever.'

Davis shook his head. 'No. To begin with, there's that uranium bomb to think about. That's somewhere between five and ten thousand tons of TNT we're talking about. Sooner or later someone's going to make one. But even if they don't, the air war is getting more destructive by the week. That wasn't a problem to them in the first war, but now it's starting to get bad – I mean *really* bad – and it's going to get very much worse. It's only a matter of time before their industry becomes physically unable to supply all they need: ball bearings, tanks, rifles. Eventually they'll even run out of bullets.' He shook his head. 'You can put your mind at ease. There'll be no repetition of 1914–18.'

Williamson was fascinated. So Davis *had* heard about the radioactive bomb, after all. 'But what if it's the Germans who invent this uranium thing first?' he objected.

Once again Davis became guarded. 'Perhaps,' he said softly, and Williamson was now certain that the American had inside knowledge indicating that they wouldn't.

'Anything else for us to worry about?'

Davis shrugged. 'Rockets, perhaps. But they'll be aimed at London. You'll be all right out here in Oxford.'

A hundred yards further on, they reached the Ashmolean Museum, where Williamson intended to take his leave. The blackout left them with just a quarter moon to see by.

'Well, this is where I say goodbye and God speed. Perhaps we can get together again some time. I'd like that. Call me the next time you're back in England.'

Davis promised to do so. He smiled as they shook hands and wished each other well. He started to turn away, then suddenly seemed to remember something. 'I almost forgot. It's a silly detail really, but my principals insisted on it. About that safe; it's hermetically sealed. You know: no air in it – a vacuum. You must make sure no one ever fiddles with the combination dial, because when it's turned the seal will break and air will get in. As I told you, inside you'll find a paper with the name of the bank you have to go to. The thing is, there's another sheet accompanying it. It bears somebody's signature. But the paper itself is coated with a chemical compound which oxidises gradually upon exposure to air. The bank will only give you the details of the task to be undertaken if they can read the signature, so you'll have about three hours after opening the safe to get the paper to the bank.'

Williamson was more than surprised. This final precaution came close to implying possible dishonesty, and it deflated him considerably. Davis sensed his change of mood and offered his apologies. 'As I say, they insisted on it. But they didn't know who I was going to choose, remember.'

Williamson was only partly mollified. Somewhat stiffly he said, 'You can tell them they have no need to worry. I'll carry out my side of the agreement to the letter.'

121

'I'm sure you will. One last point: the seal is very unlikely to break by accident, but if it does, the bank will still make you the final payment, as long as you go there on the day the announcement appears.'

'The promise of a final reward helping to curb any curiosity in the meantime?' inquired Williamson in an ironic tone.

'If you like,' replied Davis coolly.

Williamson gave him a wry smile. 'Your principals would seem to be people who anticipate degrees of relative dishonesty.'

Davis looked him straight in the eye. Gone was the amiable major, and in his place stood a man who had seen all that life had to offer. 'Relative dishonesty is the only practical philosophy in this life. Show me a completely honest man, and I'll show you one who knows nothing of law, history or people.'

Williamson held his gaze for a long moment, then he sighed. 'Yes, I think you're right. Self-interests are what motivate us all.' Suddenly he allowed himself to become formal. 'Thank you, Major Davis. It's been a pleasure doing business with you.' He offered his hand again.

Davis ignored it and clasped him by the elbows instead. 'May God bring your sons home to you safely.' They looked at each other intensely for a moment, then Davis turned and went.

Williamson watched him walk away into the night, and stood staring into the darkness long after he'd gone.

He never saw him again.

On his slow walk home Williamson pondered some of the points raised during their fascinating conversation. Davis had had inside information on all sorts of secrets: rockets, radioactive bombs, Hitler's oil supply problem. No, the infantry uniform was definitely a disguise. And what was the other thing that had come into the conversation? Oh yes, whether Italy's withdrawal from the war would speed things up. The major had become guarded and replied, '*Possibly.*' What a funny thing to be secretive about. Why not just voice an opinion?

In bed that night he was mulling over the *Times* crossword, which he still hadn't managed to finish, when Edith said, 'I'd like to bet he has Italian blood in him.'

'Mm? Who?'

'Major Davis.'

'He's got fair hair and blue eyes.'

'So? Some Italians do. But the other day in a magazine I saw a photograph of Toscanani when he was younger, and your Major Davis looks exactly like him.'

Williamson had great respect for his wife's sixth sense. He lowered the newspaper and wondered.

'Night, dear.' Edith turned over to go to sleep.

'Goodnight.' He shrugged and went back to the crossword.

Three days later came the news that King Victor Emmanuel III of Italy had arrested Mussolini.

Williamson looked at the safe standing in the corner of his office. For a long moment he stared at it, then he picked up some writing paper and began to write down a detailed account of everything that had transpired. Afterwards he wrote out three copies of the instructions Davis had given him. Finally he went out to make three copies of the key. In the afternoon, with the help of someone from an office upstairs, he moved the safe into a little storeroom behind his own office. That evening he waited until his secretary, Edna, had gone home, then began to move things around until the safe was well hidden from view.

The following morning the postwoman delivered a registered envelope with a money order. It was for fifty per cent more than the agreed amount. Williamson's first thought was that this was a mistake. Except that Davis wasn't the type to make mistakes. Then Williamson began to wonder if the major's original intention had been to test him somehow. Here was a mistake from which a not *entirely* honest man could benefit simply by sealing his lips just that bit tighter. The major's words came back to him: 'Show me a completely honest man, and I'll show you one who knows nothing of law, history or people.' Oh, yes, the major knew about people all right. He knew a very great deal about people.

This reminded Williamson of something else. Davis had suggested how Edna should be briefed on the job of scanning the newspapers daily. '*Give her a list of six words to look for, five of which will appear normally from time to time, the sixth being just the first word of the code phrase, so it too will crop up once in a while. Her task will be to circle those ads starting with any of the six words.*' It was a simple idea to which George had hardly paid attention at the time, but now he realised that this system was a good way of not arousing Edna's curiosity at the seeming pointlessness of her task, as day after day the *real* code phrase failed to appear.

From then on, George followed events in Italy with a magnifying glass. He watched the Allied armies' race to Messina in the top right-hand corner of Sicily – just across the strait from Reggio di Calabria in the toe of Italy – between Patton's Seventh Army coming along the northern shore of the island from Palermo and Montgomery's Eighth Army coming up the eastern side from Syracuse. Patton won this race. It was true that he'd had an easier time during most of his campaign, while Montgomery had needed to fight for every yard, but was there anything else behind the published facts? Something to do with Major Davis?

In an uneventful life the mysterious American major stood out for him like a beacon, and Williamson often found himself wondering what would happen if the codeword ever arrived.

The war ended, and Williamson's sons came home on the very day that Churchill was thrown out of office by a grateful but ashamed people who now wanted a larger helping of the national pudding. It was 'The Age of Socialism' and the non-believers faced a grey future decorated with golden promises, while the believers faced a golden future decorated with grey ones. *Everyone* faced a colossal reconstruction task. Europe was in ruins.

But reconstruction meant work, so Williamson's business soon began perking up, and he started to groom his sons to take over the family firm. By 1949 business was booming and the staff had grown to six. Andrew got married in 1955, and his second son David five years later. George Williamson was a grandfather twice over by this time: Patrick born in 1956 and Jane in 1958. He decided it was time to retire. So he took his two sons to dinner in a private room at the Café Royal in London's Regent Street and, after swearing them to secrecy, had the time of his life in telling them the whole story of the mysterious Major Davis. It was the one moment in his life when, just briefly, his destiny had grazed against those of the great.

His sons reacted predictably. They enjoyed the story, and the drama of a secret revealed in a private room at a posh restaurant, and were intrigued by the facts themselves. But what really had Davis showed beyond an intelligent appraisal of strategy? They weren't even impressed by the fact that the major had revealed detailed knowledge about the Atomic Bomb in July of 1943, *two years* before the first one was tested.

'I don't see anything really surprising about that,' said David. 'Hundreds of thousands of people were involved in the Manhattan Project, so it's not surprising there should have been a few leaks.'

The next day Andrew and David made time to discuss the matter together because, after all, Major Davis was still a client of theirs – and there was still the safe and the regular monthly stipends, increasing in strict accordance with the retail price index. *And* there was an agreement to be honoured. They were a family firm, after all. But they could only assume what they'd separately decided the evening before: mountains being made out of molehills. It was only boring old Dad, and nothing interesting ever happened to *him*.

George retired two weeks later, and his sons took over the company.

The years rolled by, bringing the Williamsons their share of joys and tragedies. David died of alcoholic poisoning in 1977, and Andrew's daughter Jane in a car crash in 1984. Four years later, his son Patrick married a girl he'd first met at university.

In 1990 Andrew reached sixty-seven and decided to retire. Patrick took over the management of the family firm.

Then came the black year of 1991. In January, George's wife Edna, now eighty-five, slipped on a patch of ice and broke her pelvis. She reached hospital in severe pain. For a couple of days she seemed to be making a good recovery, but then went into coma. On 1 April she woke up for two hours. George happened to be with her at the time, and was overjoyed. But this turned out to be a cruel joke of fate; for she sank back into coma, never to emerge again. Then Andrew died of a heart attack on 5 May, and his mother Edna outlived him by only six hours.

Three weeks after the double funeral, Patrick arrived at his office to find his grandfather George pouring over the small ads in *The Times*. He had the other newspapers trapped beneath a jealous arm, and the secretary who normally scanned the columns was staring at him with wide eyes. Patrick took her by the arm and guided her into his private office, closing the door behind them.

'What's he doing?'

'He's gone mad, Mr Williamson,' she whispered. 'He picked up the papers from Thompson's himself, and he won't let me near them. *And* he keeps muttering to himself.'

'What about?'

'I don't know. I can't hear. He only mutters.'

'All right, Barbara,' he murmured, patting her soothingly. 'Leave him to me.'

Barbara shook her head. 'I'm sorry, Mr Williamson, but I don't like this. If he's gone bonkers, I don't want to be anywhere near him.'

Patrick replied patiently, 'Listen, Barbara. He's eighty-nine years old. Three weeks ago he buried his wife and son on the same morning. He's *bound* to be distraught. But I know him, Barbara. He wouldn't ever be violent. He's always had a bit of a bee in his bonnet about that client. Leave him to himself, and don't worry about him. Just get on with some other work.' That seemed enough to calm her.

George spent the whole day studying the newspapers, but at five-thirty, as the office closed, he calmly got up, wished everyone goodnight, and went home.

The same pattern was repeated the next day, and the next. The day after that was Saturday, when the office was closed. Out of curiosity, Patrick rose early, drove to the office and waited outside. Sure enough, at half past eight his grandfather came walking along the street, picked up the papers from the newsagent, and went up to the office.

Patrick chewed on his lip thoughtfully. He went into a nearby coffee shop and smoked through several cigarettes while he wondered what he ought to do. Finally he decided to take the bull by the horns. He let himself into the office quietly. George wasn't at Barbara's desk. He was in the private office – now Patrick's – and sitting at what had once been his own desk thirty-one years previously. No longer worried about being overheard, he was talking aloud in normal tones.

'It's here. It has to be here.' It was a litany he repeated every minute or so and Patrick knew he must be talking about the Davis account. Years before, shortly before Patrick had gone up to university, his father Andrew had explained all about it. Uncle David had been present, half-drunk as usual, and between them they'd managed, while not openly ridiculing their father, to give the impression he wanted the whole business to seem more glamorous than it actually was.

As Patrick stepped to the door of the office, George heard him approach and looked up, squinting towards the doorway.

'It's only me – Patrick.'

'Well? What do you want?' George demanded belligerently.

'Don't you think it's time you told me all about it, Grandpa?' replied Patrick gently.

'Haven't you been through your father's papers yet?'

'I'm working through them slowly. Why?'

'You should find there some pages I wrote the day after Major Davis came to see me. The full story. You see, our memories distort things: exaggerate some things; forget others. And it was important that didn't happen here. But I'll tell you the story now, and it will be completely accurate. I've kept a copy at home, you see, and every now and again I re-read it. Just to make sure I remember it as it was.'

And he began to talk. He sounded sane, controlled and aware.

At the end of it, he looked down at the newspapers and shook his head. 'How ridiculous!' he snorted. 'Looking for anagrams, I was – anagrams and cryptic clues in the classified ads.' He gave a short bark of a laugh. 'Too many crossword puzzles over the years, I'm afraid. I wanted it to happen, you see. I wanted so much to go to that bank and find the man they want. And find out what it was all *really* about. Before I die,' he added in a whisper. He stared into space for a moment, then shook himself. Abruptly he got up and went to the door. 'Don't mind me. I'm over it now. I won't play the fool again. I won't even *look* at the classifieds any more. I'll stick to the *real* crosswords. But promise me something, Pat. If the message ever does come, you'll tell me, won't you?'

Patrick smiled. 'Yes, Grandpa. I'll tell you.'

His grandfather nodded, then went home, his end-life crisis now over.

Patrick opened his desk diary and looked inside the back cover where lay, as for nearly half a century, the sheet of paper with the instructions. He pulled out the keyring from his trouser pocket and examined the little brass key which would unlock the combination dial of the major's safe. The stipends had kept pace with inflation and now amounted to close to five thousand pounds per annum, not a fortune by any means, but nothing to be sneezed at. It was no small exaggeration to say that they had kept the firm afloat during several bad patches. But for someone to pay out so much for so long implied that there was a great deal of money in play somewhere in the world – and here was some form of failsafe device.

When Patrick reached home, he went into his study and searched through his father's papers. He found the pages his grandfather had mentioned, in an envelope near the bottom of the stack. Each one was numbered and headed: *Not to be destroyed. To be passed on to your heir.* He read them through and found that his grandfather's verbal account that morning had been remarkably accurate. To Patrick, Davis's explanation of the motive behind such an elaborate system seemed slightly unconvincing. The notion of directing a 'financial campaign' against any member of the consortium who reneged on the agreement sounded implausible. He remembered reading that new members of the Italian masonic lodge P2 had been obliged to supply documents compromising themselves, the threat of their publication thereby ensuring their own silence over the affairs of the lodge. That sort of arrangement seemed to Patrick a more likely basis for the major's scheme.

He gave a shrug. It was useless speculating. But of one thing he was sure: his father and uncle had badly underestimated Grandpa George and his mysterious undertaking.

George died the following January, managing to outlive the Williamsons' black year by a mere six days. Most of his property had been passed on to his son and then his grandson years before, to avoid death duties, so there were only the personal items to dispose of. Among them were several books about the career and downfall of Mussolini. Patrick took these home and eventually read them all, but he couldn't begin to guess how Major Davis fitted into the scheme of things. It was all academic anyway, he thought, as he put the last book down in September 1992. The advertisement hadn't appeared in forty-nine years, so it wasn't very likely it ever would.

14

Engrossed in reading a business letter, Patrick was barely aware that Barbara had come in with his morning coffee and the newspapers.

'Two this morning,' she said. 'And one of them's in five.'

Grunting acknowledgement, he reached for the coffee as he finished reading the letter. The *Times* lay on the top, folded open at the Announcements page. Barbara had ringed two items with a felt-tipped pen. One of them began: *AUTHOR wishes to talk to survivors of Soviet prison camps.* The word 'author' was one of the six she had to look out for. Patrick glanced at the second announcement, and his mind gave a sudden lurch. His heart pounding, he rapidly scanned the remaining newspapers. In four the text was identical: *WHAT'S IN A NAME? Here is the order to look, Hotspur. To look after the name Ford.* The version in *The Guardian* terminated with the word 'Frod'.

Patrick grabbed the desk diary, opened it to the back cover, and read through the instructions once again.

'The announcement will begin with *WHAT'S IN A NAME?* and the message will contain the word '*Hotspur*'. The password consists of a straightforward juxtaposition of the first and last words of the message itself. The combination of the safe can be deduced from this. The key must be turned ninety degrees clockwise.'

'Hereford,' he murmured to himself. 'The password's Hereford. But how the hell am I supposed to deduce the combination from that?'

He spent several minutes puzzling over the word before it occurred to him that the 'this' in the instructions might refer not to the password but to 'the message itself'. The order to look. To look after the name. Abruptly he got up from his desk and went into the storeroom. He shifted the files to expose the safe. Screwed into the door above the dial was a sunken metal plate with the maker's name embossed in cursive script: *Webster's.* Beneath it in tiny block capitals was the word 'OF' and below this in slightly larger capitals the word 'HEREFORD'. Webster's of Hereford.

'Look after the name!' he exclaimed and made a dive for the old toolbox that lived in the storeroom. He ransacked it for a screwdriver of the right size and, panting with excitement, unscrewed the metal plate. On the back of it were two lines of symbols engraved into the metal. The top line consisted of the alphabet from A to Z in block capitals, the letters huddled as if making a single word, and forming an arc. Beneath it, in a mirror-image arc, was the number 98172364565789049876534321.

He hurried back to his desk and, still shaking with excitement, transcribed 'HEREFORD' into numbers. He checked and rechecked this, but still could not be absolutely sure he hadn't made a mistake, because the letters and numbers curved away from each. Then it occurred to him there was a simple way to do it. He got out a ruler and laid it vertically against the plate, its edge passing through H. The corresponding number was clearly four. In a few seconds he had the combination: 42823087.

He buzzed his secretary on the intercom. Forcing himself to speak calmly, he said, 'Jenny, cancel my engagements for the morning. I've got to go out. And I don't want to be interrupted for the next few minutes.'

From his briefcase he took out the prospectus of one of his clients. It was enclosed in a rainproof plastic envelope. He extracted the document and took the envelope into the storeroom. Next he took the little key off the keyring and, squatting on the floor in front of the safe, inserted it into the aperture in the centre of the dial. He then gave it a quarter turn clockwise, and heard a brief whoosh of air. With trembling fingers he manipulated the dial. Finally he grasped the handle and smoothly turned it down to the vertical, and the door opened. On the floor of the safe lay a sheet of paper, with a block of typewritten text in the middle of the page.

Go personally, and as soon as possible, to Hamblyn's Merchant Bank. Ask to speak to the Head of Accounts or any high official of the bank. When that person appears, explain that you have come in connection with a matter concerning Account Number 12214. In his or her presence, write down the password on this sheet of paper in the space provided below, then hand it in, together with the document which accompanies it.

The password is: ....

Underneath this sheet was a single page with a signature on it. Patrick placed it carefully into the plastic envelope and pressed the air out of it. 'Something they hadn't thought of in 1943,' he murmured to himself with satisfaction, as he got up and went out to his car.

On the road to London, he wondered why Davis had made the text of the ad so unclear. The procedure had not been risky, because whoever received the message might be initially puzzled, but he would eventually be *driven* to consider the safe itself, as no other options were available, but it had all been unnecessarily complicated, Patrick decided.

Still, at least it had made him calm down. Then it dawned on him that the Major must have had exactly that intention – to complicate the procedure so that the reader of the advert, excited by its appearance, would have a chance to cool off before he could make any silly mistake. In fact, every stage of the procedure must have had a similar purpose. The frustrating task of deriving the combination from letters and numbers which curved away from each other had slowed him down. The instruction to write down the password while actually in the bank – an apparently needless requisite – had also given him pause for thought.

Williamson was amazed to realise how ingeniously Davis had arranged matters. More than amazed – uneasy. There was something diabolical about being thus controlled by a man who was very likely already dead.

An hour and a half later he walked into Hamblyn's Bank in High Holborn. The Head of Accounts was a man called Harvey, and he was at once attentive when he heard the account number. Patrick wrote down the word 'Hereford' on the sheet, and handed it to him. Harvey read the text and carefully examined the signature on the accompanying sheet, which was already beginning to brown at the top edge. Then he invited the other man to follow him. He was led into an oak-panelled sitting room and asked to sit down.

'I'll inform Sir Joshua that you're here, sir. He might be tied up for a few minutes, however. May I offer you a glass of sherry while you're waiting?'

'Thank you.'

Harvey withdrew. A minute later a male assistant brought in a silver tray with a chilled bottle of La Ina and a single large schooner. He filled the glass to within a quarter inch of the brim and set it down on a cork coaster. Then he left, but a short while afterwards Harvey came back with a tray bearing several, wax-sealed envelopes and a small silver paperknife. He was accompanied by an elderly and distinguished-looking gentleman who came forward to offer his hand. Harvey introduced the newcomer as Sir Joshua Hamblyn. The old man invited Patrick to sit again, and ensconced himself in the armchair facing his visitor. Harvey placed the tray on a sidetable next to his employer, then went to sit down on the sofa.

'May I know your name, or would you prefer to remain anonymous?' asked Sir Joshua.

Of course, thought Patrick. After all, *What's in a name?* 'Patrick Williamson,' he replied.

'Thank you, Mr Williamson.' Hamblyn opened the first envelope, pulled out a sheet of paper, and read it through. Then he looked up at Patrick and said, 'First of all, I am obliged to ask you how you acquired the password, and to require you to produce proof of the date when you learned it. Unless you can do so, we cannot proceed further.'

Patrick felt momentarily irritated. The instructions had seemed so specific, yet they hadn't mentioned this at all. Then he realised there would probably be several other unexpected queries, all aimed at ensuring that all the conditions of the agreement had been properly complied with. Deciding to imitate Hamblyn's formal tone, he turned to Harvey and said, 'May I ask you to send someone out for a copy of today's *Times*?'

Harvey at once crossed to a bellpush. The assistant opened the door immediately; he'd obviously been waiting outside. Harvey murmured something to him inaudibly, then went to sit down again. Moments later the assistant came back with a copy of the newspaper on the inevitable silver tray, which he proffered to Williamson.

'Give it to Mr Harvey, please.' Patrick waited until he had gone out again and said, 'If you'll turn to the announcements column you'll find one – I think it's the sixth up from the bottom – which begins "*What's in a name?*" The rest of the text begins with the word "*here*" and ends with "*ford*". This same announcement has appeared in four other major newspapers this morning.'

Harvey verified this fact quickly, and nodded to Sir Joshua. The latter opened the second envelope, scanned the contents, and said, 'This note confirms the correct procedure for deriving the password, which you have just explained. We are satisfied that you have fulfilled all the conditions of the agreement, and I am asked in the note to express our client's thanks. We may now proceed.' He picked up the third envelope. 'Our instructions are to ask you to read the contents of this envelope in our presence, although we are not to be apprised of them. You may make notes if you wish, but the contents must then be replaced in the envelope, which must subsequently be put into another envelope which is at present folded inside. This second envelope must then be sealed and our three signatures are to be written across the flap. It will subsequently be returned to the appropriate safe-deposit box. The letter will ask you to carry out certain lawful instructions and, upon completion of them, you must return here, whereupon we will open instructions of our own to determine whether you have fulfilled the conditions. We have been specifically asked to say that there may be several phases in the process. Upon completion of the entire operation, a sum of money will be paid to you or to any person that you designate, and in a form of your own choosing. I must now ask you whether you agree to these conditions.'

'How much money would be paid if I accept?'

'I'm not in a position to tell you. The amount is specified in the subsequent instructions. I do not, however, expect it to be paltry.'

'Very well. I accept.'

Harvey came forward to ferry the envelope tray across to Patrick. It was marked 'ENVELOPE NUMBER 3'. The paper was thick, of very good quality, but old. He broke the seal and pulled out the folded envelope promised. It was marked 'ENVELOPE NUMBER 3-3'. There was a sheet of paper also folded. The instructions were typewritten, but there was no salutation or date or signature. He read them through carefully three times, decided to make a couple of notes to be on the safe side, and replaced the sheet in the envelope. The second envelope was slightly larger than the first, so it was a snug fit. Harvey used glue to seal it and the three men then signed it across the join.

Sir Joshua shook hands with Patrick once more, and left the room. Harvey escorted him out into the hall, wished him a good day, and withdrew.

15

It was a high, back-corner shot. What everyone hated. Difficult to hit, and with a great risk of breaking the racquet. Adam leapt at the wall, twisting around at the same time, and with the flat of his foot kicked away from it, high into the air, and smacked the ball down into the opposite front corner. But his opponent was there and ready for a dropshot. Adam raced forward, but at the last instant his opponent changed the angle of his racquet and volleyed. The ball flew low, at a narrow angle to the wall, hit it two inches above the bottom line and bounced widely to the side. It sailed past Adam's racquet by six inches, and was irretrievable. It had been a match point, so it took him another five minutes to win. His opponent had played well, however, and several other players had stopped to watch them, so there was a ripple of applause as they emerged from the court and headed for the changing rooms.

Adam couldn't spend long over his shower because he had arranged to meet friends for drinks before lunch. As he left the sports club and hurried along the street, a voice called his name. 'Adam! Adam Drew!' He stopped and turned around. A man of about forty who had been standing close to the entrance came towards him. 'Do you remember me?'

Adam took a moment to identify him. 'Yes, of course,' he smiled. 'You're the man who interviewed me for the IBM job. Er, Mr Williams, is it?'

'Williamson. But I'm impressed. You've got a good memory. How're things?'

'Fine. I'm not with IBM any more, though,' he added. Then he realised that his failure to be more forthcoming sounded evasive. 'I work for an oil company,' he added.

Patrick regarded the dark-haired young man speculatively, considering the statement. He knew that it wasn't true. 'Like it?' he inquired routinely.

'Yes. Great.' Adam glanced at his watch. 'Er, look, I'd like to stop and chat but I've arranged to meet some friends for lunch and . . .'

'Cancel it.'

Adam looked at him sharply. He scrutinised Williamson's face for a moment, took note of his serious expression, then nodded. 'All right.' He went back into the sports club to phone the restaurant and leave a message, while Patrick waited outside.

Rejoining him, Adam said, 'Okay. I'm all yours.'

Williamson glanced at his watch. It was 12.05. 'It's a bit early, but how about some lunch?'

'Fine.'

'Let's find a taxi.'

Patrick had picked the Café Royal because it had private rooms. The fact that one had been reserved for them already didn't escape Adam. Neither man knew it, but by coincidence it was in this same room that, many years before, Patrick's grandfather had told his two sons all about the mysterious Major Davis.

They made their selections and Patrick waited for the maître d' to leave. Then he took out a file from his briefcase and consulted it.

'Correct me if I have anything wrong. Adam Christopher Drew, twenty-eight years old, born in New Delhi. Father a diplomat and one-time commercial attaché at the British High Commission in India. You read Politics, Philosophy and Economics at Oxford and obtained first-class honours. You rowed for the university and your other hobbies include most ball sports as well as mountaineering. You worked at IBM for two years, and then ICI for another two. Both say they'd like to have you back. When you left ICI you were earning marginally less than a backbench MP as a base, plus commissions which put you well over what the Prime Minister gets. They offered you a considerable raise to persuade you to stay. You were much sought after, and everyone speaks very highly of you.

'But then, a year ago, you started to work for Texaco. You asked for and got a one-year contract with options. Last October you walked out on them, and you haven't worked since. Texaco weren't very happy about it, although the man I talked to there was quite evasive. Would you mind telling me what happened?'

'There was a mountaineering accident. It wasn't very pleasant. I decided I needed some time to myself, to think about things.'

'I see. And the reason for the restlessness?' he asked, closing the file.

The waiters returned, one carrying their first course, and the other the wine. 'I don't really know. The only thing I can say is that I never found any of those jobs really satisfying.'

The waiters withdrew. Patrick spread some caviar on a piece of toast. 'Yet you've acted as a negotiator of some kind in all of them. Is there some particular *kind* of work that you're looking for, perhaps?'

Adam shrugged. 'Maybe.' He watched his host bite into the toast.

Williamson turned the conversation to more general topics and throughout the rest of the meal they discussed the political and economic situation of the country, the continent and the world.

Over coffee and brandies Patrick began, 'In 1943 my grandfather took on a rather unusual client. He gave his name as Major Davis – an American, who claimed to represent a business consortium. None of us ever saw him again, but every month, from that day to this, we've been paid an index-linked stipend. All we've had to do to earn the money was to scan the small ads columns of certain newspapers every day, and when one particular ad was placed to carry out certain instructions. This ad appeared yesterday – more than half a century later. The instructions turn out to be for us to look for a negotiator with your special qualities.'

'Turn out to be?'

'Yes. Until yesterday morning we didn't know what they consisted of. The profile of the person we're supposed to look for matches yours pretty closely. Male, British, well educated, not younger than twenty-seven; also fit, shrewd, patient, intelligent, and a fighter. There's one other quality in the list. The candidate must be by nature *very* careful. The precise wording of our client's instructions states: "A cautious, methodical, yet daring man who checks and re-checks his arrangements, looking for flaws, as jealous of safety as a mountaineer, a man who views his external arrangements as a mountaineer looks upon his equipment – as part of himself." That ring any bells?'

'Hm. Sounds tailor-made,' replied Adam reflectively. 'What are the terms exactly? How long a contract? How much pizza?'

'I don't know. My instructions were simply to take you to a meal at an expensive restaurant – at the client's expense – explain things in outline, so as to find out whether, in principle, you could be free to take on the job. From what Major Davis told my grandfather, it might be relatively short-term – a few days or weeks – but I can't say so with any degree of certainty. However, there is one small detail which implies a short contract. I was given a time limit of twenty-one days to find the right candidate. As for the money, I've really no idea, but my impression is that it would be well worth your while.'

'Can't you even give me a hint as to what it's all about?'

'I haven't got one to give you. But what I can do is tell you about Davis. In fact, I can go one better and let my grandfather tell you.' He took out a portable cassette-recorder from his briefcase. 'The day after Davis came to see him, he wrote down an account of it all. I was instructed not to show you any papers referring to this matter, and I've decided to interpret that injunction literally, so last night I taped it.' He switched on the recorder. A mildly distorted Williamson played the part of his mildly distorted grandfather, impressed by events, and by an American major of possibly Italian ancestry, and by a suspicion. An incredible suspicion.

When Williamson switched off the recorder, Adam murmured, 'I have to admit it all sounds very intriguing.' He was thoughtful for a

135

while, then asked. 'How many other people have you got on your short-list?'

'To be frank, no one else. But at the same time I haven't really looked. That double mention of mountaineering rang a bell with me. I knew I'd interviewed someone with that particular hobby, so I started looking through our files. Since your surname begins with D it didn't take me very long to find you. Once I read your file, I remembered you pretty clearly, and did some checking up. I'd say you were bespoke tailored for the job.'

'Savile Row, one hundred per cent woolly, only one previous owner, recent MOT,' Adam replied. 'Is that all there is? I really do need to know everything before I make a decision.'

Patrick pursed his lips for a moment, as if making up his mind about something, then added, 'There is one other thing I can tell you without contravening any conditions. It might indicate what sort of money's involved. The client's instructions state my own remuneration for finding the right man for the job would be ten times our annual stipend if you fail, and ten times *that* if you succeed. In other words, sixty thousand pounds whatever happens, and six hundred thousand if you come up trumps.'

'A powerful motive for you to find the right man.'

Williamson nodded. 'Obviously, if that's the kind of pizza the agent gets, then the principal must be staring at a very great deal of money.'

'Hm. But what if *my* offer is the whole pizza if I succeed, and the box it comes in if I fail, and I fail?'

Patrick shrugged. 'You can always turn down the job if you don't like the terms.'

Adam nodded. 'Okay. Let's say that in principle I'm interested. What happens now?'

'Are you free for an interview this afternoon?'

'Sure.'

'In that case I'll go and make the arrangements.' He went out to find a phone to call Hamblyn's Bank. Sir Joshua was lunching in the bank's private dining room, but the call was put through as soon as Williamson identified himself.

'I have a suitable candidate, Sir Joshua.'

'Excellent. It's half-past one. Shall we say two o'clock?'

They arrived punctually and were promptly ushered by Harvey into the oak-panelled sitting room. Sir Joshua Hamblyn entered at once. He shook hands with Adam, smiling pleasantly, then immediately turned to Patrick.

'I understand you were asked to prepare a dossier, Mr Williamson. May I have it, please?' Patrick took it from his briefcase and handed it over. 'Thank you. My instructions are to interview the candidate in private, but to ask you to wait while I do so. Would you mind?'

'Not at all,' lied Williamson. Still, Drew would probably tell him all about it afterwards.

Hamblyn turned to Adam and said, 'Please come this way, Mr Drew.' He led him along the corridor to his private office, a spacious room with highly-polished dark furniture and a plush red carpet. He sat down at a huge desk, waving Drew into one of the two wing armchairs set before it. He read the dossier carefully, then laid it to one side. 'I have a number of questions which I am asked to put to you, but please answer frankly and naturally, as you would do if we were old acquaintances. May I proceed?'

Adam nodded.

'I see from your dossier that you live in Chiswick. Was there any particular reason that made you choose West London?'

'Yes, it's handy for the airport.'

'Who is your favourite character of fiction?'

Adam grinned. 'Brer Rabbit.'

'And human character of fiction?'

'Phileas Fogg.'

'Do you believe in God?'

'Not very often.'

Sir Joshua smiled. 'In countries where homosexual practices are illegal, what should a practising homosexual do?'

'Practice makes perfect, so practise them quietly. Or change countries.'

'In countries where the private consumption of drugs is illegal, what should the habitué do?'

'My answer's the same as before. I don't think the State has the right to decide what people should do with their bodies.'

'I see you're unmarried. Do you have a girlfriend at present?'

'Nobody permanent.'

'What, in your opinion, should be the most important characteristic of any relationship between a man and a woman?'

'In theory, mutual respect; in practice, patience,' replied Adam without hesitation.

'And what single word, in your opinion, best describes what a father has to offer his children?'

After a moment he said, 'I suppose protection.'

'What qualities do you look for in your friends?'

Adam shot back, 'Loyalty and discretion.'

'Do you believe in capital punishment?'

'No.'

'Do you think it is reasonable to imprison those who do?'

Adam blinked. But before he could express his astonishment the banker continued, 'Very well, Mr Drew. You have given answers which, within the parameters and definitions supplied by our client, are satisfactory. I have here a letter from him. If you wish, you may read it. You will be under no obligation to accept this assignment. If you refuse it, we shall simply look for someone else. Do you wish to read the letter?'

Adam was fascinated but he restricted his reply to a nod.

Sir Joshua pulled out a plain white envelope and handed it to him. It had been signed across the flap by 'S. Davis'. He slit it open with the proffered paperknife and read.

Hello, my friend.

Forgive my informality but, since you have just passed a series of tests of my own design, I suspect that, if we were to know each other personally, we would become friends. I certainly think of you as a friend and perhaps, in time, you will reciprocate the feeling.

I have a job for you. It might be dangerous but it will be extremely well paid, and I doubt it will be boring. But in all fairness I must tell you that the danger it involves might prove fatal. You will need to have your wits about you always. I cannot say how long this assignment will last: perhaps a week or two, perhaps two months. Much will depend on you yourself, much on the world situation, and much on sheer luck. I cannot tell you yet exactly what the job is, but I can give you the essentials. I want you to save my family whom I love, as I think you will one day love your own.

Adam read the letter several times and then returned it to its envelope. He looked up to find Sir Joshua watching him carefully. 'Is this the only copy?'

'Yes.'

'So presumably you haven't read it?'

'No. In fact, if you refuse this assignment, the letter must be placed in a new envelope, which I would ask you to seal and sign across the flap. I must also ask you to sign a declaration that you received the letter from me unopened.' He leaned forward. 'I now have to ask you whether you accept the assignment. If you wish, you may have fifteen minutes to consider.'

A call for help made more than half a century ago, thought Adam. It was irresistible. 'I don't need time to consider. I accept.'

A little twinkle appeared in the old man's eye. 'Good. Now I just need to go and fetch something for you, but I also have to read the next part of our instructions, so I'll be away for a little while. I'll have someone bring in some coffee.'

★　★　★

138

Sir Joshua returned to the sitting room. 'Mr Williamson, your candidate has accepted, and we are satisfied with your efforts on our client's behalf. I understand you have been receiving monthly payments from a bank. What is the name of it?'

'Barclays.'

'In a moment Mr Harvey will give you a letter to sign, instructing Barclays Bank to stop the payments and to transfer the balance of the fund they hold to our client's account here. That act will fulfil the final condition of your agreement with him. In return you will be paid three lump sums: the first in three months' time, the other two at yearly intervals. The exact amount has to be calculated according to the value of a certain fund at the time the payment is made, but I can tell you that each payment will be in the vicinity of one hundred and twenty thousand pounds if he fails in his assignment, and ten times that amount if he succeeds.'

Patrick's lips parted in amazement. Major Davis was again paying more than promised.

'I am asked to make it clear to you that your candidate's success or failure may depend on your absolute discretion from now on. It is also a condition that you do not speak further to Mr Drew, or make any attempt to contact him until his assignment is completed. If there is any message you wish me to pass to him, please write it down now and I shall give it to him.'

Patrick thought for a moment, then he picked up a pad and wrote the words: *Good luck*. Right on cue, Harvey re-entered with the letter for Patrick's signature. A few minutes later he was outside again, in the street.

Sir Joshua waited until Harvey had returned from escorting Williamson to the door, then together they went down to a safe-deposit vault in the basement. Hamblyn unlocked the 'Davis' box himself, and gestured for the guard to carry it into one of two private rooms. Harvey followed, but stayed by the door. His presence there was merely because Hamblyn was an old man and disliked the idea of having a heart attack next to an open safe-deposit box whose contents might interest the guard more than saving his employer's life.

Hamblyn sat down at the table and opened the box. Ten minutes later he returned to his own office with a small parcel. He sat down at his desk and gazed at Adam. 'I shall leave you with this in just a moment. You may require our services when you have examined the contents. Perhaps we can make travel arrangements for you – things like that. But is there anything we can do for you now?'

'I may need to make a number of phone calls but there's nothing else for the moment, thank you.'

Sir Joshua turned the phone around towards him. 'This is an outside

139

line, and my office is yours for as long as you want. If you require anything, just buzz my secretary.' He left the room.

When Adam opened the package, he found inside several envelopes and a small jeweller's box. Inside that was a signet ring with an unusual design. There was a note saying: *Wear this at all times and, if anyone asks about it, say it has been yours for many years. But conceal it until you have left this building.* He slipped the box into his trouser pocket.

The envelopes were numbered. He opened the first and read.

Thank you for accepting.

Your specific assignment is either to protect a group of people in imminent danger or – if the threatened event has already occurred – to rescue them. This group includes my own family.

In order for you to defend them and yourself, I shall equip you with both shields and weapons. For the moment you do not need to know what these are. In fact, if you did know, it might prejudice your mission. This does not, however, apply to your greatest weapon – and it is an awesome one. I am giving you the power to prevent a political and economic earthquake.

The fact that you are reading this letter at all means that a certain mechanism, named Belvedere, has been put into operation. One effect of this was to cause the publication of an announcement (see the appendix for the exact text) in five London daily newspapers, which in turn initiated the process by which you came to be selected as my agent. But there was a second effect, and a quite separate one. On the sixtieth day after the appearance of that announcement, certain documents known as the Belvedere Accords will be published. It is this which will cause the earthquake. You and only you will now be able to prevent their publication.

I give you this power for you to use in the interests of my family. Make no judgements until you know all the facts. Reject paltry prejudice and marketplace morality. You will learn much and, when you know all you need, use Belvedere wisely – as the deterrent it was always intended to be. You must warn my opponents that they have failed to defuse the time bomb; that it will explode automatically unless they can satisfy you. And then negotiate the safe rescue of my family. When you succeed, and only when you succeed, you will receive your due reward.

Now to details.

The following instructions should be followed to the letter, as far as is practicable. Go to Russia. Travel there as quickly but as anonymously as possible. Arrange to speak to the head of a department of state, or any higher authority, and make sure that he is genuine. You may present yourself to him anonymously, or even give a false name. Give him the letter which you will find in the second envelope. It will explain to him that this matter concerns a gift made to Stalin in 1943. The letter is signed by Joseph Vissarionovich Dzhugashvili, which was Stalin's real name. He, in turn, will give you a letter signed by me, and the signature should correspond with that found on the last page of this letter. (It is in my hand though it is not my true name.) Signatures can be forged, however. To be sure that the letter is the same one I sent to Stalin in 1943, you should check the fourth, sixth and twenty-sixth lines. The second word in each should end in 't', 'k' and 'r' respectively. If that letter is genuine, simply follow the instructions therein. If it is a fake, then you must denounce it as such and demand to see the real one, which contains your further instructions and the information you will require to carry them out.

However, to ensure that the Russians themselves are unable to use that information for their own benefit, it is incomplete. The missing portions of it, which must be memorised, are as follows. In a certain city there is a firm of lawyers, which has in its possession the Articles of Association of a company whose name begins with DAVI. Articles 17, 18 and 23 explain the procedure by which the lawyers can be satisfied as to your status and bona fides. They will require from you an authentication code, which is: EVQBAN.

Should you find it necessary to offer the Russians any explanation concerning your assignment, you might suggest some kind of financial manipulation is intended.

The third envelope now in your possession is addressed to whoever is presently head of this bank. It will make available for your use considerable funds, although your final financial reward will be very much greater. If you want to know the approximate amount of this reward, ask him for the current value of the Overton Fund, and multiply that figure by three.

The fourth and last envelope contains another version of this letter – a false one. For example, the details concerning the authentication of my letter waiting for you in Russia have been changed. When you leave this building, take all the contents of this parcel away with you, then destroy everything except Stalin's letter and the false version of this one.

There is one final thing I have to tell you. For our purposes people belong to one of two groups: let us call them 'the Cappers' and 'the Blowers', to borrow the terminology of the oil business. The first group would be against the publication of the Belvedere Accords and the second in favour. The weapon I have placed in your hands is also a shield, but it will defend you only against the Cappers. You alone can now take this matter through to the end, so they will always be dependent on you for them to realise their own wishes. They dare not kill you, or even hinder you for too long. At the same time, they cannot, either through torture or threats, get out of you what you do

*not know, and, although it may test your ingenuity, you should, if
you need to, be able to make that clear to them. As a consequence of
these two points, you will always be in ultimate control of the situation,
should you come up against any Cappers. That, plus your courage
and intelligence, will enable you to succeed.*

*But, obviously, your shield is useless against the Blowers. On the
contrary, they have every motive either to immobilise you until the
sixty-first day or, if they cannot do that, to kill you, instead.*

*Your first problem is to decide who is who: Capper or Blower. I
cannot help you. I have no idea when you will be reading this letter,
or what the state of the world will be at that time.*

*Your second problem is to decide how to proceed. If you make
public the fact that you alone can stop Belvedere, you will have as
your allies all the Cappers, but at the same time you will make instant
enemies of all the Blowers. If you keep silent, you will not make enemies
of the Blowers, but the Cappers will not realise how important it is
that they collaborate with you. To me, in 1943, it seems obvious that
your safest course for the moment, until you fully understand which
group is which, is to remain anonymous. But this will not be necessarily
so. Only you can decide.*

I wish you luck and success.

S. Davis

When Sir Joshua returned Adam handed him the third envelope,
inwardly smiling at the reversal of roles, and waited while he read the
contents.

'Sir Joshua, I'm authorised to ask you what is the current value of
the Overton Fund.'

'Yes, so I see. Roughly one billion dollars. If this money eventually
becomes yours, I do hope you will elect to leave us in charge of your
financial affairs. We're really not at all bad at the banking game.
However, for this to happen, you must first succeed in the assignment
our client has given you. In the meantime our instructions are to
assist you in whatever way possible. Your financial needs in small
matters – plane tickets, hotel reservations, cash grants of a few
thousand pounds – must be taken care of without question. Cash
disbursement of larger quantities would require closer scrutiny, so
that we can justify *our* actions in the event that you fail, because
sooner or later someone is going to come and ask to see how we've
handled things. Now, how may we help and do you have any
questions?'

Adam thought for a moment: plane tickets? The client had
stipulated that he was to travel anonymously. And then there was the
point about him not putting on that signet ring until he was outside
the building.

142

'Sir Joshua, as between me and your client, how exactly would you define your responsibilities?'

'We must assist you both in your joint endeavour in whatever way we can. But obviously we must protect our client's interests first.'

Adam nodded slowly. 'But who protects *your* interests?'

The other man blinked. He could make no reply.

'If I were you, I would take a good, careful look at my family's security arrangements. And we need a password. "Black sheep" will do. If I ever send you that codeword, it means you are to take yourself and your family to safety at once. "White sheep" means there's no immediate danger, but I want to talk to you personally and under tight security.' Suddenly struck by another thought, he asked, 'This conversation isn't being recorded, is it?' Sir Joshua's surprise and hesitation lasted a microsecond too long, so both men knew it was pointless continuing the pretence. 'Is anyone listening as well?'

'No.'

'Okay. Destroy the tape *now*. Physically destroy it. Never mind your justifications. I'll be making my own travel arrangements, but I shall need some cash. Forget about "*few*". Fifty thousand pounds will be needed for a start. I shall want half of that in dollars and the rest in negotiable bearer bonds. Better include a few gold coins, too. Nothing heavy. Something rare, if possible; but I also want a couple of basically cheap but really impressive-looking coins also. Cheap and nasty. Again, light if possible.' Sir Joshua was scribbling on a notepad. 'I shall need your home phone number, your club phone number, your lover's phone number, etcetera, etcetera.'

'Anything else?'

'It would be safer for us both if I took care of everything else on my own. But there is still one thing I want from you which I'm sure will help.' He looked the other man straight in the eye. 'The name of our client.'

Sir Joshua stared back at him, his jaw muscles working ruminatively. Finally making up his mind, he replied, 'The name we were actually given doesn't matter. But I happened to be in New York once with my father in the early Sixties, and in the Algonquin bar he recognised the man who came here in 1943 to open the account. I made inquiries at the desk and learned he was called Luca Mattelli. But I noticed he was keeping close to another man – someone called Salvatore Ferrandini. Mattelli was very attentive to him, and I was told he was Ferrandini's right-hand man. Ferrandini died about twenty years ago.'

'Mafia?'

Sir Joshua nodded.

'And your feeling about that?'

'I heard some quite alarming stories about Ferrandini, but I also heard some rather admirable things, too. A Spanish writer once said,

"I am me and my circumstances." A man can't help a great deal that he is. What matters is what he does with the rest. I'm not ashamed to have him as a client.'

Adam regarded him thoughtfully. Then he gave a nod and stood up. 'I have some things to see to. I'll be back at six o'clock.'

Outside the building he took a taxi and scrutinised the traffic following behind. After a few turns he told the driver to stop. He then got out and went to a public phone. He rang Miriam and explained that he had to cancel the present course of treatment.

'I don't think that's a very good idea, Adam.'

'I've just been offered a job, and I've accepted.'

'I'm very glad to hear it. I've been telling you for months that you need to keep your mind occupied with positive things. But I still think you ought to keep up your treatment.'

'I have to go overseas for a while, so I won't be able to. I'll ring you when I get back.'

She sighed audibly. 'All right, Adam. Good luck.'

He thanked her and hung up, wondering whether they would have given him the job if they'd known he was visiting a psychiatrist. He knew his personal problem wouldn't interfere with his professional ability, but people could be easily prejudiced.

Next Adam rang a close friend at his office, giving him a short list of people to call on his behalf, to cancel appointments. That done, he made straight for the nearest travel agent to book a train ticket.

It was quarter past three. The Newspaper Department of the British Library at Colindale closed at 4.45, but visitors were not allowed in after four o'clock. There wasn't much time, so a visit would be something of a rush, but it might well be worth it.

He took the underground and reached the newspaper library at ten to four. Knowing roughly when Salvatore Ferrandini had died, he consulted the *New York Times* indexes for the last six years of the man's life. He found half a dozen references. It was one minute to four, and it generally took half an hour for the volumes to be retrieved from the stackrooms. Limited to four volumes at a time, he chose the most recent references. The girl at the desk looked pointedly at her watch, but he gave her his most winsome smile, and she processed the request slips.

Twenty minutes later the volumes arrived. The newspaper had printed a photograph of Salvatore on 11 September 1972. There was no time for thinking now, so Adam had the various entries photocopied and hurried back to the underground station.

At the same time as he boarded his train back to central London, six men were passing through passport control at Heathrow Airport. They had just landed in a private jet plane coming from Zurich.

Adam reached the Hamblyn bank at ten to six. He showed Sir Joshua one of the photographs. 'That was the man you saw?'

'Yes, that's him.' He examined the picture reflectively. 'But this doesn't convey the sheer power of the man.'

'What about his son Robert?'

'A chip off the old block, I've been told, but not quite in the same league. That's all I can tell you, really, but I could make some discreet inquiries if you thought it might help. In the circumstances, I don't feel his late father would object.'

Adam shook his head. 'No. Best not show any sudden interest in these people at all.'

Sir Joshua regarded him quietly. 'I can see that an account suddenly being reactivated after fifty years' dormancy must indicate something crucial has happened, but I also take it that in Ferrandini's letter there was some kind of warning?'

'Nothing specific. I'm just reading between the lines. But there's a law of physics which says that to every action there's an equal and opposite reaction, and I find the same thing happens in life. Salvatore's asked me to do something, and I suspect there'll be certain people who would like to stop me.'

'We've handled this account with the utmost discretion. Are you suggesting they already know of its existence?'

'I've no idea. But nothing ever happens in isolation. It might be only one stone that you drop in a pool, but you end up with a hell of a lot of ripples. And I think somebody somewhere has dropped a real boulder. You may be getting visitors.'

When Adam had left, Sir Joshua got up and poured himself a sherry. He sat down again and sipped it thoughtfully. Finally making up his mind, he consulted his desktop diary and made a phone call.

'Mr Williamson, this is Joshua Hamblyn. Two things. Through an oversight we omitted to ask you for all the material which our client left with you. Perhaps you'd be so good as to return it to us as soon as possible. The second thing is, the bank has been very impressed with the quality of your services and, as it happens, we ourselves have a certain personnel problem you might be equipped to deal with. It would involve your going to France, personally.'

'I'd be happy to oblige, Sir Joshua. Shall I come by tomorrow morning?'

'I appreciate it might be putting you out, but the matter is quite urgent, so I was hoping we could meet later this evening.'

'I'm afraid my wife has invited some people for dinner.'

'Hm. Pity. Let me think a moment . . .' Sir Joshua stared glumly at the opposite wall, where his father looked down sternly from a portrait.

It certainly wasn't worth alarming Williamson unnecessarily. Giving a shrug, he continued, 'We'll have to make it tomorrow morning, then. I could meet you at your office at eight o'clock.'

'Fine. I'll see you at eight, then. Goodnight, Sir Joshua.'

'Goodnight, Mr Williamson.'

He drummed his fingers on the desktop for a moment, then made another phone call. 'Harry? Josh here. Listen, I want to spruce up our security arrangements here at the bank. And at my home too . . .'

Stelio entered the commercial section of the Oxford public library. Half an hour later he emerged and went to a phone booth to ring a number in Sicily.

'There are six possibles, but only two advertise themselves as specialists in placement of personnel. The other four are big firms of solicitors and accountants, who offer a menu of services.'

'What's the time over there?'

'Ten to seven.'

'Offices will be closed.' Ferrandini thought for a moment. 'Go and chat to the caretakers and local bartenders. Find out if any of those companies existed in some form or other back in 1943. Ned has rounded up some people to help you. Their plane's just left Rome. Better have someone meet them at the airport. They should be there by nine.'

At five past ten Adam was lying on his bunk on the overnight train to Brussels, reading the photocopies he'd made at Colindale. Smoothly the train began to move off. Salvatore Ferrandini, caught smiling at the camera, looked back at him. Luca Mattelli had handled the Hamblyn bank, but had he also gone to see George Williamson?

It was an interesting setup. A packet of instructions, put aside for a rainy day, divided between a bank and a small firm which dealt with the placement of personnel, neither side knowing anything of the other. Organising the first was a not unduly exacting task which could be delegated to a competent lieutenant. But the second was more delicate. No, he thought, the mysterious Major Davis had been Salvatore himself. And he'd pulled off a marvellous trick. He'd trodden a delicate, even precarious line between the routine and the mysterious. He'd led Patrick's grandfather by the nose to a particular vantage point from which old George had been able to glimpse the immense and persuaded him to be vigilant with the tiny.

All to protect Salvatore's own family.

Adam studied the features of his long dead employer. Ye-es, this was a venture worth risking his life for. The concept was important to Adam, quite apart from the three billion dollars. It would be like paying off a debt. He closed his eyes and there, as always, was the

146

Eiger and that white, cold mist scudding along its sheer cliff face like an immense distorted ghost. Adam forced them open again before the cold sweat started. He didn't want to be haunted by the Eiger again for the moment.

He read his notes once more, committing them to memory, then tore them up into tiny pieces and threw everything out of the carriage window. Stalin's letter was already stored in a waterproof envelope taped to his waist. Picking up one of the books he'd bought on the history of the Mafia, he went for dinner.

Patrick Williamson reached his office at quarter to eight the next morning. The front door was already open. The cleaners must be still here, he thought, stepping inside.

In his private office three men stopped what they were doing when he walked in. 'Who are you?' he asked in puzzlement. An instant later his mind had done the simple arithmetic, and the total hit him like a physical blow. He dropped his briefcase and turned to run, too late. Two of the strangers were already on him, and a second later had him pinned against the wall with an ugly-looking knife at his throat. The third man came forward holding up the desktop photograph of Williamson's wife and children.

'Nice family,' he remarked quietly. Then suddenly he was business-like. 'Three minutes, Mr Williamson. That's all. *I* need to know some things; *you* can tell me. If I know them inside of three minutes, our business together will be concluded. If not, Marco here will relieve you of your testicles.'

Patrick went white. He knew he didn't have it in him to stand up to men like these. 'I'll tell you everything you want to know, but outside. Outside in the street.'

The other shook his head. 'Two minutes forty-five seconds, Mr Williamson.'

'Jesus Christ! Look . . . *please!*'

Stelio glanced at his watch. 'Two minutes thirty-five,' he intoned like some kind of speaking clock, counting out the seconds to the end of the universe.

Patrick swallowed. 'His name's Adam Drew. His file's in that cabinet over there.'

'Go on,' prompted Stelio, knowing full well that once they started they never stopped. In six minutes he had the whole story. Including the tape recording of George Williamson's account of his meeting with Major Davis. Including the combination of the safe. But when he opened it he found it was empty.

Sir Joshua Hamblyn parked his car in front of the building at one minute to eight. Three men walked out at the same moment, one of them carrying a slim file, but the banker didn't give them another thought . . . until he entered Williamson's private office at eight o'clock precisely to find Patrick's body lying on the carpet, a bloodstain still spreading across his shirt front. He had died less than four minutes previously.

Poor man, Hamblyn thought sadly. Were it not for your wife's dinner party, you might now be on your way to safety in France. But this was not the time to mourn the innocents. It had happened. What young Drew had warned him against had started happening.

They were here.

In his desk diary under the previous day Williamson had made a brief note: *Adam Drew, City Sports Club, 11.00*. Hamblyn went to the filing cabinet. Between '*Drayton, Charles*' and '*Drexham & Lownds, Ltd*' he found nothing. He now remembered that one of the three men leaving earlier had been carrying a file of the same type.

Sir Joshua rang his wife and told her urgently to go and stay with her sister for the next few days. 'Don't ask questions. Just leave now.' Then he made similar arrangements with his sons. He toyed with the idea of leaving quietly, but it was very unlikely that Williamson hadn't mentioned the eight o'clock meeting to his wife. With a sigh he dialled another number, catching Sir Richard Preston in the middle of breakfast.

'Dickie? It's Josh Hamblyn here. Look, I'm afraid I've just discovered a body. I'll be available to your people for questioning at my office, but I'd be grateful if you could keep the bank's name out of it.'

'I'll see what I can do. What's the address?'

After hanging up, Hamblyn looked again at the note in the desk diary. After a moment's thought, he removed the whole page and put it in his pocket. Then he went out to his car and drove back to London.

Instead of parking in the courtyard as usual, he drove into a multistorey carpark around the corner, then walked into the building through the main entrance as if he was just a client.

He briefed his secretary: 'I'm expecting someone from Scotland Yard. Send him straight in when he arrives. Also someone about the bank's security arrangements. I'm out for everyone else, and please cancel my engagements for the day. One other thing: I want to put an ad in the *Times*. It should read: *Black Sheep, our matchmaker has gone away but he left your name with some clients. Everything waterproof here but suggest you buy an umbrella. J.*'

148

16

Ned Moreno walked in and glanced around him. Stelio came up to him and said, 'He keeps his personal documents in this folder: birth certificate, medical card, and so on. His passport's not here. This is him.'

He handed over a student's card with a photograph of Drew taken ten years before, and a recent snapshot of him standing with a girl.

Ned studied the face carefully, then slipped both items into his pocket.

'If he's got a car, he must have some documentation referring to its registration number. Then we could check and see if it's parked anywhere near by.'

Stelio went straight to a drawer and pulled out a folder of bills. Amongst them was a year-old invoice for a Ford Mondeo. He gestured for one of his men to make a note, and sent him out looking for the vehicle. Ned sat down at the desk to examine the other papers more carefully. Then he wandered around the sitting room, studying the books and records.

Stelio's man came back a few minutes later, to announce, 'It's parked around the corner.'

After a further half-hour of searching, it was clear there was no clue as to where Drew had gone, so Moreno phoned Ferrandini for instructions. He also told him about their encounter with Williamson and how it had ended.

'I'm sorry, Robert. Stelio had to. They waited outside until the office cleaners had gone, and they assumed they'd have a good three-quarters of an hour to go over the place. But ten minutes later Williamson himself walked in out of the blue.'

'Then tell Stelio he killed the grandson of a man who shook my father's hand on an agreement, which he and his family honoured for more than fifty years.'

'I'm sorry, Robert, but I think he had no choice. If we're going to stop Drew at all, then he mustn't get any kind of warning.'

'Except that now all Drew's got to do is read the newspapers and he'll have all the warning he needs!'

'Which still gives us until tomorrow to find him.'

'Don't they have radio in England?' inquired Ferrandini with icy

149

sarcasm. Moreno had no reply to this. 'No, Ned. I'm not happy about the way this job's been handled. Killing Williamson was a mistake. And it was unnecessary,' he added forcefully.

Ned was silent for a moment and when he next spoke his tone was contrite. 'What do you want us to do?'

'For a start what's the name of this banker?'

'Hamblyn. Sir Joshua Hamblyn.'

'Right. Go and see him. I'd have preferred to fly over and talk to him myself, but the more time that goes by, the greater the chance he'll get to hear about Williamson.'

'Suppose he has already?'

'Then you're going to have a very one-sided interview, assuming he'll agree to see you at all. On the other hand, the account my father set up with him will probably be sizable. I shouldn't think he'll want to lose it, so you ought to be able to force an interview. You had best feed him some line about a Chinese rival being responsible for all this. Take along a photograph of me and show it to Hamblyn, so that he knows what I look like. Then I'll contact him personally by videophone.'

'What should we do about Drew?'

'Hang fire for a moment while we think about that.' Ferrandini now turned back to the other dons. 'If the Accords are in England, then Drew has had a twelve-hour start to reach them, in which case there's nothing we can do about it. I suggest we assume he's gone abroad, and far enough to give us time to stop him.'

Gabrielli replied, 'Okay. But he's unlikely to have taken a car with him, because it's much easier to trace number plates than people.'

'All right. Then by air or by train?' asked Lovegni.

Gabrielli was thoughtful. 'Airports are watched because of terrorists. Security people look more closely at passengers. This guy will want to stay as invisible as possible. Besides, his name would be on a passenger list. My bet's a train.'

The other two men nodded their agreement. Ferrandini spoke into the phone again. 'Ned, get some people over to the railway stations which deal with the coastal traffic.'

'A lot of Stelio's men haven't arrived yet. I'm a bit short of manpower for the moment.'

'Then give priority to the English Channel ports.'

At quarter past eleven that morning, one of Stelio's men struck lucky. A porter remembered seeing Drew boarding the night train to Brussels. Ned Moreno informed Ferrandini ten minutes later.

'How come the porter's still on duty?'

'Because the guy was working the evening shift until today.'

Ferrandini ferried the information to his companions.

Cattagna glanced at his watch. 'He's got a fourteen-hour start on us. You can go a long way in Europe in fourteen hours.'

'What's in Brussels?' asked Lovegni. 'The European Union, Nato . . .'

'Not in 1943,' said Cattagna. 'They didn't exist yet. Besides, it was occupied.'

'Maybe Salvatore changed the plan afterwards.'

Cattagna shook his head. 'No, Philip. Salvatore would have set the thing up properly in the first place, and remember his motto: *If it works, don't fix it*. Let's have a look at the atlas. Draw a line from London to Brussels and I think you'll find it runs almost directly east.' He studied a map of Europe. 'And that leads on to Germany and Poland or Czechia.'

'Again, all occupied by the Nazis in 1943,' argued Gabrielli. 'In fact, to reach territory that *wasn't* occupied, he'd have to go a long way east.'

Cattagna smacked his forehead. '*Russia!*' he exclaimed. The others frowned at him in puzzlement. 'Don't you see? Until recently, it was the ideological opposite of the United States. And it's still the country most likely to be independent of the US in the long run. It's the ideal place to publish the Accords. I can't understand why I didn't think of it before.'

Vitellini at once crossed to a bookcase, from which he extracted Volume V of Churchill's history *The Second World War*. He turned to a map of military operations in the Soviet Union in 1943, and quickly established that, in July, German forces still occupied Belorussia and almost the whole of the Ukraine, while St Petersburg – then called Leningrad – was still under siege.

Ferrandini turned back to the phone. 'We think he's heading for Russia, Ned. Probably Moscow. We'll get moving at this end and put some people into position to intercept. In the meantime, find out how far he could have got in eighteen hours, and get four hours ahead of him.' He hung up.

'How many men has Moreno got?' asked Lovegni.

'About sixty, but he'll have a lot more by tomorrow.'

'It's *today* that's critical. And sixty is not very many. Not to stop a man who's already got a fourteen-hour headstart.'

'And you can't rule out that he might catch a plane somewhere on the Continent,' said Gabrielli.

'If he was going to, he'd have done so already,' replied Ferrandini. 'So there'd be nothing we could do. Let's go for what we *can* stop and leave the rest to God.'

Lovegni nodded.

'One thing we haven't decided is what we're going to do with him if we catch him,' said Cattagna quietly.

'Explain that it's all a mistake,' replied Ferrandini at once.

'Suppose he doesn't believe us?' asked Gabrielli.

'Suppose he does,' replied Lovegni and the others looked at him inquiringly. 'If he knows where the Accords are, he'll have us all by the balls for ever more.'

Nobody replied.

17

The note read: *I am here as a representative of Mr Robert Ferrandini, in connection with an account which Hamblyn's has been managing on behalf of his family for many years. I have a very tight schedule and must go abroad this afternoon, so I would be grateful if you could spare me a few minutes immediately.*

Sir Joshua read it through three times. A ticklish situation. How to know for sure whether this Mr Moreno was really Ferrandini's representative?

'Better ask to see his credentials first,' he said.

Harvey went out, and reappeared a few moments later. He had been shown an employee identity card, with photograph, issued by the Salvatore Ferrandini Trust, accrediting the bearer as Director of Public Relations. It could still be a forgery, thought Hamblyn morosely.

'Show him in, but you'd better stay with us.'

Ned was studiously correct in his approach and handshake, and he made no comment about Harvey's presence.

'Thank you for seeing me at such short notice, Sir Joshua. I appreciate your courtesy. Mr Ferrandini will be contacting you by videophone. Here's a photograph of him.' He handed over a photocopy of a page from the *New York Times*. 'He would like to speak to you in person about a certain matter. It concerns various arrangements made by Mr Ferrandini's father during the war. Basically, they were intended as an insurance policy to safeguard his family. In the event of anything prejudicial happening, a bank in Switzerland would send a signal to a certain party in this country requiring him to select an agent to carry out certain tasks. Two days ago that signal was sent – but in error. The Ferrandini family is in no danger at all. The name of this agent is Adam Drew – as you know – and the man who selected him is Patrick Williamson. It is imperative we get in touch with Mr Drew to prevent him from continuing with his assignment. It could now be very damaging to Mr Ferrandini's interests – as well as to those of your bank.'

Sir Joshua gazed at his visitor, wondering if the man could be as innocent as he seemed. But there was a question he had wished to ask for several minutes, so he asked it now. 'How did you know we were the bank which approved Mr Williamson's selection agent?'

Ned gave a slight frown. 'He told me so himself.' Sir Joshua wondered about that frown. Ned wasn't happy about it either. He felt perhaps he'd overdone it, and he saw Sir Joshua's eyes narrow. Oh well, in for a penny, in for a pound. 'Sir Joshua, why did you ask me that question?'

Now it was Hamblyn's turn to throw an ounce of puzzlement into the space between them. 'Why should I not?' he inquired blankly.

Ned decided it was time to bring a little peevishness into the air. 'Sir Joshua,' he began patiently, 'I have outlined to you a highly dangerous situation for the Ferrandini family, as I also did to Mr Williamson. He naturally cooperated with us, and as far as I am aware he's the only person who *could* have told me about the role of your bank. So, the fact that you should ask who informed me leads me to suppose that there's someone else involved in this affair that we didn't know about.'

Sir Joshua looked the younger man straight in the eye. *My God, you're good!* he thought. *So damn good I* still *don't know whether you're telling me the truth.*

Rapidly he made two decisions. The companion question he also had ready, about *when* Ned had spoken to Williamson, he would not now ask. There was no point. If Moreno had been involved with Williamson's murder, he would probably know enough about the man's movements yesterday to supply an answer which he, Joshua Hamblyn, could not certainly know to be untrue.

Secondly, he would cooperate, but not in everything, because when young Drew had been apprised of his assignment, he had at once warned of the danger to Hamblyn himself. What this Moreno character was, was open to doubt. But what Drew was, was not.

'I'm sorry about the apparent thoughtlessness of my question, Mr Moreno. As far as I'm aware, no one apart from Mr Williamson knows about the arrangement. However, with respect to your getting in touch with Mr Drew, I'm afraid I can't help you at all. We have no idea what his plans were. We don't even know what his assignment is. We did offer to make travel arrangements for him, but he preferred to make his own. I hope there'll be some way you can get in touch with him. It goes without saying that if there's anything else the bank can do to help, we should be only too happy to.'

Moreno responded with the correct doses of disappointment and magnanimity. He was escorted from the premises by Sir Joshua himself. But the play wasn't over yet. As Ned kept pace alongside the baronet, he took the man by the elbow with just a hint of intimacy so that their escort following would hang back slightly.

'I don't want to worry you but I think I ought to mention that we aren't the only people interested in knowing the whereabouts of Mr

Drew. You see, Mr Ferrandini has powerful competitors in the business world, as you might expect. One of these rivals is New York Chinese. We recently discovered that they have a paid informer inside our organisation, so they might have found out about our contact in England. I tried to warn Williamson about that last night, but he didn't seem to take me very seriously.'

Hamblyn's silence lasted five seconds, then Moreno continued, 'I'm sure you've got no need to worry. Just be a bit circumspect over the next few days.' He glanced at his watch. 'Anyhow, I'd better get a move on.'

'Er, Mr Moreno. Perhaps you ought to let me know where you're staying. So if anything crops up, I'll be able to let you know.'

'At Mr Ferrandini's London residence,' replied Ned, inwardly triumphant, and pulled out a visiting card embossed with the legend '*Ferrandini*' and phone and fax numbers. The address was in Grosvenor Square.

Sir Joshua Hamblyn returned to his office a worried man; Moreno's ploy had totally convinced him. He regretted now not having told him about the death of Williamson. The enemy was obviously closer than even Moreno suspected, which meant the American might be in danger himself.

This whole affair was beginning to look extremely messy. Put a foot wrong, and the bank might lose the Ferrandini accounts, which would be a serious blow. After a moment's reflection, he rang one of the numbers on the card which Ned had given him, and left a message for Mr Moreno to call him back urgently.

Ned phoned back twenty minutes later. 'I'm sorry not to have been completely frank during our interview, Mr Moreno, but I needed time to check on your identity.' Hamblyn then informed him of the murder, and of the ad he had placed in *The Times* to warn Drew. 'There is certainly time to change the text, but I feel a final decision regarding the message should rest with you.'

'Thank you for your confidence, Sir Joshua. Let me just think for one moment.' Hamblyn's capitulation was certainly useful, but they weren't out of the woods yet. If the message did not refer to Williamson's murder, and Drew got to hear about it from some other source, he would most likely assume Sir Joshua had been got at, and distrust any further communication from him. 'Let the text stand as it is, but add the following: *Proper waterproofing is on its way, however. Contact me by phone urgently. Do nothing until you speak to me.*'

'Very well, Mr Moreno. I'll handle this personally at once.'

Ferrandini's videophone call came just after lunch. Sir Joshua was very cooperative. He explained exactly what the bank had been asked to do with respect to the selection of a candidate, and opened Envelope

155

3–3, which contained the secret instructions to Williamson, although Ferrandini already knew these because Williamson himself had told Stelio all about them. Beyond this, there was not much more that Hamblyn was able to say. The bank held no further sealed envelopes.

'How many funds did my father set up with you?'

'Four – three investment funds, currently worth about a billion dollars each, and a small operating fund, from which the expenses paid to Mr Drew were drawn, and whose value is just under six million dollars at present. The original investment in 1943 was eleven million dollars, so the average per annum capital increase has been almost 11.2 per cent. Your father's recommendations as to the particular investments to be made were very detailed.'

'How are these funds accessed?'

'By letter, signed by the client and countersigned by my own father, and a code number for each fund.'

Ferrandini nodded. This was an identical arrangement as that with the Zurich bank, where a further eleven million dollars had been invested. Eleven plus eleven made twenty-two; but the original setup fund had consisted of twenty-*five* million. He wondered what his father had done with the remaining three.

'Thank you very much, Sir Joshua. We'll keep in touch.'

Just as they hung up, and six hundred miles to the east, Adam's train was crossing the Elbe by the *Marienbrücke* in Dresden, the capital of Saxony. To his right was a cigarette factory, weirdly designed in the form of a mosque; to his left, along the riverbank, stood the baroque spires and palaces of the old town, the magnificent survivors of the Allied bombing during the war. Seeing them again stirred many nostalgic memories of an earlier visit to the city, in 1993, when he had included it in his itinerary on a mountaineering holiday in the Elbsandsteingebirge. While wandering around the Albertinum, he had met a girl named Renate and enjoyed a romantic, if brief, liaison with her among the rebuilt splendours of what had once been one of the most beautiful cities in the world.

But Adam's return to Dresden now was motivated by neither nostalgia nor tourism. His choice of route across Germany had been dictated largely by railway timetables, and in particular by the schedule of trains to Poland. His earliest arrival time in Berlin would have been 16.42, twenty minutes after the departure of the afternoon express to Warsaw. Since there would not be another train to the Polish capital until 21.00, he had decided to afford himself the luxury of a mild deception, based on the fact that there were two principal rail routes to Moscow: Berlin-Warsaw-Minsk to the north and Dresden-Cracow-Kiev to the south. He had opted for the shorter of the two but, having more than four hours to kill, rather than spend

156

them hanging around a Berlin waiting room, he had decided to devote the time to a practical purpose: confusing possible enemies, just in case any were around to be confused. So, from Cologne he had travelled to Frankfurt, then Leipzig, and now Dresden, where he intended hiring a car. He might have done this in Leipzig, which was closer to Berlin, but if anyone were to trace his movements, his passage through Dresden would suggest he had taken the southerly route to Moscow.

With German punctuality, his train pulled into the *Dresdener Hauptbahnhof* at 15.17.

Having spent so much time in the Alps with Swiss and Austrian mountaineers, Drew spoke near faultless German, and, in common with many natives, he found the '*Dreesden*' accent, with its stretched vowels, pleasantly comical. Assailed by it now on all sides, he walked through the busy station hall and out into the bright afternoon sunshine.

Few buildings in this quarter of the town could be counted among the city's glories. Built with concrete slabs, they *looked* like concrete slabs. He walked along the Wienerstrasse to the Lennéplatz, where there was a carhire firm that he had used in 1993. It was a local company and they had warned him not to drive his hired vehicle across any international frontier, so he knew that, with branches only in the Dresden area, nobody would be likely to trace their rentals, but even if someone did so, by that time Adam would be far away.

He told the girl behind the counter that he needed the car just for local journeys, and would return it within two days. His true intention was to hide it in some multistorey carpark in Berlin, then telephone the firm from Moscow to tell them where he'd left it.

Fifteen minutes later Adam was driving a wine-coloured BMW north along the *Carolabrücke*, trying to find something interesting on the radio. He tuned in a play on British Radio Four just as he was joining the Berlin Autobahn, but it finished before he'd passed Dresden Airport. A news programme followed. The last item before the sports reported a murder in Oxford that same morning. The victim was identified as Patrick Williamson.

Adam slowed and pulled over onto the hard shoulder of the Autobahn. For several minutes he sat holding the wheel and staring into space.

So, they were onto him already. He hadn't been sure before whether there was any real danger – Salvatore's security system had seemed more than adequate. But now he knew the immediacy of danger and death – as he had once known it on the North Wall of the Eiger.

He drove to the Marsdorf exit, pulled up next to a phone booth, and rang Sir Joshua.

'Thank heaven you've called,' said the banker. 'Two things.

Williamson is dead. He's been murdered. I have reason to believe a group of New York Chinese in opposition to the Ferrandini family is responsible. Secondly, I've spoken to Robert Ferrandini on the phone and he wants you to discontinue your assignment. The financial arrangements still hold, but your mission is to be aborted. Do you understand?'

'Perfectly, Sir Joshua.'

'Good. Where are you?'

'In Germany. I'll take advantage of being here to visit a friend. I'll probably stay with him a few days, and come to see you when I get back to London.'

There was a brief pause, then Hamblyn said, 'As you will.'

'I'll say goodbye then.' Adam hung up.

Abort the mission, indeed! Whoever had given that order couldn't have the faintest idea of what Salvatore had asked him to do. And the fact that Sir Joshua was cooperating with them so eagerly could mean only one thing: they'd told him that if he didn't, he could kiss his family goodbye.

Drew next rang a travel agent to ask about flights to Russia. To take a plane would be in defiance of Salvatore's anonymity instruction – though probably justified by the circumstances – but merely finding out the possible options was not. However, the information he was given ruled out flying as an alternative. The quickest air route available was via Berlin-Tegel, but the earliest connection to Moscow was not until 8.25 next day, by which time his enemies could be expected to have stationed men in both cities.

Adam climbed back into the BMW, took out his map and looked for alternatives. He was practically certain that neither Williamson nor Hamblyn could have had any inkling of his eventual destination, but that didn't mean that his opponents couldn't deduce it from whatever information *they* possessed. And if they already knew he was heading for Moscow, the obvious route of Berlin-Warsaw-Minsk would be a certain deathtrap.

Moments later, Drew was heading back along the Autobahn towards Dresden. He returned to the station, left the BMW in the carpark out front, and entered the booking hall. He spent a few minutes studying the timetable, then bought a one-way ticket to Cracow – a first-class private compartment on the 17.42 Warsaw express, with a single change at Breslau. His German pronunciation was good enough to sound Austrian to a Dresdener ear, but deliberately he put on an English accent.

After depositing his suitcase at the left luggage office, Adam walked out of the station and then along the Pragerstrasse to the old town. In the Postplatz he sat down at one of the terrace tables of the Café Schauspiel, which enjoyed a marvellous view of the Crown Gate of

158

the Zwinger. A waiter appeared immediately, and Adam ordered a small coffee with cream. When it was brought, he took out his wallet, extracted a hundred-mark note, and said to the waiter, 'There's a small service you could perform for me.'

'I should be happy to assist you, *mein Herr.*'

'Call a taxi and ask the driver to buy a second-class return ticket to Prague at the station. It will cost about sixty marks. Give him a reasonable tip, and keep the change.'

Delighted with the prospect of earning thirty marks for making a simple phone call, the waiter withdrew, leaving Drew to sip at his coffee and contemplate the splendid Zwinger. It has been almost entirely destroyed in the bombing, but the Dresdeners had lovingly restored it to its former glory.

Adam gazed at the buildings around him, conscious that on the night of 13 February 1945 this area had lain in the middle of a firestorm, and trying to imagine what it would have been like. The city had been full of refugees fleeing the Red Army and at least thirty-five thousand people had died, though no one knew the true figure. Fifteen square kilometres had been laid waste, and a mere three months before the end of the war, at a time when Germany was clearly beaten. The strategic justification had been to cut Berlin's communications with Prague and Vienna, but it still smacked of barbarism. So it was scarcely any wonder that the Dresdeners had given the Queen a rude reception when she visited the city in the spring of 1993 – shortly after the unveiling in London of a statue of 'Bomber' Harris, the man who had given the order to destroy the city! It was a tactlessness that deserved a prize, thought Adam. And as if the destruction of their city had not been enough, the Dresdeners had another nightmare in store for them. Three months later, on 8 May, the day of the German capitulation, the Red Army had marched in – and stayed for forty-five years.

All this, Adam reminded himself, had happened almost two years after Salvatore Ferrandini had journeyed to Oxford to call on George Williamson – whose grandson had been murdered that morning.

The killing *still* wasn't over.

In Sicily the five dons were discussing the recent news of Drew's ready acquiescence in aborting his mission. Cattagna studied the verbatim transcript of Drew's phone call to Sir Joshua, which the banker had recorded on tape, and shook his head.

'It's too pat. Drew's acquiescence was *too* casual.'

'It doesn't matter whether he's telling the truth or not,' replied Ferrandini. 'To cover ourselves, we must presume he *isn't* and continue the search. If we're wrong, there's no harm done.'

And all agreed.

The waiter returned with the rail ticket. Adam left the café and headed for the large bookshop in the Wilsdrufferstrasse, where he bought several maps and a guidebook. Next he purchased a travel holdall and a few clothes at the nearby Karstadt department store, then some Czech money at a Bureau de Change, after which he returned to the railway station, and retrieved his suitcase.

It was just after five o'clock, so he had forty minutes before the Warsaw train left. He would use them wisely.

The Dresden Hauptbahnhof consisted of three galleries. The middle one was the original station, and still a terminus for all the railway lines entering it. The galleries on either side were later additions and the lines were not terminated: they continued towards the southeast. The terminus platforms were at ground level; the ones in the outer galleries had been built at first-floor height. They were all numbered consecutively, however, so that one to six were in the south gallery, seven to fourteen in the middle, and sixteen to nineteen in the north. There seemed to be no platform fifteen.

The Case of the Missing Platform, thought Adam to himself as he climbed the stairs to the south gallery. From here he carefully studied the crowds in the hall below, paying particular attention to the people in the vicinity of platform nine, at which the Warsaw train was already standing. After several minutes' scrutiny, he was satisfied that, aside from station workers and passing commuters, only the layabouts that invariably hung around railway stations looking for prey were in sight.

Adam descended the steps, moved unhurriedly towards the train, registered with the attendant, and was shown to his compartment.

'I'll be getting off in Breslau. Meanwhile I don't want to be disturbed,' he told the man, handing him a fifty-mark note. 'There'll be another of them when we get there, if I'm not.'

The attendant promised to make sure the gentleman was left in peace, then he withdrew.

Adam did some rearranging of the contents of his suitcase, transferring certain items to the holdall. He spent a moment working the spine of the guidebook to and fro, creasing several pages to make it look well used, even adding some pencilled notes in the margins. Then he laid the open book face down on the seat, and left the compartment.

At the end of the corridor he stepped just around the corner, and kept a watchful eye on the passageway. A few moments later the same attendant reappeared, distracted now as he showed a middle-aged man to his compartment. Adam at once left the carriage and returned to his observation post on platform six. Partly concealed by the metal latticework of a roof support, he settled down to a long wait.

★ ★ ★

By calling in debts and promising favours, the four American dons and their Sicilian host had by now been able to mobilise a hundred and twenty reliable men who resided in various major cities of Europe. One of these was Carlo Lambetti, who lived in Berlin, and was one of three now assigned to Dresden. They arrived by car just five minutes before the Warsaw express was due to depart.

Lambetti made straight for the booking hall and spoke to the only clerk on duty, showing him false identification accrediting him to the *Bundeskriminalamt* in Berlin. When he saw the fax photograph of Adam Drew, the clerk recognised him at once. 'Cracow. First class. Private compartment on the Warsaw express. Platform nine.' He glanced at his watch. 'You'll have to hurry. It's about to go.'

Lambetti went racing through the foyer towards the train just as it began to move, his two companions running to join him when they realised his urgency. Carlo's hand came within a yard of the door handle of the final coach, but the train's gathering speed was already too great. He slowed to a stop, defeated, glaring after it. He spat an oath, then turned on his heel and ran back to talk to a station official After a brief exchange with him, Lambetti hurried towards the nearest phone.

All this had been witnessed with growing apprehension by Drew himself, observing from the gallery above.

Immediately after Lambetti phoned in his report, Moreno called Robert Ferrandini.

'He left Dresden on a train for Cracow a few minutes ago. Our people just missed it.'

'Where's its first stop?'

'Dresden-Neustadt, but we haven't got any men there. The same goes for Bautzen and Löbau. The first place where we have people who can intercept it is Görlitz, on the Polish frontier.'

'Make sure they understand they're to take him alive.'

'And if they can't?'

Ferrandini was silent for a moment. 'If there's no other way to stop him, then they can shoot to kill. But make it clear, if anybody gets a bit too trigger happy, I'll set Stelio on them and they'll wish they'd never been born.'

Adam waited until Lambetti and his companions had left the station, before going down to consult the railway timetable. What he had observed so far suggested his pursuers were putting out an extensive dragnet for him, sending agents to all the major cities and towns through which he was likely to pass. So there was a good chance Görlitz would be included. It would arrive there at 19.20, forty

161

minutes before his train to Prague was due to leave. Once they discovered he wasn't on board, they were bound to suspect some trick in Dresden station, and they would likely be near enough to get here before the Prague train departed.

Dresden was definitely too dangerous a place to hang around in, Adam decided – though the alternatives were not likely to be much less so. If it was just a matter of crossing a frontier, his best option would be to kit himself out in climbing gear and take a route through the mountains. But this would take hours and leave him stranded in Czechia, miles from anywhere, with no means of transport.

Drew wondered about the BMW, still standing in the carpark outside. Hiring it had seemed so safe. But at that time the existence of any opponents had been little more than theoretical. With the news of Williamson's murder they had become real, but had still seemed far away. Now here they were in Dresden.

Adam decided he must suppose that, assuming his pursuers had not already found out he had hired the car, they soon would. And if they were to find it parked outside Dresden station, they would know for sure he was travelling by rail and this was his point of departure. The conclusion was obvious: he must get out of Dresden as soon as possible, and hide that damned BMW properly.

But perhaps he was overlooking an advantage to be gained. If they found out about the car *after* he had got rid of it, this wouldn't matter a damn. In fact, persuading them he was now going by car might improve his chances of getting away by rail.

So deciding, he slipped around the corner of the passage leading to the booking hall, took out his car keys in readiness, and waited for the right moment. A few yards from the timetable that he had just been studying stood a hot-dog stand, surrounded by some scruffy teenagers. Just beyond this, leading to the carpark, was a tunnel continuously traversed by commuters. Adam waited for a bunching of the crowd, then, assuming an anxious expression, he ran around the corner towards the tunnel, meeting the knot of people just in front of the hot-dog stand, and contrived to bump into a passer-by. The keys went flying. He apologised, in English and in a voice loud enough for the hot-dog seller to hear, then retrieved the keys, which had landed a few yards away. His little pantomime now concluded, he hurried on through the tunnel to the carpark. After a cautious reconnoitre, in case his pursuers were still around, Adam climbed into the BMW and drove away.

Sticking to the backroads, he threaded his way out of the city and along the Elbe valley, through Heidenau and Pirna. On the rolling plain around him abrupt tors began to appear, marking the beginning of the Elbsandsteingebirge. Soon, on the top of a steep hill, the fortress of Königstein – the largest in Europe – loomed above him in the afternoon sunlight. This was the start of the *Sächsisch-Böhmische Schweiz* – the Saxon-Bohemian Switzerland, a region Adam knew well. In many places, erosion had whittled the sandstone masses into weird, towering columns – spectacular challenges for any mountaineer, and offering magnificent views in reward.

The Elbe gorge was narrow at Königstein, the road and railway line coming together to squeeze through it. Just past the next bend in the river lay the pretty spa town of Bad Schandau. The Czech frontier was a mere eight miles distant. On the mountain close above the town, and connected to it by lift, was a hamlet called Ostrau. A winding road also linked them, but by a much longer route. Adam drove up to the village, looking for a place to conceal the car. No really good hiding place presented itself, so eventually he decided it would attract less attention if he just parked it in a street. After retrieving his holdall, he walked along the footpath to the fifty-metre-high lift tower. '*Built 1904. Rebuilt 1990*', a sign announced. I'm glad to hear it, he thought, eying with misgivings the frail-looking bridge which linked the tower to the hillside.

But a few minutes later he was safely back in Bad Schandau, walking down to the quayside, where he boarded a ferry to take him across the river to the railway station.

In the system which Moreno and Stelio had rapidly set up, six regional monitors coordinated the movements of the fieldmen, who, if not equipped with cellular phones, had to call in regularly for any change of plan. This was the case for the three men assigned to Görlitz: Toni Coretti, Giovanni Napoli and Aldo Romaggio. They reached the town at 18.10. Coretti rang Berlin and learned that Drew was thought to be aboard the Warsaw train. He informed his companions, giving them instructions on how the search was to be carried out. Romaggio was to remain on the platform watching the doors, while Napoli and Coretti himself boarded the train.

'Maybe we ought to buy tickets for some place further up the line,' suggested Romaggio.

'There's no point. The train stops here for fifteen minutes. That's time enough to take care of half a dozen guys. Check your guns while you're waiting.'

Having nothing to do for an hour, Coretti left his companions and wandered along the Bahnhofstrasse. His stroll took him down to the river, where he stopped to look across at Poland. The little town of Görlitz had lost its eastern suburb when the Allies had decided to make the Neisse Germany's eastern frontier. Now it was a separate town called Zgorzelec.

Tiring of Poland, Coretti went for a cup of coffee in a nearby café. At ten past seven he was back in the station. The train pulled in two minutes late. When he showed the attendant Drew's photograph, the two hundred marks offered simultaneously were more than enough for the man to remember which compartment.

Coretti tried the handle and found it unlocked. He threw it open, then immediately swung around to Napoli. 'The toilets, quick! Then the dining car!' He turned back to the attendant. 'Go and search the whole damn train. Find him and you get a thousand marks. Now move!' He rushed to the offside window to check the tracks. Next he proceeded from door to door of the remaining private compartments. By the time the train was due to leave, they had searched it thoroughly. The conclusion seemed inescapable: Drew had either spotted them and escaped by the railward side, or he had left the train at one of the earlier stops.

Coretti picked up all Drew's belongings, shoved a further two hundred marks into the attendant's hand, muttering, 'Not a word.' While his men explored the surrounding area, he went to make another phone call.

As soon as he heard Coretti's report, Moreno was suspicious and rang to consult Ferrandini. 'I think we should send in more men, and put everyone on *all* the routes coming out of Dresden. I've already sent Lambetti back to the station.'

'You say Drew bought the ticket an hour and a half before the train left. Suppose he went ahead by bus to some stop further down the line?'

'Coretti thought of that. He promised the attendant five thousand marks to contact him if Drew reappears.'

'Even so, I'd still have men ready all the way along the line to Kiev. And on the Breslau-Warsaw-Moscow run too, because buying a ticket for Cracow might be a blind.'

Ferrandini turned to his companions to relay this latest news. Coretti's details on Drew's belongings – a suitcase, a jacket in the cupboard, an open book – everything seemed to suggest that, just as the train was pulling into Görlitz, he had spotted men waiting for him and done a bunk. The book provided a hypnotic suggestion of its own: it was a multilingual travel guide to the Caucasus mountains.

'Too contrived,' was Lovegni's instant verdict.

Gabrielli looked doubtful. 'Maybe not. That guidebook tells us he's heading for the former Soviet Union, which he's entitled to assume we couldn't have predicted otherwise.'

'And, in his instructions to Williamson, Salvatore twice mentioned a mountaineer,' Cattagna reminded them.

There was a pause. Then Gabrielli said, 'But the instructions also specified a negotiator. Why a negotiator?'

Ferrandini suggested, 'Maybe he'll have to negotiate the handing over of the Accords with whoever has them.'

'Obviously,' grunted Lovegni.

Gabrielli seemed to dismiss the point. There was another pause, then Ferrandini recapitulated, 'We can assume he doesn't trust Hamblyn any more. The question is: did he think his declared acquiescence would be taken at face value and he was now off the hook, or did he decide we'd keep after him anyway?'

They all fell silent. Eventually Lovegni said, 'It's a bluff. He was never on the Cracow train.'

Robert nodded his agreement. Gabrielli and Cattagna looked at each other, and finally agreed.

They turned to the large map of Europe which their host had provided. 'He'll try to cross as few frontiers as possible,' said Ferrandini.

'The fewest is still through Poland,' rejoined Gabrielli. 'Any other route gives him at least one extra frontier to get across. Suppose he went to Berlin to take a train from there?'

'Ned's checking that already.'

Cattagna said, 'Why draw our attention to Poland at all, if he really is going that way?'

'And if he isn't, then where?'

'I think the only feasible alternative is through Czechia and Slovakia. That route would cost him just one more frontier.'

'He could go through Austria and Hungary for the same price in frontiers,' commented Gabrielli.

Studying the map, Lovegni shook his head. 'That would involve too long a detour.'

Ferrandini phoned Ned. 'Have Lambetti find out about all trains running from Dresden to the Czech frontier this afternoon. Tell our people in Prague to stay put, and get men to all the major rail junctions in Czechia.' Ferrandini hung up and glanced at his watch. It was three minutes to eight.

'There's something we haven't considered,' said Cattagna. 'If Drew now realises that we're closing in, he might decide to go to earth somewhere in Germany, and bring in a friend from England – someone he trusts – and brief him to act as the agent.'

Lovegni groaned, 'Oh, my God!'

Cattagna's notion was sobering. After a few moments' silence, Ferrandini gave a sigh. 'It'll be a big job, but we can handle it. I'll get Stelio to find out who all Drew's close friends are, and to keep tabs on them for a few days.'

'There's another thing,' put in Gabrielli. 'Suppose Drew meets someone en route – say, while hitchhiking – and decides he can trust him to act as agent.'

'Unlikely,' grunted Lovegni.

'But possible. Especially if he's desperate,' said Cattagna.

Ferrandini replied, 'Then anyone Drew comes into prolonged contact with has got to be picked up as well.'

The others agreed. Ferrandini reached for the telephone.

18

The express from Berlin-Schönefeld Airport to Budapest-Keleti was called the *Metropol*. It glided to a stop on platform four in the Dresden Hauptbahnhof at 19.45. Lambetti and his companions hurried back into the station three minutes later. He was more than a little annoyed. Obviously this damned limey had foxed him. He and his men ran to platform four and boarded the *Metropol*.

At eight o'clock, just as the train was moving off, the three men stepped down, satisfied that Drew was not on board. They began to question the station workers. The attendant at the hot-dog stand was the first man Lambetti spoke to.

Moments later Ned Moreno was learning about Drew's collision with a passer-by, and the car keys he had dropped.

'What time did this happen?' he asked.

'Just after the Warsaw train left. I think he must have seen us, and then decided to make a run for it by car.'

'Okay. Check the local carhire firms. Their city offices will have closed by now, but airport branches stay open till late. If Drew's hired a car, they'll have a record of it on computer.'

At 20.27, the *Metropol* reached Bad Schandau – the only stop before the Czech frontier. The sun had now sunk behind the hills, though it was still twenty minutes from setting. Adam climbed aboard, acutely aware of the danger which this involved. He was banking on his pursuers simply not having had enough time to react after discovering he wasn't on board the Warsaw train.

The *Metropol* left Bad Schandau three minutes later. Drew remained standing in the corridor, ready to leap from the train, if necessary. A group of three Czech customs and passport control policemen had also joined the train at Bad Schandau, they looked bored and carried out their tasks perfunctorily.

The river Elbe varied in width, but the average was some one hundred and fifty yards. On the opposite bank, Schmilka passed by: the last village before the frontier. Immediately beyond it were the German and Czech border-guard posts, both processing short queues of vehicles. The Elbe valley was steep now, its eastern side becoming a cliff. The picturesque village of Hřensko – the lowest point of

Bohemia – clung to its side, at the mouth of the Kamenice gorge, which Adam had explored in 1993. He remembered the dozens of cigarette pedlars, mostly Arab, lining the road along it.

For the next two miles the railway line remained in Germany, while the road running along the opposite bank of the Elbe was already in Czechia, where the river was now called the Labe.

At just the moment that Adam's train entered the Czech Republic, Ned Moreno was informing his boss of the make and registration number of the car which Drew had hired that same afternoon. He also reported that Lambetti had persuaded a friend of his in the German police to put out a general alert for it.

Six miles inside Czechia, the *Metropol* pulled into Děčín. Adam was watching the platform like a hawk, but none of the passengers appeared to be hunting for anybody. The stop lasted twenty minutes. As the train pulled out of the station, Adam breathed a sigh of relief. He slipped into a lavatory to exchange his business suit for jeans, a denim shirt and a navy pullover.

It was dark when the *Metropol* glided to a stop in Ústí nad Labem's shabby and ill-lit station at half past nine. Adam was one of only a dozen passengers to detrain. He had been here before, so he wasn't surprised. Ústí wasn't somewhere many people would want to go to.

Originally a medieval town, little remained to prove it. What the nineteenth-century industrial expansion had left intact, the Allies had taken care of – three weeks before the end of the war! Before their expulsion, the town had been inhabited by Sudeten Germans – and was still called Aussig in roadsigns on the German side of the frontier – but it was difficult to find any credible motive for its destruction so late in the war. Except perhaps to reduce its value to the Russians, who were about to take it over.

A miraculous survivor of the bombing was the thirteenth-century Panny Marie Church, although its spire had been left with a lean of six feet. The rest of the old town had been almost entirely destroyed, and its reconstruction by the Communists had made it a monument to drabness. Almost the only other medieval relic was the Střekov castle, where Wagner had written part of *Tannhäuser*. Aptly called in German *Schreckenstein* – Terror Stone – it stood atop a precipitous crag high above the Labe.

In front of the station a dozen young layabouts hung around, on the lookout for opportunities. Adam walked down to the main road which ran alongside the Labe and, like a man in a hurry to get home, set off briskly upriver towards Ústí-Vaňov, two miles distant. Above him, on the opposite bank, darkly loomed Hrad Střekov on its vampiric crag – a visual analogue of the threat implicit in his own predicament.

168

Adam had no illusions. The speed with which his opponents had got on his trail was frightening and, as he had long ago learned from his job, in international operations great speed implied great power.

Spanning the river, immediately below the castle, stood a huge bridge-like structure. It was the biggest lock on the Elbe. A climbing companion who had pointed this out had then taken Adam to dinner at a restaurant called Kotva's Bar, a mile upstream and a popular eating place for bargemen and dock workers. Adam remembered its proletarian functionality – cheap furniture, smoky atmosphere, beer-stained carpet and simple but good food. Several billiards tables in an adjoining room had given it the atmosphere of a working man's club, and it had remained busy until late. This was the reason that Adam was now heading there.

More than a dozen assorted tugs, dredges and barges, packed like sardines, were moored in the dock. A few yards beyond it, on the other side of the road, stood Kotva's Bar. By this time Adam was very hungry, but to go inside would create forty witnesses.

Instead he walked further along the quayside to two barges moored against the riverbank, and looked for signs of life aboard them. On the pilothouse roof of the smaller of the two lay a black Belgian Shepherd, which raised its head suspiciously at his approach. In the faint light Adam could see a padlock on the pilothouse door. The combination of padlock and dog told him a great deal: the bargee was out; but he lived aboard the barge, so he was unlikely to be gone long. Adam walked halfway back towards Kotva's, sat down next to a bush and waited.

Soon after eleven o'clock, a young man emerged from the bar, crossed the road and came towards him. The Belgian Shepherd, tail awag, leapt down from the roof onto the deck. When its master drew level with him, Adam asked, '*Haben Sie Feuer?*' He used German because he expected anyone who travelled up and down the Elbe to have a working knowledge of it.

The young man looked up, startled, but then took out a lighter. Adam got to his feet and stepped towards him.

'Nice-looking dog. What's its name?'

'Astor.' The bargee struck up a flame for Adam's cigarette, and the illumination enabled both men to examine each other. The young man was about twenty-three years old, dark-haired, and well tanned from a life spent in the open air.

'Want one?' invited Adam, offering the packet. The bargee hesitated, but then accepted. 'Where are you heading?' asked Drew, now deliberately laying on a slight English accent.

'Prague. That's where I live. Where are you from?'

'London. My name's Peter Smith.'

'Mine's Martin Trnka,' replied the other, pronouncing it Marrteen

169

Trinka. 'And you already know what I do for living, so what about you?'

'I'm a businessman.'

'Sounds nice and vague. So am I, if it comes to that. I own the barge. Or I shall do when I've finished paying for it.'

Adam smiled. 'I buy and sell things.'

'Such as?'

He shrugged. 'Just about anything and everything.'

'Sounds high-powered,' commented Martin, in a tone which suggested he wasn't ruling out all this as pure fiction. 'So what's a big wheel like you doing here?'

'Trying to get somewhere else, of course. This is Ústí.'

Martin laughed. Then, abruptly seeing the light, he exclaimed, 'You're trying to hitch a ride.'

'Perhaps.'

'Paying?'

'How much?'

He considered. 'For a big shot like you, five hundred crowns.'

'Twenty-five dollars? Okay.'

'If you agree so readily, maybe I should have said a thousand,' grunted Martin.

'What time do we leave?'

'Tomorrow morning at half past five.'

'How much if we leave now?'

Martin shook his head. 'Barges don't work at night.'

'Is there some law against it?'

'No. But the locks don't open till six.'

Adam pursed his lips. This was a factor he hadn't taken into account. His mountaineering companion, who had shown him around the district in 1993, had told him that the Střekov lock had made the river as far as Prague navigable throughout the year. It hadn't occurred to Adam that there might be other locks.

'Do you know the lock-keepers personally?'

'Sure. I've been working this river since I was a boy.'

'How much would they want to open up at night?'

Trnka looked at him suspiciously. 'If you're in such a hurry to get to Prague, why don't you take a train?'

'If I tell you, you'll laugh.'

'Try me.'

'I'm a writer. I'm researching a plot for a thriller. The hero has to follow a certain route in Czechia in a certain time, and I want to make sure it's possible.'

'Sounds intriguing.'

'So how much do you think it would cost to ask a lock-keeper to open up at night?'

170

'If *you* did the asking, a small fortune. But I'm pretty friendly with most of them. If I claimed an emergency, they'd open up for nothing. The question is: do I want to?'

'The question is: how much would it take to make you want?'

Martin considered. 'Okay, I'll be generous. Three thousand.'

'That's *generous*?'

'I'll be losing a night's sleep, remember.'

'Okay. You haven't got any food on board, have you?'

'Only bread and cheese, I'm afraid.'

'Sounds wonderful,' replied Adam, as they walked to the barge. 'You won't charge me for it, will you?' he asked suspiciously.

Martin laughed. 'No, the bread and cheese is on the house.'

Astor subjected the newcomer to a full olfactory inspection. Adam waited a moment, then placed his hand on the animal's head and massaged the skin between its ears. The dog's eyes partly closed; they'd be friends for ever after this. Meanwhile, Trnka untied the mooring ropes, started up the engine and raised a grappling hook. Adam quickly took it out of his hands and hurried forard. He pushed it against the river bank, and the barge pulled away towards midstream. Rejoining Martin in the pilothouse, he said, 'Now, where's that cheese?'

'Take the wheel and I'll fetch it.'

'I noticed some buoys earlier on. If I'm going to be doing any driving, you'd better explain the colour system.'

'Yellow means danger. Don't worry about the others. And remember we're not on British roads. Keep to starboard.' Struck by a thought, he added, 'And when I mention the left bank, I'm talking about the bank that would be on our left, if we were going *down* the river.'

Trnka went below, reappearing a moment later with some rough-cut sandwiches and a cold beer.

The lights to starboard came to an end, as they left Ústí-Vaňov behind them. Those across the river continued for a while. They belonged to a surburb of Ústí called Brná, Martin informed him. But soon these too petered out and the river entered countryside. Its course ahead was illuminated for only some fifty yards by the barge's headlight. Beyond lay darkness. The hills stood black against a starry but moonless sky.

A road followed each shore. Very occasionally a car passed by. Adam knew that any of them might be driven by one of the men who were searching for him. He hoped that his sudden change of tactic, from fast travel to slow, would outfox them.

The *Metropol* pulled into *Praha-Holešovice* at 23.05. Jan Hurban remained by the exit gate, watching the detraining passengers, while four of his men boarded the train to search it. He already knew that Drew had not been on board at Dresden, but he'd also been informed about the deception on the Warsaw express, so any train which had been anywhere near Saxony required a second look.

A native-born Czech – though his maternal grandfather came from Palermo – Hurban had got rich under the Communists and even richer after their expulsion. He had never heard of either Ferrandini or Moreno, and knew Stelio only by reputation, but that afternoon he'd received a phone call from a friend in New York, and rapidly understood that he would be doing himself a big favour if he helped someone who would be ringing him shortly afterwards.

Hurban's men returned, shaking their heads. 'Nobody's seen him. Suppose he hitched a lift with someone?'

Without replying, Hurban opened his mobile telephone.

The sandwiches finished, Adam took a map from his holdall and studied it. 'What's our speed?'

'Twenty kilometres per hour.'

'How far is it to the mouth of the Vltava?'

'From Ústí, sixty-nine kilometres, and we've done about eight. There are four locks, and it takes fifteen-twenty minutes to fill each one. It's about a five-hour run during the day, but since we have to get the lock-keepers out of bed, you'd better add on at least another hour. Where are you heading for, by the way?'

'Slovakia, but the route can be variable. How far up is the Vltava navigable?'

'As far as Prague.'

The news wasn't welcome to Adam. He expected the Czech capital to be a dangerous place, so he wanted to get beyond it.

'And the Labe?'

'Till just past Týnec – a little town called Chvaletice.'

Adam consulted his map. Týnec nad Labem – Martin had pronounced it Teenets – lay some sixty kilometres due east of Prague. But by river, from the mouth of the Vltava, it was about a hundred.

'How much would you charge to take me there?'

'A lot more. Getting to Chvaletice and back would cost me a whole day.'

'How much?' insisted Adam.

'Ten thousand crowns more.'

Adam seemed to consider the price, but then he agreed.

'How many locks are there between here and Chvaletice?'

Martin had to think. Adam watched him count them mentally. 'Nineteen.'

'Jesus! It'll take us a month of Sundays!'

'It's you who wants to do this, remember; not me. But cheer up.

172

Most of the weirs are at the upper end. By the time we get there, the locks will have opened.'

Adam took out a notebook and, as if carrying out research, asked Martin a lot of detailed questions about the river. The Czech seemed to know everything about it and, in the course of his interrogation, Adam came to realise that rivers had as much an individual character as mountains. Trnka's knowledge of the Labe came from his father, who had worked as a bargeman on one of the government-owned bulk transporters, plying between Prague and Hamburg at the mouth of the Elbe. During school holidays, Martin himself had accompanied him. After the Velvet Revolution of 1989, which toppled the communist government, his father had decided to set himself up as a private barge operator, specialising in luxury goods, for which there was now a large demand. He'd died of cancer four years before, and Martin had taken over the business. His usual cargo on the downriver route was Bohemian cut class, but upriver he carried everything from fruit to television sets. His present cargo consisted of eight hundred refrigerators, which he'd picked up cheaply from a wholesaler who was closing down his business.

The first lock was at the town of Lovosice, nineteen kilometres from Ústí. As it was approaching, Adam said, 'By the way, I forgot to ask, but where exactly would the hero hide? He's supposed to move around without people seeing him.'

'Down in my cabin.'

'I want to do everything exactly as the hero is supposed to, so I'd better go below.'

Martin shrugged. 'Suit yourself.'

Adam climbed down the steps into Trnka's cramped and untidy living quarters. The noise of the engine dropped, the barge slowing. Martin tied up directly before the lock gates.

It was half an hour before they were on their way again. Once they were safely swallowed by the darkness, Adam went topside and along the deck to the prow. Now there was only the hypnotic throb of the engine between him and the silence of the night.

They're out there, he thought, staring into the blackness. Searching for me. The idea turned the surrounding night into something tangible and alive. A sightless beast sending out fingers towards him. Like the cold grey mist of the Eiger when the sun went down, leaving just the two of them alone – Adam and the killer mountain.

But the Eiger had been mindless. This hostile night had intelligence behind it: Cappers and Blowers who could observe and deduce. And decide.

19

The patrol car glided discreetly along the *Ostrauer Ring*, as if reluctant to disturb the sleeping inhabitants of the street's complacent houses, and stopped beside a wine-coloured BMW.

Twenty minutes later, aboard a private jet flying at twenty-six thousand feet above Belgium, a telephone rang. Ned Moreno awoke, picked up the receiver and listened. He snapped instantly to attention and grabbed the map lying nearby. 'Where the fuck is Ostrau?' he demanded. 'It's not on the map.'

'It's a suburban hamlet of Bad Schandau,' Lambetti replied.

'Okay, got it.' Ned hung up, then dialled the number of Tommaso Vitellini's country villa.

Ferrandini and Cattagna were sitting in comfortable chairs in the darkened loggia, sipping grappa and watching the moonless Sicilian night while they quietly conversed.

Ferrandini answered the telephone and learned of the existence of a place called Ostrau. He switched on a table lamp and studied the map. Then he said, 'I want the border guards questioned, as well as all the station personnel along that line. In the meantime, go and have a look around that village yourself. I want to know if there's any place he could have hidden his car where it wouldn't be found.'

The second lock, only eight kilometres beyond the first, was at a little village called České Kopisty. Adam again went below to hide. But this time, when he came up afterwards, he caught Trnka looking at him suspiciously. Obviously the Czech was beginning to doubt his passenger's story. What worried Drew was that Martin might think he was a criminal on the run and ask one of the lock-keepers to phone the police, which was a risk that Adam absolutely could not run.

After some thought, he decided his best course would be to tell the truth and, by exaggerating the danger to Martin himself, frighten him into keeping silent. He approached Trnka and offered him another cigarette. 'I made up the story about being a writer. The truth is I'm being hunted by a Mafia group.'

Martin stared at him. 'Why?'

Adam chose his words carefully. 'Because of something someone told me.' He paused to allow Trnka to absorb this. And now he dropped his bombshell. 'I'm afraid I've put you in danger.'

Martin gaped. 'What do you mean?'

'Because I might have told *you* about it. They won't be *sure* you know, but if you're dead they *will* be sure that no one else will.' He grunted. 'Human life is very cheap to some people.'

After getting over his initial shock, Martin rapidly grew angry. 'What fucking right did you have to involve me?'

'What do you think I should have done – commit suicide?' replied Adam hotly. 'Show me the man who's falling off a cliff and won't grab hold of someone to save himself.'

'That's different. That's instinctive. You had time to think about this.'

'Exactly. I had time to decide whether I wanted to commit suicide or not. I decided I didn't. But if *I'm* okay, then so are you.'

Martin put his anger on simmer. 'What do you mean?'

'I admit I've put you in a spot. I'm sorry. I had no option. I had to get off the roads and railways. But if I can evade them, you'll be okay. And I'll make it up to you. Help me, and I'll give you twenty thousand dollars, five thousand when we get to Chvaletice, and the rest when I'm back in London.'

'And I'm going to believe a simple promise, of course,' grunted Martin.

'It doesn't matter whether you do or don't,' replied Adam with deliberate brutality. 'You're still in trouble. If you get *me* out of it, you get *yourself* out. If you subsequently receive a gift of fifteen thousand dollars in the post, you'll know I keep my word. If not, you'll know I don't – or I'm dead.'

Martin considered all this, and Adam decided to push home his advantage. 'You haven't got a van by any chance?'

Trnka shook his head. 'At the moment, I haven't even got a driving licence. I was banned from driving for a year. I've still got two months to go. Why does it have to be a van, anyhow?'

'Because people can see into cars. What about your friends?'

Martin shook his head. 'Nobody I trust. But I do have one good friend with a driving licence. He could hire a van.'

Adam shook his head. 'The carhire firms will be the first thing they'll think of, and tomorrow's Saturday; in the Prague area there'll be less than a dozen vans hired on a Saturday, and all easily traceable.'

'Only the police can trace hired cars,' said Trnka, now suspicious again.

'Yes, I know,' replied Adam quietly. 'The people who're chasing me can pull a lot of strings.'

Martin blinked at him.

* ★ *

175

At quarter past four Carlo Lambetti drove slowly along the Schanzenweg, the last street in Ostrau to examine. At the end of it, he stopped and awaited instructions from the man sitting beside him. Moreno took out his mobile phone, and dialled his boss. 'I think he was really trying to hide the car. I don't think it's a bluff. But we can't get confirmation on whether he boarded the train. The railway people have gone off duty.'

'Okay. Assume he's gone into Czechia. Pull out all the stops.'

When Ned hung up, Lambetti asked, 'Where now?'

'Take me to Prague.'

Lambetti gave an inner sigh, but complied without hesitation. He drove back down the mountainside to Bad Schandau. As the car rejoined the main road, Ned looked across the Elbe to the lights of the railway station, wondering whether Drew had hitched or taken the train. To the river itself he spared no thought.

The sun had been up for an hour when the square white tower of Mělník's priory church came into view. It stood almost on the cliff edge of an escarpment, on the north side of the Labe, overlooking its confluence with the Vltava. The pretty little town – the centre of Bohemia's wine-making region – spread down the escarpment and along the river, limiting itself to the 'right' bank; the 'left' was virtually countryside, lushly populated with trees. The dwindling hills were still in evidence to the north, but south of the river, the central Bohemian plain stretched uninterruptedly to the horizon.

Knowing Smetana's famous symphonic poem *My Country*, Adam had expected the meeting of the two rivers to be violent but, to his surprise, he found that the Vltava swung around in a gentle curve, and merged with the Labe in perfect tranquillity. He commented on this to Martin, who at once pointed to a bay scooped out of the north bank, beneath the cliff and directly opposite the mouth of the Vltava.

'The confluence wasn't always so calm. Smetana composed the music before the locks were built.'

Adam stared at him. The idea of man overcoming the rage of a God he didn't really believe in, he found obscurely blasphemous.

Once past the confluence, the Labe lost fifty yards of its width, slimming now to ninety; the trees, lining its sides, closed in intimately. The intimacy seemed to be contagious, because Martin asked, 'Is your name really Peter Smith?'

'No. It's Adam Drew.'

'Married?'

'Not yet. You?'

'Next year, with a bit of luck.' He grinned. 'Or lack of it.'

Adam laughed. 'What's her name?'

'Jana. She's a nurse.'

'Does your mother have a job?'

'She handles my accounts, and looks after my younger sister. I'm the breadwinner of the family.' Then Trnka asked, 'Where exactly are you going in Slovakia?'

'It's Russia that I'm heading for.'

'That's a long way.'

'You're telling me,' murmured Adam.

A pair of swans glided past indifferently. Astor stared after them in fascination.

'What will you do when we get to Chvaletice?' asked Martin.

'Find somebody with a van, if I can. If not, I'll just have to hitchhike, and trust to luck.'

Trnka seemed to consider this. 'If these people catch you, they're going to want to know your movements while you were on the run, won't they?' Adam nodded. 'Will you tell them about me?'

'I'll try not to.'

The Czech looked at him, nodding slowly. 'Are you afraid?'

Adam took a deep breath. 'Yes, Martin. I thought getting to Russia would be a doddle. When I realised they were on my trail in Dresden, I was badly frightened.'

Again Trnka was thoughtful. 'You're serious about the forty-five thousand, aren't you?'

Drew sighed. 'If you think about it, there was absolutely no point in mentioning it at all, *unless* I was serious.'

From the direction of these questions, he knew that the Czech was leading up to something. At last Martin brought it out into the open. 'I've thought of someone I know who has a van – Karel Juránek. He lives just outside Týnec.'

'Do you know him well?'

'Reasonably.'

'You realise you'll be putting him in the same mess as us?'

'*I* don't want to commit suicide, *either*,' said Trnka quietly.

Drew nodded slowly. It was a triumph that gave him little pleasure. 'What does Karel do for a living?'

'He's a painter and plasterer.'

'So twenty thousand dollars would probably interest him. But I could only offer the same terms as to you: five on delivery, the balance when I'm back in England. He's not likely to want to risk his life for a deal like that.'

Martin replied, 'If I tell him how powerful your friends are, he'll be too frightened to help us at all.'

'So how would you explain things to him?'

'I'll just tell him some bad guys are looking for you, and you need to get to Russia. You don't need to offer so much. Five thousand

177

dollars is already a lot of money. Anything you decide to give him afterwards is up to you.'

Assuming there *is* an afterwards, thought Adam grimly.

20

The first glimpse of the sun's orb was matched, moments later, by a dazzling reflection off the Potomac. The chauffeur at once lowered the eyeshade but, a few hundred yards further on, the highway veered to the left and the glare disappeared. David Ewing, sitting in the back, opened his copy of that morning's edition of the *Washington Post* and began to read the lead article. It covered a forthcoming meeting of the leaders of G7 and what the US should push for. Ewing yawned. What a way to start the day, he thought. What a bunch of crap! A roadsign announced the exit for Langley, and the chauffeur jockeyed the Lincoln over to the right-hand lane.

As they were approaching the CIA headquarters, some fool of a kid on a bicycle swung out in front of them. The chauffeur had to brake so sharply that Ewing's briefcase slid to the floor. The kid barely glanced back, then pedalled unconcernedly away. Damn brat, thought Ewing; hope he has a fatal accident. The incident put him out of sorts. When the car came to a stop, he stepped out in a bad temper. To a greeting from the duty officer, he limited his reply to a surly grunt. Few people were around that early and on the way to his office he encountered only a pair of patrolling guards, and then Makin. The bleary-eyed young computer genius, his hair uncombed and tie askew, had obviously been up working all night. At the sight of him, Ewing shook his head sadly.

Makin spotted him, and at once came towards him along the corridor. 'Ah, Director. If I could just have a word—'

'Later, Dr Makin. Later.' Ewing swept past him into his secretary's office. He touched a button on her intercom, to transfer calls automatically to his own phone, and once inside his inner office, he switched on the Cona machine. There would just be time before his appointment for it to warm up. When his phone rang, he was already sipping a cup of hot black coffee.

'Mr Richmond to see you, sir.'

'Send him up.'

A short while later a guard knocked at the outer-office door, then Alan Richmond walked in. 'Coffee?' inquired Ewing.

'Please.'

Ewing poured him a cup and waved him to a chair. 'All right, Alan. What's the flap?'

'Twenty-four of the richest men in America have suddenly disappeared. Their families too. Gone underground. Italian-Americans, all of them.'

Ewing nodded slowly. 'I see. What's it all about?'

'We don't know,' replied Richmond, watching him closely.

'Who are we talking about? Lovegni? Ferrandini?'

Richmond nodded. 'And Patellini, Cattagna – all the biggies.'

'Sciacca?'

'No, not Sciacca. He's big, but he's too much of a newcomer. And he's too clearly involved with lower-grade CN activities. We don't think he's a member of the Curia.'

Ewing noted how routinely Richmond used that word. The last time he'd heard it mentioned, it was still only a theory. Clearly the FBI – or at least Richmond's faction of it – now believed the Curia really existed. 'But what's all this got to do with the CIA? It's strictly your country, I'd have thought.'

'We think Ferrandini's in Sicily. Maybe some of the others, too. Also, yesterday, at least fifty men, whose names are on our files, emplaned for various European destinations. We know they all work for Stelio Mascagni, who's officially independent, but it's an open secret that he takes his orders from Ferrandini.'

'Which destinations?'

'Major cities in Germany, Poland, Czechia, Slovakia, Austria, Hungary, Belorussia, Ukraine, Russia.'

'All contiguous. These men of Mascagni's, what are they exactly? Technicians, muscle, buttonmen, what?'

'A bit of a mixed bag. But mainly his best – the ones with heads. The ones he can rely on.'

'Hm. Sounds like a hunt.'

'We think it is. That's why I've come to you.'

'Yes, I appreciate that. But why all the urgency? Phoning me in the middle of the night, a dawn meeting. Couldn't you have waited until office hours?'

'Possibly. I'm not sure. What bothers me is the fact that *these* particular twenty-four families are involved. You see, we have a long-standing directive which requires us to ask the Attorney General's office for permission before touching any of them. Yet on two occasions in the early Eighties – when we wanted to investigate a couple of them, Jack Valacchi and Paul Vanzetti – we rang upstairs as required, and they told us to leave them alone. Hell, we weren't even after *them*; we just wanted to probe their connections with known members of CN.'

Ewing frowned. 'Protection? Is that what you're suggesting?'

Richmond shrugged. 'If it is, I can't see why they even need it. As far as we know, neither Vanzetti nor Valacchi themselves are up to anything; they're too rich with legitimate businesses to bother. Hell, they even have clean dossiers with the IRS! And I'm talking about the *secret* IRS dossiers – the ones they fill up with trivia about somebody deducting a three-martini lunch when he only had two martinis.'

'If they're such good little boys, why did you want to investigate them?'

'Because we thought they were *really* pally with the bad guys, and *in vino veritas* – a boozy dinner together, and a black hat weeps on Vanzetti's shoulder about what a terrible year it's been because he's only shifted fifty million in cocaine.'

'I see. But if you weren't supposed to investigate Ferrandini & Co, how did you find out they'd done a bunk?'

'We heard it on the grapevine, and decided to look into it. We're investigating their disappearance as possible *victims*, not their activities as possible felons, so we're in the clear.'

'Just how long-standing *is* this directive of yours?'

'That's another thing that bothers me. In fact, there are *two* things bothering me. The first is the *age* of the thing: ever since I've been with the Bureau – twenty-five years. I naturally assumed it was one of Hoover's little arrangements. You know what things were like in those days. But when it still hadn't been rescinded after he'd been dead a year, I began to wonder. I spoke to a few oldtimers, and found out it had been in force since World War II. So I came to the conclusion that the directive was some kind of payment for services rendered. You know, for their help in Sicily in '43 – Lucky Luciano and all that.'

Ewing nodded. 'You said there were *two* things bothering you.'

'Right. The directive has been updated several times – I don't know how many. The wording is the same each time, but with new names added. In the early 1950s there were only three or four names on the list. Then it gradually got longer till it reached twenty-four names in 1980. Since then, there's been no change.'

Ewing pulled out an unused pipe from a desk drawer, and sucked on it for a moment. 'You wouldn't have come to me unless you'd spoken to Pollard first.'

'He doesn't know anything.'

'How can you be so sure?'

'He's just not that good an actor. Come on, David. I know how to spring surprises on people just as well as you do, and Pollard's not very bright, even when he knows he needs to be.'

Ewing was dry: 'I'm glad you work for him instead of for me.'

'So am I,' replied Richmond with feeling.

'All right,' said Ewing, suddenly businesslike. 'I get the picture. An agreement between Cosa Nostra and either the Justice Department or J. Edgar, or both, under which they help us out in Sicily, and the FBI turns a blind eye to their other activities. Dollar for dollar, I'd say we got a good deal. Besides, I thought the Curia was supposed to be almost legit. That's what you told me at that cocktail party at the White House last year, anyhow. And if Valacchi and Vanzetti are as clean-nosed as you make out, then it still is. Now all of a sudden it panics over something, and everybody hits the mattress. What do you want me to do, Alan?'

'Two things. One's official: find out what's going on in Europe. The second's off the record: talk to the AG's office and State. This whole deal is obviously some super-secret, unofficial arrangement at the highest level. You've got better contacts than I have: you're Ivy League; I'm public school.'

'Maybe. But if they haven't told me before, why should they tell me now?'

'Because something's happened, David,' replied Richmond with a suspicious glint in his eye that made Ewing realise the other man momentarily suspected him of holding out on him.

Abruptly Ewing felt annoyed. It was partly because of the stupid incident with the boy on the bicycle – what the hell was he doing riding a bicycle about when the sun hadn't properly got out of bed, anyway? – and partly because of Richmond's uncalled-for innuendos and his wholly irritating, superb imagination and his equally irritating on-the-nose hunches.

'In case the point has escaped you,' he replied acidly, 'what you're suggesting is that the government of the United States has contrived some agreement with an entity regarded as non-sovereign, the existence of which agreement being known to neither its internal nor external security services.' No one was the equal of Ewing when it came to improvising professional-sounding language in the field of public international law.

Richmond regarded him speculatively. 'I know,' he replied.

When Richmond had gone, Ewing sucked on his pipe for a minute more. He glanced at his watch. It was twenty past six. He reached for the telephone and dialled Phil McCarthy, the chairman of the State Department Policy Committee. McCarthy was an early bird. He would be doing his daily workout in his private gym.

'Phil? It's David Ewing. Listen, the FBI has a standing directive basically amounting to a hands-off order concerning twenty-four Italian-American families. You wouldn't happen to know anything about it, would you?'

There was a pause, but McCarthy's reply was relaxed. 'As a

matter of fact, yes. Why? Any problem with it?'

'I don't know. All I can tell you is that the heads of those families have all suddenly disappeared. Run to earth, by the sounds of it. But there are indications which suggest they've meanwhile organised some kind of manhunt in Europe.'

Now the pause was longer. 'I think, David, it might be a good idea if you came over for breakfast.'

'I'm on my way.' Ewing hung up.

It took him twenty minutes to reach McCarthy's detached suburban house. McCarthy himself, dressed in a tracksuit, was sitting at a table on the verandah sipping orange juice. He waved Ewing to a chair opposite and poured him some coffee.

'Tell me what you know,' said McCarthy, and Ewing gave him an account of his meeting with Richmond. When he had finished, McCarthy sat in thoughtful silence for a long while. 'I don't like the sound of it,' he said at last.

Ewing's reply was patient. 'Phil, if I'm to be at all useful in Europe, I'm going to need to know what's at the back of this.'

McCarthy looked at him for a moment, then nodded. 'The truth is it might be something involving only themselves – some private problem – or it might be connected with something called the Belvedere Accords. Basically those were a set of agreements between the United States government and certain members of what is conventionally called the Mafia.'

'How come the CIA doesn't know anything about it?'

'Why should you? The Accords were signed in 1943. They predate the existence of the CIA. And I'm afraid, David, I can't tell you the whole story even now. You know the *Need to Know* rule as well as I do. But what I can tell you is that, in essence, the agreements were, on the side of the government, a promise of protection; and, on the side of the Sicilian families, an undertaking to assist us in the prosecution of the war.'

'If you're talking about what Lucky Luciano did, I already know about it. I thought that was more or less common knowledge.'

McCarthy shook his head. 'No, David. I'm afraid there's more to it than that. What I can tell you is that the families kept the original contract as a guarantee against the government's reneging on the agreement afterwards. If it were ever made public, it would do us the most immense damage. I'm going to have to take advice on this – I'll talk to the Secretary of State this morning – but, for the time being, my advice to you is to give this matter top priority. Try and find out what they're up to in Europe if you can, but what's more important . . .' he paused ' . . . is that you provide assistance.'

Ewing blinked. '*Help* them? Help the Mafia?'

'Yes, David. Help them. If those twenty-four families are out looking

183

for somebody, I'd say it's in the vital interests of this country that they find him.'

Ewing could only shake his head in wonderment. Then a thought occurred to him. 'Suppose they want to kill him?'

McCarthy's expression became suddenly inscrutable. 'I think, David, I've already made myself quite clear.'

21

McCarthy spoke to the Secretary of State at ten past nine. The latter rang the White House requesting an urgent meeting. At ten o'clock the President received both men in the Oval Office.

'Well, what's up? I've cancelled two engagements for this.'

McCarthy began at once. 'Mr President, in 1943 there was a secret agreement, known as the Belvedere Accords, between the United States government and the patriarchs of at least twenty-four private families. Those families were all of Sicilian descent.' He took a deep breath. 'The Mafia.'

The President blinked. 'The *government* of the United States of America signed a secret agreement with the *Mafia*?'

'I'm afraid so. More precisely, with certain members of CN who formed a commission, called the Curia.'

'What the hell for?'

'Because of the situation in the European theatre of war.'

The President went over to a sideboard where a Cona machine was bubbling gently, and poured himself a cup of coffee. 'Sounds like a good plot for a thriller. So 1943, you say. Stalingrad was in January, Kursk in the summer. We wrapped up North Africa and invaded Italy. All right, I'm in the time frame. What was the matter with the situation?'

'Put briefly, we weren't in control of it. I don't know how much you know about the political side of things during the war, Mr President, but there were two main factors influencing most of the decisions taken at the top level: Stalin's intentions in postwar Europe, and the A-bomb.'

'I know the basics. The American public was hankering to get back at Japan because of Pearl Harbor, but the government decided Germany was the more dangerous enemy as it was scientifically more advanced. There was a danger they might develop the bomb before we did, so the war plan we agreed with the British was designed to defeat Germany as quickly as possible.'

'Exactly, Mr President. That was the paramount aim of the war. The point is, if you look at the geography of Europe, it's easy to see that Germany's southern flank was very well protected. The Alps form a nearly impenetrable barrier, and the passes through the mountains could have been defended by the Germans with just a couple of regiments. It would have been impossible to defeat Germany that way. So even invading Italy and knocking her out of the war would have been of practically no strategic value.'

The President grunted. 'In the First World War, Italy fought *against* the Germans. That had practically no effect at all.'

'Right. Italy's presence on one side or the other couldn't seriously affect the main battle against the Germans.'

'Okay. The attack had to go over the Channel and through France – which it did. Go on.'

McCarthy pulled out an ancient file from his briefcase. 'This was a top-secret study carried out – on President Roosevelt's orders – by the State Department, in preparation for the Casablanca conference.' He passed the file across the desk. 'You'll find a summary at the end.'

The President turned to the back page and read the conclusions. 'Hm. I had no idea things had been as black as this. Were the British told about this study?'

'No, sir. In fact, Roosevelt pulled a fast one on them. At the press conference at the end of the Casablanca meeting, he made an announcement – without prior consultation with Churchill – to the effect that the Allies were demanding the unconditional surrender of the Axis powers. Italy wasn't exempt. Churchill was not very happy about it. The general public belief has always been that Roosevelt spoke without thinking. In fact it was an essential part of US government policy.'

'Where does the Mafia come into all this?'

Now McCarthy pulled out a second file. 'This is a copy of the Belvedere Accords.' He passed it to the President – and watched the colour drain from his face as he read through the three pages it contained.

'Christ in Heaven!' the head of state breathed. 'Why haven't I been told about this before?'

'It's always been regarded as a dormant issue, Mr President. It was never expected to come to light. Its access has always been restricted to as few people as possible, by direct order of President Roosevelt himself. None of his successors needed to be told, except Kennedy.'

The President blinked at him. 'What's happened, Phil?' he asked quietly.

'As I said, this is a copy. The original document was given to the Curia as a protective guarantee to dissuade us from taking action against its members. They then set up a system which would lead to the automatic publication of the Accords if we ever violated them. And, as you can see, the political damage ensuing, if all this got out, made it too dangerous to probe their scheme. We have never known

186

for sure exactly how many families were involved. President Roosevelt dealt directly with Salvatore Ferrandini, who was supposed to select the other members of the Curia in secret. Ferrandini agreed to limit the total membership to between twenty and thirty men. This arrangement was designed to make it difficult for us to discover who had taken custody of the original document.

'However, J. Edgar Hoover persuaded Roosevelt that, even if no action was to be taken against the families, the government should still know how many were involved, and who they all were. He wanted to initiate a long-term investigation. Roosevelt finally agreed, but he would not allow any of J. Edgar's lily-white boys to have anything to do with it, and, much to Hoover's annoyance, gave the task to the Attorney General. Whenever a family was identified, Justice would add its name to a standing hands-off order. By 1980, that order listed twenty-four families, and none has since been added, although there was no guarantee that there weren't a further six still lurking in the backwoods.

'This morning I was informed that, five days ago, the current heads of those twenty-four families disappeared. We have reason to believe that several of them are now over in Europe. Additionally, a large number of men has been sent to various central European countries on an unknown mission. The pattern of their activity suggests some kind of manhunt is in progress.'

McCarthy looked pensive for a moment. Then he turned to the President. 'I've given all this careful thought. I've tried to imagine all sorts of reasons for this sudden activity. But I'm very much afraid, Mr President, that there is only one convincing rationale. The fact that all twenty-four of them reacted simultaneously, as if they were in personal danger, leads me to believe they received warning from some source that they *were* in fact in danger.' He paused again, to select his words with care. 'So it is my belief that the mechanism to make public the Accords has been set in motion. And I think whoever the families are hunting is the agent designated to do so.'

There was absolute silence as the President absorbed this analysis. Then he murmured, 'If you're right, then we're smack bang in the middle of the greatest crisis since Watergate.'

The Secretary of State shook his head. 'Watergate was peanuts in comparison.'

McCarthy nodded his agreement. 'Watergate was messy, but it was a domestic issue. This one has wide international dimensions, too. Among other consequences, it would tear NATO apart.'

The President regarded him tensely for several moments. 'How does their system work?'

'We've never known. We don't even know who set it up. In fact, the members of the Curia themselves don't know who set it up. They used a secret lottery to select one of their number to do it. In the envelope with the Accords, Ferrandini included a page outlining a series of possible systems, so that whoever won the lottery would have an idea of what to do. But it was agreed that the winner would never divulge either his identity or how the system operated. He would take the secret with him to the grave, but the mechanism would be designed to remain operational for well beyond the lifetimes of all the original members of the Curia. Both Roosevelt and Harry Hopkins, his closest adviser, suspected Ferrandini himself would take charge of the Accords, but J. Edgar thought that was too obvious. He couldn't believe that Ferrandini would place the Accords – and by implication, his own fate – in the hands of the one man positively known to be a member of the Curia.'

'Suppose it was a double bluff?'

McCarthy shrugged. 'Who knows? In fact, that's the whole point of Ferrandini's scheme: it could very well be a double bluff. But since it might not be, we didn't dare touch him, because if we were wrong, it would have triggered the system. Ferrandini's been dead for nineteen years, in any case; and we can be sure that, even if he did set it up, he wouldn't have told anybody how it operated, because that would have endangered his own son. Only one member of the original Curia is still living, but he can't have been the man who set up the scheme, because otherwise he would know how to stop it. So we're talking about a system which is still in place, yet no one alive knows how it works.

'This is a list of the twenty-four.'

McCarthy handed another sheet of paper to the President, who stopped his pacing to peruse it. 'God, these are some of the richest men in the country! I thought they were all legitimate.'

'With respect to mainstream CN activities, they are. They have no need to involve themselves. In fact, that was one of Ferrandini's objectives. He wanted to take his family out of the rackets. That suited Roosevelt because his concern was to avoid the government being endlessly blackmailed by the families. By making everybody too rich to want to, he eliminated the danger.'

'But, for God's sake, the government *has* been blackmailed! Ever since the war!'

'Only within the terms of the Accords. No new demands have ever been made.'

'None needed to be,' the President replied drily. 'How were we supposed to give protection to these families, if we didn't know who they were?'

'Ferrandini supplied a list of coded messages. If anyone entitled to protection required it, he would send a message to Justice. He'd be identifying himself, of course, but at least he'd get the police off his back. In fact, only two men have ever required it, and *they* were being investigated incidentally.'

The President resumed his pacing. 'Who signed these Accords?'

'The original document had a fourth page – a letter, written by Roosevelt, explaining the rationale for certain clauses in the agreement, and signed by him, J. Edgar, five top members of his cabinet and the US ambassador to the Vatican. They're called the Belvedere Accords because the document was notarised in the Belvedere Palace in the Vatican City. It was witnessed there by two men: Eugenio Pacelli and his secretary Giovanni Montini. They're better known as Popes Pius XII and Paul VI.'

22

The river banks were densely populated with willows – mainly Northern and Triandra, with the occasional weeping Babylonica – which screened Adam Drew from hostile eyes. From time to time the trees thinned, revealing meadows and wheatfields which spread away flat as far as the eye could see, the landscape sprinkled with poplars whose tops were uniformly bent towards the northwest, betraying the direction of the prevailing wind. Sometimes a line of pylons strutted across the plain, like alien invaders. And here and there in the distance was a church spire or onion dome surrounded by its clutch of houses.

The sun beating down made everything seem lonely and sinister.

But the loneliness had given Trnka an opportunity to get some rest, because now Adam could take the wheel in safety. By now, their relationship had subtly evolved into friendship. Although Drew had forced the alliance, the Czech had come to terms with the situation.

Some houses were approaching, so Adam called down, 'Wake up, Martin. We're just coming into Kolín.'

Trnka groaned and came up to take the wheel, while Drew went below.

At Kolín, the Labe ran through a shallow gorge. The river banks were connected in the centre of the town by three bridges – pedestrian, road and rail – each separated by about a hundred yards. Between the first two bridges stood a lock – the seventeenth Drew had passed through since leaving Ústí. The downstream gates already stood open, so Martin guided the barge directly inside.

The water had almost risen to the upriver level, when over the road bridge above there passed a Mitsubishi Galant, its sleek lines and dark metallic colour combining to give it a sinister aura.

Tomáš Palacký slowed sharply. The Saturday afternoon traffic was light, and the road over the bridge was four lanes wide, but someone had run out of petrol and was now pushing his ancient Volkswagen along the slower of the two southbound lanes. Momentarily trapped behind him, Palacký yawned, glancing down uninterestedly at the barge in the lock. Then a gap opened up in the fast lane, so he was able to overtake the Volkswagen. Once past it, he put his foot down.

A slight frown came to his face, as he realised something was now bothering him.

But before he could identify it, a Fiat in the slow lane suddenly swung out in front of him, forcing him to slam on his brakes. Palacký narrowly averted running into the back of it, and a string of murderous expletives passed through his mind. A moment later he was able to overtake the Fiat. He treated its negligent driver to a cool look. But the incident had made Palacký forget his troubling thought.

Its innocent cause was now emerging from the Kolín lock. Drew came back up on deck when the town was behind them. 'Do you want me to take over again?'

'No, I'm okay now.'

Adam walked along the catwalk towards the prow, lay down on the cover of the forward hold and smoked a cigarette, thinking about his situation.

Until this present assignment he'd never given much thought to crime as a full-time activity, but the books he had now read had already brought him to adopt more ambivalent attitudes. Some criminals were engaged in straightforward theft, an activity universally condemned because it deprived someone else of the fruits of their labour. But others, although technically breaking the law, involved themselves in activities which could not be condemned so easily. Bootleggers, for example, had supplied alcohol to countless ordinary citizens who considered Prohibition a bad law and happily disobeyed it. The American government had eventually agreed with them and repealed the ban. Should those men who had engaged in supplying alcohol when it was forbidden still be classified as criminals when it wasn't? And didn't the same argument apply to a whole range of illegal activities, such as prostitution, gambling and the distribution of narcotics?

True, the organisers frequently had to resort to violence and even murder, but, equally true, this arose because the law refused to protect those activities that it had declared illegal, which was a point the general public tended to overlook. So, if a bootlegger signed a distribution contract with his supplier, since this agreement was unenforceable in law, he had no option except to provide himself with the same protection that man had employed throughout most of his existence – self-defence. If he couldn't turn to the law of the land, he would turn to the law of the jungle.

Simplistically, the general public saw only two groups: those who broke the law of the land and those who tried to enforce it. But in the jungle, matters were not – could not – be so simple. There were as many enemies as conflicting interests, and alliances shifted constantly under the pressure of changing circumstances.

But whatever Salvatore's background might have been, he had not asked Adam to commit any crime; instead, he had entrusted to him the safety of his own family. And Drew had given him a solemn undertaking to do so – an undertaking given in reality to Salvatore's representatives, but emotionally to his ghost.

The sun made Adam drowsy. He closed his eyes and saw a different ghost – the cold, white mist, skimming along the sheer face of the Eiger towering impossibly above him – as menacing as the Belvedere Accords.

Jan Hurban lived in a sumptuous apartment overlooking the Charles Bridge in Prague, and Ned Moreno was now using it as his headquarters. He picked up the telephone to ring Ferrandini.

'We've finally had a positive sighting. The border guard who checked his passport between Bad Schandau and Děčín remembers he was definitely on board the Prague train last night.'

'But not when it reached Prague. In how many places did it stop on the way?'

'After Děčín, two: Ústí nad Labem and Lovosice. I've put a dozen men in all three towns.'

'But why should he get off at any of those places? What's there?'

'Not much. Maybe he's got a friend in one of them. Some mountaineering chum, perhaps.'

Ferrandini grunted. 'What's the situation with the police?'

'Hurban's very well connected. He has a dozen high-ranking contacts ready to help. The story being put out is that Drew's wanted in connection with a bank robbery in Prague last month, but they're not giving out his nationality, because the British embassy would start asking a lot of awkward questions.'

'Okay. What about the frontiers?'

'There are thirteen border crossings between Czechia and Slovakia,' he reported, 'but the frontier's like a sieve. There are scores of places where he can just walk across. The risk of getting caught is minimal. But there wouldn't be any advantage to him in going to Slovakia at all, unless he intends crossing into the Ukraine directly, because if, instead, he goes north into Poland or south into Hungary, he just gives himself one more frontier to cross.'

'How many crossings are there into the Ukraine?'

'Just one.'

'And on the other frontiers?'

'Seven into Poland, two into Austria and twelve into Hungary.'

'But what if he crosses into Poland from Czechia, and then into Belorussia? That gives him the same number of frontiers.'

'I've already thought of that. There are nineteen Polish checkpoints and I've got them all well covered.'

192

'And if he takes some route over the mountains? He is a mountaineer, remember.'

'If he does, he'll just be giving us more time to get organised in Russia. His only hope is to move fast.'

As the lock gates opened, Adam looked out of the porthole in Martin's cabin at the townlet of Týnec nad Labem. Most of it lay on the far side of a low hill, so that what remained in view was a charming little village, with pretty cottages standing among an abundance of weeping willows and poplars. A hundred and fifty yards upstream of the lock stood a bridge and, just beyond it, was a small harbour, now empty, for laying up river craft. Its mouth faced upstream so that, if any vessel unmoored, it wouldn't float away.

Martin backed the barge into the harbour, then tied up at the quayside. There didn't seem to be anyone around, but, following Adam's advice to do everything he would normally do if he was alone, Trnka locked the pilothouse, sent Astor up onto the roof to stand guard, and walked across the bridge to the village, whistling.

While he was gone, Adam kept watch from the cabin porthole. Few vehicles used the bridge, but he listened carefully to the noise of their engines for any sign that the drivers might be taking an interest in the barge.

An hour later he heard the door being unlocked, then Martin climbed down into the cabin. 'He accepts your offer. He also knows someone in Košice who can get you into the Ukraine. A smuggler.'

Drew didn't much like the sound of the idea. A smuggler might easily regard him as just another commodity to be haggled over, then *handed* over. 'We'll think about that later. What about the Slovak frontier?'

'That's no problem. There are lots of places where you can just walk across. Karel knows one of them. I'll have to come to Košice with you – to translate. Karel only speaks Czech.'

'What about your barge? Someone might steal the cargo.'

'That's a risk I'll just have to take. If I'm going to get that twenty thousand, I'd better make sure you're still around to pay it.'

They waited until nightfall. At half past nine, a cream Skoda 1203M van came across the bridge, turned down on to the quay and pulled up beside the barge. Adam and the dog climbed into the back, while Martin slid in alongside the driver. The vehicle reversed along the quay, turned around and drove back across the bridge, watched idly by Old Peter who was walking in the other direction to his usual spot, where he would lean against a parapet as he puffed on his pipe, enjoying the peace of the still evening. Sometimes he looked upriver, towards its birth – 1390 metres up, in the Riesengebirge – the Giant Mountains – between Czechia and Poland; sometimes he looked downriver, towards its death – 1165 kilometres old – in the North Sea.

Karel Juránek was an amateur footballer with a strong body. He was too broad-faced to be handsome, but he made up for it with an easy, ready smile. He lived in a small house just outside the town. His dark-haired wife Sylva had won the local beauty competition the year before their marriage, and Karel sometimes called her 'Miss Týnec'. The evening meal that she'd prepared was a grotesque-looking stew which turned out delicious. Adam ate four helpings. Neither Karel nor Sylva had much German and their English was worse, so everything had to be translated and the conversation was slow.

Adam asked Karel, 'What's the name of this smuggler?'

'Miro Čarnogurský.'

'How did you get to know him?'

'I did my military service in Košice. That was way back in 1989, before Czechoslovakia split up. I earned a bit of pocket money doing a few jobs for him. Back then, things were really bad here. Just about everybody was working some black-market deal or other. You had to. In those days a weekly wage was less than fifteen dollars, whereas a decent Western-made shirt cost at least twice that much.'

Adam nodded. He knew all this. 'Yes, but what exactly *were* those jobs you did for Čarnogurský?'

Karel was vague. 'A little bit of this; a little bit of that.'

Adam shrugged.

By now, both he and Martin were very tired, so they turned in early. They fell asleep to the faint sounds of some Western on the television downstairs.

Karel woke them at four in the morning, and they were fed again. By half past they were on the road to the east, Adam staying out of sight in the back. It had rained during the night and the sky was still overcast, so the dawn was depressing.

It was Sunday and almost no other vehicle shared the road with them, which made Adam feel uncomfortably conspicuous. At least they could make good time, however, and they reached the Moravian capital of Brno in under two hours. Here Karel took the road to Trenčín, which brought them by eight o'clock to a village called Starý Hrozenkov, just two kilometres from the Slovak frontier. The van stopped a few hundred yards outside it.

Adam, Martin and the dog got out and, following Karel's directions, set off through the trees of a pine wood. In different weather it might have been a pleasant walk, but the rain collected by the trees during the night now dripped incessantly on them. Drew felt they were aiming for him deliberately.

They came back to the road three-quarters of an hour later, and Karel picked them up again. Adam was now in Slovakia. The crossing had been very easy, but he wasn't surprised. The untraumatic mitosis of Czechoslovakia had left the daughter states with too many interconnections for them to be truly separate. The border was more a matter of cultural and linguistic pride than a serious attempt to seal off either state from the other. But the Ukrainian frontier, Adam knew, would be very different.

A quarter of an hour later they passed through Trenčín, dominated by its ancient fortress on a craggy hill above the river Váh. Cliff-top castles appeared regularly along the valley, while mist clung to the wooded hillsides in the pale light.

Soon it was raining again. Adam wasn't surprised. They were approaching the Tatras, where the summer months were often the wettest. The rain didn't last long, however, and shortly after they'd passed Žilina, gaps in the clouds began opening up.

They stopped for a lunch of ham rolls and beer at a layby just outside Východná. The scenery was spectacular. To the south stood the Low Tatras, the mountains with a silly name; to the north, were the High Tatras, the youngest range in Europe. Clouds hugged the summits of both sierras, while the sky over the valley between them was clear blue.

They drove on, passing futuristic hotels nestling among the pines. As they approached Poprad, the valley broadened into a great plain, the Tatras rising out of it like an immense saw. Just as the van went by, a TU 134 passenger plane was landing at the city's tiny airport. Poprad – a mass of white, high-rise buildings, bright in the afternoon sunlight – functioned as a base for tourists wanting to explore the mountains.

Tomáš Palacký had lunch at a bar in Týnec nad Labem. He was tired. He'd spent the whole morning and all Saturday driving around eastern Bohemia, brandishing Drew's photograph. Later as he was driving down the hill towards the bridge over the Labe, he spotted a solitary barge tied up in the little harbour, and remembered the one he had seen in the Kolín lock the day before. Palacký was a middle-ranker in Hurban's organisation, so he wasn't paid to think. But now he wondered whether the big shots had ever considered that Drew might be travelling by river.

Then it dawned on him that this barge was very similar to the one he'd seen the day before.

Palacký drove down onto the quay, and got out. The padlock on the pilothouse door made it clear no one was on board. The registration number of the barge was L Pa 282 Cs, which meant it came from Prague.

'Went off in a van, they did,' said a gruff voice behind him.

Palacký turned to see an old man shuffling along the quay, an unlit pipe clenched in his teeth.

'How many?'

'Two men 'n' a dog. And the driver of the van.' Old Peter came to a stop beside him. 'Friends o' yours, are they?'

'Sort of,' replied Palacký. He whipped out Adam's photo. 'Was this man one of them?'

Old Peter looked at it, rubbing his chin. 'Mighta been. Couldn't see very well. It was dark.'

Palacký felt a tingle at the base of his spine. 'What time did they leave?'

'Not long after sundown. Musta been about 'alf past nine.'

Palacky glanced at his watch: quarter to two.

'What kind of van was it?'

'Skoda 1203M. Cream.'

'Did you notice the registration?'

'Nope. Didn' look. What they do, rob a bank?'

'Thanks for your help.' Palacký hurried back to his Mitsubishi and sped away.

Old Peter shuffled along to the bridge, to light his pipe and lean against the parapet watching the river drift slowly by – just as he had done for twenty years – and wait for death. It would not be long in coming now. Quietly one night in his sleep, he hoped, with a final tired gasp from a tired old man, consoled by the knowledge that his river would still be drifting by in the morning.

Jan Hurban was unbuckling his seatbelt aboard Ned Moreno's plane, just after takeoff, when Palacký called to tell him his suspicion about the barge. Hurban at once relayed the information to a friend in the Prague police, Captain Havel, who fed the barge's registration number into the police computer. Trnka's particulars came up on the monitor at once. Havel phoned Martin's home number, but there was no reply. He drummed his fingers on the desktop for a moment, thinking. Then he turned to his assistant. 'The passage of river craft is logged by the lock-keepers, isn't it?'

'I should think so.'

'Okay. Start phoning them. Find out what time this barge last went through.' He handed him a note with the registration number. 'Start with the Střekov lock.'

A short while later, the assistant reported, 'The barge passed through Střekov at 5.15 yesterday afternoon. That's more than four hours before the *Metropol* arrived at Ústí. It weakens the hypothesis that the third man in Týnec was Drew.'

'Maybe not. The locks close early. Somewhere around six or seven at this time of year. Let's find out where Trnka stopped for the night. Phone the next lock along.'

Within minutes, the assistant was excitedly informing his chief, 'It travelled by night! The keeper says barges only do so in an emergency!'

Havel grabbed his telephone and quickly informed Hurban, who accepted the news with equanimity. 'What about the Skoda van?'

'That's not such a useful clue. There are thousands of 1203Ms, and cream is the most common colour. In the area of Týnec alone, there are more than a hundred. We've started checking up on their owners, but that's likely to take some time.'

'Too much time, considering Drew has more than a sixteen-hour lead on us,' replied Hurban. 'Okay, thanks.' He hung up, then phoned a police contact in the Slovak capital of Bratislava and asked him to put out a general alert for a cream Skoda van with any Czech registration number.

Still travelling eastwards, Adam and his companions came out of the high mountains and reached the university town of Prešov just before four o'clock. They were now only some fifty miles from the Ukrainian frontier. Košice lay due south, connected to Prešov by thirty-five kilometres of modern motorway. Karel was not very familiar with the city, so he merely followed the signs for Košice. Just as they went by, a policeman was relieving himself behind a tree. He had heard the general alert only ten minutes previously, so watching the van disappear around a bend he finished the business in hand and made a beeline for a phone.

None of the occupants of the Skoda had spotted him, but as they were approaching the motorway, Martin suddenly exclaimed, 'There's a police roadblock!' Seeing it in the same instant, Karel braked sharply, just managing to take a turn-off into a housing estate of high-rise apartment blocks. The police had set up their checkpoint only minutes before, but sealing off all the southern exits from Prešov would require two more roadblocks and, before they were in place, Karel managed to slip through the backstreets to the old road to Košice, which ran parallel to the motorway.

At just that moment Ned Moreno's plane was touching down at the little airport of Košice, the capital of eastern Slovakia. He was accompanied by Jan Hurban and a top-notch marksman called Frank Zucca from Chicago, sent in by Stelio. Hurban had supplied him with a pre-tested Heckler & Koch rifle, with infrared nightscope, in a long rosewood case.

Twenty minutes later the party reached police headquarters, where

197

they were greeted by Janko Tajovský, the Colonel of Police. Czech and Slovak were mutually comprehensible languages, but out of politeness he spoke in Czech.

'A cream Skoda 1203M van with a Kolín registration number was spotted passing through Prešov twenty-five minutes ago.'

Hurban translated the report into English, and Ned crossed to study a wall map of the region.

The single border crossing into the Ukraine, at a village called Vyšné Nemecké, was approached by just one main highway from Michalovce. Few minor roads joined it. If Drew intended crossing by road, the border guards would pick him up. And if he intended taking some cross-country route, a dozen correctly-positioned roadblocks would prevent him from reaching the frontier at all.

Tajovský came alongside Moreno, looking worried. 'The frontier is a hundred kilometres long, and that's a lot of ground to cover. The problem is that most of my people are a long way from Prešov, covering other areas. It will take too long to reposition them.'

When he heard the translation, Ned looked up sharply. 'Where the hell has he deployed his men?'

The Colonel began pointing to some red markers on the map. Moreno had noticed them before, but hadn't associated them with the manhunt for Drew. Now he studied the map, his jaw rapidly clenching. Tajovský was an imbecile! He'd deployed the bulk of his men too far back. The Colonel had thus left himself with just a few dozen men to cover a hundred kilometres of frontier. The idiot had turned a bowl into a sieve!

Seeing Moreno's expression, Tajovský explained defensively, 'I picked the best places to cover all the frontiers.'

'There was no need to worry about the north and south,' replied Ned. 'I thought I made that clear. If Drew was going into Poland, he'd have crossed from Czechia. So what now?'

Hurban questioned Tajovský, then translated. 'He says the only way we'll have a chance of catching him now is to use the off-duty police, and that's going to provoke a lot of questions.'

'What questions?'

'Up till now he's been playing this business as a routine police matter, and it's already public enough. But if the off-duty police are called in, that would imply a very dangerous person was on the loose. The press would be down on it at once. He says it's up to you, but either we play it quiet and there's a chance he'll slip through, or we go all out and raise a lot of eyebrows.'

'Then raise their fucking eyebrows,' replied Ned coldly.

At once Hurban turned to Tajovský and gave him instructions. The man clearly wasn't at all happy. Police operations of this sort invariably provoked the curiosity of the busybodies in Bratislava. The

Ministry of the Interior would want to know what was going on.

Hurban was politely sympathetic. 'Let's just call it a *big* favour,' he replied quietly.

Tajovský gave a deep sigh and went to the phone.

Zucca sat patiently in an armchair, quietly observing.

23

At just that moment the cream van was spotted a second time. In the little village of Lemešany, eighteen kilometres north of Košice, a police patrol car had stopped a motorcyclist. While one patrolman was idly examining the rider's papers, his companion was leaning in through the window of the police car for the radio microphone, to check up on the motorbike's registration number. So neither man noticed the van approach until it was actually passing. The officer with the radio glanced casually over his right shoulder, did a double take, and yelled out to his companion, gesticulating towards the Skoda.

Drew saw it all. It was unmistakable. He was rumbled.

'Hide the van as quick as you can or we're sunk!'

The road through the village curved to the right. A short distance past the bend, Karel turned off into a narrow street which climbed steeply among detached bungalows with walled gardens. At the point where it levelled off, he made another right turn and stopped.

Adam's companions turned to face him inquiringly. He looked back at them grimly. 'Martin, you'd better warn him this has complicated matters – especially for him.'

A look of uncertainty came over Karel's face when he heard the translation. 'What do you mean?'

'I mean they can trace you through this van. They want me badly. Legal niceties won't bother them. 'You'd better ring Sylva and tell her to get out. *Schnell!*'

The German adverb together with Sylva's name jolted Karel into action. He raced off to find a phone.

Sitting up uneasily, Astor watched him disappear around the corner. He looked up at Adam for reassurance.

'Don't worry,' murmured Drew, stroking the dog's head. 'They won't think *you* know anything.'

Karel returned a few minutes later. 'She's going to stay with an old schoolfriend.'

Adam nodded. It was probably barely secure, but it would have to do. There followed a brief conversation between the two Czechs, then Trnka said, 'He wants to know what the options are.'

'I don't think there *are* any. The people who are after me aren't going to waste their time in trying to sort out who knows what. They'll treat all three of us the same way. As far as I can see, there's only one course open to us – unless we want to be lemmings. If I can get to Russia, there's a chance I can do something to get us all off the hook.'

After Martin had translated this, Drew continued, 'I think there's only one way they could have connected me with this van: someone must have seen us getting into it; which means they can now trace you through your barge registration number.'

'At least they'd know that my family can't be involved,' replied Martin, glancing at Drew for confirmation.

Adam toyed with the idea of lying to him, but after a moment said, 'That doesn't follow, Martin, I'm afraid. They're not clairvoyant. They couldn't be sure some member of your family didn't come aboard at some point.'

Martin remained frozen for a moment, then started to climb out of the van. Adam grasped him by the shoulder.

'Wait Martin; listen to me. I advised Karel to send his wife away because she'd actually met me. Her reactions to their questions would have told them so, and they'd have put her through the mincer. But none of *your* family knows anything about me, so they'd be bewildered by the questions and look it. It wouldn't take long for the police to realise they don't know anything. That wouldn't be so, if they suddenly did a bunk. It would strongly suggest they do know something.'

Martin whispered whitely, 'So everything depends on my mother convincing a bunch of thugs she knows nothing about you?'

'It will probably be the police who'll call on her, Martin; not thugs. And there's another thing. When they find out Sylva has gone to ground, they'll guess we warned her. Since we didn't do the same with *your* family, it will suggest we didn't think it was necessary, because they haven't got anything to do with it.'

Martin nodded slowly. 'Yes, I see that.' He swallowed. 'But Sylva could be in serious trouble.'

'A lot less now than if she stayed at home,' replied Adam, hoping his advice to everyone had been right.

Karel demanded to know what had been said, since he'd heard Sylva's name mentioned several times. The two Czechs quietly discussed the situation among themselves. After a long moment's consideration, Karel pronounced his verdict, and Martin translated. 'Neither of us thinks we have any choice. We're going to have to depend on you.'

His words brought the Eiger erupting into Adam's mind. *Tell me to cut the rope!*

What would you say, if you knew I woke up sweating every night? thought Adam darkly.

'What now?' asked Trnka in a resigned murmur.

Adam wiped a thin layer of perspiration from his brow and turned his attention to the question. 'Find somebody with a car who would like to earn a week's wages overnight.'

'Leave that to me,' said Karel, as if deciding enthusiasm was the best antidote to fear, and got out of the van again. He had called Sylva from a bar called the Drink Pool, on the main road just before the bend. He'd noticed one of the other customers – a man in his late twenties – glancing his way surreptitiously. And too often. Karel returned to the bar and ordered a beer. The man was still there. He was sitting on a bar stool at the counter, watching four hearty types play dominoes at a nearby table. No one else was around, apart from the bartender.

Karel sipped his beer and, when the young man next glanced his way, said, 'Know anyone with a car? Mine's broken down.'

He'd spoken in Slovak, but the young man detected his nationality and replied in Czech. 'I've got one. Where do you have to get to?'

'Just into Košice. I'd pay you for your time.'

The young man smiled demurely. 'That won't be necessary. I was intending to go into town later, anyway. There's nothing to do in Lemešany on a Sunday. Or any other day, if it comes to that. My name's Ján Lodice.'

'Mine's Václav Tyl. Would you mind if we went now? I'm in a bit of a hurry.'

Lodice shook his head and followed him out. As soon as they were in the street, Karel said, 'Look, I really would prefer to pay you. You see, I'm with two friends.'

If Lodice was disappointed, he gave no sign of it. 'I'd charge you if I ran a taxi service, but since I'm a schoolteacher I'll just correct your Slovak.' Karel laughed.

Lodice lived in a house just up the hill, close to where the van was parked. His car was a Citroën ZX which he'd bought second-hand a few weeks before. The two men climbed in, then drove around to pick up the others.

In Karel's absence, Drew had studied one of the detailed maps of the area, which they'd bought at a filling station near Poprad. Less than half an hour had passed since they had been spotted by the police patrol, but he now expected roadblocks to be set up all over the district. The road from Lemešany to Košice ran parallel with the motorway from Prešov. The roads merged five miles to the south, which was the obvious place for a roadblock, and Adam was too realistic to hope they might get through before it was set up. But halfway between Lemešany and the junction was a turn-off which ran over the motorway to a hamlet called Ploské. From here a minor road linked a series of villages and eventually joined the main highway to Michalovce, which would enable them to enter Košice from the east.

Adam had then concocted a little plan with Martin, so when Ján Lodice climbed into the Citroën, Drew was introduced to him as a BBC producer, on the lookout for suitable locations for a television drama set in the days of the Austro-Hungarian empire, who wanted to take a look at Ploské and the neighbouring villages. Intrigued, Lodice was delighted to oblige. Adam sat in a rear corner, massaging Astor between the ears, while keeping a watch on the road behind.

Tajovský's manpower problem gave Adam and his companions the bit of luck they needed. They reached Košice safely.

Karel's smuggler friend lived in the well-to-do Atrium district, but, playing safe, they had Lodice drop them off several streets away.

After they had taken leave of him, the schoolteacher glanced at his watch. It was only quarter past five – far too early for the bars – so he headed for the Petrovov Sad park, intent on cruising. It was a dangerous place after dark, but in the afternoon there were sometimes some interesting people around.

Captain Sabinov, Tajovský's assistant, came into the Colonel's office. 'The van's been found in Lemešany, but there's no sign of the passengers.'

'Have the villagers questioned. *Somebody* must have seen them.'

Walking up the hill towards the Atrium district, Drew asked, 'What exactly were those jobs you did for Čarnogurský?'

Now forced to trust him, Karel replied, 'I ran a few shipments of guns across to Prague for him in an army lorry. Miro fixed things with an officer, so I had all the right papers.'

'Obviously well-connected, then.'

'By every finger, and every toe.'

'Is he married?'

'No, but he's very popular with women. Rich people always are,' replied Karel, ringing the smuggler's doorbell. 'And Miro has a limp, too. From an old bullet wound. He was shot in the knee by a border guard twenty years ago.'

Čarnogurský answered the door in person. On seeing Karel, he broke into a grin. 'I always wondered when *you'd* turn up again.'

'Can we come in? These are friends of mine,' said Karel.

Miro was a dark-looking man, in his early forties, with a beak for a nose, suspicious eyes, and a furtive way of glancing around almost constantly. Astor didn't like him, and everyone knew it.

'The dog too?'

'He'll stay outside.' Martin instructed Astor to lie down and the dog meekly obeyed. Miro limped along the corridor and led the three men into a well-furnished sitting room, then waved them into chairs.

Lying open face down on a table beside his own armchair was a John Le Carré paperback, in English.

'This isn't exactly a social call,' explained Karel. 'I'm bringing you some business.'

'Even better. Are you buying or selling?'

'Buying – a ticket over the border.'

An immediate change came over the smuggler. His eyes swivelled towards Adam and stared. After a moment, he asked in excellent English, 'Is your name Drew?'

'Yes.'

Miro pursed his lips. He did not look at all pleased with this answer. 'A lot of people are looking for you.'

Drew scrutinised the man's expression closely, and waited.

'That's what I gathered from a chat with a friend in the police earlier on. The funny thing is that I had a phone call this morning from a friend in Prague, who's in much the same line of business as me, and he gave me a slightly different version. He said that certain people are prepared to pay a lot of money to get their hands on you – and for anybody who comes into contact with you.' He paused significantly. 'Which would now seem to include me.'

'I'm like King Midas: everybody I touch turns to gold – for some *other* headhunter.'

Miro did not smile. Obviously barely controlling his temper, he asked, 'So what do I do with this leper, who's just walked into my home?'

'What about helping me?'

'Why should I?'

'The people who are after me are trying to stop me doing something. Once it's done, they obviously won't be able to – end of story. Everyone that I've contaminated will be miraculously cured. So your best option is to help me succeed.'

'Help you in what way?'

'To get across the frontier to Užgorod.'

'On its own, *that's* not going to do anything. Where are you heading for?'

Adam looked into the other man's eyes. 'Maybe your best chance would be not to know anything which could help the other side to trap me.'

Miro nodded slowly. 'I suppose that makes sense.' With grim humour, he added, 'This would seem to be the commercial equivalent of a shotgun wedding. I can do business with you, and you alone, but if the other side finds out, maybe I'll soon be able to urinate through my stomach.'

In a serious tone, Adam asked, 'Do you think you should charge me for something which may help you?'

Miro's eyes flashed. 'Let's say you just spilt gravy on my suit, and it's you who's going to pay the dry-cleaning bill. Thirty thousand dollars.'

'I accept. But deferred payment.'

'I've never in my life worked on any basis that wasn't cash on delivery.'

Adam replied patiently, 'Mr Čarnogurský, for me to succeed, I may need every penny I've got.'

The other man pursed his lips. Then, shaking his head morosely, he said, 'I must be out of my mind.'

'One other thing,' said Adam. 'We're going to need transport on the other side. And guns.'

'No problem. Weapons are ten-for-a-penny in the Ukraine. And cars are cheap too, because they're usually stolen. I'll arrange something for you.'

Adam turned to Martin. 'Miro's just confirmed there's a price on all our heads. So we're all in the same boat, and *I'm* the only one who can get everyone off the hook. Now, you and Karel have got to stay out of sight for a while, in any case; but if I have you two with me, and all three of us are armed, we triple our chances of survival. What do you say?'

Martin translated and Karel nodded his agreement at once. Adam felt considerably relieved.

Miro said, 'Okay. Now, the more time that goes by, the tighter they're going to draw the net. Your best chance of slipping through is to move quickly. I'll try to get you to Užgorod tonight. Karel, make something to eat for everybody. I've got some phone calls to make.'

Lieutenant Nálepka hurried out of the Drink Pool to his car and grabbed the radio microphone. Almost at once he was speaking to Captain Sabinov. 'I've just spoken to the owner of a bar in Lemešany. He says a stranger came in around half past four this afternoon and got talking to one of his regular customers – a schoolteacher by the name of Ján Lodice. They left together a few minutes later. Lodice has a car – a red Citroën ZX. The barkeeper doesn't know the number.'

'Okay. Check Lodice's home, in case they're there.'

Sabinov broke the connection and passed on the information to the Colonel. A few moments later, the police computer supplied the registration number of Lodice's vehicle and Tajovský put out a general alert for it. Then he went over to the wall map, where Hurban and Moreno were examining the red markers, which now indicated the locations of the repositioned roadblocks. Just as he was informing them, Sergeant Štúr came in carrying a report which he handed to the Colonel.

Tajovský glanced at it, then said irritably, 'What are you bothering me with *this* for now?'

The sergeant, who had been idly looking at the wall map, apologised, retrieved the report and withdrew. He returned to his office, phoned Miro and told him where the roadblocks were. This was all the information Miro had asked for, and Štúr had assumed he needed it so that one of his routine smuggling operations wouldn't get snared by the manhunt. So, although he heard about the general alert for a car owned by some schoolteacher living in Lemešany, it never occurred to him that Miro might be interested in the information. So he didn't tell him about it.

Ján Lodice left the park at five past seven, feeling very disappointed. He walked back to his car, inserted his key in the lock, and was promptly arrested.

Ten minutes later, the badly frightened schoolteacher was being interrogated by Tajovský personally. What interested Moreno, watching from behind a one-way window, was Drew's route into Košice – from the east – yet he had not offered to pay Lodice to take him closer to the frontier.

Afterwards, conferring with Hurban and Tajovský, he said, 'It looks to me as if they were heading for this city deliberately. I'd say one of them must have a friend here, and close to where they asked Lodice to drop them. Show me on the map.'

Tajovský went over to the street map on the wall and pointed to an intersection close to the police headquarters.

Hurban looked thoughtful. 'If they've taken refuge with just an ordinary friend, they'll be trapped here. But if I was in Drew's shoes, I'd be looking for someone who knows the frontier.'

He'd spoken in English, so only Moreno understood. 'You mean some mountaineering friend?'

Hurban pursed his lips. 'Possibly. But I was thinking of someone like a smuggler.'

Ned looked up sharply. 'Quick! Tell Tajovský!'

But, despite the urgency in Moreno's voice, the Colonel reacted very calmly. He grunted, 'In Košice we've got more black marketeers than telephones.' Turning to Captain Sabinov, he asked 'Which smugglers live near Vojenská Street?'

'At least a dozen, sir. But most of them are small-timers. Andrej Hirka and Miro Čarnogurský both live in the Atrium. They're about the biggest.'

'Okay. Have some men search the homes of all the known smugglers in the district. They can start with Hirka and Čarnogurský. And cordon off the Atrium,' he added as an afterthought.

At eight o'clock, when Adam and his companions left Miro's house, a heavy black cloud lay over the city, but the sun, still quarter of an hour from setting, shone brilliantly from the west.

Miro led the way down a narrow road towards Vojenská Street. He looked about furtively and the others did likewise. Astor, leading the way without knowing where he was going, glanced back occasionally to see if anyone agreed with him.

Miro owned several vehicles, parked in various garages around the neighbourhood. The car they needed today was a Range Rover, and this was kept in one of a cluster of garages, at the bottom of the hill, but on the other side of Vojenská Street. Therefore, technically, it was not within the Atrium district. On driving out from the group of garages, Miro turned left, away from Vojenská Street, just as the first units of the police cordon were arriving. None of the occupants of the Range Rover happened to glance back before the police vehicles disappeared from view, so they were unaware of their narrow escape.

Miro took the main road towards Michalovce. Fifteen kilometres to the east of Košice stood the north-south ridge of the Slanské vrchy. It was not a particularly imposing barrier to the eye, but it had cost the Red Army twenty-two thousand men to capture during World War II, the smuggler informed Adam. The road due east ran through the Dargov Pass. Miro already knew that the police had set up a roadblock there, as at the other three road routes through the Slanské vrchy. But there were far too many footpaths across the ridge to cover them all.

What was worrying Miro, however, was the look of the sky. He had intended to wait at the end of one of the footpaths till dark – so as not to be visible to any patrolling helicopters – and make the crossing without headlights. Since he knew the footpaths well, there would be little problem. But if it rained – and the black cloud above them threatened a deluge – the ground would become a mire, which even his four-wheel drive would need some light to cope with. True, heavy rain was likely to ground the helicopters, but the Range Rover's headlights would be visible a long way by ground forces. It might be better to try to cross in daylight, and hope it rained.

Lightning flashed in the east.

Finally making up his mind that he couldn't risk the long footpath he had originally decided on, he turned off the main road, taking a narrow lane which threaded its way, parallel to the ridge, through a series of villages to Červenica, fifteen kilometres to the north. By the time they reached it, it was almost dark, and that was when the heavens opened. After stopping to attach chains to the wheels, Miro – soaked through – climbed back into the Range Rover, then started along the muddy footpath.

* * *

Captain Sabinov made his report in an excited voice. 'They're with Čarnogurský! A neighbour says she saw him leave his house with three men and a dog, half an hour ago.'

'What about the cordon?'

'He left the area before it was in place.'

'Do we know which part of the frontier Čarnogurský operates?'

'I'll try and find out, sir.'

'And put out an alert for all vehicles under his name.'

Five tortuous miles later, the Range Rover came down into the village of Zámutov, on the far side of the Slanské vrchy. The rain was now much less intense. The villages here were in total darkness.

'Rain must have knocked out the power supply in this area,' explained Miro. 'It still happens now and again. Seven years since we gave up planned inefficiency, and a drop of water still knocks everything to hell.'

Captain Sabinov came into Tajovský's office, accompanied by Sergeant Štúr. 'Tell the Colonel what you told me.'

Štúr looked nervous. 'Well, sir, I did hear one rumour about Čarnogurský. I was told one of the sections of frontier he operates across is near Husák.'

Hearing the translation, Moreno said, 'Then let's go there. I want to see for myself. Ask Tajovský to call up a helicopter.'

At just before ten o'clock, the Range Rover reached Michalovce, where the narrow European railway gauge came to an end and the broad Russian gauge began. The street lighting was working here, though it might have been better for the town if it hadn't been. Miro drove into a housing estate of cheap apartment blocks, built in horrendous postwar Stalinist style, and pulled up before a grim, nine-storey tower in a street appropriately named after Kiev. Stepping out, he hurried through the drizzle into the building. In a first-floor apartment he made several telephone calls. One of them was to Sergeant Štúr.

On returning to the Range Rover, Miro's expression was grave. He climbed in, restarted the engine and drove off at once.

'What's up?' asked Adam.

'The police know I'm involved. There's an alert out for all my cars. Including this one.'

'My God,' breathed Adam. 'Is there anywhere you can hide?'

Miro shook his head. 'If it was just the police who were after me, then yes. But your friends are putting the word out in the underworld too. Pretty soon, everybody I deal with will know there's a price on my head. There are two or three people in Košice I could count on, but the police can easily find out who they are.' He paused. 'To be absolutely frank with you, I don't think our chances of reaching the frontier now are at all good, but there's nowhere else for us to go. If we succeed, then maybe you'll be able to do something for me. In the meantime, I think my best bet's to lie low in some log cabin in the Ukraine. It wouldn't be comfortable, but at least I might live to write a book about the experience.' In a quieter voice – more marvelling than resentful – he said, 'This afternoon, I was quietly reading a novel, the doorbell rang and Mr Catastrophe walked in.'

There was a pause while he let Adam absorb this. Then he continued, 'So, my friend, I'm in this up to my neck. If you don't succeed, I think I'm a dead duck. So I'd better do the best job I can.'

'What's the plan?'

'You'll go in an ambulance – and you'd better pray the driver hasn't yet heard how much you're worth. We'll meet at the place where I'm going to try to get us across the frontier.'

'Why aren't you coming in the ambulance too?'·

'Because we're going to need the Range Rover. A friend of mine in the police has put everybody on the wrong track, so maybe the place where I want to cross won't be so closely patrolled. But there's a mile of open ground that we'll have to cover – and fast, because the helicopters will be passing frequently. You three can run; I can't.'

'Did your police friend tell you where the roadblocks are?'

'The fixed ones, yes. The problem is that there are a dozen mobile units and God knows where *they'll* be. But we've got to move right now, because the later it gets, the less traffic there'll be on the roads and we'll be too conspicuous. Now, since I've got to take the Range Rover with me, anyway, and this is one of the vehicles the police will be watching for, what I've decided to do is to provide a bit of a diversion. I'll be driving ahead of you, then if I'm stopped, with any luck the cops will be too busy talking to me to pay any attention to the vehicles following. It's no sacrifice, of course, because I'm just as likely to get nabbed if I'm doing something intelligent, like distracting the men who nab me, as I'd be if I was just sulking over what a bastard you are. But it would be pointless just getting you close to the frontier, if I can't get you across it. So I've arranged some backup for myself. A friend of mine is on his way. He's one of the people I said I could count on. I doubt the police will have put together a list of my friends yet, so he shouldn't have any problem. If anything happens to me, he'll show you the way. He may take a while in getting here because he's coming from Košice.'

They soon left the town behind them. The rendezvous Miro had arranged was on a quiet, unlit road on the northern shore of the so-called Slovak Sea, a big reservoir created in the 1960s for industrial purposes. The ambulance was already waiting for them. The driver was a fat woman in her forties called Božena. She was accompanied by a pimply young man, grinning incessantly, who nobody bothered to introduce.

Miro drove away at once. Božena waited a minute, then followed. Their route swung all the way around the Slovak Sea and, at a small town called Sobrance, returned to the main road eastwards, which they were obliged to use for two kilometres because no safe backroads were available. And it was just before the village of Tibava, in which they were supposed to turn northwards again, that Miro was flagged down by the police. He knew both patrolmen, and had even bribed them to look the other way a few times, but he doubted it would work today.

'Sorry, Miro. Nothing personal, but we've got our orders to bring you in.'

'On what charge?'

'Aiding a criminal.'

'Where's the criminal?'

'That's what Tajovský would like to know.'

'Well *I* haven't got him. See for yourselves,' he announced blandly, jerking a thumb over his shoulder. They peered into the rear of the vehicle, barely noticing an ambulance pass by.

'So where've you stashed him?'

'I don't know what you're talking about. A man came to see me earlier and he had a couple of pals with him. One of them wanted to hire a car, so I let him have an old Zil which I don't have much use for. They had a bite to eat, and off they went. One of them will be bringing it back tomorrow.'

The patrolmen looked at each other. 'What's the number?'

'I'm not sure – ZV-something, because I bought it in Zvolen, about five years ago. It's black.'

One of the men hurried back to the patrol car, to radio in this information. Returning, he said, 'I'm sorry, Miro. The captain's adamant. You've got to come in for questioning. With a bit of luck, they won't keep you more than a couple of hours.'

That's what you think, thought Miro blackly.

The ambulance had turned left at Tibava onto the Ubl'a road, and was now moving to the northeast. Around them lightning flashed frequently, but the rain was light and intermittent. They left the storm behind them when they entered the Vihorlatské vrchy, the foothills of the Carpathians.

Three kilometres further, just before the village of Podhorod, the ambulance turned right, onto a narrow country road, which came to a dead end at the hamlet of Inovce – only a mile from the frontier.

Where the road ended, there was a potholed lane leading to the right. This ran up a shallow little valley; half a mile along stood an abandoned mansion, boarded up and semi-ruined, some nobleman's hunting lodge in the days of the Austro-Hungarian Empire. There the ambulance came to a stop and Božena got out. She opened the rear door and said, 'Miro was stopped by the police, though I shouldn't think it's anything serious. He may take a while to get here. But we've got to get back at once to avoid suspicion. You'll just have to wait for him.'

A moment later the ambulance was jolting back along the lane. As the bouncing headbeams disappeared into the trees, the darkness of a moonless night closed in. Adam observed one of the strangest weather systems he had ever encountered. The western half of the sky was taken up by the storm, with thick pillars of lightning frequently seeming to hold up the clouds; the eastern half was limpidly transparent, the stars shining more brightly than he could ever remember seeing them. There was something other-worldly about the scene; like the surrealistic cover designs of science fiction paperbacks.

Martin and Karel sat down on a low wall, murmuring to each other. Listening to a conversation which he couldn't understand didn't have much appeal, so Adam decided to take a stroll around the house. Astor seemed to agree and came with him for company.

At the back of the mansion was an expanse of overgrowth, which Adam suspected had once been a garden lawn. The dark sky was cut by the darker mass of the Carpathians, rising beyond the black conifers of the nearby forest. From there came the howl of a lonely wolf, and Astor jerked to attention, his nostrils frantically sniffing the air.

'Friend of yours?' inquired Adam.

Astor glanced at him impatiently, then resumed his urgent nasal quest. Adam walked on, wondering whether dogs thought sounds came to them through their noses.

From somewhere overhead nearby came a different sound: the beating rotors of a helicopter.

Another helicopter was following the main Michalovce-Užgorod road towards the village of Husák. Jan Hurban leaned towards Moreno and had to shout above the noise of the engine, as he translated the message which the pilot had just relayed to Tajovský.

'They've picked up Čarnogurský. On the main road just a mile or so ahead of us. He was alone.'

'Where are they taking him?'

'To the police station at the frontier.'

'Tell the pilot to take us there, then.'

After passing on the order, Hurban leaned forward to scrutinise the scanty traffic on the road below, on the lookout for a black Zil. As the helicopter flew over Tibava, he saw an ambulance just west of the Ubl'a turn-off, but he thought nothing of it because it was heading the wrong way.

They reached the frontier post a few minutes later. Rather than have his pilot do nothing, Tajovský told him to join in the search, so the helicopter dropped its passengers in a carpark in front of the duty-free supermarket, then took off again.

The Colonel led the way through the first checkpoint, where a policewoman stood to attention and saluted him. A few yards further stood a single three-storey building with the proportions of a shoebox, and comparable charm. It was shared by the Ukrainians and the Slovaks, and housed the police, customs and passport-control sections of both nations. As usual it was busy, but the flow of traffic was westwards. 'It doesn't look as if many people want to go to the Ukraine,' commented Ned.

'If you'd been there, you'd understand why.'

Miro was now in the police section, being interrogated. He was trying to seem as friendly and cooperative as possible, because almost all the policemen around were at least customers, if not collaborators. Tajovský walked in, followed by Moreno and Hurban, and then Zucca. The latter was carrying a long rosewood case. Miro decided Adam was in bad trouble.

Ned muttered to Hurban, 'Let's not waste our time with this guy. The cops will get what they can out of him. Let's talk to the guys who picked him up.'

Hurban murmured a translation to Tajovský, and the patrolmen were summoned. After a few preliminary questions Hurban asked, 'What about the cars before and after the Range Rover?'

'Single drivers,' replied the senior officer. 'I knew most of them. Locals on their way home.'

'And the vehicles following Čarnogurský?' The man looked uncomfortable. Hurban smiled amiably. 'Don't worry, man. Take your time and have a think.' The policeman frowned in concentration, but nothing came to him. His partner couldn't remember, either.

Moreno broke in, 'Ask them if there was any lorry or van.'

'All the vehicles that passed us were cars,' said the junior. 'Apart from an ambulance.'

Hurban blinked once, then called out to Tajovský.

The patrols on the road to Michalovce quickly got the word and, a few minutes later, one of them waved down the ambulance. Božena's young companion took fright and started talking.

Within moments, Hurban was racing out of the door. Tajovský commandeered the only remaining patrol car, jumping in alongside a startled novitiate, while Moreno, Hurban and Zucca piled into the

212

back. As the car lurched forward, Tajovský was shouting orders by radio to the helicopter pilot.

Adam completed his circuit of the mansion and rejoined his companions. He started to say something, but just then they heard the sound of an approaching vehicle. 'Quick! Hide!'

The three men ran for cover.

A few moments later, a car pulled up in front of the mansion. Its driver got out and, in English, called, 'It's okay. I'm a friend of Miro's. My name's Alois.'

Adam stepped out from the trees. 'Miro's been picked up.'

Alois nodded. 'He said there was a good chance of it. Three men and one dog, that the cargo?'

'Yes, and Miro said he'd organise a car for us in Užgorod.'

'Organise a car?' Alois sounded puzzled.

'Yes, find us a car.'

'Oh, I see. That won't be much of a problem.' The others had also emerged from the trees, and came over to shake hands with him. 'I suggest we go now. There are a lot of patrols about, so we'll have to do without lights — ' He broke off and cocked his head to listen, as Astor had been doing for several seconds. Then they all heard the car. It was approaching fast, but its sound was suddenly drowned by a new noise, and abruptly a helicopter burst into view overhead, its spotlight flooding the whole area.

All four men scattered, Adam running after Alois. Seconds later, a police car tore onto the scene, and Moreno was already leaping from the back. The pilot rapidly informed Tajovský on where the fugitives were heading, but Zucca already had one in his sights. When he fired, the running figure arched his back in agony, and fell to the ground.

The helicopter was now in pursuit of a second man. Zucca raised his rifle again and scanned the area on the chopper's starboard side. A second target presented itself, and a bullet took away the top of Martin Trnka's head. Astor approached his dead master cautiously, fearfully. He sniffed at the blood and somehow knew that licking *this* wound would do no good, so he lay down beside the body and waited for his own pain to go away.

Zucca now scanned through his telescopic lens towards the east – and the frontier. He spotted the other two targets a quarter of a mile away, running up the mountain slope towards the encroaching forest. The second man fitted Drew's description perfectly. Zucca rested the Heckler & Koch's barrel on a low branch and took careful aim.

A moment later, he fired.

24

Robert Ferrandini went across to the drinks cabinet to pour himself a brandy. 'Anybody else like something?' he inquired.

The men behind him declined with polite murmurs.

It was late. Moreno's reports, coming in regularly throughout the night, had supplied them all with a nervous energy to keep them well awake, but at last they were showing signs of wilting.

Lovegni commented, 'If the Ukraine's as tight as Slovakia, I don't see how we can fail to catch him.' There were murmurs of agreement from the others. 'Anyhow, I'm all in. I'm going to bed. If anything happens, wake me up.'

'I think I'll do the same,' replied Gabrielli, staring down at the map they had been using to follow Drew's route. 'You know, this has all been quite exciting, in its way.'

No one replied to that. Maybe they were too tired. But their total lack of reaction made him think they may have considered it a childish thing to say, and he coloured slightly. Soon afterwards, Vitellini and Cattagna retired to their rooms.

Alone now, Ferrandini went over to the window to stare out at the Sicilian night and sipped thoughtfully at his brandy. There was something at the back of his mind which kept warning him that they were committing a mistake.

Gabrielli was right: it *had* been exciting. And there was something wrong about that.

On the large coffee table several other maps lay spread open. That of Slovakia was large scale, so Drew would now be within an inch of the red line marking the frontier. He had done well so far, but to slip through their net now would take a miracle. Ferrandini began folding the maps away. The last covered northern Europe, and Ferrandini traced a finger along the route Drew had taken: Brussels, Dresden, Ústí, Týnec, Prešov, Košice.

He frowned. This was all so improvised, so risky – absolutely anything might go wrong. Everything else in Belvedere was designed to run like clockwork – each operation entrusted to long-standing and meticulous institutions.

Ferrandini and his colleagues knew practically everything about it now. The Swiss banker Zaunmacher had given them Adriano Lupillo's list of three possible successors and one of them, Bruno Toscana, had been interviewed. Adriano had paid Toscana a social call shortly after taking up the estate manager job. Over a discreet glass of wine he had broached the real purpose of his visit, claiming he was merely a messenger boy for a friend who was one of the Friends.

'I can't tell you who he is,' Adriano had said, 'but he's a man of his word. He's looking for someone to do a job for him after he dies. He's only in his forties at present, so we're talking about something a long way off. But it would be very well paid.'

'What is the job?'

'I don't know exactly. The only thing he would tell me was it's a question of looking after something for someone.' At which point Lupillo had glanced around to make sure nobody was near, then lowered his voice. 'Between you and me, I think that that someone is an illegitimate child, living in America.'

'Sounds all right. You can tell him I'm interested.'

'Good. When the time comes, you'll get a letter from his lawyers giving you all the details, but there is something now which he wants you to remember: "Make sure the pious one is warm." '

Ferrandini had at once sent someone to fetched the picture of Pope Pius XII from Adriano's bedroom. On warming it, they discovered the guardian's detailed instructions written on the back in invisible ink.

Even his newspaper-reading activity had been reduced to something routine. Adriano had been on the lookout for information concerning certain families. Again, Salvatore had disguised the vital among a mass of trivia, because the list not only identified the families of the twenty-four Codeholders, but also sixty others – major families in the world of politics, business, and even the American Cosa Nostra. Adriano had been required to classify the news items, then award it a corresponding number from a list of criteria, and multiply this by the number set against the family concerned. The results of these calculations had next to be added to certain of the circulating numbers, which were simply share prices. Almost all those criteria were quite meaningless, but hidden among them were '*sudden disappearance*' and '*acute difficulty through US government or police action*' and '*unnatural death*'. These bore high multiplicands, and since the multipliers set against the twenty-four families were also high, the products were large figures. When the Swiss bank received a figure over a certain limit, the Belvedere process automatically came into operation.

In this way had Salvatore, posthumously for nineteen years, controlled his system and, through it, maintained his threat to hurt the world if the world dared to hurt his family.

Belvedere was a tight system, depending on people carrying out routine tasks in ignorance of their real significance. But, with the all-important exception of Adriano, everyone else involved was an *institution* of some kind. So why the need now for a single individual to have to cross the whole of Europe – with all the attendant hazards of such a journey?

In fact, why the need for 'an agent' at all?

Abruptly an image of his father came into his mind, saying, '*Never make a threat which you cannot or do not intend to carry out.*' Robert had been a child when he had first heard this, but his father had repeated the maxim many times throughout the boy's subsequent apprenticeship. What was nagging at him now was the discrepancy between Salvatore's lifelong rule and this exciting but fundamentally ad-lib 'excursion' across Europe. If Salvatore had behaved true to form, the Belvedere scheme was already set to run its course. But Drew was human, and therefore fragile. Blow-awayable. He could not possibly be necessary to its operation. Salvatore would never have entrusted such a *vital* process to a single individual and sent him on such a precarious chase.

But if so, then what the hell has Drew got to do with it?

In an electric moment of stark clarity Robert suddenly saw the answer.

They'd got the wrong end of the stick! Drew wasn't part of the publication process at all! He was the insurance policy! The man selected by his father to *stop* it!

'You *mustn't* kill him! Detain him if you can, but under no circumstances must he be killed, Ned!'

Standing a yard away from Zucca, Moreno saw the man's finger squeeze through the first pressure – a millisecond from firing. His hand knifed out to knock the barrel of the rifle into the air just as the marksman pulled the trigger.

'What the hell . . . !' exclaimed Zucca.

'Fucking hell! Did you hit him?'

'Of course I bloody didn't!' Zucca peered through his nightscope, and saw Drew was still running towards the treeline. 'He's getting away.'

'Can you shoot to wound, but guarantee not to kill?'

'At this range and with a moving target? You gotta be joking.'

Ned put down the phone, snatched the rifle out of Zucca's hands and, through the infrared scope, watched Drew disappear into the forest – and into the Ukraine. He picked up his phone and explained to his boss why they had had to let Drew get away.

In Sicily, Robert blinked, alarmed by the fact that Ned had misunderstood his instructions and nearly given the order to wound a man he now believed to be on their side.

'Don't do anything for the moment. Let me consult with the others, and I'll get back to you.' Ferrandini hung up and went to wake his three American colleagues.

Gabrielli and Lovegni came down to the sitting room in dressing gowns, but Cattagna had taken the time to dress. Robert invited them all to sit down. 'A short while ago Zucca had Drew in his sights. He was on the point of firing, but I managed to get through in time to stop him.'

Gabrielli jumped to his feet in astonishment, exclaiming, 'Why, for God's sake?'

'Yes, why the hell did you do that?' echoed Lovegni. Cattagna remained imperturbable knowing that they were about to hear the explanation anyway, so there wasn't much point in asking for it.

'Because it would have been a mistake.'

'A mistake? Why?'

Ferrandini regarded them thoughtfully, realising he was going to have to handle this very carefully if he was to continue to retain their support. He looked out of the window at the dark Sicilian landscape. 'You know,' he said, contemplating it, 'if you forget about the nuts and bolts of the system and just think about the philosophy of it, then my father was returning to his roots. To the people of this land, who shared the same ideas and loyalties as he did. But he did all this because he would either be powerless – because our opponents had acted against him – or dead. But suppose he were still alive – and free.' He turned around. 'Vincenzo, what would he do? What would *you* do?'

'Now or fifty years ago?'

'Now – but let's suppose you're young again.'

Cattagna was thoughtful for a moment. 'In 1943, Salvatore's problem was how to protect his family against the government if it decided to break a fundamentally unenforceable contract. But the main danger wasn't that the government would simply break its word, but that it would try to keep the whole agreement secret by eliminating everyone who knew about it.' He pursed his lips. 'If I thought they'd really tried to move against us, believing they could stop Belvedere in time, I'd now make it clear to them that they'd failed. I'd give them a chance to make peace with us, and then set up another Belvedere.'

'Right. But once the Accords were made public, you'd have nothing left to bargain with. You'd be totally impotent.'

The other men looked at him. 'Conclusion?' asked Gabrielli.

'He wouldn't publish *immediately*.'

'I still can't see what you're getting at.'

'Obviously, he'd do something else first.'

Lovegni shook his head exasperatedly. 'That's all very well. Perhaps he would, *if* he were alive. But he's dead, so he can't.'

217

Cattagna looked at him. 'Can't he? Hasn't everything we've learned over the last few days shown us just how much a man can do even when he's dead?'

Ferrandini sat down and leaned forward, with an intense expression. 'Let's think about it. The focus of Belvedere has been in Sicily for fifty years. Then it moved to Switzerland, and then to the United Kingdom. But why Britain?'

'It's a communications and financial centre,' replied Gabrielli. 'It has close ties with both Europe and the States.'

'What about the people?' asked Ferrandini.

'Easy-going but class-ridden,' said Lovegni. 'Disciplined when they want to be.'

'Where are you taking us, Robert?' asked Cattagna. 'What's the point of this?'

'I'll tell you where I'm taking you. Sicily, Switzerland and Britain. Three countries with highly stable internal structures, their own long-established traditions, the population being individualists who conform voluntarily to those traditions. My father once said, "If I hadn't been a Sicilian, I would have liked to be British." All three of them are islands – even Switzerland, really – because they've been able to develop their own systems without reference to the outside world.'

'I suppose I understand what you mean. But I still can't see what you're driving at.'

'Let me ask you this, then. If you wanted to find someone sympathetic to us who would carry out your wishes unquestioningly twenty years after your death, where would you look?'

Cattagna shrugged. 'Exactly where he did look – Sicily.'

'Right. And if you wanted a banker who would obey your instructions to the letter and do his utmost to respect your privacy, where would you look?'

'All right – Switzerland. So what kind of agent was he looking for in Britain?'

Ferrandini lit a cigarette, closed his eyes, then expelled a long plume of smoke. 'Someone like himself.'

There was a silence. Then Cattagna said, 'It's an intriguing idea, Robert. Salvatore always put great faith in human beings, but very little in systems. I must confess, in all my musings about the setting up of Belvedere I tended to fiddle around with checks and balances and cross-checks in the form of lawyers and banks, whereas of course a truly foolproof system must also be proof against fools, and it really can't be unless there is one overriding authority fully aware of all the facts and able to make decisions without interference. Salvatore *must* have foreseen the possibility of people throwing a spanner in the works without realising what they were doing, and he was never one

218

for simply giving up in the face of difficulties.'

Lovegni said, 'I can't see why he'd limit himself to England.'

'Can't you? There's one very important attribute of the people of England that we didn't mention: they speak English.'

His listeners blinked at him. Then Gabrielli said, 'That's a good point, Robert. But I have the feeling that you're attributing more importance to it than the rest of us are.'

Ferrandini nodded. 'I'll come back to that in just a minute, Peter. What I want you all to consider now is this. Everything else in Belvedere has worked like clockwork. It's used banks, lawyers, firms of long standing. So why the need now for a single individual to cross the whole of Europe, with all the risks that might involve?' He let them dwell on this question for a moment. 'Why the need for an agent at all? Why not keep the Accords in a safe-deposit box and have the bank just send them to a reputable newspaper?'

Lovegni objected, 'Your father couldn't be sure the newspaper wouldn't consider the whole thing a hoax. He needs an agent to make sure the matter is made public.'

'Very well. He needs an agent to broadcast the news. But why have a single man cross a continent to fetch them?' Ferrandini could see Lovegni was going to make another objection, but he preempted him. 'And haven't we just decided that publishing the Accords would mean using up all his trumps? He'd have *nothing* left to bargain with.'

Cattagna nodded slowly, and Robert decided to press home his advantage. 'My father used to say, "Never make a threat which you can't or don't intend to carry out." It was his life rule. I'm certain that Belvedere is already set to run its course, and it does not depend on the success or failure of any individual's mission. Even if Drew was killed, nothing would change. The Belvedere Accords would be published anyway.'

Gabrielli said, 'Yes, all right, Robert. You've made a good case. Given the urgency of the situation, I think you were right to abort the operation. I'll back you up in the Curia.'

The others nodded their assent. Lovegni said, 'So what's the purpose of this Drew character? What's Salvatore really using him for?'

It was Cattagna who replied. 'I think the answer's obvious. If Drew's function is *not* the publication of the Accords, then it must be the opposite. He's supposed to *stop* it.'

Robert nodded. 'It's a failsafe device. He's a negotiator. He's supposed to negotiate our release if we'd been arrested.'

'And since we haven't, what happens now?' asked Lovegni.

'That's just the point. Drew probably doesn't know that. What's more, if he's to be convinced that we don't need saving, he's going to have to see us living our lives normally and without threat. So I propose we all return to the States tomorrow morning and carry on as usual.'

Cattagna nodded. 'That makes sense. It's coherent, anyway, even if you're mistaken.'

'There's something else. I instructed Ned to detain Drew if possible, but not to kill him. He then asked Zucca if he could shoot to wound instead. What worries me is that my instructions were so easily misinterpreted. I don't want to take any more chances. I want to call the manhunt off.'

Lovegni gasped. 'Have you any idea of how much all this has cost?'

'A lot less than it will cost us if the Accords are published. By chasing him all over Europe, we're raking up the hostility of a man I think is actually on our side, and since two of his companions were killed, God knows what he thinks of us now. I think we should stop running unnecessary risks.'

Gabrielli said, 'But we're going to have to get in touch with this man *somehow*.'

'Then we'll just have to think of some other way. We can't have a lot of trigger-happy headhunters messing up our chances of talking with him reasonably.'

Cattagna nodded. 'All right, Robert. You have my approval.'

Ferrandini turned to the others. They glanced at each other, then yielded. He phoned Moreno with their decision.

'Call off the manhunt – in Slovakia, the Ukraine, everywhere. Take care of this personally, Ned. Tell all your people to go home now and make sure the local police understand that they are absolutely not to proceed any further. Understood?'

In Slovakia a puzzled Moreno replied, 'Check.' His boss had spoken clearly and that was that.

In Sicily, Peter Gabrielli asked, 'Why is it so important that Drew speaks English?'

'Because if the balloon *had* gone up, my father would need a man of intelligence and resourcefulness to help us. But that person would also need to know what Belvedere consisted of, to understand the value of the threat he was making. So my father instructed Williamson to find an individualist. Someone who would judge a situation on its own merits, rather than by any preconceived notions of right and wrong. Those were the initial qualities my father was looking for, but they weren't enough on their own. Not to persuade his agent to exercise his power to stop Belvedere. For that he would need to *talk* to him, to show him things, to offer him a new way of looking at the world. To be able to deal with the US government, it would be useful if the negotiator spoke English, but not essential. To comprehend my father's ideas, however, every nuance of English would be important.'

'Then why didn't he pick a Sicilian and write in Italian?' asked Lovegni.

'Because Britain has a population ten times that of Sicily. My father wanted a large pool of men to choose from.'

'Then why not Italy? It has a bigger population than Britain.'

Ferrandini shook his head. 'Now, yes. But the bulk of it was inaccessible in 1943, because most of Italy was occupied. But there's another consideration. Fifty years ago the population of Sicily was divided too sharply into the rich and the poor. A poor man would be unlikely to have the educational requirements to undertake complex negotiations, and a rich man would probably hold loyalites which might easily bring him into conflict with my father's wishes. An Englishman's loyalty would be a lot less cluttered up by religious considerations, and we already know from Hamblyn that my father instructed him to rule out any candidate with strong religious convictions.'

Gabrielli replied, 'You're very persuasive, Robert. But will your father have been?'

Robert shrugged. 'He's given himself the best chance.'

'There's also the financial reward if Drew fulfils his assignment,' Lovegni reminded them.

Cattagna shook his head. 'If he controls Belvedere, he can ask his own price.'

25

Adam knew that Martin and Karel were dead. The singleness of each shot, the lack of any cry of pain, the subsequent behaviour of the helicopter – all had contributed to his inner certainty.

An inner certainty upholstered with guilt.

He had ensnared two innocent men, deliberately deceiving them, in order to save himself.

Trekking behind Alois through the endless Carpathian forest, Adam felt disembodied. The wolves – which he never saw – provided a counterpoint to his remorse. Alois said there were three of the beasts – curious about these two invaders of their domain. But just curious, because it was early summer and food was plentiful.

So Adam swung between apprehension and remorse; between thinking of his own survival, and trying to convince himself that Martin and Karel would have thought of theirs.

A dull pain under his ribcage, caused by a collision with a branch of a tree, as he had fled into the forest, occasionally reminded him of the wider world that lay somewhere beyond the hypnotic infinity of dark pines.

Adam and Alois reached the edge of the forest. The wolves, having escorted their guests to the exit, stayed behind, watching them walk down through a steep meadow – where sheep might safely graze only if the shepherd had a gun. The valley below was sprinkled with a dozen clusters of lights, whose sparsity and dimness promised poverty. For Adam, the thought of a helicopter suddenly swooping out over the trees, its searchlight probing, was so vivid that he cocked an ear at the slightest sound.

The wolves had the right idea: they had stayed in hiding.

The meadow flattened and the dark mass of a huge barn loomed towards them – a fossil of collectivisation. Nearby stood an old log cabin, the remnant of an earlier age: the dwelling of some peasant long dead and as long forgotten. Alois made straight for its entrance and lifted the latch. Adam followed him into a makeshift safety. Alois lit a match, its flare revealing one large room. Against a wall stood two bunks bearing cheap mattresses and dirty blankets. There was no other furniture.

Adam glanced at his watch. It was nearly three o'clock. They had been walking for more than three hours. Exhausted, the two men climbed onto the bunks and fell asleep.

They were awakened by the sound of a tractor passing along a nearby track. Through a dirty window, Adam saw a sunny morning already at odds with his mood.

Alois struggled to his feet, then threw some water over his face at the filthy sink in the corner of the room. He turned to his companion. It was the first time Drew had been able to see his face clearly. Alois had the same beak-shaped nose as Miro. He was obviously a son.

'You won't get far alone. Do you want me to come with you?'

'Yes. I was going to ask you to.'

'Okay. You wait here. I'll organise a car.'

'A van would be better. How long do you think you'll be?'

Alois blinked at him in puzzlement, then guessed what the sentence meant. 'As long as I am now,' he said, laughing. 'Perhaps two hours.' He went out.

Adam lay back, staring at the ceiling, a long while thinking of Martin and Karel. In London, Drew's assignment had seemed a great adventure – almost a game. In Dresden the game had grown serious; in Slovakia deadly.

Then remembering that the life of a third man, Miro, now depended on him, he jumped down from the bunk, stripped off his clothes and went over to the sink. He washed himself thoroughly, using yesterday's shirt as a towel. By the time Alois returned, he felt halfway decent again. The van was a white Opel Combo. It looked new.

'Stolen two weeks ago in Austria,' explained Alois. 'I got it cheap because it has no papers, but if we're stopped, it won't matter whether we have or not.'

Adam climbed into the back and was pleased to find several cushions and blankets, still in their polythene wrapping. Alois handed him a thermos of coffee, a bag of buns and two German Makarov Pistole Ms with a box of ammunition.

'They used to be standard issue to the East German STASI,' he explained, as he let out the clutch. 'They're chambered for the Russian 9 × 18-millimetre cartridge. They'll be handy to have around.'

After breakfasting, Adam examined the guns and wondered why that marksman had let him escape. Considering how far his target had been from the cover of the forest, the only rational explanation was that he had run out of bullets. Unlikely as that seemed, nothing else made any sense. Giving a shrug, he turned to watching the Carpathians creep past.

And, when the mountains were behind them, the endless miles of the East European Plain.

'I've wrapped up everything here,' reported Ned. 'I'm flying back to Prague in an hour or so. I should be in London tomorrow. What do you want me to do then?'

'Stay there for a week or so. I may need you to talk to Hamblyn, if Drew contacts him again. Though I doubt he will.' Ferrandini stared out at the clouds over the Atlantic, wondering what he could say to Drew if they ever managed to meet.

Alois drove throughout the day.

Adam slept, dozed, rationalised, healed. Beyond the windows, kilometres became miles, which became meaningless. It was the spatial equivalent of the time dilation effect.

Adam took the wheel during the hours of darkness, allowing his companion to sleep. Headlights forged a tunnel through distance, an aching shaft through aching flatness, mercifully shrouded in agoraphobic night.

A dimness in the east awoke an uncertain blue around him; distances becoming what he thought they were, and perspectives all shot to hell. Adam was drunk on distance.

On farness.

On sheer, bloody endlessness.

The sun decided to rise, but it seemed to be in two minds about it. Of course, all that flatness would put anybody off, thought Adam, witnessing for the first time in his life a dawn that he did not like.

It was here, in all this tremendous foreverness, that Hitler had received his comeuppance. Napoleon, too. Two bad judges of . . . distance. For a landscape like this, Drew could not understand why either of them had bothered.

Adam, a mountaineer, was moving through territory where the majority of inhabitants had only ever seen a mountain on television.

A town was approaching. Drew slowed to a stop and shook Alois awake. He climbed into the back, and fell mercifully asleep.

At noon, Alois awakened him. Adam sat up and looked out through the windscreen to see a familiar cluster of palaces and towers ahead.

The Kremlin.

Olga Pavlovna Petrovskaya, the permanent head of the Ministry of Finance, looked up as her secretary Kozyrev entered the office. 'This letter just came for you. Handed in at the desk downstairs.' Kozyrev gave it to her, then withdrew.

Petrovskaya glanced at the envelope, noting it was marked 'Personal – Urgent'. She opened it and took out two folded sheets of paper – the first, very old and of good quality; the second, ordinary notepaper. A glance at the signature at the foot of the first page made her blink three times, then sit up. Petrovskaya read through both letters twice, then sat back in thought.

After a few minutes, she summoned Kozyrev.

'Nikolai Sergeyevich, there's something very important that I want you to do for me. Take a car from the ministerial pool, but something very ordinary and discreet, and go to the Moscow Zoo. A man will be sitting on a bench somewhere near the pandas. He'll be wearing jeans and a dark-blue pullover. He's English and doesn't speak Russian. Just say that you're a friend of Olga's. Don't ask for his name; he'd probably give you a false one, anyway. Drive him out to my dacha in Zhukovka, and install him in the guest house. Here's the key. Make sure he has everything he needs, and stay with him until I arrive. I ought to be able to join you by six o'clock.'

The village of Zhukovka lay fifteen miles west of the Kremlin. Hidden in the forest nearby were scores of country homes for rich and powerful Muscovites. Petrovskaya's dacha was a roomy log cabin, and the guest house just a smaller version of it, facing its parent across a patio and swimming pool.

Kozyrev proved a considerate host. He was about thirty, slim and quietly pleasant. He seemed very familiar with the premises, so maybe his relationship with Petrovskaya went beyond the mere professional.

At ten to six, Kozyrev escorted him to the main house and introduced him to Petrovskaya herself. A woman in her late thirties, elegant rather beautiful, she obviously looked after herself.

After studying Adam for a moment, she invited him to sit. 'Would you like a drink?'

'No, thank you.'

She smiled. 'How very un-Russian.'

He returned her smile. 'Perhaps that's not surprising.'

Suddenly businesslike, she picked up an envelope from the coffee table that lay between them. 'This document was entrusted to us in 1943. We were paid one million dollars to look after it indefinitely, and promised a further payment if certain conditions were met. Now, in 1943 a million dollars was a great deal of money, but we were told that the further payment would be ten times as much. Moreover this sum was to be invested – mainly in oil, so it has far outpaced inflation. I haven't had the time for an exact calculation yet, but a rough estimate puts the value of the fund somewhere around three billion dollars.

'The conditions specify that this envelope should be preserved intact and unopened, and must be surrendered to the bearer of Stalin's letter, who may present himself anonymously – as you have done. We must treat your visit with the utmost discretion and make no attempt to discover your true identity. To do so might prejudice the value of the fund. Upon receipt of this envelope, you should satisfy yourself that nobody has tampered with it. You may read the contents without supervision, and destroy them afterwards, if you wish. Subsequently, you will give us certain instructions. We have no idea what they will be, but obviously we can refuse to carry them out if we consider them prejudicial to Russian interests. If, however, we find ourselves able to accept them, and comply with them to your satisfaction, we shall then receive the money promised.'

Petrovskaya handed him the envelope and a paperknife, and walked out of the room. Kozyrev followed her out, closing the door behind him.

Adam slit open the envelope, and extracted what he instantly recognised as another communication from Salvatore.

We meet again, my friend, and I hope you have had an easy journey.

I obviously cannot know the current political state of the Soviet Union as you read this letter. Before the German attack in 1941 it was evident to me that communism simply was not working. In fact, it is a wonderful nonsense, and sooner or later the Russians themselves will junk the ideology. But the present war may postpone that.

My choice of Russia to act as the custodian of this letter was dictated not by its ideology but rather by its economic potential. The country must always be a rival to the United States because of its vast size and because its wealth of raw materials is second to none.

The Russians will have a financial interest in helping you. They can probably supply you with all that you need regarding legal experts, diplomats, spokesmen and representatives, economists, detectives, bodyguards. Whatever you decide, the Russians will undoubtedly find the best men available to fight our case. When you have the backup team you need, then proceed yourself to New York. If you decide you must enter the country incognito, our Russian friends ought to be able to arrange that too.

Once you are in New York, you must go to a firm of lawyers called Barton & Willis, mid-morning. By the time you read this letter, their name or address may have changed, but you should have no difficulty in tracing where they have relocated. For their current address and particulars, see the appendix that follows.

You will claim to represent a client of theirs: S & Associates. Since they will require proof of this, they may ask questions which only you can answer. Once they are satisfied, they will give you the next letter of instructions from me, although they will only do so if you walk into their premises alone.

Your goals are the same: to find out what has happened to my family and associates, and why; to negotiate an agreement under which they can be brought to safety; and to devise suitable mechanisms to ensure they remain safe. This is no easy task. Whatever system any man might be clever enough to invent, there will always be a cleverer man to penetrate it. But perhaps you should consider one very important fact of life: the two most powerful motives in human affairs are money *and* love. *They have more in common with each other than we like to think. But there is one major difference between them. The first is convertible into other commodities and back again. A man may accept a smaller amount than he originally intended if there is a corresponding increase in something else which he happens to value – such as some gain in personal prestige, for example. But love is not convertible. It cannot be negotiated or reduced by decree or threat or bribe. It's an absolute. Nonetheless, money and love can, in the real world, be made convertible. The point of interchange lies within the man who loves. He will, when he has an interest in doing so, place a value on his own life in terms of dollars and cents. This is the amount which he perceives himself to be worth. But he will readily give up that same life to save the loved one. Therefore, since he can't pay more than the supreme sacrifice, he has, in effect and unintentionally, put a value on his love.*

This is perhaps an unusual way of stating a well-understood truth, but it may still provide a framework within which the basic motives of human life can be cross-referenced and tamed into well-behaved elements within a mathematical equation.

But perhaps you're asking yourself: is there any purpose in such a branch of mathematics? The answer is I don't know. But there might be. It might enable us to devise more workable political structures than the ones we have at the moment. I don't think the state, for example, is going to prove a very satisfactory entity in the long run, because there is no horizontal love permeating humanity. Love is arranged vertically from generation to generation, from father to son, with small horizontal extensions from son to brother and cousin. This is why I think communism will fail, because you can't ask a man to place a financial value on his sacrifice for someone he doesn't love. So if the mathematics had existed in 1917, perhaps the Russians would not have swallowed the certainly attractive but basically inedible bait which was offered them.

But even if I'm right, I still have to be constructively critical. So what alternative is there to the State? *One answer could be to break up the impersonal relationship that exists between the individual and the state and put him into a self-regulating emotional unit. On the one hand, increase the authority of the family over its members, whom it will seek to control not merely through punishment and threats, but also through love; and, on the other, to make each family a single unit responsible for its actions (and any of the actions of its members) to a general collective of families.*

I really am not at all sure how this arrangement would affect such problems as crime, but I do know that each individual would then enjoy a feeling of belonging, and whatever problems he might face, however weak and ill-equipped he might be, he would have the support of people for whom he too felt responsible.

Thousands of years ago the world had the beginnings of this system. Then the State was created. And it is a living thing and, like all living things, fundamentally selfish and determined to perpetuate itself. It has sought to make itself strong at the expense of the family, and has gradually debilitated it to the point where in advanced countries it is no more than an extension of the womb – an incubator of the individual until he becomes old enough to accept a contractual relationship with the State.

The above reasoning has not led me into being an enemy of the State (or of any state), but I am certainly no friend to it and I am deeply suspicious of its motives.

Why not? The State is Other People. And Other People have motives of their own. They even have Other Motives.

As I am sure you must have considered deeply over the last few days.

Good luck.
S.

Drew read through the letter three times, then memorised the information in the appendix. After burning all the pages, he crushed the ash to flakes. Then he sat back thoughtfully.

For three billion dollars, the Russians would certainly be accommodating. Could he use them to do something about Miro's predicament? No doubt, Slovakia was anxious to remain on good terms with Moscow, so the Russians would pull a lot of weight in Bratislava. It was tempting, therefore, to ask them to pull it in the smuggler's favour.

But matters were not so simple. The corrupt prefect Tajovský and his paymasters would lose interest in Miro, once they knew that he did not know where Adam had gone. No doubt, Miro himself was doing his best to persuade everybody of his continued usefulness, giving out – Scheherazade-fashion – the names of Ukrainians who might have given Adam refuge. And since this might still lead to Drew's capture, no one would see any reason to stop Miro talking – yet.

But if the Colonel now received a phone call from Bratislava, ordering him to release his prisoner, Tajovský and his paymasters might easily decide that matters would be safer for everybody, if Miro met with an unfortunate accident.

Besides, there were the Russians themselves to think about: they might want to be obliging, but they were not going to act like robots,

228

obeying Drew's commands automatically. They would serve their own best interests at every juncture. Their motivation was money, so their services would be subject to the laws of the marketplace, in which case they might decide to sell to the highest bidder. This worried Adam greatly. The steps his opponents had taken to stop him carrying out his mission had included the mobilisation of the police forces of several countries. Evidently, a great deal of money was at stake. But where was it coming from?

Drugs seemed to Drew the only credible source. His opponents' huge expenditure strongly suggested that whoever controlled the Belvedere Accords must control the international drug-distribution network. He could think of nothing else which could justify the astronomical sum of *three billion dollars*, which Salvatore had promised to pay him – and the same amount to the Russians.

When Adam had first learned what his payment was to be, he had felt like laughing. The figure had seemed nearly infinite. But now he was assailed by a suspicion that it might not be enough! Clearly Don Salvatore had been astute in his choice of investments. Although he could not have had an inkling – not in 1943 – of what the Arabs were going to do to the price of oil thirty years later, he had still foreseen the ubiquity of motorcars and the consequent importance of their fuel. But the performance of oil as a *legal* investment had been far surpassed by that of narcotics as an *illegal* one. So, although the payment which Salvatore had promised seemed huge, it was a paltry amount in comparison to the value of the drug market itself, whose estimated worth was 'in excess of' two hundred billion dollars per year.

Moreover, what might be an immensity for a single man was a droplet for a government, yet Salvatore – equating them – was proposing to pay the Kremlin the same amount.

Sure, if anyone asked Adam, 'Do you really believe that the modern Russian government would involve itself in the drug market?' he'd say no. But was it so impossible – when the country was mired in an impossible past, and striving towards a possibly impossible future? Might not taking control of the drug market – or, at least, raking off a decent percentage in return for their cooperation – be too strong a temptation to a government which could not see any light at the end of the dark economic tunnel that the country was trudging through?

Besides, it wasn't just the Russian government that Drew had to worry about; any *member* of it – even Petrovskaya – was a potential operator; and, hence, a potential enemy.

No, Adam told himself firmly; he dare not use the Russians to pry Miro out of Tajovský's hands, while he himself was in theirs. In fact, he would need to tread very carefully in his dealings with them.

Drew spent a few minutes considering the phrasing of the questions he wanted to put, then he went to the door and called to his hostess. Petrovskaya reappeared at once, and unaccompanied. She's a cautious one, thought Adam appreciatively.

'What exactly do you wish us to do?' she asked.

'I won't know until I've done some preliminary research. I need detailed reports on the fifty richest people in the United States, and as urgently as possible. I want to know everything about their lives and their families. Also, I need access – and tonight – to a library which keeps American newspapers and financial magazines.'

'That won't be difficult. I'll go to arrange it.'

Shortly before nine o'clock, with the sun still three-quarters of an hour from setting, Kozyrev drove Adam to the Russian Foreign Ministry, on the Garden Ring. Its library kept all the major foreign publications on microfilm. Kozyrev sat discreetly in a corner of the room, while Drew scanned the recent editions of the *New York Times*, looking for references to the name Ferrandini or the Mafia, expecting to learn almost immediately the reason for the activation of Salvatore's system. After going back through several months and drawing a blank, he tried some of the other American newspapers, but again found nothing. Robert Ferrandini's name cropped up quite frequently, but always under perfectly routine circumstances.

Mystified, Adam walked over to the patient Kozyrev, saying, 'I've finished. Now I need to do some thinking. I'm going for a walk. Would you mind waiting for me?'

'Not at all.'

On leaving the building, Drew zigzagged through several streets, to make sure no one was following, then entered a phone booth to ring Alois 'The best thing you can do to help your father is to stay in your hotel for forty-eight hours. If I haven't phoned by then, go home.'

'Can you do anything to help him?'

'I don't know. But if anybody associates you with me, that might prejudice his chances. So lie low.'

At eight o'clock the following morning, the telephone on the bedside table in the guest house rang. Adam picked it up.

'Good morning,' said Petrovskaya. 'Did you sleep well?'

'Yes, thank you. The bed's very comfortable.'

'Good. You should find everything you need for breakfast in the kitchen. And the reports which you requested are ready.'

'You're very efficient.'

'They were put together by a team of seven researchers, working throughout the night. I'll send them over to you now. I'll be working at home today. If you require anything, just pick up the telephone and dial zero.'

The doorbell rang a moment later. Drew answered it, to find the ubiquitous Kozyrev, holding a stack of files two feet high. He carried them inside, deposited them in a chair, and withdrew.

Adam felt sorry for Petrovskaya's team of researchers. They had laboured in vain on forty-nine of the reports, because he had requested them only to camouflage his real interest. The dossiers were ordered according to the subject's wealth – Ferrandini's was the fourteenth. It was a very complete report, covering in great detail the intricacies of the Ferrandini business empire – or, at least, the visible part of it. His companies seemed well run and paid their taxes. There was no hint of any fiscal irregularities or any other motive for US government intervention. The dossier didn't even make particularly interesting reading – unless one liked riches-to-riches stories.

Ferrandini's social life was less well-documented. He seemed a somewhat retiring man, preferring to avoid the public eye; but not unduly so. He was clearly very much of a family man and spent a lot of his time with his wife and children. The dossiers on the social lives of these were fuller, including several articles taken from society magazines. Ferrandini's wife Barbara was a duplicate bridge player of some note, and participated in most major American tournaments. Robert played too, but he preferred the cut-and-thrust of rubber bridge – and at high stakes. He also played poker regularly, winning in a single evening the sort of sums that most people earned as annual salaries.

Ferrandini's three sons were all sportsmen of some kind. The eldest, Robin, played tournament golf and was a middle champion in major-league tennis. His two brothers were following in his footsteps. Their sister, Diana, was a dancer of both classical and modern ballet. Her dossier was detailed enough to mention the times of her dancing classes. There were three photographs of her, taken from society magazines, and she was clearly a very attractive young woman.

The report on the Ferrandini family was up-to-the-minute and there wasn't a word to suggest he faced any problems. It was all very perplexing. Adam had expected to find – at least in the newspapers – if not an explicit mention that Ferrandini had been arrested, then some report of his disappearance, which he could interpret as arrest and detention by the United States government, pending some form of judicial process. Adam's job would then be clear: to call upon the Russians for appropriate experts in American law and finance, and a series of go-betweens to enable Drew to negotiate Robert's release with Washington.

None of this now seemed necessary, and the 'backup team', which Salvatore had mentioned had nothing to back up, so what was the point of putting one together?

Yet the Belvedere system *had* been put into operation. So now the

Accords would be publicised on schedule – which would provoke some political and economic earthquake. But for no apparent reason.

Adam frowned. It was all so mystifying.

Perhaps everything would become clear when he reached New York and read Salvatore's next letter.

Giving a shrug, Drew went into the kitchen to make himself an elaborate breakfast, which he ate while flicking idly through the rest of the dossiers. He wanted to take Ferrandini's with him to New York, as a reference manual, but this would show the Russians which of the fifty millionaires he was really interested in. He didn't want to lug a two-foot-thick stack of files around with him, however; so he selected six pages with essential information on the Ferrandini family, and withdrew equivalents from the other dossiers.

At half past ten, he walked across to the main house, to see Petrovskaya.

'I have to fly to New York. But I want to keep my movements as undetectable as possible – at least, for the time being. So I would like you to arrange a false identity for me – as an American businessman, born in New England, with at least one American parent but with a personal history to account for my English accent.'

Petrovskaya nodded without hesitation. She had obviously expected some such request. She smiled. 'Perhaps dyed hair and a false moustache?' she inquired with gentle mockery.

Adam returned the smile, murmuring, 'Why not?'

Petrovskaya looked at him. 'Plastic surgery, too?' she suggested.

His smile became a grin. 'You obviously have a critical eye.'

Petrovskaya laughed softly. They were friends now. 'How do you want to get to New York?'

'Can you suggest anything undetectable?'

Petrovskaya pursed her lips. 'Nothing's *truly* undetectable; not if you want to fly the whole way. But I suggest you go by submarine from St Petersburg to Finland.'

'No questions asked?'

'Perhaps somebody might want to know whether you take milk in your coffee.'

'What happens in Finland?'

'You'll be put ashore near Helsinki. A car will be waiting to take you to the airport. I suggest you fly via London or Paris.'

'How do I get to St Petersburg?'

'I can place a Ministry aeroplane at your disposal. We normally use Sheremetyevo Airport, but I could arrange for you to use a military airfield, if you wish.'

'No, let's keep things looking as routine as we can. As long as Kozyrev accompanies me, so that I don't have to open my mouth, no one will have any reason to believe I'm not simply a civil servant. But

I'd like to leave as soon as possible. The quicker I get to New York, the better.'

The Russian President looked up from the report into the worried eyes of the Minister of Finance. 'Seems pretty cut and dried. We sneak him into Finland with a fake moustache and passport, and get paid three billion US dollars. I'm not surprised Petrovskaya's so delighted.'

Ilyenko looked doubtful. 'But we suspect his intention is some form of stock-market manipulation, probably in New York. I hardly think the White House will be happy about that, especially if they find out it's happened with our collusion.'

'Stuff the White House. Think of our balance of payments.'

'Yes, but we need the Americans' backing for our new IMF loan.'

The President sighed, then addressed Ilyenko patiently. 'Boris Denisovich, you have a number of options at your disposal: you can deny everything; you can deny the more succulent bits of it; you can claim you didn't know what he was going to do; you can claim you *did* know what he was going to do, but it was nothing to do with us, and, in any case, he hadn't broken any Russian law – or even an American one, because to *intend* to manipulate the stock market does not constitute a manipulation thereof. We're talking about *three billion dollars* and, unlike the loan, it's money which we wouldn't need to pay back. I don't know what this is all about, but I know a good deal when I see one, and this, believe me, Boris Denisovich, is a good deal.'

'So we okay it,' replied Ilyenko flatly.

'Of course. But what should be occupying your thoughts is not whether to use your little rubber stamp, but whether there might be some further gain to be obtained here. Maybe this man – whoever he is – really is going to manipulate the stock market. But maybe he's up to something else entirely. I think it would be in the interests of our country to know just exactly what's behind all this, because no one, Boris Denisovich, absolutely no one shells out three billion dollars without a bloody good reason.'

26

McCarthy stared at Ewing. 'They called it off?'

'Exactly that. They had him in their sights, but the order came through not to shoot.'

'No explanation?'

'None.'

McCarthy's gaze went out of focus for a moment. Then he got up and began to pace the room. After a minute he stopped and turned back to Ewing. 'Then we do likewise.'

The other man blinked at him. Shaking his head, he appealed, 'Phil, you and I have known each other for a long time. It would help enormously if you'd tell me just what the hell is at the back of all this.'

McCarthy raised his eyebrows. 'David, I said: we do likewise,' he replied, putting equal emphasis on all the words. 'And that's a direct order.'

His tone got Ewing's back up.

'An order? Phil, you're chairman of the State Department's Policy Committee.'

McCarthy stiffened visibly and his reply was icy. 'If you require it, the President will issue you with a written order within the hour.'

Ewing's eyes blazed angrily but impotently. 'No, Phil. That won't be necessary. Was there anything else?'

'I don't think so.'

'Then, good morning.'

'Good morning.'

Ewing walked out of the office, fuming. What the fuck do these shits think I am? A messenger boy? His thinking continued in this vein all the way down to his car.

'Langley,' he told the chauffeur curtly. But as the car moved off and his temper began to cool, a new feeling came over him. He suddenly saw that his career was effectively over. He had risen as high as he was ever likely to get. His lack of a politically-saleable personality ruled out a try for the White House, and there was absolutely no point in being just a senator or a representative. His intelligence was high, but he did not reach the top flight, so he did not expect to be offered the State Department or even a senior place on the Policy Committee. The truth was he was head of a department of dirty tricks when the world just did not need dirty tricks any more. Not on the same scale of importance as during the Cold War, anyway. He had to admit now that joining the CIA had been a major mistake.

So what was left? Private industry? Who would take him? None of the big names – and to join a lesser company would be social suicide and his wife would leave him. Start a business of his own? And where would he get the money for it? It was true there were one or two little side deals he had managed over the years, which had realised gratifying little 'rewards', but at his age any business would have to start at least medium-sized, and that meant something like ten million dollars. Where the hell would he ever get ten million dollars? It would mean selling something. But who would buy? The United States just did not have any enemies with that kind of money, apart from a handful of countries who would not be interested in anything he had to offer.

His brow furrowed. Maybe there *was* something he could sell. Ewing spent a moment working out the details, and then abruptly ordered his chauffeur to take him to the airport. On the way he rang his secretary, telling her to cancel his engagements for the rest of the day. On hanging up, he sat back and allowed his face to assume a relaxed half-smile. Who the hell did McCarthy think he was, anyhow?

Two and a half hours later Ewing sat in a taxi crawling through the maze of streets forming New York's Chinatown. Once he reached his destination, he hurried inside. On the car phone, when he had arranged this meeting, he had stipulated maximum discretion, and this was now provided – Ewing was greeted by a single middle-aged Chinese man who did not even search him, but led him politely but unceremoniously straight through several red-wallpapered rooms to an inner sanctum, where a leather-skinned man, close to seventy, wearing a dark grey suit was waiting to receive him. He bowed, and Ewing did likewise. A chair was offered, and Ewing sat, glancing over his shoulder towards the escort. The old man seemed to make no gesture, but his assistant withdrew.

'May I offer you tea? Or perhaps you would prefer something stronger?'

'Nothing, thank you. I want to be out of here in five minutes.'

'A great pity,' replied Lee Kwan, with scrupulous exactitude, sitting down himself.

'I have something to sell you. The price is ten million dollars, clean money, and it's non-negotiable.'

'Indeed? Then it must be very valuable. May one inquire what it is?'

Ewing gave a slight smile and a surprising reply. 'No.'

Lee Kwan maintained his impassivity. He reached for a nearby cigarette box, offering one to Ewing, then lighting his own with some ceremony. In all, it was nearly a full minute before he selected a response, and inquired politely, 'May I ask one question?'

'Go ahead.'

'If I decline to buy, to whom then will you offer the merchandise?'

'To nobody,' replied Ewing, inwardly triumphant, but keeping his expression casual. He had done all his thinking beforehand.

Lee Kwan allowed his still-impassive gaze to wander to the clock. If Ewing had been exact with numbers, they had less than two minutes left. In spite of himself Lee Kwan was intrigued. This was the most unusually presented business proposition he had ever encountered. But there were two things which absolutely could not be ignored: firstly, Ewing was operational head of the CIA; secondly, however many resources a powerful man might have at his disposal, there was no way he could be certain of evading vengeance if he were to commit the eternally unforgivable crime of swindling Lee Kwan, and Ewing would know this. So what was at hand? Had Ewing suddenly found out he was suffering from an incurable cancer and was selling his rotten body for the most he could get? No. In the first place, revenge could be taken against the beneficiaries. In the second, if some fraud was involved, Ewing would have set this whole thing up more elaborately, and he had the entire resources of the CIA to call on.

No, the offer was genuine. This man possessed some extremely valuable information. The fact that he had come so openly, and without protection, meant that he had likely taken precautions against being kidnapped and tortured, but even if he had not, who in his right mind would risk making a personal enemy of the whole CIA? Besides, the man was only asking for a mere ten million.

Even so, there were still one or two questions to put. 'How can you be so sure I do not already possess the information you have to sell?'

Ewing grunted. 'I'm *not* sure. In fact, I suspect you might know one or two items which form part of the complete package. But I can promise you one thing: when you've bought it, you'll be satisfied I couldn't know exactly how much you knew, but I had good cause to believe you knew relatively little.'

Lee Kwan raised his eyebrows as if in doubt. 'That hardly seems a satisfactory consolation if, in fact, I did possess this information beforehand.'

Ewing smiled. 'Let's just say that if you do, my confirmation of it would be worth ten million dollars to you.'

'The most expensive "yes" in history,' replied Lee Kwan, allowing himself a thin smile.

'You miss my point,' answered Ewing, employing his standard in-house down-talk terminology. 'I'm offering information which I sincerely believe you do not possess, but if you *do*, you will be satisfied

236

that I couldn't know it, and in any case my confirmation of it will in itself be valuable to you.'

Lee Kwan would have liked to take this head-swollen palooka apart, word by word or sinew by sinew. To him the method was much of a muchness, and the effect the same, because he considered vengeance only in terms of the satisfaction it brought *him*, and not in terms of the pain inflicted on his opponent.

'Might this information have anything to do with certain recent events in Slovakia?' he asked, strongly suspecting his question would disconcert.

Ewing felt suddenly uncomfortable, but his reply was delivered smoothly enough. 'I'm afraid I can't provide any hint as to what the information might be by either confirming or denying supplementary details.'

Lee Kwan wanted to terminate his interview with this distasteful man as soon as possible. 'How would payment be made?'

'In cash, or cash equivalent.'

'Negotiable bearer bonds?'

'Fine.'

'I shall have to call a meeting of the Chinese Council to consider your offer. Your name will not be mentioned. I can give you an answer by this afternoon. Where can I reach you?'

'At the Waldorf. But I'll call you.'

'Very well. Shall we say half-past two?'

'Fine.'

The Council met at two o'clock. Lee Kwan decided to speak in English and his explanation for the convocation was brief. 'We have been offered information by an unimpeachable source. The offer is apparently to us alone. The price is ten million dollars in negotiable bearer bonds. The offeror would not disclose the nature of the information he has to sell, but I suspect it concerns our Italian friends' recent activities in Slovakia.'

The eleven other men glanced at each other, but no one had anything to say. Lee Kwan's presentation had said it all. A vote was called. Eight hands went up immediately, three more with less enthusiasm, and everyone looked to the twelfth man, and waited. After a moment he nodded.

It was five past two.

Ewing's call was punctual. 'We have decided to accept your offer and we are ready to make the payment.'

'Good. I can be with you in half an hour.'

'At three o'clock, then.'

★ ★ ★

237

Ewing arrived five minutes early. Lee Kwan wasted no time. He passed across a foolscap envelope containing the bearer bonds, and that morning's edition of the *Wall Street Journal*.

Ewing checked the current prices of the bonds, then counted the certificates contained in the envelope. He took out his pocket calculator. The total was twenty-three thousand dollars short of the ten million.

Lee Kwan pulled out a wad of one-hundred-dollar bills from his inside jacket pocket and handed them over to him. 'Two hundred and thirty. Count them if you wish, but they're all there.'

'Clean?'

'You have my word.'

Ewing pocketed the money without counting it, and began to talk immediately.

'In 1943 the US government and a representative of twenty-four Italian-Americans signed a set of agreements called the Belvedere Accords.' He took out a sheet of paper and handed it over. 'That's a list of the Italians. The representative was Salvatore Ferrandini. I don't know the precise terms, but I do know that basically the government offered protection to those twenty-four men and their families, in return for their help in prosecuting the war. And, ever since, the FBI has had a standing hands-off order from the Attorney General's office. The Accords documents were given to the twenty-four families as an insurance policy, in case the government decided to renege on its agreement. Last week the current heads of those twenty-four families suddenly hit the mattresses. They disappeared, along with their immediate families. Then Ferrandini, Cattagna, Lovegni and Gabrielli turned up in Sicily.

'Ferrandini's assistant, Ned Moreno, subsequently went to London, and over the following days a manhunt was organised. Hundreds of men were brought in, some from the States, others from various European countries. Moreno also used local police forces in the former Czechoslovakia and in the Ukraine. The man they were hunting is called Adam Drew.'

Ewing opened his briefcase, pulled out a large manila envelope, and passed it to Lee Kwan, who extracted from it six pages, obviously photocopies, and a photograph which had evidently been sent by fax from London.

'That's a dossier we've put together on Drew. Moreno also brought in from Chicago a crack marksman called Frank Zucca. Three nights ago, Zucca actually had Drew in his sights while he was on the point of crossing the frontier into the Ukraine. But suddenly an order came through from Ferrandini not to shoot. So Drew got away, and the manhunt was called off.

'A few hours later Ferrandini and his friends arranged to fly home.

At the moment they seem keen to give the impression that everything's hunky-dory and just like normal. Drew, of course, has dropped out of sight. Now, here's the trimmer. When the Chairman of the State Department Policy Committee was told about this manhunt, he ordered me to help in any way I could, even if that meant terminating Drew. But when everyone was ordered to forget about it, he told me to do the same. There's just one final detail I have to add: neither the CIA nor the FBI currently knows about the Belvedere Accords, though I have reason to believe that J. Edgar Hoover did.

'Everything I've told you so far is fact. This is my supposition, based on bits and pieces I've picked up. The Accords were carefully hidden and a system was set up so that if anything ever happened to harm the families, they'd be published. Last week that system was activated by accident, but Ferrandini and Co thought the government was about to take them out, so they went into hiding. Then they realised it was all a mistake, but the system was still operating, and Drew was somehow part of it.'

Ewing put the bonds into his briefcase, snapped it shut, and stood up. 'It's been a pleasure doing business with you.'

'The pleasure was all mine,' replied Lee Kwan, rising to his feet. They bowed to each other again, the middle-aged man appearing from nowhere to escort Ewing to the street.

Once Ewing had gone, Lee Kwan sat down again and pondered what he had just been told. A whisper that the Italians were pulling out all the stops to find an Englishman called Drew had already reached him. So many people had been involved in the manhunt that it would have been surprising if one hadn't. But practically everything else Ewing had just said was new to him. It had long been clear that *some* faction in the government was in the pay of the Italians and affording them protection. Now it turned out that this protection reached cabinet level. Interesting. Lee Kwan was not sure how useful this information would turn out to be, but it was definitely worth the ten million he had paid for it.

The Council reconvened at four o'clock, and by quarter past it had degenerated into a babbled mix of Chinese and English. Lee Kwan, at the head of the table, remained impassive, listening carefully to the three men present he had most respect for. It was soon clear that a consensus of opinion was emerging. That the Accords should be published was obviously against the Italians' interests, because they'd have no further hold over the government. Their sudden about-face regarding Drew could only mean they had changed their mind about his role. They had first assumed him to be instrumental in the publication process – and therefore to be stopped at all costs – and then for some reason decided the opposite was true: Drew was somehow essential in stopping publication, so he had to be kept alive at all costs.

ZhouTsiao put forward the interesting suggestion that, since Drew's dossier made it clear he was a negotiator, his role might be to negotiate the release of the Italians once they'd been arrested. Lee Kwan inclined to this view also, because he had known Salvatore personally and had always held the greatest respect for his intelligence. If the publication system was his device, then there could be little doubt it had been well set up, and that the Accords would be published automatically and soon – but allowing Drew enough time to complete the negotiations.

He raised a finger, and the group turned to look at him.

'Publication will clearly prejudice the interests of the Italians, but will it favour ours?'

Deng Siang, in his late twenties and the youngest man present, spoke up at once. 'Anything that hurts them has to be good for us.'

Several men nodded their agreement with him.

Lee Kwan replied, 'Our existing arrangements with the Italians and the Colombians have made us all rich men. It's true we're the junior partners of this consortium, but we mustn't forget that the ten million dollars we have just paid out amounts to less than one week's income. Do we really want to rock the boat? Doesn't desire for more of the cake, when the cake is already so big, just mean greed?'

Deng countered, 'Speaking for myself, I'm tired of having to kowtow to the Caucasians, of *whatever* nationality. We've been under Italian orders for long enough. Here's our chance to become independent.'

'We have never been under Italian orders. We have negotiated agreements with them from time to time, and they, for the most part, have respected them – and even taken punitive measures against their own people who infringed those agreements.'

'I'm not surprised. They know it's in their interests to keep us happy.'

'Isn't it in *our* interests too to keep us happy?' inquired Lee lightly.

'I for one would be a lot happier if we weren't under their thumbs.'

'Again, I do not consider we are under their orders,' replied Lee patiently, 'still less their thumbs.'

Zhou interposed, 'What is Deng Siang proposing to do about all this, anyway?'

'The negotiator can't even start negotiating until he knows all the facts. Sooner or later he's going to have to get in touch with Ferrandini, who's now back in New York. My guess is that Drew will come here personally. So we keep a watch on Ferrandini and his visitors, and when the Englishman turns up we either kidnap him and keep him locked up until the Accords are published, or we take him out immediately.'

Lee said, 'What Deng Siang is proposing would lead to all-out war between ourselves and the Italians.'

'It could only lead to war if they found out we were behind it, but in any case it would be a war in which they no longer had the protection of the government. We'd be fighting on equal terms, and our people are better than theirs.'

'But do we want a war, anyway?' asked Zhou.

'If it gives us control of the distribution networks, then of course we want war! And if we're the ones who start it, we'll have the advantage of surprise. We could take out their best people before they even knew what was happening.'

The opportunity was there for all to see: a real chance to place the worldwide drug-distribution network in Chinese hands. This was a dazzling prospect, and very soon there was a polarisation of views around the table, the older generation siding with Lee and the younger men with Deng. When at last the vote was taken at six o'clock, it was a tie. As chairman, Lee Kwan used his casting vote, and the formal decision of the Council was to do nothing for the time being and to wait upon events.

But Deng had not finished yet. 'Exactly how does Lee Kwan propose we find out about these "events"?' Lee Kwan eyed him inscrutably but did not reply. 'Let us at least keep Ferrandini under close observation.'

This matter was briefly discussed, and Lee called for another vote. Now Deng's position was stronger because he was merely proposing surveillance, not open hostility. Those in favour raised their hands: again six. But this time, when a count of the opposers was taken, Wang Tsu decided to abstain. So the motion was carried and Deng was authorised to make the necessary arrangements. Reluctantly Lee surrendered to him the photograph of Adam Drew.

As soon as Deng Siang left the building he went to visit his younger brother, and told him what had happened. Kim agreed that it was stupid to throw away such a golden opportunity. 'Stupid isn't the word for it,' grunted Deng. 'It's criminal.' He threw himself onto a sofa, picked up the phone and dialled a number.

'What are you going to do?'

'Put a contract out on Drew.'

'But you'll be breaking the sacred covenant if you defy the Council,' objected Kim. 'They'll order your execution.'

'Only if they find out about it. So I'm not going to use Chinese. I'm going to hire outsiders.'

27

On Friday morning, Drew's Air France *Concorde* landed at Kennedy Airport punctually at 8.45, Eastern Daylight Time. Now holding an American passport, he experienced minimum delay in getting through the immigration checkpoint. He was carrying papers in the name of Richard Andrews, indicating that he had been born in Connecticut of an American father and Canadian mother, but had been brought up in England by an aunt since his parents died in a car crash when he was eight years old. The special effects department of the Russian Security Service still benefited from years of heavy investment during the Cold War, he noted, as he flicked through the items in his wallet. Credit cards, club membership cards, private bric-à-brac, driving licence and business cards proclaimed him to be a business consultant, with an office and secretary that actually existed.

The Russians had done well with Drew's papers, but with Drew himself they had done even better. On the flight over, he had gone to a lavatory four times, needing to look at himself in a mirror again because he could not get over how different he appeared – hair dyed blond, with a different cut, a false moustache that could withstand a shower and even heavy petting. His own mother would need to look carefully to recognise him.

Once out of the airport terminal, Drew took a taxi to the Hilton Hotel, on the corner of the Avenue of the Americas and Fifty-Third Street. He chose it because, with more than two thousand rooms, the hotel would make him feel comfortably anonymous. He could hide from everybody – except the Russians.

Adam hadn't spotted any yet, but he suspected they were somewhere around. Probably in groups of three, in contact with each other by shortwave radio, or even mobile phone. And they'd be the best, too, because to put a tail on him contravened the conditions, and if Drew spotted one he could consider the agreement with the Russians void.

This was why he wasn't absolutely sure they were there at all. Petrovskaya might have taken at face value all his little deceptions aimed at persuading her to limit to the bare minimum the number of people informed. But even if Petrovskaya herself now believed that their best course – meaning that which would bring them the best financial return – was to follow all Drew's baton cues, her superiors might easily have decided on a tempo of their own – an *allegro con brio* colliding with Drew's *andante furtivo*.

Expecting all the mysteries and doubts to be clarified when he read the letter held by the law firm, Adam postponed any escape from his possible surveillance until he knew what he would want to do afterwards.

Barton & Willis was now called Barton, Willis, Lord & Hooper, but the firm's offices were still located in Pearl Street in the financial district.

'I represent a client of yours,' Drew assured the receptionist. 'By the name of Davis & Associates.'

She frowned. 'That name doesn't ring a bell with me, I'm afraid, and I've been here six years. If you'll just hold on one moment, I'll ask Mr Greeley.' A moment later she invited Drew to take a seat. 'He'll be with you in a few minutes.'

Unlike the red-carpet treatment generally offered to anyone representing Don Salvatore, the reception Drew was given now seemed routine. Greeley, a man in his mid-forties, came out to escort Adam to his office.

'I'm sorry Sandra didn't recognise the company name. It's been a very long time since their account has been active. Well, Mr Andrews, exactly what can I do for you?'

'Is that the confidential file for Davis & Associates?' Adam asked, indicating an ancient folder lying on the desk in front of Greeley. The lawyer nodded. 'Somewhere in there you should find a copy of the Articles of Association. Please read articles seventeen, eighteen and twenty-three.'

Greeley opened the folder, leafed through several documents and pulled out a bound deed. Greeley read the articles, then looked up. 'According to this you're supposed to provide proof of your claim to represent the firm of Davis & Associates by citing an authentication code which we've been keeping in a sealed envelope in our trust. I presume that must mean in the safe. If the code is cited correctly, we are to regard you as endowed with full power of attorney. I take it you do know the code, Mr Andrews?' Adam nodded. 'Then if you'll just wait one moment, I'll go and fetch the envelope.'

When he returned he asked first, 'What is the code, please, Mr Andrews?'

'It should read: E, V, Q, B, A, N.'

Greeley opened the foolscap envelope. Inside it lay two smaller envelopes. Typewritten on both he saw: *The authentication code is EVQBAN. Escort the representative to a private room and hand over to him all papers concerning Davis & Associates.*

'Everything seems to be satisfactory, Mr Andrews. If you'd like to come this way.' He led Adam to the deserted company library, saying, 'Tell the receptionist, when you've finished, and I'll join you as soon as I can.'

Adam ensconced himself in an armchair, and began to examine the two envelopes. One of them looked much newer than the other and bore the date January 1967. Beside the date were the words: *This replaces the first envelope.* He opened both and discovered their texts were practically identical, but in the second one a line had been added to cover the invention of new technology which had not existed in 1943.

Trust me and do exactly as I say. It is practically certain that you are being followed by our Russian collaborators, as I expect you already know, and you must get rid of them at once. It is possible they have concealed a tracer in your clothes or shoes, and you may need to buy replacements before following these instructions further. You will find some keys in labelled envelopes in the confidential folder. One of these envelopes is marked Barrow Street, but should any lock have been changed or augmented, a copy of the new key, or keys, again in a labelled envelope, will have been delivered to this law firm and included in the folder. Any additional key will bear the date it was brought to the firm, as well as an indication of which door it opens.

All these keys belong to a brownstone building, owned by Davis & Associates, in Barrow Street in Greenwich Village. Since the name of the street may have changed by the time you read this, I have enclosed a map to show you exactly where the brownstone is.

Put all the interior keys pertaining to Barrow Street in one pocket, and the main outside door key in a different one. Take all the papers and documents concerning Davis & Associates away with you, but tell Barton & Willis that there is something you need to attend to right away, and that you will contact them again within a few days.

Leave the building at a purposeful pace, but taking care not to give any impression of urgency. Take a cab to the Barrow Street brownstone. Go down into the basement, then along to the boiler room at the end of the corridor. At its far end there is a locked door. From behind this a long passageway leads to an identical arrangement in a building in the next street. Turn right out of this second building and a few steps will bring you to Seventh Avenue, where you'll find plenty of transport options. Get to some place quiet where you can read the rest of this letter. Go now!

It was the concealed tracer which, of course, received no mention in the original 1943 text.

First Drew called in to explain his departure to Greeley. Then, going down in the empty elevator, he used one of the keys to tear a large and visible hole in one trouser leg. This provided him with an excuse to enter the first men's store he came to. There he bought a new pair of shoes and some outer clothes as similar as possible to those he was already wearing. It was only the trousers he put on immediately; the rest could wait until he reached the boiler room.

Following Salvatore's elaborate instructions to the letter, a half-hour later Drew emerged on East 33rd Street, close to the Empire State Building. He went straight into a café, ordered a coffee, and settled down to read the rest of the letter.

Those two brownstones you have just visited belong to Davis & Associates, a company I set up in the early Forties – a straw company owned by people who never existed. It is managed by a large firm of lawyers (although its documentation relating to you has been in the possession of Barton & Willis until today), who think the owners are several rich Midwestern families who are all devotees of an obscure right-wing Protestant sect. The lawyers run the company, rake in the profits, subtract a percentage as their fee, pay the taxes due, and send off the rest to a drug-addict rehabilitation centre run by Protestant nuns near West Point, who pay what they think is a nominal rental to Barton & Willis, but this is actually that firm's retainer.

So why construct a phantom company instead of a charitable institution? It is one of the ironies of American life that business is allowed to function in an untrammelled manner, but charities are subject to stifling controls because of the tax advantages available to them. So, acting as a charity, our setup would be periodically investigated, while as a company it is left alone. Every year the rehabilitation centre, on behalf of the Protestant sect, sends an auditor to check the lawyers' books, the IRS investigates the nuns from time to time, and everyone's happy. A perfect circle, going around and around on its own forever.

By the way, all that stuff about Barton & Willis moving their business somewhere else was hogwash, in case the Russians should read the Moscow letter. I am the sole owner of that building, and the firm enjoys an open-ended lease at an extremely low rent, this being apparently in return for a favour which Mr Willis once did me. The motive behind this generosity, however, was simply to guarantee that the firm would survive, and so ensure that you would eventually receive this letter. If Barton & Willis had gone out of business, its various clients would have been passed on to other law firms, but how could you possibly have found out which? Then the link between us would have been broken.

Well, the link has not been broken. You are here, in New York, probably with a false identity, protection and expert assistance. And now you are on your own.

You may wonder why it was necessary to break free of the Russians so soon, but it is now essential that you become a truly free agent, so I have done my best to help you.

I suggest you now find a safe place where you can stay anonymous if you decide to get rid of the Russians permanently. While there, you might like to reflect on the following questions. Do manufacturers of guns pray for an end to war? Do manufacturers of hearing aids pray for an end to deafness? Will drug suppliers cease to exist when the addicts do? Will drug addicts cease to exist when the suppliers do? Is it the case that drug addicts destroy themselves because they become addicted to drugs, or do they become addicts in order to destroy themselves?

If the world destroyed all drugs, would it 'destroy' the drug addict? Or would it destroy him?

Well, my friend, I must leave you to ponder those questions and I must leave you. This has been our final meeting. The appendix to this letter gives you a list of the twenty-four men whose families and descendants it is your assignment to rescue. My own real name is the last on that list, although I strongly suspect you will already know it. I give you my sincerest thanks for all you are doing for the people I love, and I sign myself.
Your friend, Salvatore.
Goodbye

Adam turned quickly to the remaining documents in the ancient folder. They consisted of an assortment of stamped and notarised papers, dealing with the formation of Davis & Associates as a company and its registration with the IRS and other government departments. He read the Articles of Association minutely, but almost everything there was standard legalese, with the exception of the articles granting him power of attorney.

He paid for his coffee and walked out.

Goodbye. And that's it? That's all you've got to tell me? What am I supposed to do *now*?

He headed west, towards the Hudson River. 'This is fucking *absurd*,' he murmured loud enough to attract the attention of a passer-by. The Empire State Building now towered over him. He stopped to stare up at its impossible defiance, but its phallic power seemed only to mock his own sense of impotence. *For God's sake, Salvatore, you haven't told me how to stop Belvedere! You haven't even told me what it is!*

He walked on. *Goodbye?* What kind of a termination was that? Has this man *ever* used a word without thinking? No! The bastard's still speaking to me. Even when he says 'Goodbye'.

Suppose the final instructions are going to be posted to me?

But no sooner had he formed the notion than he discarded it. The enemy would have his London flat under surveillance, and there was nowhere else to send any letter, because no one knew where he was. Not even me, Adam thought grimly.

What particularly concerned him was Salvatore's reference to the 'protection' and 'expert assistance' Drew was supposed to have around him. Nothing more clearly indicated that something had gone awry, because Salvatore obviously expected him to have brought his backup team to New York – complete with bodyguards! But what for, when they didn't have anything to do?

Moreover, he'd made Adam go through the rigmarole of escaping from his Russian tails, before Adam had been able to establish whether he *had* any. That was doubly annoying, because it would have been very useful to know how the Russians were handling this affair. Besides that, of course, if they *had* been tailing him, they would now know all about his escape route, so if Adam later needed to call on the Russians for anything, he wouldn't be able to use it to get away from them afterwards.

Suddenly he was fed up with being shunted around and supplied with unreliable allies. And he definitely did not want to fall back on the Russians, if he could help it. He needed a base and allies of his own: people he knew and trusted. The problem was he did not have any close friends in New York.

Then suddenly he realised there *was* someone he could call on. Not a close friend, perhaps, but certainly someone he could trust – a fellow mountaineer called Lawrence Turner. They had been partners of the rope, when each had held the life of the other in his hands.

He went to a phone booth and rang Turner to make sure he wasn't out of town. A butler answered and said he was expecting his employer home at any minute.

Lawrence Turner lived in the penthouse of a forty-storey glass tower on Fifth Avenue, near St Patrick's Cathedral. He was the son of a wealthy oil broker, who gave him a vast allowance which he spent on women and sport. He was also a mountaineer of note, and Adam had been a member of his four-man team, which had scaled the Matterhorn three years before. Turner had financed the whole expedition and been generous with the extras to boot. Adam had vaguely liked him, but did not consider him an intimate, as off the mountains they belonged to very different worlds.

Drew phoned his apartment from the lobby, and this time found him at home. Turner's greeting was expansive.

'Adam! Where are you?'

'In your lobby.'

'Then come straight up.'

Lawrence himself opened the door. Seeing Adam's newly blond hair and moustache caused him some surprise, but he brushed it aside and welcomed him enthusiastically. He led his visitor into a large sitting room occupying one corner of the building. Its two walls consisted of floor-to-ceiling windows separated by narrow steel struts, and the view offered a spectacular array of towers, crammed together with amazing economy of space.

'Throw yourself down somewhere.' Turner waved an arm towards three sofas. 'Drink?'

Drew took a beer.

Lawrence came to sit opposite him. 'I . . . I was sorry to hear about your brother.'

Adam nodded but made a gesture indicating he did not want to discuss the matter.

Lawrence tried again. 'So what brings you to New York?'

'Actually there's a favour I wanted to ask you. Could you put me up for a week or two?'

'That wouldn't be a favour. It'd be a pleasure.'

'Thanks. But the thing is I'd be grateful if no one found out I was here.'

Lawrence looked at him. 'Are you in trouble?'

'Depends what you mean by trouble. Not with the police, anyway. I've taken on a sensitive assignment, and there are certain people who might like to stop me.'

'And they wouldn't care how they did it – is that it? And I suppose that's the reason for the moustache and the dyed hair. Okay, mum's the word. You can stay here as long as you like, but I'll be going away the day after tomorrow and I'm taking my butler with me, so you'll have to shift for yourself.'

'I expect I'll survive,' replied Adam drily.

Lawrence looked at him askance. 'I don't know about that. I remember your cooking at the Matterhorn base camp.' Adam chuckled. 'Talking of food, I'll be lunching out. Shall I get Philip to rustle you up something?'

'No, thanks. I have to go out, too.'

Turner gave him a set of keys for both the apartment door and the basement carpark, and showed him to a guest room.

A visit to a nearby department store enabled Drew to stock up on the basic necessities and several changes of clothes. After dumping his packages back in Turner's apartment, he went out for lunch in a restaurant on Fifty-Second Street, and there re-read the whole Davis & Associates folder thoroughly. He even warmed the papers with his lighter, in the faint hope that some new message might have been written there in invisible ink.

Adam stared at the opposite wall, completely flummoxed.

Something significant had happened, obviously – otherwise the Belvedere system would not have been triggered. Yet Ferrandini and his family did not appear to be in any danger. But suppose Salvatore had set up his scheme so that it could detect danger, and react to it, before the newspapers got wind of it. Suppose there was some preliminary step that Ferrandini's enemies had to take, which had been detected by the system – like a burglar alarm going off because the burglar first tries to deactivate it – but the newspaper reporters hadn't found out about it yet. Or perhaps Ferrandini's enemies had planted a fifth columnist *inside* his organisation and close to him, and this person had committed some hostile act which the system itself had registered, while nobody else was aware of it.

Adam considered the merits of simply picking up a phone and calling Ferrandini in person. The idea was tempting, because to do so might clarify matters at once.

But it had three drawbacks. The first seemed slightly absurd to Drew, but he could not think of any safe way of surmounting the difficulty: he didn't know Ferrandini's voice. Multimillionaires didn't answer their own phones, so Adam would have to go through several underlings, all trying to protect their boss from bothersome strangers. He might easily find himself talking to someone who took him for a lunatic and tried to humour him. Or perhaps someone apparently loyal to Ferrandini, but secretly hostile, who could now see a way of hurting him. In fact, Adam might even wind up talking to the fifth columnist himself, and not know it!

The second difficulty was that, even if he did succeed in getting through to the real Ferrandini, the man might react unpredictably – even panic – if he did not yet know what was happening. The third drawback was that Ferrandini, even if he wasn't a normally panicky type, would have every reason in the world to panic when he learned that Adam still didn't know how to stop the Belvedere process.

And that's what it all came down to: not knowing. He didn't know Ferrandini's voice, how he'd react, whether there was a fifth columnist, who or what had set off Belvedere, the terms of the Accords, why their publication would cause a political and economic earthquake – and, above all, he didn't know how to switch Salvatore's bloody machine off!

Adam left the restaurant in a dour mood, heading towards the East River. On reaching Park Avenue, he was sorely tempted just to pay a call on the Ferrandinis in person, because he knew they lived in the penthouse of a thirty-six-storey tower a few blocks to the south, near the Pan Am Building.

But Ferrandini's enemies would be expecting Drew to try to contact him, so it was on the cards that there would be men nearby, ready to stop him. And with guns.

Rather than wind up in jail for trying to smuggle a weapon into the United States, Adam had abandoned his Makarov in Russia, so he was now unarmed again. While he remained so, it would be folly to give up the only protection he had left – concealment. Until Drew learned more about what was happening, better not to let anyone else know he was even in New York.

So Adam resisted the temptation of dropping in on the family, crossed the avenue, and continued eastwards.

Yet, sooner or later, he and Ferrandini had to meet to discuss the situation face to face. And preferably when Adam would have some idea of how the man was going to react. He needed to study Ferrandini – somehow – yet without him knowing. And without the opposition knowing.

The next avenue after Park was Lexington. As soon as he saw the name, Adam remembered a little detail from Petrovskaya's report: every afternoon at five o'clock, Ferrandini's daughter Diana took dancing classes – under the name of 'Diana Jones' – in a school on Lexington near Gramercy Park.

Drew took the subway. A quarter of an hour later, he strolled past the dance school, pondering the pros and cons of trying to reach the father through the daughter. It was now ten to four: a little late to find anything else useful to do today.

After several minutes' thought, he went in and enrolled.

Adam bought some gymwear at the reception desk, changed his clothes and joined the aerobics class, together with some two dozen streamlined bodies – mostly female. Glad of the physical exercise, he still felt depressed. Everything had gone wrong. Three men were dead. Half the planet seemed to be looking for him, and he had the distinct impression that the other half was only biding its time. He didn't know a fraction of the things he felt he should. And, to cap it all, the only approach he'd been able to come up with now had him jigging around on a dance floor, wondering how he could con his way into the life of a twenty-two-year-old girl. It was pathetic.

And he felt afraid. He'd bitten off more than he could chew, and he had no idea how he was going to get out of the mess he was in. Before, despite all the scares in Europe, he'd felt a kind of security because, in acting as an agent within the framework of Salvatore's masterplan, it was as if Salvatore himself was watching over him. Now he was on his own. He was expected to improvise, but with what? He had no tools for the job. He felt as if he'd opened some tremendous Pandora's box, and something diabolical had flown out and was now flapping around, hunting for him, while he hunted for the crucifix to ward it off.

In the middle of these depressing thoughts, Diana Ferrandini herself danced into the room, greeting several friends, her fair hair bouncing with the beat. Blue eyes glanced at Adam and . . . did a double take!

For a moment he felt a sense of panic. Somehow certain that her father would not have involved her, Adam had not even considered the idea that *she* might recognise *him*. Clearly she must know who he was!

But now Diana merely joined in the aerobics, thereafter ignoring him.

It dawned on Adam that the double take might have a more obvious explanation; if so, making friends with her might be easier than he had imagined. Moreover, another avenue of approach was through some friend, and she had just pinpointed half a dozen for him. One of them was a friendly young Hispanic called Pablo, who had struck up a conversation with him during a break earlier on. Adam now decided to cultivate the acquaintanceship.

But this was another plan that went wrong, because Pablo soon departed. And shortly afterwards, it was time for Diana's ballet class, so she went off to some other room – as did everyone else she had earlier greeted.

Stumped, Adam took himself off to the gymnasium for a bit of weight training. 'And now we'd fall back on Plan B,' he murmured to himself. 'If we had a Plan B.'

In its absence, he tried masochism for an hour, which at least kept his mind off the distant dangers. By the time he stepped into a cold shower, he'd worked up a satisfying sweat.

Soon afterwards, he was standing outside in the hall near the reception desk, apparently studying the announcements on the notice boards, but keeping an eye on the door to the women's changing room.

Diana emerged with some friends fifteen minutes later, and passed him by without even a glance. Congregating near the reception desk, the women were soon joined by male companions, and all departed together. Adam followed them to a nearby coffee-bar discotheque, where many of the group at once invaded the dance floor, though Diana herself sat at the bar, watching and tapping her foot to the beat. Then she spotted a friend and went across to chat to him. There was a chance she might return to the bar, so, in the absence of any better strategy, Adam went over to the counter and sat on the stool which Diana had just vacated.

A few minutes later she returned. As she approached, Adam saw her hesitate a moment, then step confidently up to the bar counter. He stood up, offering her the stool. A faint smile came to her lips. She nodded her thanks and, as she sat down, said, 'Did you know that in Holland it's considered a breach of etiquette to offer a woman your seat?'

'As a matter of fact, I did. But do they still think so?'

'The old timers do, I think. Are you British?'

'No, but I was brought up in England. My father was American.'

'Was?'

'My parents were killed in a car crash when I was eight, so I was brought up by an aunt.'

'Do you have any brothers or sisters?'

'No. There's just little me. What about you?'

'Three brothers, all at various stages of evolution from little pest to smart-ass.'

He smiled. 'I'm Richard Andrews.'

She mouthed the name, as if savouring it, then nodded her approval. 'Solid-sounding. I'm Diana Jones.'

The ease with which he had got to know Diana made him suspicious. Could it be that she *did* know who he was, after all, and was a really smooth operator?

But this just did not seem compatible with her peculiar combination of sophistication and innocence, so again he dismissed the notion.

The ice was now broken, however, and the conversation became relaxed and friendly.

Half an hour later somebody came up to them. 'Hi, Diana. 'Scuse the interruption, but there'll be a come-as-you-are party over at my place tonight. Wanna join us?'

'Sure. What time?'

'After dinner. Say ten. Bring your friend.'

'Okay. See you then.'

He drifted away. 'Who's that?' inquired Adam.

'David Rochester. He's nice, but not very bright. He lives in a building more intelligent than he is.'

Adam chuckled. 'Perhaps that's why.'

'Yes, but it must be kind of hard to get an inferiority complex from your address. Want to come to his party?'

'Sure. Maybe we could discuss Wittgenstein with his building.'

She laughed. Deciding their relationship was already trusting enough to withstand a little intimacy, Adam said, 'But the party's at ten. Do you have plans for dinner?'

'What do you suggest?'

'Somewhere quiet. Good food. Italian maybe. I'm in the mood for Italian.'

Diana nearly admitted she ate Italian seven days a week. 'How about Greek?' she countered. 'There's a little place I know on Third Avenue.'

'Sure. So long as you don't want to break any plates.'

'Don't worry. I'm a member of Plate-breakers Anonymous.'

Dinner was surreal. Adam oscillated between suspicion and seduction, unable to come to terms with the ease with which he had managed to have Ferrandini's daughter sitting opposite him and the tremendous danger that this might represent.

Yet in no time at all it was ten o'clock and they went to David Rochester's party.

Their host lived in a large, modern split-level studio in Soho, everything white and black and spick and span, and totally without personality. The guests were all beautiful and terribly aware of it, and Adam decided he was facing, collectively, a million man-hours spent in gymnasiums. Two token intellectuals who had just had books published were being lionised. There were several gays with terrific musculatures and eying Adam aggressively, but no blacks, which he commented on.

'David's a hypochondriac. He thinks racial mixing increases the risk of mutant diseases like Aids.'

Adam blinked at her. Just then Rochester himself came over to join them.

'Everything all right?' he inquired.

'Yes, fine,' replied Adam. 'We were just thinking of making up a bridge four with your building.'

Diana struggled not to laugh.

Rochester looked blank. 'I'm sorry?'

'It's okay, David,' she managed. 'A private joke.'

Once he had wandered away, Adam hissed, 'Come on, Diana. Let's get out of here. All these people ought to be stuffed and exhibited. They're nothing but hunting trophies of each other.'

She looked pained. 'They're my *friends*.' Then she grinned. 'Even if they *are* dweebs. We'll have to stay a little while.'

'All right,' he sighed, wondering how in the world their relationship had developed into conjugality so soon.

'Let's mingle,' she suggested.

'I'd rather do that on our own,' he answered slyly.

She smiled flirtatiously, but didn't reply. And it was that absence of a verbal riposte which suddenly told Adam she was still a virgin. Diana had been brought up on Roman Catholic leftovers and somehow or other muddled through all the standard temptations to reach her twenty-two years without actually succumbing to the Big One. But she's been wondering what it feels like for years, he thought. And recently her body's been screaming at her to find out. Then I walk into her life at just that moment, and I'm her type. My God, we've only just met, but I could take her to bed tonight!

But it didn't happen.

They spent the evening chatting senselessly with senseless people, their eyes meeting constantly, while Adam's imagination played out juvenile fantasies of hauling her off to a bedroom, but when it was time to go, they merely strolled around the streets for a while, talking aimlessly, until they returned to Diana's car. A bluish-grey McLaren F1 which looked like a spaceship, it was a birthday gift from her father, according to Petrovskaya's report, and she was obviously in love with it. She offered to drive him home, but an inner voice suggested it might be wiser not to show her where he lived – at least, not for the moment. So he told her he was in the mood for a good hard walk.

'Have dinner with me tomorrow night?' he suggested.

'I'll think about it.' She got into the car and lowered the window. 'I'll let you know at the dance school tomorrow.' She blew him a kiss and drove away.

Adam headed south to Wall Street through the dark, deserted canyons of the financial district, and then on to Battery Park at the tip of Manhattan Island. Across the dark water stood the Statue of Liberty, floodlit. To his left was Ellis Island where so many millions of immigrants had been processed on their entry into the United States.

Among them, in 1912, was a young boy called Salvatore Ferrandini, whose granddaughter Adam now found it hard to keep out of his mind.

And that was something else that, for all his foresight, Don Salvatore could not possibly have taken into account.

Diana took less than ten minutes to get home. Her descent into the basement garage was observed by a television monitor located in a van parked across the street. Hua Sheng stifled a yawn, glancing at his watch. Only another fifteen minutes before the end of his shift. The man about to relieve him was standing in a phone booth less than fifty yards away. He had just dialled, and someone answered immediately. He heard the volume of a television in the background being lowered.

'Mr Violi?'

'Who's calling?'

'I have a message for you from your son.' He placed the mouthpiece next to a tape recorder, and switched it on. The voice was that of a young man of twenty-two. The message lasted less than a minute – during which Alfredo Violi, Ferrandini's butler, died inside. Once it had finished, the caller spoke again. 'Mr Violi, if you want to see your son again, we shall require your cooperation.'

Fredo asked dully, 'What do you want me to do?'

'Has an Englishman called Adam Drew been in touch with your boss yet?'

'I don't know.'

'If he hasn't contacted him, he soon will. So keep your ears open. We shall want to know exactly what is said. Who arranges security?'

'Mr Moreno.'

'How often does he check the place for bugs?'

'Two or three times a week. But he's over in London at the moment.'

'You'll find a packet of bugs waiting for you at the porter's desk. Instructions included. Plant them in all the phones the family uses. Understand this. It's Drew we want, not Ferrandini. As soon as we have him, we'll release your son unharmed. Both you and he will then forget this ever happened.'

Lin Teng hung up and went to relieve Hua Sheng from his shift.

28

Around eight o'clock the next morning, Adam Drew stuffed a handkerchief in his mouth before phoning a woman called Samantha Graeme who lived in Brooklyn. She was a political journalist he had met two years previously in Washington – they had even gone to bed together – but he didn't want her to recognise his voice. Instead he claimed to be a freelance reporter from London, researching an article on drugs and needing to talk to an expert on the Mafia. He explained that a mutual acquaintance had suggested her as someone who knew her way around the world of journalism.

Samantha was able to give him a list of five suitable people living in New York itself. Immediately he began to ring round. The third of them was home and agreed to see him at ten that same morning, since Adam was offering to pay for his time.

Mario Fanucci lived in a large apartment in Little Italy – together with several tons of books and a herd of cats who inhabited them, hid behind them, and sharpened their claws on them. He was a corpulent man in his late forties, almost bald but with several thongs of hair arranged unconvincingly to conceal the fact. He waved Adam towards a deep armchair, then flopped into its partner.

'So what can I do for you, Mr Andrews?'

'I'm told you're an expert on the Mafia?'

'*Which* Mafia?'

'How many are there?'

Fanucci shrugged. 'Nobody knows.'

Adam waited for him to elaborate, but the other man just lit up a cigarette and began to puff smoke reflectively.

Suddenly Adam felt irritated. 'If you need such precise questions before you can answer, then I'm probably wasting your time.'

Fanucci blinked at him. 'Look, my friend, let me try and put you in the picture. Let's divide the world into haves and have-nots. Naturally, the have-nots want to join the haves, but if too many of them succeed, there'll be fewer havables to go round, and the haves show an understandable reluctance to become have-lesses. So what do they do? They make it *difficult* for the have-nots to join their club. The way they do this is very complicated, mainly because they've been doing it for so long – gradually constructing a complex interconnecting system involving religion and guided morality, totems and prizes, lawyers and priests, policemen and courts, prisons and gallows. But the bottom line is simple enough to understand: the havables are not only *desirable*, but also *givable*; so turning some of the have-nots into have-mores, they can be divided – and therefore ruled. In other words, the havables give the haves *power*. The structure as a whole is called the State.

'If any have-not refuses to recognise the authority of the State and decides to write his own laws, then he's a potential *mafioso*. He may only *vaguely* understand the unfairness and the hypocrisy of the system, but that doesn't matter. What counts is his preparedness to operate *outside* the system. But he soon finds out that it's very difficult to work on his own. He realises he needs allies – a club of collaborators who share his views and who have developed an organisation able to outwit the system. If he has brains or strength or some talent, he'll be of use to some club somewhere. And if nobody's taking in new members this year, then he'll start his own with a few of his pals. He may find he needs permission from the local Mafia. Perhaps he'll even have to pay an operating tax. But so long as he's not treading on any toes, they'll probably give him the nod. If the club makes money, its members will stay with it; if it doesn't, they'll leave it and go join a new one.

'How do these clubs make money? Some run protection rackets, some sell drugs, some limit themselves to collecting debts. What sort of character constitutes a club member? You get all sorts. Some have pleasing personalities, some are vicious psychopaths, some have a type of nobility, and others are just plain thugs. If you want to know how the Mafia operates, read English, French and Spanish history. It's all the same story, the same method, the same philosophy. The only difference is that the descendants of the older mafias have to be addressed as Your Majesty and Your Grace.'

Adam smiled. 'All right, I get the picture. But a moment ago you said a new club might need an operating permit from the local Mafia. You seem to be talking about some entity *above* the little clubs.'

'No, I'm not. I'm talking about alliances between certain clubs that are more important than others.'

'All right. So let's talk about the most important clubs.'

Mario gave an amused grunt. 'That's easy. The US government, the Japanese government, the Vatican, General Motors. The list is quite long, but I think you could write most of it yourself.'

Adam smiled again. 'You *know* what I'm talking about – the Sicilian Mafia and the American Mafia.'

Mario sighed. 'Yes, okay.' He stood up and began to pace around the room. 'Certain big clubs *are* in contact with each other – if for no other reason, just to agree on territorial limits and jurisdictions. They'll collaborate if they have a motive to do so. Some of them share the same rules, customs and traditions. Maybe there even exists an *inner* Mafia, but how inner is inner? How high is high? If that's what you're asking about, I can't help you. When you came in, you said I was an expert on the Mafia. The truth is *nobody's* an expert on the Mafia. Not on the modern Mafia. It's too big and complicated; it's too diverse; and it's too hidden.'

'What about all those films we've seen?'

Mario grunted. 'Joe Valacchi – mainly, anyhow. But that's all *old*. The Mafia is an evolving creature just like any other organism. It's moved on a long way since then. And Valacchi's testimony was only a tiny part of the story, in any case. He was too low down to see everything that was going on. Buscetta was much higher up, but he was very selective in what he was prepared to talk about.'

Adam replied drily, 'On the basis of what you've said so far, it sounds as if I'll be paying you just for explaining why you can't tell me anything.'

Mario smiled and sat down again. 'What I've said so far explains why I can't answer the question you originally asked.'

'Well, you've convincingly explained why you can't know very much, yet you obviously do know *some* things. So where does your information come from?'

'A rumour here, a hint there. And a lot of guesswork. But it's enabled me to build up a picture over the years. What exactly do you want to know?'

'To what extent might any particular "club" be protected by the government.'

'I think that goes on all the time. You're bound to find corrupt men in high places. People talk, they do deals together, they turn a blind eye. It's a cinch. Look at Italy.'

'No, I'm not talking about corrupt politicians as individuals. I'm referring to the government itself.'

'Same thing,' replied Mario with a shrug. 'The corrupt individuals, instead of merely being in high places, actually get to the top. As in Panama, for instance. You got to remember the drug trade has made some men rich enough to buy whole countries.'

'What about the United States government?'

Fanucci looked at him. 'What are you suggesting? That the President's on the payroll? Well, why not? A few of them have been on the payroll of big corporations, and some of the Mafia clubs are richer than General Motors. Besides, money isn't the only motivation. Suppose someone found out that the President's a fag. Most men would let their arms be twisted a long way to stop that information being leaked to the public. It's one of the reasons why party leaders vet their candidates so closely. But I think it's fair to say that blackmail

258

isn't used very often these days. Not by the Mafia, anyhow.'

'Why's that?'

'Because it's not good business to make an enemy of a man who's still breathing.'

'Then why was it before?'

'Because *then* they couldn't afford to bribe him; and *today* they can. In any case, attitudes change. You got to understand that, although the Mafia was born in Sicily, and imported Sicilian ideas when it set up shop over here, its attitudes have inevitably been influenced by simply being in America. Take its attitude to the State, for example. Originally the Mafia consisted of have-nots – and not just have-nots, either; sometimes stolen-froms, too. You see, Sicily's been invaded by just about everybody, and most of the time the rulers didn't treat the people at all fairly – particularly the Bourbon kings. It's no accident that *three* major mafias grew up in the territories the Bourbons ruled: the Kingdom of the Two Sicilies spawned Cosa Nostra in Sicily, the Camorra in Naples, and the 'Ndrangheta in Calabria.

'These societies came into being because, when people couldn't get justice from the State, they turned to each other, to the family, to the stronger members of their society. But, above all, they turned to themselves and to their own resilience. There's a word for this which you may have come across: *omertà*. It's in all the books about the Mafia. A lot of the time it's translated as something like "the law of silence", but that's not what it means. Its real meaning is: *to be a man*. If someone did you a wrong, you didn't complain to the courts about it; you took justice into your own hands and sought satisfaction directly. But it was dangerous just to hurt the man, because then he could hurt you back, so you killed him. Hence the vendetta.

'Not ratting on your friends was also part of it. I believe you have something similar in Britain. Your laws demand that you denounce a criminal, otherwise you're an accomplice after the fact, but the public school ethic forbids people to tell tales. In Britain it was the ruling classes that developed that concept; in Sicily it was the peasants who did. But in both cases what evolved was a secret society – in Britain the old boy network; in Sicily the Mafia. The difference is that, in Britain, since the old boy network forms a ruling elite, they don't need to be quite so secretive.'

'An interesting point, though the comparison seems a bit lopsided.'

'That's only because Britain's *mafiosi* made their loot centuries ago, and now all they need to do is hang on to it. They've become respectable now, and write the laws telling people not to steal back from them what they stole in the first place.'

Adam laughed. Then he prompted, 'You were explaining how the Mafia's attitude towards the State changed.'

'Yes. The Sicilian immigrants brought with them their disrespect

259

for authority, and *omertà*. They were rejected by the original WASP inhabitants, so they closed ranks. Other ethnic groups found themselves in the same position – notably the Irish and the Jews. But the Sicilians had several advantages over them: a secret society which already existed; widespread support for it and fear among the Sicilian population; and, as its central creed, *omertà*, which far-sighted members strengthened by rituals and initiation rites: blood mixing, formal oaths, rolled-up paper burning in your hand, and so on. So the *mafiosi* were already better placed to take advantage of the opportunities they found here – particularly Prohibition. Before then they had just been street-wise hoods engaging in small-time criminal activities, though ready to use any means to achieve their ends.

'It was Prohibition which put them on the map. That must rank as the stupidest legislation in the history of the universe. Most intelligent Sicilians hadn't been very impressed by a secret society whose members consisted mainly of thugs preying on their fellow Sicilians, and whose creed of manliness often degenerated into simple bullying. But now the thugs were getting rich, and by a means which few could object to, since they were breaking a law generally considered asinine, and hardly any outsiders were getting hurt. So the Mafia quickly sucked in bright young men who rose rapidly to the top. The Mafia stock became greatly improved in quality, and their secret society began to evolve into a formidable organisation – or, I should say, organisations at that time, because it was divided into territories. You see, *omertà* had a few disadvantages, too. It had led to blood feuds in Sicily, and the immigrants had now brought those feuds over here.

'It was Lucky Luciano who realised that all this was bad publicity, hence bad for business. His solution was "the Commission". The feuds were stopped, and he drew up rules for dealing with future frictions. Whereas disputes had previously been settled by gang warfare, they were now settled by the Commission itself. And if anyone stepped out of line, his case was passed over to the executive arm of the Commission – Murder Incorporated.

'There you have an example of the Mafia adapting itself to the changed conditions of its new environment. Lucky Luciano didn't *make* the Mafia evolve. That would have been impossible. He was simply the man who put into words what the rank and file already felt, since *their* attitudes had changed. What Luciano *did* do however, was to make sure these new attitudes didn't change back. One of the first things he did as head of the Commission was to close Cosa Nostra's books, to use his expression, meaning that no more Sicilian immigrants could be sworn in.'

'A Sicilian wanted to shut out other Sicilians?'

'Yes, and very logically. You see, one of the effects of the gang wars had been to eliminate the Neanderthals – the "old moustaches", as they were called – from positions of power. So by now Cosa Nostra consisted of men with a modern outlook. Luciano didn't want a lot of country bumpkins contaminating his new organisation with primitive Sicilian ideas about vendettas and manliness. He wanted a corporation devoting itself to supplying those services and commodities which the US government had so obligingly made illegal.

'So, whereas the Mafia in Sicily had been made up of rebels distrustful of the State, in America it evolved into a group which accepted the need for authority; for a state within the State – with its own legislative, judicial and executive functions.'

'I see. How did drugs affect this picture?'

'Considerably. You can see to what extent the Mafia's attitudes have changed since it established itself here by comparison with its Sicilian counterpart. The Sicilians frown on prostitution, but they reckon dealing in narcotics is okay – though their own members aren't supposed to indulge. Their American cousins, on the other hand, take a liberal view on prostitution, but dislike getting involved with narcotics.'

'Does that reflect their adoption of WASP attitudes?'

'In fairness, I think most of them felt genuine revulsion at the prospect of kids becoming addicted. They saw drugs as a pretty dirty business, and they were doing well enough with their other interests. Also they knew that involvement with drugs would bring a lot of heat down on them from the police and politicians. But there was one major factor which swayed them in the other direction: the need to keep other people out. To stop others from growing as powerful as themselves. That would have been fatal, because whoever controlled the drugs business would soon become immensely rich, and could then take over all the other criminal activities.'

'So they went into drugs *despite* all the flak they'd get from the police.'

'No, they didn't. The way they solved their dilemma was quite neat. Can you guess how?'

Adam thought for a moment, then shook his head.

'Simple. Since they didn't want to get involved themselves, but their Sicilian cousins didn't mind, they gave the job to them.'

'When was this?' asked Adam.

'In 1957. It was Lucky Luciano who set it up. He called a meeting of both Mafias in the Grand Hotel delle Palme in Palermo, and made the proposal. A few weeks later during another meeting, at Apalachin in upstate New York, the Americans agreed to stop dealing in drugs. That was the famous episode when the police burst in on them, and the dons scattered all over the countryside. The press treated the affair as a hilarious joke, but some very important decisions were

261

taken at that meeting. Thereafter, a few Americans did continue to deal in drugs, but it was very much against official Mafia policy. Luciano's idea was that if the Americans leased out their territory to the Sicilians and merely collected rent, it would look as if they had nothing to do with the business.

'That was the theory, anyhow. In fact, the Sicilians moved in on a huge scale. In the early days, if you were a member of one Mafia, you could automatically become a member of the other. But Luciano had put a stop to all that. So, although the Sicilians were well received by their transatlantic cousins, and vice versa, in order to do business on each other's turf you had to obtain permission first. When the Sicilians started doing a lot more business without bothering to ask, their American cousins did little more than protest. They were reluctant to take them on, you see. By this time, the American Mafia had become diluted, whereas the Sicilians still came from pure Mafia stock. You might say the Americans were flabby in comparison.'

'I see. And where do the Colombians and the Chinese fit into the picture?'

'As far as the Chinese are concerned, there's a popular misconception that they're the main suppliers of heroin to the West, because they control the so-called Golden Triangle of southeast Asia – Thailand, Laos and Burma. In fact, the Chinese have a big market of their own to supply, so only about a fifth of the heroin reaching Europe and the States comes from that area. The main source of opium reaching the West is the Golden Crescent in Turkey, Iran and Pakistan. That's collected by the Turkish Mafia, then routed to Sicily where it's refined, before being sent on to the European and American markets as processed heroin. So the Chinese play a relatively small role in drugs in either Europe or here. And in fact the Sicilians handle a lot of their distribution for them.

'There is even some evidence that the Sicilians fostered the Turkish supply to stop the Triads from becoming too powerful in the West. The weakness of the Chinese and Japanese position is that you can grow poppies anywhere, so the Asiatics only have real power in the areas they control directly, mainly the Far East. But cocaine is something different. It grows only in the high mountains of Colombia, so the Colombians hold the monopoly. The Sicilian and American Mafias have done a special deal with them. Opium is shipped from Turkey by the Sicilians, processed into heroin in Sicily, then sent over here where it's paid for by the Americans with cocaine, which they buy from the Colombians and ship in the other direction. The operation was set up that way in the early Eighties.'

'From all you've said, it seems the Sicilians are by far the most important group.'

'In drugs, certainly. They've had to cope with competition from a lot of other ethnic groups – everybody from the Vietnamese to the Ukrainians. But they're weathering the storm very well. Although Cosa Nostra has suffered its setbacks in both the USA and Italy, there will always be a Mafia, because drugs provide such a vast income.'

Adam was thoughtful. 'All these well-publicised *mafiosi*, the *big* names like John Gotti and Salvatore Riina, are they the men who really control things, or are there invisible puppeteers behind them?'

'The Curia theory,' grunted Fanucci.

'What's the Curia theory?'

'It was someone in the FBI who first brought the word into use, round about the time of P2 and the Vatican Bank scandal, but I don't know where he got it from. During that Palermo meeting of 1957, which I mentioned earlier, Lucky Luciano persuaded the Sicilians to set up their own Commission. It's called the *Cupola*. Basically the Curia theory says that these commissions don't have the last word – that there's a higher authority, supposedly called the Curia. Nobody knows how many members, or who any of them are. In fact nobody knows for sure that the Curia even exists. That's why it remains just a theory. But if it does exist, then there are some extremely wealthy Italian-Americans who are likely members.'

'For example?'

'Philip Lovegni. Robert Ferrandini. Men like that.'

'What do you know about Salvatore Ferrandini?'

'Ah, the great Salvatore. A remarkable man. Highly intelligent, very astute. I'm pretty sure he was involved in some Mafia business in the late Thirties, and his rise to wealth after the war was so spectacular that I wouldn't be surprised if he got a lot of help from the Friends.'

'And his son, Robert?'

Mario shrugged. 'Who knows? As I say, if the Curia exists at all, there's a distinct possibility he holds a seat. But he's so rich he wouldn't need to bother with the Mafia. The family's main interests are in computers and microchips, but they own a lot of real estate too.'

'What would be the function of this Curia?'

'To arbitrate between the warring factions, I should imagine. As I say, no one knows whether it even exists.'

Adam nodded thoughtfully. 'Changing the subject, exactly what role did the Mafia play in Italy during the war?'

'A fairly considerable one. It was probably Lucky Luciano who organised that, too. He seems to have had fingers in a lot of pies. He was in prison serving a thirty-year sentence on a prostitution-racket conviction, and the story is that the government made him a proposition: get the Sicilians to help us, and we'll let you out, though you'll still have to be deported. He accepted, and the Mafia went in with the American army. It wasn't officially the Mafia, of course. In theory, they were supposed to be just native Sicilians who acted as pathfinders and coordinated with resistance leaders behind the lines. But in fact they were true representatives of the Mafia.

'There was something else, too. Mussolini had seen most of the Mafia leaders jailed without trial. When the Americans arrived, anyone they found in jail or under investigation was assumed to be anti-fascist, so they installed them in local government. I'll give you an example: Calogero Vizzini. His criminal dossier included thirty-nine murders, six attempted murders and sixty-three charges of extortion. The US military governor of Sicily gave him a gun permit "for protection against fascist attacks", and made him mayor of his home town of Villalba. He ran a thriving black market from the town hall. So you see, the Mafia became very much more powerful in Sicily than it had ever been beforehand.'

'And after the war Luciano was thrown out of the States?'

'Yes. He went off to live in Naples. But he still remained head of the American Mafia.'

'Was Salvatore a friend of Luciano's?'

'Yes. And pretty close, I'd say. They were both born in Lercara Friddi – only a few years apart too. Luciano was born on 11 November 1897, and I think Salvatore in 1904. As a matter of fact, I once heard it was Salvatore that Luciano used as a go-between with some of the Sicilians.'

Adam felt an inner excitement. He knew this had to be a connection. He was getting warmer.

When he got back to Lawrence's apartment, Adam found Philip the butler preparing lunch.

'Where's Mr Turner?'

'Upstairs in the roof garden. That's where he's having lunch. Shall I set a place for you?'

'Please.'

Adam had not been up to the roof before, and the view from there of huddled skyscrapers was as impressive as anything he had ever seen. Most were taller than his own, and the RCA Building in the Rockefeller Centre soared a further thirty floors towards a blue sky. The roof garden took up about a quarter of the available surface, the rest being devoted to elevator motor rooms, ventilation shafts and other architectural essentials. A table had been set up for lunch with an elegant white tablecloth and silver cutlery, but Lawrence was nowhere in sight. Adam eventually found him in a storeroom adjoining the elevator motor rooms, sorting through some scuba-diving equipment.

'Need a hand?'

Lawrence glanced up. 'Yes, as a matter of fact you could check those gas cartridges for the harpoon gun. Any empties, you can chuck away.'

Adam looked around at an amazing array of sports, diving and mountaineering equipment. There were flippers, wetsuits, snorkels, masks, squash and tennis racquets, golf clubs, polo mallets and a variety of balls. Even a cricket bat. For mountaineering there were ropes, pulleys, climbing boots, pickaxes, skyhooks, abseil pitons, karabiners, helmets. There was even a grapnel with rocket charge and a Very pistol, because Turner was also a mountain-rescue volunteer.

'Jesus, where's the kitchen sink?' he murmured, and began sorting through the cartridges.

After a while he helped Lawrence carry his selected equipment downstairs to one of the spare bedrooms. On the way back up he noticed two keys hanging on hooks by the door leading out onto the roof. One must be for that door itself and the other for the storeroom, but fixed to the wall beside them was an ultra-complicated alarm clock.

'What's this for?'

'It's a time switch for the roof lights.'

'What do you need that for?'

'A lot of New York buildings display different coloured lights for special occasions. I follow the Empire State: red, white, blue for 4 July; orange and white for Halloween; green, white, red for Christmas. I also put on white and blue for my birthday, and New Year's just peachy: red for the old year, then – wham! – white for the new. With a time switch, I don't need to worry about countdowns.'

'What system is it set for now?'

'White and blue. I had a birthday six weeks ago,' replied Lawrence, stepping out onto the roof again.

Adam surveyed the lawn with its border of shrubs and flowers. 'Who looks after your garden?'

'A Mexican called José Antonio de las Eras.'

'With a name like that he could run for mayor of Acapulco.'

'He comes in twice a week. His wife does the cleaning.'

They sat down to table, and Lawrence poured some wine from a bottle which had been chilling in the bucket nearby.

'Tell me, how's your assignment going?'

'Making progress. But I was thinking maybe I ought to get myself a gun.'

'I've one I can lend you.'

'Terrific. I had visions of having to fix a deal with some shady character in a seedy bar.'

'The gun merchants here all wear three-piece suits, and they're rolling in it. In New York these days, not owning a gun is like playing Russian roulette. Things are going mad down there.' He nodded towards the world beyond the railing – where the jungle was. Adam looked around at the sheer cliffs of a different kind of jungle arising out of it – Corporate America. There was something surreal about the contrast.

'I suppose drugs are responsible?'

Turner nodded. 'Most muggings here are committed by people desperate for their next fix.'

Philip appeared carrying a tray with two bowls of vichyssoise, then quickly withdrew. They ate in silence for a while, till Adam asked, 'What's the solution?'

Lawrence gave a shrug. 'Search me.'

'How about legalising drugs?'

'What good would that do?'

'Their high price is due to the fact that they're illegal. The distributors take compensation for the risk of going to jail if they're caught, by charging whatever the market will bear. Since all the zones are regulated by the Mafia, and no competition is allowed in any zone, customers are obliged to pay a very high price, which is why the business is so profitable. It also provides the pushers with a motive for deliberately hooking customers – which I suppose is why they're called pushers. If drugs were legalised and sold at government retail outlets, their price would drop through the floor. The pushers then wouldn't be able to compete, and would go out of business, in which case nobody would have a motive to get people hooked. And addicts would have less incentive to mug people, because they could now afford the price.'

Turner looked doubtful. 'I don't think you'd reduce the number of muggings that way. As things stand, the addict mugs victims because he's desperate for a product, then goes to the pusher, hands over the money and gets the product in return. You make drugs legal and maybe you would eliminate a few addicts, but how's the pusher going to earn a living now? He'll mug people directly instead of getting the addict to do it for him. Legalising drugs wouldn't solve the problem it would just cut out the middle man.'

Adam laughed.

'Okay, I made a joke out of it, but when it comes to muggers, I'd rather the addict than the pusher. The addict is dangerous because he's often out of control, but once he's got your money the only thing on his mind is securing his fix. The pusher is a worse risk because he's a man in control of himself and knows you could identify him, so he might not take the risk of leaving the witness alive. As far as I can see, the breakdown of law and order here is because too many people just don't value human life.'

'*They're* victims, too.'

'Maybe so, but what you've got to realise, Adam, is that killing people is too damned easy. It's the films which make it look difficult and dramatic. They give you all that jarring music with hysterical violins, to make you think God's about to put in a personal appearance, but the reality is that killing someone is routine. You shoot, he falls down, and that's that.' He finished off his soup and went on. '*That's* what few films manage to get across. For some people, killing is as routine as chopping wood.'

Adam looked doubtful. 'I'm not so sure. I seem to have seen quite a number of films try to express that idea.'

Philip reappeared with two plates of lightly grilled sole and a bowl of lettuce salad.

Lawrence continued, 'In that case I've failed to get across to you what I'm trying to say. So let's try something different. Think about prison. There are two things most people don't realise about it. One, just how terrible it is. Two, just how easy it is to get yourself in there. Since you're a mountaineer, I'll talk about something a mountaineer will understand. Imagine you're scaling a sheer cliff like El Capitán or the Eiger. You're careful. You don't put the pitons in like they're made of glass. You rely on your tools, and put them in like they're pitons, made of good metal, as they're supposed to be. You don't check and recheck and double-check and triple-check. You give a couple of good sharp tugs and accept that they're properly anchored. And you *believe* in them. You have faith in the work of the guy who made them, and in your own skill in testing them. That's life: uncomplicated, but sturdy, intelligent, adventurous life. And then that certain unpredictable something happens, and you die. What are we going to say? That the system failed? No! The occasional failure is *part* of the system.'

'What are you implying? That every now and again we jail people who are innocent?'

'No! Or rather, yes, we do. But that's not what I'm talking about here. What I'm saying is that every guy who's in prison failed to do what he intended to do. It doesn't matter whether you're talking about someone really clever or a complete idiot. He *failed*. And what reduces the number of people ready to commit crime is the same thing that reduces the number of people who'll ever take a crack at the Eiger – fear of failure. Fear of *routine* failure.'

'Yes, but what's all this got to do with how easy it is to kill?'

Lawrence shook his head. 'I express myself really badly sometimes,' he muttered. 'Adam, the prisons are full.' He watched the other man's expression, before continuing. 'Most of the time the pitons hold.'

Adam examined his host from under lowered eyelids. 'Hm,' he murmured thoughtfully, picking up his fork.

Lawrence had to leave for an appointment immediately after the dessert. Alone now, Drew sipped his coffee, thinking about their conversation. He got up from the table and walked over to the railing. Around him towered the cliffs of wealth – the visible wealth and power of America, wielded by invisible men behind the dark windows. In a natural association of ideas, Robert Ferrandini came into his mind. The Ferrandini building on Park Avenue was only a few streets away, but it couldn't be seen from Turner's roof garden because of intervening skyscrapers.

Adam lowered his gaze – and instantly knew what he was going to see.

There it was: the gaping void into which his brother, staring upwards, endlessly fell.

But forty floors down to the street was a mere five hundred feet, whereas they'd been two thirds of the way up the six-thousand-foot North Face. James had fallen four times the height of this building.

Tell me to cut the rope!

Dear God, have pity on me. At least let me forget.

He turned away.

Philip was now clearing the table, oblivious to the nearness of the Eiger.

Adam went down to his room and stripped off. He went into the shower, turned the cold tap on full and let the water blast him. He stood enjoying the discomfort until his teeth were chattering, then subjected himself to some brisk towelling. After that he lay on the bed and stared up at the ceiling. The sheer whiteness disturbed him. That, too, reminded him.

Jesus Christ! I can't look at anything! Is this what hell is going to be like? Because if it is, then I'm there already!

He reached for his cigarettes and lit one.

I'm in a mess, he decided. And it's getting worse. I'm living with a mountain inside my brain. I've somehow got to break free.

But what about Salvatore's mission? And what about Salvatore's granddaughter?

Adam suddenly seized his briefcase, as if the demons which haunted him were hiding inside. But all the briefcase contained were the notes he'd taken earlier in Mario Fanucci's apartment. The notes on Salvatore Lucania, alias Charlie 'Lucky' Luciano. He skimmed through them for a while, then lay back thinking about the man's extraordinary history.

In 1917 Luciano had teamed up with Frank Costello and two Jews, Meyer Lansky and Ben 'Bugsy' Siegel. When Prohibition began in 1920, the group had engaged in bootlegging and become very successful. They attempted to remain independent of the two big warring crime organisations run by Joe Masseria and Salvatore Maranzano, who were fighting over the control of New York. The war became particularly bloody in 1930, and Luciano was one of many who abhorred the bad publicity, which threatened to provoke a crackdown by the authorities, but Masseria resisted a peace settlement. So, on 15 April 1931, Luciano lured him to Scarpato's restaurant in Coney Island, where he was gunned down, while Luciano was washing his hands in the restroom.

After Masseria's funeral, Maranzano presided over a convention attended by five hundred men in a hired hall in the Bronx. Here he outlined a new system of control and government of the underworld, in which disputes would be settled by a committee of the heads of all the Families. Maranzano himself was the *capo di tutti capi* – the boss of all bosses – and received financial contributions from all the other Families. This new era of universal peace, however, was not intended to embrace Luciano, the *capo* of one of the five New York Families, whom he regarded as a dangerous rival. But while Maranzano was still plotting to kill him, Luciano acted first. On 10 September four gunmen entered Maranzano's offices, posing as IRS inspectors, and shot him down.

Luciano now became the boss himself, although he did not claim either the title of *capo di tutti capi* or the tribute due to it. In a private meeting room at the Blackstone Hotel in Chicago, in which Al Capone played host to delegations from all over the country, Luciano was acclaimed as the 'president' of what was now, through his efforts, a national crime corporation operating on accepted business principles and practice.

In 1935, however, the New York special prosecutor Thomas Dewey gathered enough evidence to convict Luciano on charges of owning and running a string of brothels, and in 1936 he was sentenced to imprisonment for thirty to fifty years. From his cell Luciano continued to rule his empire, and when the luxury liner *Normandie* blew up in New York harbour in 1942, Naval Intelligence sought his help in preventing further Nazi sabotage. Since the Mafia controlled the Longshoremen's Union, he gave the order and the sabotage was halted.

The story about the further help he provided the US government in arranging local assistance for the American military invasion of Sicily had never been confirmed by any government source, and Luciano himself denied it. But, whatever the truth, in 1945 he was paroled, and on 11 February 1946 was deported to Italy. From Naples he continued to exercise a powerful influence on the American Mafia until his death from a heart attack in January 1962.

Adam found it intriguing that there should be so much detail in the story of a supposed visit by Luciano to Sicily before the American invasion. But more obvious to him was that the US government, with such a plentiful supply of Sicilian-born agents at its disposal, could not have failed to take advantage of the opportunity they offered to facilitate the invasion and thus save thousands of Allied lives. If Luciano himself had not gone to Sicily, then somebody else had.

29

When Diana arrived at the dance school at five o'clock that afternoon, to Adam's embarrassment she came over to watch him. He stopped at once. 'I can't do this with you looking on.'

'How did you get in such good shape?' she asked, eying the muscles outlined by his tight black vest.

'Mountaineering, mainly.'

She looked away, and began some stretching exercises.

'Well? Are you having dinner with me this evening?'

She sighed. 'Oh, I suppose so.'

'That sounds really enthusiastic.'

'What do you expect? For me to swoon all over you?'

'Isn't there some happy medium?'

She stopped exercising and cocked her head to one side. 'Why do I get the impression with you that mediums aren't very happy at all?'

He blinked at her, then turned away. Suddenly he felt like a troublemaker – a Jonah – for those around him. She had hurt him, although he couldn't tell her why. As if sensing this, she asked tentatively, 'I obviously touched a nerve. I'm sorry. Where shall we go for dinner?'

'Somewhere quiet, where the food's unutterably expensive and wonderful.'

'There's a French restaurant I know, in the Village.'

'Sounds good.'

'Have you ever met anyone under the clock at Grand Central?'

'No.'

'You'll never feel like a real New Yorker till you do. See you there at seven thirty.'

The evening passed uneventfully; quietly romantic, with passion stalking at a safe distance – along with other menaces. Adam felt in limbo. The debts of passion were mounting. For both of them. There was an inevitability about it, which Diana too recognised. He knew she was at heart spoiled, but was she reining in her selfishness during this courtship and was even worse than she seemed?

At one point during the evening Adam had a premonition that their relationship was going to end really badly. He somehow knew he was going to die because of Diana.

He pushed the thought out of his mind, but it was never to abandon him entirely. Despite it, he persisted in his involvement with her, putting it down to a death wish born out of the debt he owed to his brother.

When they reached her car, he asked, 'What about tomorrow night?'

'I'm supposed to go to a party.'

'Don't.'

'I think I have to.'

He shrugged. 'Have to is have to.'

She nodded and sighed. 'I can have coffee with you in the afternoon, though.'

'That's a fair consolation prize.'

She smiled. 'Yes, isn't it. Five o'clock?'

'Under the clock at Grand Central?'

'That'll do. Bye.'

Adam watched her taillights disappear, feeling a strange mix of disappointment and relief.

He walked home wondering how cold was death.

The following morning his host Lawrence left for his deep-sea fishing and scuba-diving vacation in the Bahamas. He remembered to leave Drew the promised pistol: a Ruger P91.40 which fitted Adam's grip comfortably.

Its clean lines, promising sudden but permanent solutions, hypnotised him.

Finally finding the object ugly, he decided he would not need it yet, and put it away in a drawer in his room.

'Do you want to come to this party tonight?' she asked him over coffee.

He almost said yes, but an alarm bell rang in his mind. He guessed the party would take place in Ferrandini's own apartment. His mild disguise would not stand up to close scrutiny.

'I'm afraid I've already made other arrangements.'

Diana's 'Oh' sounded casual, but he knew she was disappointed. 'Is she pretty?'

'Not bad. But I tell you what: you get out of your thing, and I'll get out of mine.'

She liked that, he could tell. 'Are you normally so fickle?'

'No,' he answered, leaving the monosyllable to do all his flattery for him.

'What would we do?'

'I'm looking after a friend's apartment while he's away on holiday.

272

We could cook ourselves some dinner and watch a video.'

'Sounds quite domestic.' She considered a moment longer, then agreed.

It was two hours later, while preparing salad in the kitchen, that they kissed for the first time. Within minutes they were both out of control. He picked her up and carried her into the bedroom.

'I've never done it before,' was all she said.

'I know,' he murmured.

Arriving home at ten to four in the morning, Diana found her father waiting up for her.

'Where've you been?' he demanded coldly.

'I went out with a friend. Someone I know from the dance school.'

'Who?' he persisted.

Suddenly she felt angry, but mostly because of her sense of guilt. 'No one you know. He's just a friend.'

'A man you know well enough to spend half the night with?'

'I . . . I like him.'

Her reply had spoken volumes, and she hadn't wished it to.

Ferrandini stared at her for a long moment. 'Have you anything else to tell me?'

When he'd asked that same question a year ago, she had held his gaze and said sincerely, 'No, Dad.' Now she said nothing.

He turned away. 'We'll talk tomorrow, Diana.'

'Goodnight, Dad.'

For the first time in her life, her father did not reply.

Adam spent the next morning in the New York Central Library, reading up on the Sicilian campaign and its immediate aftermath. But he found it hard to keep his mind on the task because Diana kept invading it. Then he turned a page and something caught his interest. Soon he was reading with complete absorption. After a while he began to take notes.

July 3rd: Intensive air attacks initiated against Sicily.

July 10th: Invasion begins.

July 13th: Fascists call on Mussolini to convoke a Fascist Grand Council on 24th.

July 17th: Leaflets dropped calling on the Italian people to surrender.

July 19th: USAF bombs railyards & airport at Rome.

July 22nd: Palermo taken.

July 24th: Fascist Grand Council meets in Palazzo Venezia at 5 p.m. Grandi proposes a resolution calling on the king to assume his responsibilities. Mussolini opposes it but the voting

273

is 19 to 7 in favour with 2 abstentions.

July 25th: Mussolini requests an audience with the king at 5.00 and is arrested. Marshal Badoglio forms a new government. In reaction Hitler orders Rommel to assemble a force in the Alps for a possible entry into Italy if events should go unfavourably for Germany. Rommel exceeds his brief and seizes the Alpine passes. He subsequently infiltrates more and more troops into Italy despite Italian protests.

July 28th: The Badoglio government enters into secret negotiations with the Allies via agents in Lisbon and Tangier. The British and US governments both have accredited representatives in the neutral state of the Vatican but this convenient channel of communication with Badoglio cannot be used because neither possesses a secure code! From July 28th to August 3rd there is much toing and froing of telegraphs between London, Washington and Eisenhower on the terms of surrender to be offered to Italy: the so-called 'Long Terms', originated in the British Foreign Office at the instance of Foreign Secretary Anthony Eden, and the 'Short Terms', devised by Eisenhower and his political advisers.

Aug. 5th: Catania falls to British Eighth. Churchill leaves the Clyde aboard the *Queen Mary* for Canada.

Aug. 6th: US Seventh takes Troina and Cape Orlando on 10th and Randazzo on 13th and the enemy breaks contact.

Aug. 9th: Churchill reaches Halifax and entrains for Quebec.

Aug. 16th: Americans take Messina.

Aug. 17th: By 10 a.m. last German soldier flung out of Sicily. Roosevelt arrives in Quebec.

Aug. 19th: Quebec Conference starts.

Sept. 1st: Rommel already has 8 divisions in northern Italy.

Sept. 3rd: The Short Terms of surrender are signed in Sicily by General Giuseppe Castellano, whereupon he is presented with the Long Terms.

Sept. 8th: German army begins encirclement of Rome. Radio Algiers broadcasts Italian armistice. After dark the Italian battle fleet, obeying Allied instructions, sets sail from Genoa and La Spezia to surrender at Malta on September 11th but on the 9th German aircraft attack it and the flagship *Roma* blows up.

Sept. 9th: The Allied landings at Salerno begin.

Sept. 12th: The Germans stage a spectacular rescue of Mussolini at Gran Sasso in central Italy.

Sept. 14th: Mussolini meets with Hitler and at the end of September, guarded by German troops, sets up a puppet government called the Italian Social Republic at Salò on the shores of Lake Garda in the north of Italy.

Sept. 29th: Marthal Badoglio, under protest, signs the Long Terms before Eisenhower aboard the British battleship *Nelson* at Malta.

Adam put the book down and considered. One of the more unfortunate aspects of the story was that the news of the Italian armistice was broadcast just when the Allied invasion armada was approaching Salerno bay near Naples, for the main assault on mainland Italy. It had the effect of making many of the attackers think they could walk in unopposed, whereas the Germans were already digging themselves in. The resulting battle was fierce, and the Allies barely held on by the skin of their teeth till help arrived in the form of the British Eighth Army, commanded by the ultra-cautious Montgomery, after a leisurely stroll up from the toe of Italy.

The effect of an ineptitude of gargantuan proportions by the Allies was that Italy was invaded simultaneously at both ends: in the south by its ex-enemies now wanting to be friends, and in the north by its ex-allies having to become enemies. The king and Badoglio fled Rome, the Italian army surrendered wherever anybody gave it the opportunity to do so, and eventually the Germans and the Anglo-Americans settled down somewhere halfway up the leg to slog it out together. Civil war broke out in several areas of the country, and huge numbers of people were either murdered outright or handed over to the Gestapo and *then* murdered.

The Allies, slowly, and at great cost in human life, continued to crawl up the peninsula, fighting all the way until almost the end of the war. The remnant of the Wehrmacht in northern Italy surrendered on 2 May 1945, only six days before the general German capitulation.

In the meantime the civil war continued unabated and with a savagery on a par with the atrocities committed in Bosnia. The worst butchery took place in the notorious 'Triangle of Death' – the provinces of Bologna, Modena and Ferrara, where the slaughter of entire families was frequent. It was impossible to know how many people died, because so many simply disappeared, but the death toll could have been a hundred thousand despite an official figure – still held to by the Italian government – of 17,322. The participants included not only communist partisans and fascists on the run, but also German units preferring the excitement of war to an internment camp in Germany.

A suspicion was now beginning to form in Adam's mind. He remembered something he had read the previous day in Volume V of Churchill's history of *The Second World War*. He took the book out again, and spent a quarter of an hour hunting for the reference. He found it eventually on page eighty-nine, and proceeded to read the whole chapter with fascination.

At lunchtime he got up and walked out of the library, deep in thought.

30

The unhurried footsteps echoing on the stone floor came closer. Somebody had all the time in the world, he thought. In this place *everybody* has all the time in the world. The footsteps stopped outside his cell.

'Charlie, you awake?'

Lucky Luciano opened a single eye. 'My parole come through?'

The warder laughed. Good ol' Charlie. Always in good humour. 'Then you really *would* be lucky. Got another thirteen years to go before you're eligible.'

'Don't remind me.'

'Come on. Up you get. Ya gotta visitor.'

'It ain't visitors' day. So who is it?'

'Search me. I just do as I'm told. The governor says you gotta visitor, you gotta visitor. Come on.'

'Whatever you say, Mike.'

The warder opened the cell gate and they walked along the corridor at a pace closer to a mild stroll. This was jail speed, and he'd been walking at this pace for seven years. Seven years!

They passed through several electronic gates, until they reached central control. Luciano started to turn right towards the communication booths but the guard pulled him back and they proceeded straight on to the administration block. The warden himself opened his office door and beckoned Luciano in. Mike started to follow, but the warden gestured him away and closed the door.

Standing by the fireplace was a man in his mid-thirties with quick, sharp eyes in a slightly pockmarked face.

The warden said, 'Mr Harding, this is Salvatore Lucania. I'll leave you to it.' He withdrew.

Harding studied the prisoner wordlessly for a moment, then stepped forward and offered his hand. 'Please sit down, Mr Lucania.'

'Everyone calls me either Charlie or Luciano – or Lucky,' replied Luciano. 'Great sense of humour, huh?' he added, gesturing at his surroundings.

'Maybe they're not so far out,' replied the other mysteriously. 'Cigarette?'

Luciano accepted one, and Harding lit it for him.

'What do you mean?'

'Mr Luciano, I won't beat about the bush. You've already been a great help to us in this war, through your efforts over Nazi sabotage on the New York waterfront. Frankly, we're impressed by your ability to continue controlling events from inside prison. I'm here as an official representative of the United States government, to make you an offer. We know you're the head of the Mafia here in America, and that you also have contacts among the Mafia in Sicily. As you well know, Mussolini has had many of its leaders imprisoned without trial – but not all. A great many are still free and we can reach them through you.'

'Why do ya wanna do that?'

'Because we want them to organise a resistance movement behind the lines when we invade.'

Luciano pulled on the cigarette and blew out a plume of smoke. 'Interesting idea. But you used the word "offer". I ain't heard no offer yet.'

'The deal is this: release but deportation after the war, in exchange for services rendered now.'

'Deportation?'

'Back to Italy. You're not wanted for anything there. But from there you can go anywhere else you want, except for United States territory.'

'How much time have I got to set it up?'

'Maybe three months. Maybe a bit more.'

Luciano nodded slowly.

'Well? What do you say?'

He went through the motions of considering a while longer. 'Yeah, I think I might be able to help ya out.'

'Good. What will you need?'

'Not what – who. The world isn't built on whats. It's built on whos.'

'Very well. Who do you need?'

'Someone who knows Sicily. Someone I trust.'

'Have you anyone in mind?'

Luciano nodded. 'Salvatore Ferrandini.'

Vincenzo Cattagna entered the room with a pretty girl on his arm. Smiling broadly, Salvatore stepped forward and took him by the elbow. They gazed into each other's eyes a moment, then fell together in a bear hug. Breaking away, Salvatore stood back to examine the younger man.

'A whole year, Cenzo,' he said quietly.

'Don't tell me you can see the difference,' responded the other in mock alarm.

Salvatore laughed. 'Only in your ankles.'

Now it was Cattagna's turn to laugh. He turned to the girl waiting patiently by his side. 'This is Myra. She's a friend of Meyer's. Her surname's Polish. I can't pronounce it yet, but she's giving me lessons. Myra, this is Salvatore.'

The girl offered him her hand to shake, but Ferrandini deftly turned the back uppermost and bowed his head over it for a token kiss. All in one suave movement. Then he guided her towards his wife.

Sofia was an attractive woman who managed to combine grace with her rather large bones. She and Vincenzo had met often before, and he warmly kissed her on both cheeks. Then Cattagna and Myra went over to pay their respects to the baby lying in the cot, its blue eyes wandering curiously over them. Robert Ferrandini was one year old today.

Then the couple went off to mingle with the crowd, and it was nearly two hours before their host could signal for Vincenzo to join him in his study for a private chat.

Passing his friend a glass of brandy, Salvatore asked, 'What's new out in Chicago? Any problems with upstairs?'

'Nothing I can't handle. Everyone likes to think he's another Capone, but it's all fart and no shit.'

'Amen,' replied Salvatore with feeling.

'No, I think all's quiet on the Midwestern front – at least as far as our business is concerned. But maybe something's happening in a rather unusual area.'

'Oh? Which?'

'Science,' replied the younger man, then switched to Italian. 'An experiment was performed at the university last December. Very hush-hush but everyone was pretty excited about the result. It took me a while to find out what it was all about, but I can tell you if you're interested.'

'Does it interest *you?*'

'Yes.'

'Then I'm interested.'

Cattagna switched back to English. 'Okay. Uranium. It's the most complex element that exists naturally, although there are others which can be formed artificially. One of them's called plutonium. The more complex an element is, the more bits it has in each atom. But some complex elements throw out some of their bits naturally, and at more or less regular intervals. The bits fly out at a terrific speed and can hit other atoms, causing them to explode, and then they in turn blow others apart. It's called a chain reaction. In other words, a bomb. But a bomb working on a completely different principle from ordinary ones. And very powerful.'

'How powerful?'

'The Bronx,' he replied gravely.

Salvatore blinked twice, then reached for the box of cigarettes on his desk. 'Go on,' he prompted.

'What they did at Chicago was to dampen the effect by introducing a heavy medium, making it difficult for the bits to get through to other atoms. Originally they wanted to use something called heavy water, but then they found out that graphite was almost as good and it was easier to get hold of, so that's what they got. By using a dense medium, the process can be controlled so that you don't get an explosion but a continuous supply of heat. Heat which can be turned into electricity. The whole process could prove a terrific boon for mankind – but all that's in the future. For the moment it's the military and the government that are calling the shots, and you can guess what *they're* after.'

'The bomb.'

'Too right. And the principle's simple enough. It's all a question of numbers. Imagine you've got two atoms and one explodes. What are the chances a bit will hit the other?'

'Next to nothing.'

'Right. Imagine you've got a hundred. What are the . . .'

'Okay, I've got the picture. The explosion will occur when you've got enough atoms to guarantee that if one explodes, they all will.'

Vincenzo was impressed. 'Not quite. It doesn't have to be all of them. Just enough to ensure a chain reaction. The scientists call this critical mass.' Then he gave a shrug. 'But they don't know how much it amounts to in weight yet. They think it's somewhere between two pounds and twenty.'

'Does it matter? Make a bomb of twenty pounds, and there you are.'

'Apparently, it's getting hold of the right kind of uranium which is the problem. You have to purify it by a very long and expensive process. Plutonium's even more difficult. They could only produce it after this Chicago experiment.'

Salvatore looked doubtful. 'It doesn't sound as if they're very close to anything practical yet.'

Vincenzo shrugged. 'Maybe closer than you think.'

Salvatore was busy refilling their glasses and missed the undertone. 'How did you find out about all this?'

'One of the guys working on the experiment was homosexual. I made friends with him, and one thing led to another. I'm afraid I even had to sleep with him.'

'Have to go all the way?' asked Salvatore, intrigued.

Vincenzo nodded. It was time to play his ace, he decided. 'What impresses me is that most of the Chicago people have since moved away. They're now working at a place near Knoxville, Tennessee. A year ago it was just open countryside. Now it's a town of fifty thousand people, and heavily guarded by the army. There's related work also going on down in New Mexico. Again a town springing out of nowhere. The whole operation's called the Manhattan Project and it's run by an army engineer called General Groves, the same guy who built the Pentagon. The government's pushing a lot of money into this, Tore. Too much for a bum steer.'

Salvatore frowned. 'But if we can do it, so can the Germans.'

'That's the problem. My friend says it's a race.'

Salvatore replied gravely, 'Maybe it's one race we can't afford to lose.'

The following morning Salvatore received a phone call from Lucky Luciano. Within a quarter of an hour he had cancelled his engagements for the day and was packing an overnight bag. By eleven o'clock he was aboard a military plane, heading for Dannemora prison in the extreme north of New York State, close to the Canadian border. There he had lunch with Luciano himself in the warden's private dining room.

'A bit different from your suite at the Waldorf Astoria,' commented Salvatore, looking out of the window.

'You can say that again,' replied Luciano drily.

Salvatore broke some bread. 'So what's the deal exactly?'

'Parole when the war's over, then deportation to Italy. Public opinion wouldn't like it if I stuck around,' the chief added wryly.

'So what exactly do you want me to do?'

'A lot of the guys had to skedaddle when Mussolini let Mori loose on them. They're broke now, most of 'em. The cake's only so big. They'd be glad to get back home to Sicily. The idea is that they go in with the troops, to pave the way a bit. But what's more important is that our friends still in Sicily know what's gonna happen. You're gonna have to be real careful about who you talk to, because if a word gets back to the Germans, they'll throw in all the reinforcements they got. It'll have to be just the top people who know, the ones who can really get things moving at short notice. Like two days at the outside.'

'I can fix things up with my own contacts, but what will I do about yours?'

From his jacket pocket, Luciano took out a little black notebook and tossed it onto the table in front of his guest. 'That's a list of them. Calogero Vizzini's the most important. For each guy I've put down a coupla items of information you couldn't know about unless it came from me. Any messages you send them, wrap them up in a yellow silk kerchief stitched with a black *L*.'

'Sounds okay.'

'Do a good job, Sal. The sooner this thing's over, the sooner I'll be outa here for good.'

'I'll do what I can, Charlie, you know that. But what I don't understand is why they're going for Italy anyhow.'

'It's ripe for falling. I don't think even the big-cheese generals realise just how ripe. Everyone's sick and tired of Musso. He pushed them into a war they didn't want, they're being shelled and shot up all over the place by the Brits, who used to be our friends, and now they just want out.'

'I realise that, but what I mean is they're not going to defeat Hitler by going through Italy. Anyone who looks at a map can see that.'

Luciano shrugged. 'Talk to the guys in the Pentagon. Maybe they'll tell you. Your contact's a guy called Leone. He's a colonel. Second-generation Italian from Naples. Maybe that's why they picked him. He'll be waiting for your call.'

'Okay. I'll go see him tomorrow.'

'There's one other thing. A lotta those guys Mori put away are still in jail. When the army goes in, it'll be locking up all the fascists and letting out the anti-fascists, and anyone in jail's gonna look about as anti-fascist as you can get. But some of them are commies. The boys you send in with the army maybe oughta point that out to the brass hats. When it comes to picking mayors and councillors, we gotta make sure it's the *right* kind of anti-fascist who gets picked.'

Salvatore wasn't slow to see the possibilities. 'This is going to make you one hell of a popular guy with our friends there.'

'Sure. After all, I'm gonna have to live over there in a little while, remember? So I'm gonna need friends in high places. As high as I can get them into,' he added with a sly smile.

Salvatore reached the Pentagon at a quarter to ten. He was impressed by the size of the complex, which he had previously seen only in newsreels. Its construction had finished just in time for the war. Upon arrival, Salvatore was promptly escorted by a guard to a quiet office on the second floor, where Colonel Leone waited to receive him. He was a tall man of generous proportions and generous smile. They shook hands briefly and he waved Salvatore to a chair.

'Okay, where do we begin, Mr Ferrandini?'

'That's what *I* was going to ask.'

Leone smiled faintly. 'Yeah. Pretty unusual, huh?'

'Pretty.'

'Well, the basic point is that the High Command hasn't decided yet where they want to hit the Germans next. But *if* they decide on Sicily, our job will be to fix up in advance a behind-the-lines operation.'

Salvatore gave him a polite nod, but he didn't swallow the '*if*', with or without the emphasis. The US government wouldn't be dealing with Cosa Nostra on the basis of any *if*.

'Perhaps you'd care to tell me why we're thinking of going into Italy at all.'

Leone gave a wave of his hand, as if brushing the question aside. 'Technical reasons.'

'What are those reasons?' insisted Salvatore.

'You really want to know?'

'Sure.'

'Well, basically the issue is we've got to help the Russians and be *seen* to be helping them. We no longer think they're going to collapse, but one reason for that is that the threat of an invasion in the west is forcing Hitler to keep forty divisions ready in France. He thinks that if he can throw us back, he'll then have a breathing space to send all his divisions against Stalin. So the threat of invasion alone is taking a lot of pressure off the Russkies, whereas if we actually went ahead with it and failed, it could mean we'd lose the whole war.'

Salvatore nodded.

'So the invasion of France has to wait until next year, by which time we'll be strong enough to be surer of success. But at the same time Stalin's screaming at us to engage the Germans in battle *somewhere*, to reduce the pressure on him further. First we went for North Africa, which is now almost completely in our hands, but we'll soon have all those men sitting out there with not much to do. Churchill wants to use them in a lot of pinprick attacks in Italy and the Balkans. But on this side of the Atlantic, the general feeling is that if we get too involved in scattered pinpricks, we won't be able to put enough into the main push in France. They'll draw off our available resources in men and materiel, especially landing craft.

'Now, Eisenhower reckons we ought to go for just Sicily, and stop there. His argument is that it would help clear the sea lanes which are very important to the British. And keeping Britain afloat is the be-all and end-all of this war.' He lowered his voice. 'Very few people know how close they came to collapse last year. Their empire's top heavy. They've got too many people in the metropolis – forty million in one not very big island. Without open sea lanes, they couldn't even feed themselves, let alone carry on a war, and last year the Germans were sinking shipping at the rate of one and a half million tons a month. Fortunately we've got that problem pretty well licked now, but if the Germans came up with some new kind of submarine – and we know they're working on one – then the war could start to go badly the other way.'

'So it'll just be Sicily?'

Leone shook his head. 'No. Either the invasion will be a success, or it won't. If it isn't, we'll pull back; if it is, then nobody's going to tell the armies to stop, although personally I think that would be a good idea. What the hell do we want Italy for anyway? The plain fact is you can't get at Germany from the south.'

Salvatore pulled out a pack of cigarettes and offered one to the colonel. 'You know, the Italians may be much closer to packing it in than the Allied High Command realises.'

'Don't I know it. Frankly, I think that if the invasion's a success, they'll boot Musso out and sue for peace. We've already had a few feelers from them about how we'd react if they offered to switch sides.' He shrugged. 'Though I can't see anyone taking them very seriously, because nobody's interested in Italy strategically. Not when the enemy is Germany, anyhow. The Italians *were* on our side in the last war, and we had to divert a lot of aid just to prop them up. They turned out to be more of a liability than an asset.'

'They?' inquired Salvatore lightly.

Leone looked sheepish. 'Yes, okay. I haven't forgotten who I am. Look, I don't like what's happening over there any more than you do. But I'm an American now and, besides that, I reckon the best way we can help the old country is by ending this war as soon as we can.'

'Then let's get at it.'

They turned to discussing the best places for Allied landings in Sicily and the ways in which a built-in fifth column could assist this invasion. They continued talking over lunch in an officers' dining room, then throughout the afternoon and until the late evening. Finally, at half past nine they agreed to call it a day, and to carry on early the following morning. Leone offered his collaborator a ride to his Georgetown hotel.

Salvatore had some beers and a plate of sandwiches sent up to his room. After showering, he sat in a comfortable armchair, munching on the sandwiches and listening to Jack Benny on the radio. Then came a music request programme, which began – inevitably – with Glenn Miller and Salvatore fell into a doze.

He woke up again at ten to midnight and got up to brush his teeth. He was gazing absent-mindedly at himself in the bathroom mirror when pieces of his conversation with Leone came to his mind. The colonel's arguments had been sound and logical, but Salvatore had the impression there was something missing. His brushing slowed as he tried to pinpoint exactly where.

It was no good. He couldn't remember. He lay in bed for a while, smoking and staring at a map of Sicily which Leone had loaned him, then switched off the light and tried to sleep.

An hour later he rolled onto his back, lit another cigarette and stared up at the darkened ceiling. At some moment, through his subconscious, it had come to him that one thing which had been totally absent from Leone's discourse was *politics*. The colonel had spoken solely in terms of military strategy and the necessity of ensuring British supplies. The more Salvatore now thought about it, the more it seemed to him that Leone's thinking was defective as a consequence. He switched on the light and made a note of the several significant questions he wanted to ask when they reconvened.

His wake-up call came at seven, and at eight thirty he walked back into Colonel Leone's office. The other man poured him a mug of coffee and they got down to work at once. At ten o'clock, when they broke off for more coffee, Salvatore asked casually, 'Tell me, when the invasion of France takes place next year, where do you expect the Russian front to be?'

Leone grunted. 'You a mindreader or something? I must have spent a hundred hours on that question last January. I know more about the Pripyat Marshes than the Byelorussians who live there.'

'Who asked you to assess it?'

'The order came down from the chiefs of staff, but I think the President himself was behind it. Churchill's worried about the future of those countries in eastern Europe which get liberated by the Soviets, so Roosevelt wanted something ready for the Casablanca conference to show he'd done his homework.'

Salvatore crossed to look at the wall map of Europe. 'So we and the Russians would then be about equidistant from Berlin.'

'About that. Assuming the same rate of advance as currently.'

'And, assuming the two armies move at the same speed, then they'll reach Berlin at about the same time. So Poland, Hungary and Czechoslovakia will be liberated by the Soviets.'

'Only if Hitler doesn't surrender first,' replied Leone.

'You mean, only if Hitler doesn't surrender unconditionally.'

Leone made a wry face. 'Yes, a lot of people think that was a mistake. It played right into the Nazis' hands and gave them a terrific propaganda weapon. And including Italy in the package was just plain stupid.' He was referring now to the declaration of policy which Roosevelt and Churchill had made jointly at the Casablanca conference, calling on the three principal Axis powers to surrender unconditionally. In the press and in bars across the country it was claimed that the German generals would never overthrow Hitler and end the war if that meant accepting their homeland being occupied even in part by the Russians. What had particularly irked many people was the inclusion of Italy in this declaration, when it was known that Mussolini had a far weaker hold over his people than did Hitler or the Mikado over theirs.

'You weren't by any chance there, were you? At Casablanca?'

'Yes, I was. Roosevelt took his full planning team. So did Churchill. Some of those Brits are *real* sharp, so we had to keep on our toes.'

'Did you sit in on all the discussions?'

'That'd have been impossible. A lot of them were running

simultaneously. But I was there for the really big ones between Roosevelt and Churchill, and between Marshall and Brooke.'

'So you must have attended the discussion about unconditional surrender.'

Leone shook his head. 'There wasn't one. The matter wasn't discussed at all. Roosevelt pulled it out of his hat in the press conference at the end. I'm told it really shook Churchill. He hadn't been expecting it at all. Of course, he then had no choice but to back the declaration when it was his turn to speak. But he didn't like it one little bit.'

Salvatore again offered his packet of Lucky Strike. 'You were saying yesterday that nobody would take very seriously any Italian offer to switch sides, because no one is interested in Italy strategically—'

Suddenly he stopped speaking, as he remembered Leone's *exact* words. His eyes shifted to the wall map behind Leone's head, and abruptly he saw to what extent a name can be seriously misleading. Had he lived his adult life in Sicily, instead of America, he might have noticed it sooner.

The colonel was waiting. 'Yes, what about it?' he prompted.

Salvatore turned back to him. 'You're a *military* strategist. Who's advising the President on the *political* issues of the war?'

'Heaps of people: Hopkins, Stimson, Acheson, Hull, Morgenthau, the State Department. Any particular reason you're asking?'

Salvatore regarded the other man thoughtfully for a long moment. Abruptly he made up his mind. 'Colonel, I'd like to suspend these discussions for the moment and have a private interview with the President in person.'

Leone stared at him in surprise. 'What for?'

Ignoring the question, Salvatore said, 'Please pass on my request to the President.'

The colonel searched his face for a moment and then, with a shrug, he reached for the telephone.

31

That afternoon at four o'clock Salvatore walked into the Oval Office and found himself face to face with Franklin Delano Roosevelt. He stepped around the desk to the man in the wheelchair, and they shook hands.

Looking up at him, the President studied his face for a moment, then said amiably, 'Help yourself to coffee. Pour me another cup, too, would you?' The man knew how to put people at their ease. He waited until his visitor was seated, then prompted, 'Mr Ferrandini, you asked to see me.'

'Mr President, I'll come to the point. The government of Italy is extreme right-wing, but Italy itself, after twenty-one years of fascism, is red. If free elections were held tomorrow, the communists would win by a landslide.' He watched Roosevelt's face carefully. 'And I believe you know this already.'

'What makes you think so?'

'First, the inclusion of Italy in your demand for unconditional surrender at Casablanca. That was no slip of the tongue. You don't want the Italian generals to overthrow Mussolini, because if they did there'd be a popular demand for free elections within a month. Second, you're ignoring the peace feelers already put out by prominent Italians.'

Roosevelt regarded him mutely for a moment, and then said, 'Let's suppose for one minute that Italy surrendered next week. How would you see the war developing?'

Salvatore decided there wasn't much point in having a card up his sleeve if he wasn't prepared to play it. And Vincenzo had given him a trump.

'You mean if the war ends before Groves succeeds in getting one of his squibs to work?'

Roosevelt blinked at him. 'How did you hear about that?'

Salvatore was tactful in his choice of words. 'A discreet friend whispered something in my ear.'

'How much do you know?'

'Of the science, just the basics. But I know you're pushing a lot of money into it. Too much for you not to believe it's going to work.'

'How much?'

'I've no idea, but I heard you're building two towns out of nothing, and that's not cheap.'

'Do you know where they are?'

'Tennessee and New Mexico somewhere. I don't know where exactly.'

'Is there anything else you know about this?'

'It's called the Manhattan Project, and the result will be a bomb capable of destroying the entire Bronx. But I'd like to ask *you* a question, Mr President. Are the Germans working on the same thing?'

'We believe so. Most of the important theoretical work was done by them before the war. Many of them are now over here working for us, either because they didn't like Nazi politics or because the Nazis didn't like theirs. But the Germans still have several important brains working on their side.'

'Do we know how far advanced they are?'

The President scratched his chin. 'The short answer is no. Not in terms of the pure physics. But there are other ways of gauging things, and one of them is cost.' He gave a small grunt and murmured almost absently, 'Money is what makes the world go round, and ultimately it's money that will make it stop.' He leaned forward and placed the tips of his fingers together. 'Our best estimates indicate that the development of the bomb is just too expensive for the German economy.'

Salvatore considered this. 'How close are *we* to making one?'

Roosevelt shrugged. 'We haven't even produced the raw material yet, so we're at least a year away from a test bomb. Maybe two, maybe three years. We're not counting on having one to defeat Hitler.'

'Do the Germans have any other surprise up their sleeves?'

The President nodded. 'Rockets, we think. We *hope*. Effectively, for a single conventional bomb they'll be building a method of delivery costing as much as an aeroplane. Our experts' opinion is that's a serious mistake. It's not only costly, but it's keeping a lot of clever people tied up in the pursuit of a not very worthwhile objective. More serious worries are the new types of submarines and aeroplanes which we know they're also developing. However, the air offensive is increasing week by week. There have already been a few thousand-bomber raids. Our intention is that within a few months raids of that size will be taking place every night. In short, Mr Ferrandini, we're not taking any chances. Our aim is to destroy Germany's industrial potential absolutely. Whatever they need to keep their existing war machine functioning, or to bring into operation these new weapons, will be hit repeatedly – fuel, spare parts, production factories, ball bearings, etc etc.'

Salvatore considered all this, then said. 'So, effectively, there's a good chance that the rest of the war will be fought with more or less the same weapons as hitherto.'

Roosevelt nodded. 'So perhaps now you can answer my question about how you see it developing.'

'If Italy surrendered next week?'

'Yes.'

'Is there enough time to organise an invasion of northern France this year?'

'Not with any high probability of success, no.'

'Then we'd invade in the spring of next year. If we were successful, we and the Russians would then gradually close in on Germany. Not because of any great generalship on our part, but because we were continually hammering their factories while our own are out of range. Sooner or later their army would overthrow Hitler and make peace.'

Roosevelt nodded. Looking at the other man he asked slyly, 'And is that a desirable option, do you think?'

Salvatore's gaze became alert. His answer was cautious. 'It would end the war and stop people dying uselessly.'

'That was the argument for accepting the German offer of an armistice in 1918. What the German people were told, and came to believe, was that their army had been stabbed in the back by the politicians and a few treacherous generals. Ten million men died in the first war. That same number is what the Russians alone lost in just 1941.'

A deep silence descended as both men regarded each other, one curiously, the other with a growing wariness. At length the latter inquired, 'Are you going to betray the German generals who send out peace feelers?'

The President remained expressionless for a while and then asked, 'What would *you* do?'

'It might be very risky,' Salvatore replied cautiously. 'You could scarcely count on the discretion of Hitler himself. If the Germans ever found out that the generals had offered peace and that then we'd gone on to destroy their country, it would take centuries before they forgave us. But, leaving aside arguments of that sort, as long as you insist on unconditional surrender followed by occupation of their country, I should think you'd be able to arrange matters so that the German populace believed their army was beaten in the field.'

Roosevelt nodded. 'That's my view also.' He stared thoughtfully into the middle distance. 'And what about Europe after the war?' he asked after a while.

Salvatore had his answer prepared. 'The Russians will probably occupy Poland, Hungary and the Balkans. Italy is likely to turn communist too, if it holds free elections. If Germany is occupied by both us and the Russians, Stalin will have half of Europe in his hands.'

'What would be the effect of a communist Italy in the postwar world?'

Salvatore cocked his head to one side. 'Colonel Leone said to me yesterday, "Nobody's interested in Italy strategically. At least, not when the enemy's Germany". He's right, of course. The Alps supply the Germans with all the protection they need on their southern flank. But if the enemy is Russia it's a different story. I realised this morning, while I was looking at a map of Europe, just how misleading is the expression "Mediterranean Sea". It's not one sea; it's two. And it's Italy which cuts it into two. If Italy goes communist, then the Russians will control the eastern Mediterranean, so I can't see how we could stop them then taking over Greece, Turkey, Syria, Palestine and Egypt as well.'

The President pulled a small key from his pocket and unlocked a drawer of his desk. From there he took out a green folder and pushed it across to Salvatore. 'That's precisely the conclusion of this top-secret study which I ordered for the Casablanca conference. I'll give you an oral resumé of our expectations.

'Case one: Germany surrenders while no principal battle is being fought on home territory, and with her industrial capacity still more or less intact, though making some attempt to wring minor concessions from the Allies in order to claim this was a negotiated surrender. In that scenario, the general view is that in twenty years we'd be seeing a *fourth* Reich, though some think it might be a preferable alternative to Soviet domination of half the world. I don't happen to be one of them, however. Germany has to be beaten to her knees. The Germans must not be allowed to develop yet another myth about her army being stabbed in the back by the politicians, so they need to be shown categorical proof that their army has been beaten on the field of battle, which means the country must actually surrender unequivocally. Both Churchill and I believe that continued prosecution of the war with the purpose of destroying Germany's industry, and a demand for absolute and unconditional surrender followed by military occupation is the right policy, and the majority of our advisers agree with us. It goes without saying that, given the current popularity of Uncle Joe and the Russian people, there is absolutely no way in which present public opinion in Britain and America would entertain the idea of our doing any kind of deal with the German generals behind Stalin's back, or of trying to exclude the Russians from their share in the occupation.

'Which brings us to cases two and three: Germany either surrenders unconditionally while she is still able to fight, or is beaten until the extinction of her capacity to continue the war. In either of these cases Germany would be restored to her frontiers of 1937, and partitioned into zones of occupation by Great Britain, the Soviet Union and the United States. The exact boundaries of those zones have yet to be determined, and are presently being negotiated with the Soviets. But it seems pretty clear that, given the tremendous damage the Russians have suffered, they won't settle for much less than East Prussia, Silesia, Pomerania, Mecklenburg, Brandenburg, Saxony and probably Thuringia too. In other words, the line of demarcation between the British and us on the one hand, and the Russians on the other, is likely to be the river Elbe. Our observations of what they perpetrated in Estonia, Latvia, Lithuania and eastern Poland during the twenty months in which they occupied those lands, before the Germans attacked them two years ago, give us a good idea of what to expect in any territory occupied by the Red Army.'

Roosevelt screwed another cigarette into his holder, and angled it high to direct the smoke away from him. 'You're a very astute man, Mr Ferrandini. What I'm going to say now, I never said.' He glanced at Salvatore for a confirming nod. 'We do not think there is any way in which we can realistically prevent the Russians from gaining control of eastern Europe. We expect Tito in Yugoslavia to maintain his independence, even though he is a communist himself. The fate of Bulgaria remains in the balance, but we already know from reliable sources within the Red Army that Stalin has ordered his generals to plan a southward swing into Bulgaria, and the Russians already have very strong influence there, for historical reasons. Even Greece may fall. There's a strong communist party there, ready for insurrection when the time is ripe, and if they call on Stalin for help, it'll go under. The loss of Greece would be a serious blow to us, but we could stand it. But if Italy goes red, it would be a geopolitical catastrophe of the first magnitude, for precisely the reasons you have already elucidated. That has to be prevented at all costs.

'So you're quite right. Including Italy in my call for unconditional surrender was not a slip of the tongue. I didn't discuss the matter with the British prime minister beforehand, although I have since explained things to him in confidence.

'In Italy itself there is a large party of men grouping themselves around the king, and led by Marshal Badoglio, who want to negotiate a capitulation in secret, and then to declare war on Germany. Their interest in declaring war is twofold. Firstly, they would expect softer final peace terms. Secondly, they're fully aware of the political situation in their country and think it would be easier to keep control by imposing martial law, which they couldn't justify unless by claiming a national emergency – such as the continuance of a state of war, but against a different enemy.'

'Then why are you ignoring their offer?'

'Because we don't think they can do it. There'd be a repetition of 1917, when the czar was overthrown and replaced by Kerensky's social democratic government, which made the mistake of agreeing to continue the war. The people wanted peace at any price, and it was the Bolsheviks who gave it to them. That's not far from the present situation in Italy. King Victor Emmanuel has allowed Mussolini to rule as a dictator for twenty-one years, so he isn't very popular himself. Certainly not popular enough to rally the support necessary to withstand a call for his abdication by the communists, if they were organised about it, which they will be. We've looked at the matter carefully, but it's our opinion that the king is already a lost cause. Italy is going to become a republic, whatever happens. That doesn't particularly matter, but we believe the only way we can stop it from becoming a *communist* republic is if we actually conquer and occupy.'

Salvatore nodded slowly. After a while he said, 'If the invasion of Sicily is successful, Mussolini's position will be weakened even further. The Italians are going to realise that the war is lost, and the king and Badoglio may have to act to forestall a popular revolt which could easily turn into a communist revolution.'

'That's what we think, too. The difficulty, from our point of view, is that our declared war aim is the elimination of Hitler and Nazism – *not* the German people – and, by extension, Mussolini and Fascism and *not* the Italians. So if the Italians themselves get rid of him, we'd have no excuse to go on fighting them. After all, we could hardly be warring against Hitler in the north of Europe and against the Italians in the south.'

'Hm. And if Badoglio surrenders to us, you'd have a tough job persuading people of the need to occupy his country.'

Roosevelt nodded vigorously. 'Exactly. In fact, I don't think public opinion would wear it, and especially not Italian-American public opinion.'

'Particularly if Badoglio also declared war on Germany.'

'Precisely. There'd be no possible justification for occupying the country punitively if Badoglio was himself cleaning out the fascists, nor administratively when the civil service was clearly intact and Badoglio capable of running it effectively, nor even occupying it militarily, because we can't attack Germany through the Alps. Worst of all, to maximise our chances of preventing a communist takeover, we'd have to keep the Italian population well fed, and in effect that would mean our supplying *another* vital island, because effectively a hostile Germany would convert the Italian peninsula into an island, and one with an even larger population than Britain's. About the only thing that can be said in favour of an Italian surrender is that it would give us two new fleets: the Italian navy and that part of the British navy which is presently containing it. Frankly, we see the situation as practically hopeless. Two advisers have even suggested that we shouldn't invade Sicily at all, but should send the army somewhere else, like the Balkans.'

Salvatore shook his head. 'That would just postpone the problem. It wouldn't solve it. Mussolini's finished. His days are numbered. As soon as he goes, the communists will take over, either through revolution or by free elections.'

Roosevelt nodded his agreement glumly. He watched Salvatore's thoughtful expression, and after a while asked, 'Does any solution occur to you?'

Salvatore's eyes refocused on him. Then he said, 'I imagine Badoglio's plan must be to hammer out the details of an agreement with some representative of the Allies first, and then to present Hitler with a fait accompli: arresting Mussolini, surrendering to the Allies, declaring war on Germany, blowing up the Alpine tunnels to prevent any Germans from escaping, and taking prisoner all German troops in Italy, all on the same day. Mr President, am I right in thinking the Germans have been pulling back their industry, out of range of our bombers, to southern Germany and Austria?'

'Yes.'

'So if Italy now joined the Allies, the Germans would be faced with a new air menace from just the other side of the Alps. In that case, suppose Hitler had advance warning of Badoglio's plans? What would he do?'

Roosevelt blinked at him. 'That's a very intriguing idea, Mr Ferrandini. Yes, I think you're right. He'd invade. I think he'd have to. To keep our bombers as far away from southern Germany as possible. From the air, it's practically defenceless.'

Roosevelt summoned his three closest advisers to discuss Salvatore's idea, but it was soon obvious there were a number of practical problems to be solved before a completely coherent strategy could be formulated. And, given the need for maximum discretion, it would not be possible for them to delegate any of the preparatory work, so the five men were faced with a long session. The President therefore told his secretary to arrange a dinner for five in his private dining room. When the meal was ready, Roosevelt invited Salvatore to wheel him in. This action was not lost on the others. They were witnessing the formation of a new alliance.

During the meal itself the subject of the meeting was abandoned, because the servants were coming in and out constantly, but over coffee and brandy the debate resumed. Salvatore listened carefully to their arguments, and with a growing conviction that the plan by itself would not be sufficient to avert the danger which all five men believed to be very real.

While they were talking amongst themselves, he murmured to his host, 'I'd like to speak to you again in private afterwards.'

Later, when they were alone, Salvatore began, 'Mr President, I think I ought to go to Italy and find out for myself what the situation is.'

'Out of the question. You know far too much. Quite apart from all we've discussed today, you know about the Manhattan Project. If you were to fall into the hands of the Gestapo, it would be a catastrophe. Yesterday your job was to liaise directly with the Sicilians. Today it's something quite different, and much more important. We'll find someone else to do the liaising. I couldn't possibly let you travel into enemy territory.'

'Mr President, let me remind you that I'm a native Sicilian, and in Sicily the Germans are hated. I'll have friends everywhere, while the Germans have only enemies. Secondly, what I know about the Manhattan Project is what German scientists already knew in 1939. The only information I have that they're unlikely to know is that there are two new cities which have sprung out of nowhere, and I know the names of the states where they're located. Nothing else. I don't even know the names of the nearest towns. Thirdly, as far as our discussions here today are concerned, I can't see that I know anything dangerous, since the whole objective is to let the Germans know in advance of Badoglio's plans.'

Roosevelt gave him a wry smile. 'All very convincing, I'm sure. But why do you want to go?'

'This evening we've been discussing how to bring about a German invasion, in order to justify an Allied one to counter it. That plan is going to turn my native land into a battlefield. But will it still be enough to prevent a communist takeover after the war? That's what I doubt. And if it isn't then we must think of something else. So please let me go and judge for myself. The risk of my being caught by the Germans is next to nothing.'

'But not nothing.'

'Perhaps not. But remember the *real* value of what I know. And there's another thing to bear in mind. For us to gauge whether our plan will work, someone must study the situation on the ground. But whoever is sent would have to be let in on our secret. Yet we obviously want as few as possible to know it, so whoever goes should be one of the five men here tonight. And I'm the only Italian among us.'

Roosevelt regarded him with wry amusement. 'You're a very persuasive man, Mr Ferrandini. Thank God I'll never have to run against you in politics. When do you want to leave?'

'As soon as possible.'

The President picked up the phone and spoke for a while. Then he turned back to Salvatore. 'There'll be a plane ready for you tomorrow afternoon. I'll have someone drive you to the airfield. By the time you reach Tunisia, I'll have arranged a way to smuggle you into Sicily.'

'I can arrange my own way in and out, if you just find me a seaplane and a reliable pilot with some guts.'

'How much time do you think you'll need there?'

'Four or five days. I'll fix up a communications system with a few friends, while I'm there.'

'Make sure they *are* friends, Mr Ferrandini.'

'Mr President, in *my* world you learn who your friends are before you have any.'

Roosevelt watched him help himself to some brandy. 'Like another drop?' inquired Salvatore, raising the bottle.

'Please,' replied the thirty-second president of the United States – who didn't, but somehow felt it would be a breach of etiquette to decline.

32

Salvatore landed in Bizerta on 14 May, the day after the German surrender in Tunisia. The entire North African coastline was now in Allied hands. It was without doubt a victory on a par with Stalingrad and El Alamein, although it was too soon to know how many prisoners had been taken, because they were still being counted. But provisional figures suggested in excess of two hundred and thirty thousand, of which more than half were German troops. On the radio it was reported that the church bells were rung all over Britain. In North Africa itself, everyone wearing Allied uniform was either throwing a party or throwing up after one. The Arabs were happy, too, because the soldiers were splashing their money around most liberally. Even most Italian prisoners were smiling, because the victory had brought the end of their nightmare closer.

The plane was met by a Colonel Harris, who introduced himself as the intelligence officer taking care of Salvatore's needs. Harris led him out to a jeep and got behind the wheel himself. During the drive to his office, they discussed possible ways of slipping into Sicily. Salvatore's original thought had been to fly by seaplane to Lake Fanaco, and then make his own way across country on foot, but that would mean crossing the Agrigento-Palermo railway line, and Harris warned him that the Germans had recently tightened security on the line and increased the number of patrols along its length. It was too risky now, he said.

'Stateside the newspapers claim we've got air control over Sicily. Is that right?'

'More or less. The Germans are short of fuel. They only send up their fighters if they think it's a worthwhile target. And the Italian airforce seems to have grounded itself voluntarily.'

'What would constitute a worthwhile target? A fighter plane?'

Harris shook his head. 'That would be pointless. We're not short of planes, pilots *or* fuel, so any German pilot would be on a hiding to nothing. If he succeeded he wouldn't even dent our capacity, and if he failed he'd just have used up precious fuel to no purpose. That's assuming he's not shot down in the process. No, the only reason for the Luftwaffe to go up would be to take on a squadron of bombers. Then the average German pilot could up his kill ratios a bit.'

'So there wouldn't be much risk if I went in a reconnaissance plane.'

'Shouldn't think so. It would have to be a two seater, of course, and have the range. A P-38 with a supplementary gas-tank would fit the bill. It's a fighter-bomber, although we're only using them for photo-reconnaissance these days, because now we've got more up-to-date machines, like the P-47. But a P-38 isn't very easy to jump out of. You're likely to get clipped by the tail.'

'I wouldn't want to jump. I've never done any parachuting. I'd want it to land.'

'Oh, I see. I'm not so sure that's a good idea. On a clear day you can see a long way in Sicily, and there are blackshirt observer patrols about. If someone spots a P-38 either just before landing or just after takeoff, they're going to realise someone was dropped and they'll cordon off the whole area.'

'Yes, but at night those blackshirt patrols do the sensible thing and stay safely locked up in their homes.'

'Oh, you want to go by night. But how will your friends know to lay out lights for you? A prearranged radio code?'

'It would be beautiful if we had one. Unfortunately we don't. What's more I don't know of a suitable landing place close where I need to get to. I'll have to fly over and drop a message telling them to pick a field and put out landing lights.'

The colonel pulled up before a low, white building at the edge of the airfield. He frowned. 'The only drawback is then they've got to tell us roughly where that field will be.'

'That's no problem,' replied Salvatore mysteriously. He jumped down and picked up his bag.

Just before dawn next day, a P-38 flew low over the Sicilian coastline, to the west of Agrigento and moving northeast. In ten minutes it had reached Villalba, a little town situated on a steep slope halfway between Corleone and Enna. The sun was still below the horizon, but in the pre-dawn light Salvatore had no difficulty making out the narrow streets arranged in a regular grid. A quarter of a mile outside the town, but hidden from it by the brow of the hill, stood a farmhouse surrounded by a vegetable garden. They flew low over it twice, in wide circles, till two of the house's occupants had come out in night clothes to see what was happening. On the third pass Salvatore dropped a tight roll of material which landed in the vegetable garden. At once the plane flew off in a westerly direction, back to Bizerta. One of the two men retrieved the roll and brought it over to his companion, who began to unravel it. A yellow silk kerchief, on which was stitched a black *L*, was wrapped around a sheet of paper rolled into a tube.

* * *

297

At ten o'clock that night, the P-38 returned. This time, however, it passed Villalba a mile to the west. Salvatore soon spotted an arrangement of eight lights in a field. Three formed an isosceles triangle pointing the direction they had to proceed. The other lights indicated a distance of five kilometres. Having already examined several maps that afternoon, he knew they were being directed towards the rolling plain between Villalba and a narrow river called the Torrente Belici. The pilot veered to the southeast, and less than a minute later Salvatore saw two rows of lanterns ahead.

Don Calogero Vizzini watched the plane feel its way down to the ground, then bump along the dark earth to where he stood at the head of the makeshift runway. He made a gesture and Vito ran forward. When Salvatore jumped down, Vito escorted him towards Vizzini.

'*Buona sera*, Don Calò.'

'*Buona sera*, Don Salvatore.'

'Any problems?'

'No.'

'Good.' Salvatore used a torch to signal to the pilot, who had already turned the plane around. At once the sound of the engine increased, and the P-38 trundled back along the crude runway. A man lighter now, it had no difficulty lifting into the air. Moments later it was gone.

Three other men emerged from the darkness to collect the lanterns. They seemed in no hurry, which Salvatore took as a good sign. By night Sicily belonged to them.

Vizzini took him by the elbow and guided him towards an Austin Seven parked at the edge of the meadow, the solid, silent Vito proceeding ahead to open the doors for them.

'Unusual car for Sicily,' commented Salvatore, as he climbed into the back.

'Yes. It belonged to an Englishman doing a tour of Europe just before the war. He got himself into trouble over some woman, who turned out to be the wife of the local police captain in Enna. I sorted things out for him, and he made me a gift of his car.'

In the darkness, Salvatore grinned.

Half an hour later, guest and host were seated alone at a candle-lit table set up outside the farmhouse, near the kitchen door. The plain stretched away below in darkness – the starlight and a thin crescent moon unable to make any features discernible. No artificial light could be seen anywhere.

Vizzini's amply-proportioned sister Rosaria ferried bread, cheese, pickled onions, salami and good Sicilian wine from the kitchen into the pool of light cast by the candles. Salvatore found it all wonderful.

'A gift for you, Don Calò,' he said, and pulled out of his kitbag four cartons of Camel cigarettes, four thick bars of chocolate and two pounds of coffee beans. His host smiled and nodded his thanks.

Vizzini was an avuncular figure, large and heavy-jowled, sixty-six years old. His two younger brothers had taken the cloth – one remaining a simple priest, but the youngest, Monsignor Giovanni, rising through the hierarchy to become a bishop and Vicar General of the diocese of Muro Lucano. Calogero too was unmarried, but he had lived a far from celibate life. Joining the Friends during World War I, he had risen to a position of great influence – committing at least thirty murders, it was said – and was now recognised as head of the Mafia in the province of Caltanissetta. He was a man worthy of respect, who respected few things, but those he did respect he would never betray.

For a while they talked about activities in America, and the doings of mutual friends and shared enemies. Vizzini obviously had his own sources, because he seemed well informed of recent events. As they finished eating, Vizzini gestured to Rosaria, who picked up the bag of coffee beans and went off to make a pot for them.

Salvatore found it instructive to watch his host's face as he tasted his first cup of real coffee in a very long time. He suspected Vizzini would have access to German supplies, either through straightforward pilfering or black-market dealing, so it was clear that even here, in what the Wehrmacht now considered a front-line zone, its officers were no longer being supplied with the real thing. Clearly the Anglo-American naval blockade was beginning to bite.

Vizzini, however, had his own lavishness to display. Another murmured instruction to Rosaria produced a bottle of fine old Napoleon brandy. Salvatore had kept back one final gift, and brought out a pair of Partagas cigars.

'Luciano himself gave me these, to smoke with you,' he explained. 'They're the only ones remaining of a consignment Meyer Lansky originally sent him from Cuba.'

At a candle-lit table in the midst of a darkened Sicily, while all Europe went hungry around them, two men enjoyed the best luxuries that human ingenuity could provide.

As conversation turned to the course of the war, gradually the purpose of Salvatore's visit became clearer.

Vizzini said, 'I myself can give you the information you need about Sicily, but for the rest of Italy you'll need to talk to someone else. I'll take you to him tomorrow.'

It was three o'clock in the morning before Vizzini escorted his guest to a bedroom. Salvatore had energy enough only to brush his teeth, before he climbed into bed and fell asleep.

Only four hours later he was awakened by Vito, who led him to another room where a hot bath awaited. Afterwards he found his host seated at the outside table. Breakfast was fresh orange juice, local bread, butter, German jam and coffee. At last Salvatore could view the landscape in daylight: the fields forming a patchwork of faded greens and browns spread over an uneven, arid-seeming terrain, with bald hills jostling each other roughly.

The house was surrounded by half a dozen eucalyptus trees, strategically sited to provide shade, but without depriving the vegetable garden of sunlight. It felt like an oasis.

Half an hour later Vito appeared with the Austin, to drive them to Palermo. Colonel Harris had provided Salvatore with false papers, but had not been able to include a viable travel permit because the Italians, in imitation of the Germans, kept changing the design.

'The Italian patrols probably won't stop us,' explained Vizzini. 'The Germans are supposed to be guarding only their own installations and the principal railway lines, but they've become a law unto themselves these days, because they know Sicily's likely to be the next Allied target. If they do stop us, just tell them your permit was stolen, and don't make a fuss if they arrest you. They'll only hand us over to the Italian authorities, so we'll be out and free in ten minutes.'

Although they did pass two patrols, one German and one Italian, the three-hour journey over badly surfaced roads passed uneventfully, allowing Salvatore to enjoy the evolution of the scenery of his native land, from the bumpiness around Villalba to the precipitous mountains of the Palermo hinterland. Almost all other vehicles on the road were horse-drawn: further evidence of the success of the Allied blockade.

At one point Vizzini remarked, 'Lot of bandits in the hills these days. Army deserters, most of them. Wehrmacht too, though they're the clever ones. Most German ranks and file still believe they're going to win. A lot of officers too, though they tend to be fanatics. It's an odd sensation to know something for sure, while so many around you believe the opposite. It gives one a hint of what being God must feel like.'

Salvatore smiled.

Suddenly the Mediterranean was before them: the Gulf of Palermo cupped by a wall of mountains, as if an immense volcanic cone had sheared and half of it had slid into the sea.

The streets were hot and crowded but, even here in the island's capital, few other motor-driven vehicles were in sight. Petrol rationing had caused a mass extinction. In their place was an amazing variety of carts and carriages, drawn by horses and donkeys and even the occasional dog. Most people went about on foot, patiently enduring the endless privations of a war foisted on them by alien Rome. There were many who simply stood around in groups, a disturbing purposelessness in their expressions and gestures. They were clearly not contented. They wanted to be somewhere else. They wanted to be *somewhen* else. They wanted change.

300

Vito drove straight to the cathedral, one of the myriad glories of Sicily, a perfect marriage of Arab and Norman architecture, reflecting the diversity of conquerors who had coveted the island's choice real estate. As its dome came into view, Salvatore remembered the first time he had seen it, as a boy. Knowing only poor, drab towns like Lercara Friddi, he had wandered wide-eyed through the avenues and boulevards of this city which had then seemed to him the capital of the world.

Now a resident of its *true* capital, New York, he smiled at this recollection of his own naivety.

At the cathedral's southwest corner stood the episcopal palace, and Vito pulled up near its main entrance. Vizzini and Salvatore climbed out and walked inside. A few minutes later they were ushered into the presence of the Cardinal-Archbishop of Palermo.

A light white wine was offered and they were invited to stay for lunch, a singular honour in rationed Italy, where even the Roman Church's abundance was constrained. It was a mark of Vizzini's local importance. Lasagna was followed by haddock pie. Dessert was zabaglione. German ersatz coffee was then served, but nobody drank it, not even the Cardinal. They contented themselves instead with a passable Armagnac.

Afterwards the three men strolled among the palm trees in the courtyard, and their discussion turned to how they imagined the map of Europe would look after the war. It was soon evident that the Vatican had reached the same conclusions as the Pentagon planners, and also expected the Allies to invade Sicily, although Salvatore couldn't decide whether they had acquired inside information. The political situation in Italy itself seemed about as dismal as could be. In March there had been widespread strikes in factories in the north, in protest against deteriorating living conditions and shortages. In some areas the communists were canvassing more or less openly – with the tacit consent of local fascist leaders, who were meanwhile assuring Rome of their doing everything to stop them. Palmiro Togliatti, leader of the Italian Communist Party and now in exile in the Soviet Union, was making regular broadcasts urging rank-and-file members of the Fascist Party to join forces with the liberal and left-wing parties. And, whenever he spoke, the hungriest two-thirds of the adult population of Italy listened.

'Italy is going to pieces, my young friend,' warned the Cardinal, as he led his two guests back into the palace. 'You'd better get here quickly.' He extended a hand, and both men bowed to kiss his ring. Then abruptly he turned about, and withdrew to his private apartments.

As Vizzini and Salvatore walked out into the Piazza della Cattedrale, they found the streets almost deserted. Siesta hour. Vizzini suggested they do likewise, and Vito drove them to the Grand Hotel delle Palme, where Vizzini usually stayed on his visits to Palermo. Though receptionists and hall porters treated him with great respect, their deference was Sicilian and unobtrusive. As Vizzini and his guest were escorted to rooms on the first floor, they could hear the loud voices of a party of German officers in the bar.

At five o'clock, Salvatore was awakened by a knock on his door. Vizzini entered and said, 'Now let's go and listen to the people.'

They left the hotel to head along narrow streets towards the harbour. Their route took them through a crowded food market, near the little inlet called *La Cala*, and they stopped to examine the scanty goods on offer. Most of the fruit and vegetables were near rotten, but this didn't discourage the sellers from singing out their wares, the protracted last syllable always dying away in the Palermitano fashion – a lament appropriate for the lamentable choice available.

Salvatore watched two crates of fresh cod carried in, the crowd pressing forward eagerly. The fishmonger had no time for singing in the impromptu auction which now developed. He sold to the customers who waved the most banknotes under his nose.

'Have you seen enough?' inquired Vizzini at last.

Salvatore nodded, and they left the market. Vizzini now took him on a guided tour of working-class cafés, sometimes listening to the general talk, sometimes engaging the customers in vociferous conversation. What impressed Salvatore was that no one seemed concerned about fascist informers. The mood was clear: fascism was on its last legs. Even most fascists already realised this, and were being careful not to antagonise people with whom they would have to somehow coexist when it was all over. German military invincibility had become a myth of the past, laid to rest by the string of defeats on all fronts. The general opinion was that the Allies would not be long in coming, and when they did the Fascist government would fall.

Already occupying people's minds was what would follow, and the communists sounded both convinced and convincing. They pointed to the Soviet Union as living proof of what Marxist organisation could achieve. That rotten barn which Hitler had thought he could flatten within three months had become a fortress repelling the invader, and soon to send its own legions into his home territory. Italy, too, they said, could be just as strong and, more important, the Italian people would then have food on their tables and jobs to go to. Work, they said, and work at a fair wage was a right. And any government which did not guarantee that right was cheating the people.

Salvatore noticed a few groups of German soldiers wandering among the hostile population, trying to get a little pleasure out of their few hours' leave. They were only tolerated because they had a little money to spend, though this was a decreasing asset since there seemed less and less to spend it on. As the sun went down, however, these Germans returned to their barracks. The Sicilian capital was too dangerous for them after nightfall. And as darkness descended, a sullen resentment settled over the city.

Palermo was waiting for something to happen.

Vizzini took Salvatore back to their hotel.

The following morning their tour continued, starting with the Stazione Centrale. A troop train from Messina was pulling in as they got there. Messina lay in the northeast corner of Sicily, just across the straits from Calabria, so the troops had probably come from the mainland. They formed up in ranks along the platform, talking excitedly, and Salvatore could hear a variety of accents: Neapolitan, Roman, Florentine, Milanese. These were little more than boys, he noted sadly, knowing that they would fare badly against the battle-hardened Americans and British, and many would not return. He watched them march off to a different platform and a different train, moving closer to their impending ordeal.

Vizzini raised an eyebrow, inquiring whether his companion wanted to move on, and they started towards the exit. Outside, a horse-drawn taxi was waiting. Beside it, a heated row was in progress between a porter and an elderly man with a grizzled beard, who had just arrived from Agrigento. The old man was protesting that he was being overcharged, and the porter claiming they had agreed the price beforehand. To the amusement of all the onlookers, the porter suddenly heaved the man's suitcases back on to his trolley and wheeled them back to the Agrigento train.

'I think I've seen enough of Palermitano insanity for the time being,' said Salvatore.

'As you wish, my friend,' replied the imperturbable Vizzini.

On the drive back to Villalba, Salvatore was silent. Vizzini sat quietly alongside, letting him do his thinking. At one point they passed a signpost indicating the turn-off for Lercara Friddi, Salvatore's birthplace. He and his parents had emigrated in 1912, but many of his kinfolk still lived there. In the 1930s, he had twice returned to visit them. Vizzini glanced at him, in case he might want to make house calls now, but Salvatore remained huddled in thought.

At length, however, even Vizzini's apparently infinite patience proved to have a limit. 'What exactly is troubling you, my friend? You *know* what the solution is.'

Staring out at the passing countryside, Salvatore murmured, 'Oh, yes. I already have the solution.'

'Then what's the problem?'

'The man with the beard in the station is the problem.'

303

Vizzini glanced at his companion. 'The one who was arguing with the porter?'

'Yes. The old man cheated him.'

Vizzini considered, then gave a shrug. 'He had to carry his suitcases himself, though, didn't he?'

'Yes, because the porter was able to restore the status quo ante. But he had to be *alive* to do that. Didn't he?'

33

That evening Salvatore took a stroll on his own. Vizzini sent two men, armed with shotguns, to accompany him at a suitable distance. For two hours Salvatore walked across dry fields, smoking endless cigarettes and brooding on ways to stop this country from electing its own perdition. By the time he returned to the house he had decided upon the basis of his plan.

Next morning the P-38 was back. Its pilot noted the carpet left out as if to dry, and flew away immediately. Sometime after breakfast Salvatore suggested to his host that they go for a walk together, and Vizzini, knowing his guest had a purpose, readily complied. Followed by the inevitable Vito, but also by two bodyguards carrying *luparas*, they took a route which brought them to the river Belici. Several miles further along, they came to a small hill which Vizzini insisted they climb. Waiting for them on its summit, to Salvatore's amusement, were two chairs, a sunshade and a table already laid for a picnic lunch. Since no other human being was in view, the effect was almost surreal. Vizzini grinned broadly at Salvatore's reaction to his little joke.

They had been walking for nearly two hours, so the crisp white wine in its ice bucket was very welcome. As Salvatore sipped, he enjoyed an unparalleled view of the Sicilian landscape. The plain stretched far towards the southwest, and was interrupted by two sugarloaf hills, one topped by the Manfredonic castle at Mussomeli, the other by a church at Sutera. In the distance, a flight of Mustangs flew over a Wehrmacht encampment, no doubt to annoy the German troops, then scattered leaflets over the surrounding villages, which urged the inhabitants to rise up against the government in Rome once the Allies invaded. Salvatore knew that similar drops were being made in Sardinia, Corsica, Greece and even the south of France, all to keep Hitler guessing where the real blow would fall.

Vizzini served them himself, so they could continue to talk in privacy, and it was there, on that Sicilian hill over a leisurely lunch, that the details of Salvatore's plan were hammered out.

That night the Austin took Vizzini and his guest back to the meadow where men were already setting up the landing lights. Vito again produced the bottle of Napoleon brandy, and in the half-light of the moon Vizzini and Salvatore silently toasted each other and their joint enterprise.

A short while later could be heard the drone of an aeroplane. As the P-38 landed, the two men embraced each other on both cheeks.

'*Sabbenedica*, Don Salvatore.'

'*Sabbenedica*, Don Calò.'

Moments later Salvatore was airborne. He watched the dark land, invisibly violent, pass below. On the approaching sea the crescent moon cast a shimmering path towards the hopeful west, for the plane to follow. They crossed the coastline. Then Sicily faded into the eastern gloom.

The following day saw him boarding a DC-3 for the long haul back to Washington, but this time he spent most of the flight in deep thought, working out the details of his complex plan, and mentally preparing what he was going to say.

'Mr President, I have to tell you that neither a German invasion nor an Allied one will prevent the formation of a communist government in Italy at the end of this war.'

Roosevelt stared back at him with doleful eyes. 'That means we shall have no option but to force a war with the Soviet Union at the soonest possible moment.'

Salvatore regarded the chief executive coolly. 'I said our plan wouldn't work. I didn't say that *no* plan would.'

Roosevelt looked straight into the other man's eyes, and felt a chill run down his spine. To save Italy, something terrible was about to be proposed. And he knew that he would have to give his assent to it.

Harry Hopkins found the President out in the Rose Garden. He was staring down at the petals of a blossom in the palm of his hand.

'Well? What did he say? Do we go ahead as planned?'

'No, Harry. The plan won't work. If the Germans do invade, the Communists will work with both the underground and the Allied armies to help throw them out. As soon as the Germans have gone, they'll crawl out of the woodwork, fully organised, with seventeen different plans to set up a communist government, whatever the circumstances. We'll have turned the whole country into a battlefield for nothing.'

'So what is he proposing?'

'Something similar, but with a new angle.' The President threw the rose petals away, withdrew a notebook from his pocket and consulted it. '*Point one*: we confront the king directly. We convince him he has no earthly chance of keeping his throne, but ask for his patriotic cooperation. *Point two*: the king will then put Mussolini under arrest, as and when we tell him to, and he will order Badoglio to form a new government. *Point three*: the king will arrest Mussolini *personally* and with enough witnesses to ensure it becomes common knowledge in Rome by nightfall, but in such a way that the Germans are unable to interpret events with certainty.

'*Point four*: Badoglio will give the German ambassador to understand that Italy intends to maintain its alliance with Germany, and he will do nothing overtly to contradict this posture. *Point five*: a series of rumours will be spread throughout Italy by the Mafia, to the effect that the new government is planning to surrender to the Allies and declare war on Germany. *Point six*: the same people will spread a second rumour that the government plans to legitimise itself by holding parliamentary elections as soon as possible, with the aim of catching the Communists off guard. *Point seven*: the Mafia will take note of the people who start coming out in praise of Stalin, especially those who kept silent earlier. At the same time they will advise the right-wing democrats to remain quiet.

'*Point eight*: if the Germans have not already seized the Alpine passes, information will be sent to them indicating that both the Italian capitulation and a declaration of war on Germany are imminent. *Point nine*: when the Germans invade, the king and Badoglio will remove the official Italian government to safety in some city in the south. *Point ten*: the names of all the Communists and their sympathisers will be leaked by the Mafia to the Germans, and those who manage to escape the Gestapo will be hunted down by the Mafia themselves – this last task to be continued after the war ends.

'In a nutshell, Salvatore is proposing we organise a civil war in Italy as a smokescreen for the wholesale murder of all leading communists.

'*Point eleven*: throughout all this, the American and British governments will do all the wrong things, demonstrating a constant state of amiable confusion, well-meaning ineptitude and good-natured imbecility. Specifically, he wants the British to propose one set of surrender terms and us here to draw up a different set. At the critical point, discussions over which set of terms to hand to the Italians can be drawn out over a considerable period.

'*Point twelve*: Allied military operations should proceed rapidly until Mussolini's arrest, to give us a solid military base, and then become slow and unadventurous. Ideally, the king should wait until Sicily is almost in our hands before he acts. *Point fourteen*: friends of Salvatore's will go in with the American army. Many members of the Mafia have been imprisoned by Mussolini without trial. As anti-fascists, they

307

should be released and entrusted with all the local civil administration. They can be relied upon to take care of the communists within their jurisdiction. The same policy should then be applied on the Italian mainland.

'In effect, Salvatore wants us to make the Mafia a powerful force in postwar Italian politics. He says that is the only way to ensure the communists are kept under control.'

Hopkins watched the President screw a cigarette into his holder. 'What do you think?'

'It's monstrous. Diabolical.'

'Yes. You're right. That's why it will work.'

'A plan to cooperate with the Mafia?'

'You were all in favour of seeking Luciano's help in using the Mafia to pave the way for the Allied landings.'

'That was different. There's no comparison. If this ever got out, we'd be discredited for a hundred years.'

'Only a handful of people will know the true story. To everyone else it will just seem ineptitude on our part, and opportunism on the part of the Mafia. Not even King Victor Emmanuel and Churchill need know the full story. We can keep it in the family.'

'But the Mafia would know! They'd be able to blackmail us forever.'

'Ferrandini tells me he could limit those who'd ever know about it to six, if he wanted to.'

'If he wanted to?' echoed Hopkins.

'He thinks it might be better, for everybody, to clue in a few more than that.'

Hopkins dismissed the point. 'Even so, is there any difference between being blackmailed by six or six hundred?'

'I'm very much inclined to trust Ferrandini, and to trust his judgement too.'

'And if he makes a mistake?'

'Do we have a realistic choice? It was you who warned that a communist Italy would give Stalin eventual control over the Middle East, and we already know that America will need Arabian oil by the 1960s. If we hand over Italy to Stalin, we'll be giving him one half of the world and the chance to economically blackmail the other half. No, Harry. Ferrandini's plan is the best we've got. The *only* way to stop Italy turning red is to kill off the leading reds there, and the *only* non-fascist force capable of doing so is the Mafia. We're going to have to cooperate with them. So wheel me in and let's have some coffee.'

In the Oval Office the President turned to study a map of Italy. 'If we're to move fast initially, we'll need an aggressive commander in the field, but . . .'

'Patton's already been designated. He's ideal.'

'Yes. But how do we persuade him to become slow and unadventurous afterwards?'

Hopkins grunted. 'That, I can promise you, is impossible.'

'In that case, we'll have to let him in on our plan. I don't think we need worry; he's about as anti-communist as Hitler is. The problem will be people wondering why he suddenly slowed down so noticeably.'

'That's simple. Relieve him of his command.'

'After a successful campaign in Sicily?'

'Get him doing something insubordinate. That'll be easy for him, because he does it all the time. In fact, you might not even need to bring him in on this at all. If he doesn't provide Ike with a genuine excuse to shelve him, then you can ask him to provide a fake one.'

'All right. Then we put in some slowcoach. But we'll still have to make it look as if we're at least trying.'

'We could fix a landing somewhere along the coast where we know the Germans are well dug in.'

'Ferrandini tells me the far south of the Italian peninsula is much like Sicily: dirt poor, absentee landlords, therefore a lot of communists. But he doesn't think the Germans will bother to defend it. It would stretch their supply lines too far. So if we don't take over, the locals will. Then it will go red, and act as a focus for other districts to coalesce around. In that case I think our best plan, after Sicily, would be to capture the whole area up as far as Naples.'

'I'll tell Leone to provide a list of alternatives. And *I'll* provide a list of alibis. Because you need to be out of town while a friend is murdering your wife, Franklin.'

'I've already thought of one: a conference with Churchill, but on *this* side of the Atlantic, and somewhere where we can credibly claim a communications breakdown if we need to. I was thinking of Canada. We'd both be off home base, and neither of us would be in close touch with our communications. After the conference, we'd go on holiday to different places. Like that, both of us can make ourselves inaccessible at the critical moments.'

'But won't people say it was odd that the two directors of the war put themselves so far away from the scene of the action at such a critical moment?'

'Not if we dress it up properly. Churchill can suggest London as the venue for the conference, and I'll accept – initially. That'll look as if we nearly put ourselves close to the action. It will also suggest that it's the turn of the British to be hosts. Then I'll claim I can't go, because some important domestic issues have cropped up, and propose Canada as an alternative location. Since it's part of the British Empire, it will look like a compromise. If anybody questions the domestic-issue angle, I can always drop a few hints that the real reason I wanted to get out of a conference in London was that I didn't fancy

Churchill lording it over me. A petty excuse about personalities always fascinates people. It's a lesson I learned in politics a long time ago,' Roosevelt added drily.

Hopkins smiled. 'Okay, a conference in Canada. What about somewhere in the French-speaking area, like Montreal? The occasional language difficulty might prove useful.'

'I agree. But not Montreal. It's too big a city and international communications would be too good. I was thinking of Quebec. Everybody's heard of it, so it won't sound like the sticks, and it's a pretty town – ideal for a spot of sightseeing afterwards.'

'A nice leisurely conference, while on the other side of the world Italy goes down the toilet.'

The President looked at him, but did not reply.

Hopkins went over to the sideboard to pour two cups of coffee. He handed one of them to his chief, who accepted it absently.

'That is *all* Ferrandini wants, isn't it?' he asked, suddenly suspicious.

Roosevelt glanced up at him. 'No, Harry. I'm afraid it isn't.'

34

The sun's globe, red and bloated on the horizon, engulfed the finger of the Washington Monument. It would now be shining yellow above the battlefields of Europe; the red there would be supplied by the wounded and dying.

Red, thought Salvatore. The colour of blood, by nature. The colour of communism, by adoption. How strange they should have chosen it for themselves. What dangerously contagious psychological need had it fulfilled in the weirdly organised minds of the idealists who equated their clammy pleasures with the sweat of peasants and workers?

His mind abruptly forged a connection between this thought and something completely different. In the 1920s and '30s the Midwest had suffered a plague of frauds based on invitations to invest in newly-discovered perpetual motion machines. One of them was ingeniously simple. It consisted of a glass tube, wide at one end, narrow at the other, like a horn twisted back on itself so that the narrow end hung a few inches above the wide one. The naive and unschooled mind, when told that this apparatus would be filled with water, would have no difficulty in imagining the weight of water at the wide end would be heavy enough to force water from the narrow spout down into the wide end again, and so on *ad infinitum*. Salvatore had heard of one man brazen enough to go from door to door with a glass model of the apparatus, about the size of a French horn, but with a crack in it – which he claimed was the result of his having dropped it the day before. His glib patter, however, was good enough to render a working demonstration unnecessary, and hordes of people handed over their life savings upon seeing the professionally elaborate share certificates he offered.

To avoid falling into that trap, reflected Salvatore, one needed either to know something of basic physics, or simply to understand that in this world no one ever gets something for nothing. The glass horn was a succulently presented free lunch, because the notion of a heavy weight displacing a lesser one was so beautifully and irresistibly 'obvious'.

There was just one drawback. It didn't work.

Salvatore compared this device to the appeal of communism, and decided a lot of people were going to fall for that too.

How brightly obscure the future was, he reflected, watching the fast-rising sun and wondering about all the future dawns, day after day, year after year, into an ever more brightly obscure tomorrow. Had he stood in this same spot in 1900, would he have had any notion of the invention of flight a mere three years into the future? Some men had. Not the principle of the wing, perhaps, but they had sketched their visions of the future and filled the skies of their own tomorrows with flying dirigibles.

That wasn't predicting the future, he decided; they'd merely extended past into future.

He lit a cigarette and blew smoke towards the new dawn.

Machines were one thing; ideas were something else. 'Communism is the single greatest threat to the progress of man, because of its appeal,' Roosevelt had said. 'The immediate danger from Germany and Japan must be countered first, because it is military. But the philosophies currently prevalent in these countries have virtually no external appeal.'

'You're very quiet,' said Cattagna by his side. 'What are you thinking about?'

'The future. How to predict it.'

'When you've figured it out, let me know what stocks to buy.'

Salvatore smiled. 'Shall we go and pay our respects to old Abe?'

'Sure. But what's *he* got to do with the problem?'

The two men turned and strolled alongside the Reflecting Pool towards the Lincoln Memorial.

'Maybe more than you think,' replied Salvatore at length. 'You can fool some of the people all of the time, and all of the people some of the time, but you can't fool all of the people all of the time.'

'I wasn't intending to.'

'Maybe he missed a line. You can fool yourself for as long as you want.'

'I hope that's not personal.'

They reached the huge figure, nineteen feet high, seated imperially in a posture of patient, fatherly wisdom. The two men stared up at it, each coming to terms with his own sense of awe in his own way.

'Know who carved him?' asked Salvatore quietly.

'No. Who?'

'Two brothers called Piccirilli from New York.'

'We Italians get everywhere.'

Salvatore turned to the South Wall, on which was inscribed the Gettysburg Address. 'Read out the last part,' he said.

Vincenzo obliged. ' " . . .*That we here highly resolve that these dead shall not have died in vain; that this nation, under God, shall have a new birth of freedom; and that government of the people, by the people, for the people, shall not perish from the earth."* ' He stood for a moment silently contemplating the words, and then breathed, 'Magnificent.'

'Yes. It is. But now read the first sentence.'

Again Vincenzo obeyed. ' *"Four score and seven years ago our fathers brought forth on this continent a new nation, conserved in liberty and dedicated to the proposition that all men are created equal."* Sounds very biblical.'

'Sounds very false,' replied Salvatore. 'All men are *not* created equal. Some are clever, most are not. You can fool some of the people all of the time, remember. He *believed* that, Cenzo. He believed it because it's true.'

'Don't I know it. But where are you trying to take me with all of this?'

'What's going to be the biggest source of illegitimate income in this country after the war?'

'That's easy. Drugs.'

'Have you seen what happens to people who get addicted?'

Cattagna's reply was delivered in an almost resentful tone. 'Yes. It's what most makes me question the existence of God. It's disgusting that any human being can get into such a state.'

'Suppose you cut off that human being's supply of drugs?'

Vincenzo shrugged. 'He'll find some other way of going on vacation from life: alcohol, LSD, meths, the nitrites. A chemist friend of mine tells me there are heaps of ordinary domestic products which will give you a high – even glue. Some drugs *can't* be made illegal, because we need them for legitimate purposes.'

'So, to you, the problem isn't just a question of supply?'

'No. It has to do with the make-up of the individual. Some people are going to crack, whatever happens. They just can't take it, so they get off the bus.'

'All men are created equal?' inquired Salvatore softly, regarding him speculatively, almost slyly.

Vincenzo turned to look at him quizzically. 'Tore, you're leading me somewhere, but I can't see where exactly.'

'What'll happen if we don't take control?'

'Of drug distribution? We *have* to. If we don't, the Jews, Irish and Hispanics will.'

Salvatore nodded and began to walk away. 'Bye, Abe,' he murmured. 'Thanks for your help.' Vincenzo hurried to catch him up. 'What about selling to children?'

Cattagna considered for a moment. 'I think basically it's the same situation. It's appalling to think about, but the truth is that if there's a market, someone will fill it. Our best chance of controlling the situation is to control the distribution networks. We exact an oath from our distributors that they won't sell to kids, and from time to time we make an example of those who break it. We'll never stop it entirely, but at least we might seriously curb it.'

Salvatore nodded. 'How come *you* realise all this, when no one in government has the faintest idea of what's going to happen?'

Cattagna snorted derisively. 'Since when has any government realised what was going to happen *before* it happened? Governments are made up of college graduates with their heads up their asses. And college graduates are the last people in the world to understand how hard life is for the people out there who aren't equipped to compete – which is half the population.'

'How big a thing do you think it's going to be?'

Vincenzo grunted. 'It's a bomb looking for a place to go off. Those college graduates have no idea how many bastards there are who'll offer those poor under-equipped people an hour of heaven as a way of escape from life.'

'So what's the solution?'

'It's obvious. Eliminate the bastards' profit motive?'

'Legalise narcotics?'

'Sure. Remember what happened under Prohibition? Selling booze suddenly became criminal; so, suddenly, only criminals sold it. Since they were criminals, they used criminal means to eliminate competitors in their neighbourhoods. With no competition, they could charge what they liked, and the price of alcohol went sky-high. That's why bootlegging was so profitable. The same thing's going to happen with drugs.'

They had now arrived back at the Washington Monument. Cattagna stopped, and pointed to the United States Capitol ahead of them. 'See that building? That's where they make our laws.' Now he turned and pointed to their left – the White House. 'And *that's* the home of the man who's supposed to enforce them. We're talking about the *government* of the United States, Tore. Those damn college graduates invented Prohibition. They turned small-time hoodlums into lords of a criminal empire stretching across a continent. And what for? To stop any man doing what he wanted, even when he was doing no harm to others. They thought *they* knew better. They thought it was okay to interfere in other people's lives. And what did the rest of America do? It quietly went out to a speakeasy for a drink.'

Vincenzo shook his head. 'Tore, I think you'd have to visit a lot of planets to find a government as stupid as ours. And you can take it from me: they haven't learned a thing. With drugs, they're going to do exactly the same.'

Salvatore nodded. 'But suppose they didn't. Suppose they decided to legalise drugs. How would that affect the number of addicts?'

Vincenzo gave a grunt. 'Tore, that question makes as much sense as asking: if they legalised potatoes, how many people would switch over from turnips? The answer is: all the people who prefer potatoes to turnips. The problem isn't legality or availability or price. It has to do with personal weakness. The basic truth is that you can't stop people doing what they *must* do anyway. It doesn't matter whether you're talking about something that we *all* do, such as eating, or something that only *some* people do, such as fornicating. They're going to do it anyway, because that's what the word "must" means.'

'Which was why Prohibition was a bad law.'

'Sure. It made half the population criminals simply for having a drink. It's hard to think of anything stupider than that.'

They walked on into the Mall. Cattagna inquired, 'You said a little while ago that there was a line missing: "You can fool yourself for as long as you want." What did you mean exactly?'

'Let me answer your question with another question. What do people think of Cosa Nostra?'

'That we're a bunch of cheap hoods. Capone, Masseria, Mad Dog Coll, Dutch Schultz, you, me – it's all the same to them. Except you and I aren't very well known. But they'd lump us all together if they heard about us. The average guy in the street thinks people like Dillinger and Bonnie and Clyde were in the same line of business as Charlie Luciano and Meyer Lansky.'

'And what does this average guy think of doing business with us?'

'That he'd better fulfil his side of any contract or he's going to need medical insurance.'

'But suppose he knew he could break his word and we couldn't touch him?'

'Oh, sure, he'd break it all right.' Vincenzo grunted. 'Probably think he was doing his country a favour.'

'Right, Cenzo,' replied Salvatore softly. 'He probably would. That's what I mean by the missing line.'

Cattagna frowned for a moment and threw his friend a look of annoyance. 'You're not being exactly lucid this morning.'

Salvatore stopped and faced the younger man. 'Okay, Cenzo. I'll spell it out. The average guy thinks it's okay to stop the negroes from voting. He thinks it's okay that Congress should pass laws about what he can and cannot do in his own bedroom. He thinks it's okay to have a drink in a speakeasy, but he also thinks that the people who supplied the booze are cheap hoods. He thinks that when said cheap hoods try to stop outsiders from muscling in on their territory and raising the prices of booze, that's wrong. He thinks the cheap hoods are subhuman and it's okay to chisel them because he'll be doing his country a favour, and the only reason he doesn't do it himself is because he's worried about getting a bellyful of lead.' He paused and then in a quiet voice summarised, 'When it comes to thinking, the average guy in the street should stick his head up his ass so he can smell the result.'

Vincenzo regarded the other man with silent appraisal, and waited.

Eventually Salvatore reached the bottom line. 'They'll renege, Cenzo.'

Cattagna continued his scrutiny of his friend for a moment longer, then with a sigh looked away. 'Roosevelt's scarcely the average guy in the street. He respects you, Salvatore.'

'Roosevelt's president today. Who'll be president next year? Besides, it doesn't have to be Roosevelt who gives the order.' He turned Vincenzo around to face him and began enumerating the points on his fingers. '*One*: the guys we're dealing with have the power to make the decision. *Two*: they don't respect us and think we'll blackmail them. *Three*: they won't listen to Roosevelt. *Four*: they're going to give us the go-ahead to cause a civil war in Italy and have the communist leaders murdered. *Five*: they're going to provoke a German invasion of Italy.' He shook his head. 'No, Cenzo. They *can't* let us walk around with that kind of a hold on them. And it's not just *their* position they'll be worried about. It's the effect on American relations with Italy, and the Soviet Union. They'll have every patriotic reason in the book for making sure we don't reach Christmas.'

Cattagna's eyes went out of focus as he visualised the likely outcome. Demonstrations whipped up by agitators to furious riots in the major Italian cities. American businesses destroyed. American troops and civilians lynched. Italy breaking off diplomatic relations. Protests from dozens of other countries. It would be the diplomatic gift of all time to the Soviet Union. Then the political uproar would be followed by economic turmoil, as people hurried to move their dollars into gold and safer currencies. A run on the dollar – and on the stock market. A repetition of 1929.

At length, the grim catalogue of disasters reviewed and considered, Vincenzo commented, 'If all you wanted to say to me was that you think they're going to double-cross us, you could have told me so in six sentences. But you haven't taken me all around the mulberry bush for nothing.' He lit a cigarette, watching Salvatore over the flame. 'You've got a solution, haven't you?'

Salvatore looked him in the eye and gave a single nod.

After a while Vincenzo asked with irritation, 'May one inquire as to what it is?'

Salvatore gave him a half-smile. 'Suppose you've got someone in your Family that you think maybe talks a bit too much, and you and he have done something illegal together. What do you do to keep him quiet?'

'I give him something to do which will *really* bring the roof down on him, if it ever gets out. Okay, so how are you going to do this to Roosevelt?'

Salvatore gave him a sly look and said quietly, 'I'm going to make this President pay for the lie of one of his predecessors, and I'm going to make him pay a lot of money.'

Vincenzo grinned. 'I knew you'd get some benefit out of this.'

'Ah, but this is different, Cenzo. I'm going to save Italy, yes, but I'm also going to make damn sure my kids don't end up without a daddy to look after them. Here's the scheme: twenty-four men – I'm one of them and I select the other twenty-three, but Roosevelt won't know who they are. In fact, he won't know for sure even how many there are, because the agreement will state "between twenty and thirty". We'll call this group "The Curia", unless somebody can think of a better name.'

'Am I going to be a member of this exclusive little club?' asked Vincenzo, grinning.

'Of course. In fact, you're going to help me pick the others.'

'Thanks. But why so many?'

'To make it as difficult as possible for the government to take out the whole lot of us at one go.'

Cattagna blinked at him. 'I see. Okay, we're twenty-four and the government would rub us out, if they knew who we were. Frankly, Tore, I'm not sure I want to be a member.'

'Wait till you hear the rest of it before you make up your mind. Roosevelt and his advisers will sign a contract, *before* the invasion of Sicily, and the terms of said contract will make it clear, among other things, that the government is deliberately hiring the services of Cosa Nostra for the murder of the key men in the Italian Communist Party. The contract will be entrusted to me, representing the Curia, and on the understanding that it will be hidden in a safe place by one of the members – to be chosen by lottery. The hiding place will be equipped with a warning system – a sort of burglar alarm, if you like. But an alarm with a difference, because it will go off not only if a burglar tries to steal the contract, or to deactivate the alarm beforehand, but also if he attempts to take us out.'

Cattagna nodded slowly. 'That's an interesting idea.'

'And it gets better.' Salvatore explained his idea in detail.

At the end, Vincenzo said, 'So the system can function perfectly well, even when the designer is dead.'

'Of course. In fact, Cenzo, it will be a whole lot safer for the whole group, including my own son, if I don't tell him exactly how it works.'

Cattagna nodded thoughtfully. 'There's just one thing that bothers me about all this. Won't Roosevelt be worried about being blackmailed?'

'No. That's why it's all going to cost him a lot of money. People who resort to blackmail need money. The members of the Curia won't. We're all going to be very rich.'

317

'I'm glad to hear it, but how?'

'Through legitimate businesses. The government is going to finance us.'

Vincenzo gaped. 'And you seriously believe Roosevelt will go along with this?'

'He already has, Cenzo,' Salvatore said lightly. 'He had no choice. I told him I didn't want to see Italy go communist either, but I said it was either the full deal or nothing. He didn't want to surrender completely, however, so he made a few conditions of his own. The only one that really matters is that no member of the Curia can have served any time in prison – which rules out Charlie. Still, I'll make sure he's okay.'

Vincenzo shook his head incredulously. 'So Roosevelt agreed to give us funds to enable us to make ourselves rich?'

Salvatore nodded blandly. 'Sure. Why not? *Somebody* has to make motorcars, but does it really matter that it's Henry Ford?'

'How much is Roosevelt prepared to cough up?'

'Fifty million.'

Cattagna's mouth dropped open. '*Fifty million!*' he exclaimed.

'To stop Italy going red, it's cheap at the price. About half the money will be needed to set up the burglar-alarm system. Roosevelt's not going to know that, of course, because it would signpost me at once.'

'But how's Roosevelt supposed to get Congress to okay an expense of fifty million?'

'No problem. It'll be buried in the Manhattan Project budget.'

'Just like that?'

'Sure. It's amazingly easy. The project's already gone way over budget. Roosevelt says that if they finally make a bomb for less than one and a half billion, he'll be delighted. So all they've got to do is claim something called the gas diffusion filters they've got don't work properly, and they need a million square feet of new ones to be made by hand – things like that. The jobs will be offered for tender to firms set up by us, so there won't be any record of an unaccountable payment. The Manhattan Project accounts will be top-secret for decades, even after the bomb is built. By the time they're opened for inspection, the few people still living who might know anything about the project won't remember the details. It's the perfect cover. Hide one top-secret project inside another. How about some breakfast?'

At his hotel, Salvatore stopped at the reception desk to order breakfast brought up to his suite. 'Orange juice, ham and eggs, toast, coffee. Everything twice.' Up one flight of stairs, they entered Ferrandini's suite. 'Go on out to the balcony. I'll be with you in a minute.' He crept into the bedroom quietly, to avoid waking his wife and child.

They had arrived by train from New York the previous afternoon. Salvatore picked up his baby son from the cot and carried him out onto the balcony. Robert looked up into his father's face and gave a happy gurgle of recognition.

Vincenzo looked on smiling, thinking of the day when he too would feel an overpowering need to hold his own child in his arms. Salvatore's face held an expression of such complete absorption, it was as if he was transferring information to Robert through their eyes, whereas the message was simple: *You're my son.* Vincenzo had known, from the moment of their first meeting, that Salvatore would be successful in life. But now for the first time he saw the vast empire that would be built around this child who bore Ferrandini's name.

Feeling suddenly very tranquil he turned to look out across Washington – the city where Salvatore had wrought the unholy covenant which would make them both rich and powerful beyond their wildest dreams. Then, remembering something that had not been explained, he asked, 'What did you mean by Roosevelt paying for the lie of one of his predecessors?'

Without looking up, Salvatore replied, 'I'm going to get the thirty-second president of the United States to agree that the sixteenth president was wrong – all men are *not* created equal.'

'But what does it matter if Roosevelt says so? Most people would expect him to *think* it, anyway. In fact, the whole purpose of this agreement with him is to stop Italy being taken over by a political group which believes the opposite.'

'That's what it started out as, sure. But along the way it got a lot bigger. It's going to happen because the West needs Italy, otherwise it will lose the whole Middle East, but in the long run it'll be the other clauses in the contract which will have the greater effect. I don't think Roosevelt himself quite realises it, because he's too busy with the war and the postwar strategic picture to think about domestic issues.'

'But what *are* these other clauses?'

Salvatore looked up at his friend and his eyes became hooded. 'I want to use the Curia to control organised crime,' he murmured, with earnest intensity.

Cattagna stared at him. 'But I thought your aim was to get us *out* of illegal activities.'

'It is, Cenzo. We can control without participating.'

'But why on earth would you even *want* to remain involved?' demanded Cattagna, beginning to feel angry.

Salvatore sighed. 'Because I agree with you, Cenzo: the government is made up of college graduates with their heads up their asses. Prohibition proved that.'

'For God's sake, Tore! Let them go to hell their own way!'

319

And now Salvatore too began to look angry. 'No, Cenzo! I have to live in that hell which they manage so incredibly incompetently. *Think* about it for a minute, will you? Think about Prohibition. The government of the United States passed a law which made a bunch of some of the worst thugs and madmen in history absolute *millionaires*! The *government* of the United States thereby showed *it had absolutely no understanding of human nature whatever*! And do you think any *other* government would make a better job of things? What about the British and French, for example? They threw away a whole generation – ground into Belgian mud – in the most incompetently conducted war on record, then they threw away the peace and, as a consequence, this present conflict is going to cost even more lives! No, Cenzo! I am *not* prepared to have my son grow up in a world run by fucking baby-kissers, who don't know one end of a baby from the other, without giving him *some* chance to defend himself against their stupidity! This miraculous opportunity has given me the power to do something about it, and I'm going to use it, with or without your approval!'

Salvatore had come close to shouting and now one-year-old Robert began to express his unease by whimpering. His father rocked him back to security, then continued more calmly.

'I'm sorry I bawled you out, Cenzo. But let's look at this rationally. If the US government could make such a mess of things in 1920 with booze, then it can do exactly the same with drugs.'

'I should have thought it would have learned its lesson.'

'Maybe it has, Cenzo, though I wouldn't bank on it, but what bothers me is that it may have learned the *wrong* lesson.'

'What do you mean?'

'A little while ago we were talking about legalising drugs. I agreed with practically everything you said. Those people who aren't equipped to compete will go under, whatever happens. If they can't opt out with drugs, they'll do it with something else. So all men are *not* created equal. Now, I have one question for you. No one in the US administration is currently considering legalising drugs, because they don't know how big the phenomenon is going to become in a few years' time. But when it is, some of them will remember Prohibition and think that maybe legalisation can't be such a bad idea, if the Mafia is against it. It's not going to matter to you financially, Cenzo, because you'll be sitting pretty, but would you be in favour of it?'

Cattagna considered the matter for nearly a minute. 'I don't know whether legalisation would reduce the total number of addicts, but it would certainly make for fewer Al Capones.'

Salvatore scrutinised his friend's face. Then he murmured tensely, 'Wrong, Cenzo. The Al Capones will all still be there.'

Cattagna blinked at him.

320

Then, abruptly, he saw the light.

For a moment, he remained impassive. Finally he asked, 'Have you included in the contract a clause to cover this?'

'Of course. I told Roosevelt the Sicilians were insisting on it, but *I'm* the one who's insisting. Vizzini's an astute man, but he didn't have the advantage – as I did – of a chat with Leone and Roosevelt, so he doesn't realise how powerful the current circumstances have made him.'

Vincenzo was silent for a long time. At length he said, 'You can't fool all of the people all of the time, Tore.'

Salvatore looked up from tickling Robert and threw him a cynical smile. 'Which? The *equal* people or the *unequal* ones? If I can fool *some* of the people all of the time, can I pick out the unequal ones to do it with?'

Cattagna replied quietly, 'One day, Tore, you may have to answer to only *one* Person.'

Salvatore noted the suppressed anger and his flippancy dropped away. 'Yes, Vincenzo, one day I may. But, as I see things now, I have a son to care for, and that's the highest of the missions God has assigned to me. As for the rest, He can make up His own mind. He made me what I am, so until He decides He'd rather have me different, He'll just have to let me take care of my family as best as I know how.'

Salvatore gazed down into the face of his son, and smiled.

Vincenzo looked across at the man he loved most in the world and quietly prayed for him. Men would die by the thousands because of the unholy agreement which Salvatore had drafted. Perhaps God would forgive him, but on the day Salvatore died, He would need to be in a very good mood.

The sun was up now. In Europe it was early afternoon.

In Europe men were dying by the thousands every day.

35

'How about *not* going to your dance class?' suggested Adam.

'Any particular reason?'

'Yes.'

'That's a very convincing argument. Where are you?'

'In the New York Central Library.'

'What are you doing *there*?'

'Reading.'

'What a funny thing to do in a library. Okay, I'll put my face on and meet you out front in, um, an hour.' She hung up, turned around, and came face to face with her father.

'When do I get to meet this man?' asked Robert.

Diana registered her father's pained expression. 'Tonight?' she suggested gently.

He sighed heavily. 'I can't. I've got a meeting. It'll be a late-night session.'

She noted the fatigue in her father's voice and regarded him with concern. 'Dad, is everything okay?'

'Not exactly, but I'm working on it. Just don't worry your head about it.' He kissed her forehead. 'What's his name?'

'Richard Andrews.'

'Where's he from?'

'Connecticut. He's a business consultant.'

'How long have you known him?'

'Not all that long,' she replied accurately, but feigning an expression of casual innocence.

Robert, unfooled, remarked quietly, 'He must be very special.'

'He *is*, Dad,' she replied with complete sincerity.

'Bring him along for a drink tomorrow evening. I ought to be back by then.'

'Okay.' She pulled away. 'I'd better go and get ready.'

As she hurried along the central passage, she saw Ned Moreno come through the front door, carrying a suitcase and a briefcase. Just back from London.

'Hi there, stranger.' She gave him a kiss on both cheeks. 'Thought you'd died.'

'Sorry to disappoint you.'

'Next time, huh?'

'That's a promise. Is your father home?'

'Sure. He's just gone into his study. See you later.'

Ned dumped the suitcase in his own apartment. Back in the corridor he encountered Fredo the butler, who was wearing a constrained smile. 'What's the matter with Fredo?' he asked his boss a minute later. 'He didn't look too happy a moment ago.'

Robert shrugged. 'Nothing I know about.'

'I don't suppose there's any news of our friend?' Ned took a photograph out of his briefcase and handed it over.

'Nothing new. Maybe we finally frightened him off,' replied Ferrandini, studying Drew's features properly for the first time. 'Patellini's called a meeting of the Curia tonight, to decide what we do if the Accords get published. Personally I think it's a waste of time, because there's nothing we *can* do. Not as a group, anyhow. It'll be every man for himself.'

He put the photograph away in a drawer.

'Where's the meet? Burnham?'

Robert nodded. 'I'll go on my own, Ned. You'd better stay here in case Drew decides to phone or make contact. I was just about to ring Stelio about security, so will you do that for me?'

'Sure.'

'Tell him not to spare the hospitality. We'd better get everybody there in a good mood. And ask him to make sure the place is properly clean. Last time there was dust everywhere.'

'The Torinis are getting old.'

Robert's reply was irritable. 'Then tell Stelio to retire them – from principal duties, anyhow. They can live in the gatehouse. It's been empty for years.'

'Okay.' Moreno crossed to the telephone.

'I'll see you later. I'm going to take a nap. I'm not sleeping too well at nights. You can guess why.'

After making the necessary arrangements with Stelio, Moreno picked up his mail and headed back to his apartment. On the way he caught sight of Diana leaving by the front door. She had obviously spent time with her make-up.

After a shower, Ned sat down to deal with his correspondence, then decided it was time to tackle his normal security chores. Opening a drawer, he hunted around for his microphone detector, fruitlessly. In the dining room he found Fredo polishing silver. 'You haven't seen my debugger, have you?'

The butler looked up. 'No, Ned, I haven't.'

Robert himself must have used it and forgotten to put it back, thought Ned. He would ask him for it later.

* * *

Lee Kwan's invitation to Deng to call on him was not far short of a summons. 'I understand you have had his butler's son kidnapped,' he began expressionlessly.

How did the old buzzard find out about that? wondered Deng in irritation. But his bland reply betrayed no sign of his surprise. 'Of course. The Council authorised me to keep Ferrandini under observation. How was I supposed to observe him without some internal cooperation?'

'The Council authorised surveillance, yes – but as a non-hostile act. You have exceeded your brief and made a direct attack on the Italians. Your action has compromised us all.'

'Only if they find out,' replied Deng brazenly.

Lee Kwan regarded him curiously. What a stupid megalomaniac you are, he thought. 'I've called a meeting of the Council tonight to discuss the matter.'

The news did not unduly disturb Deng, who knew that the old dodderers usually approved initiatives post facto, because they were ever anxious to avoid schisms.

'Suits me,' he responded calmly.

When the icy interview was over, Lee lit a cigarette and considered. He toyed with the idea of letting Deng have his way. The reasoning that Drew would at some point get in touch with Ferrandini was almost certainly correct. And it made sense to assume he did have some power to prevent the publication of the Accords. But was that all there was to it? What if the Accords did get published, and the Italians thereby lost the protection of the US government? Was it possible that the government might then decide to legalise drugs?

What had Salvatore once said to him? *If it works, don't fix it.* The more Lee thought about it, the more it seemed a wise policy to leave well enough alone. It was the intelligent course when one didn't have all the facts.

Besides, Deng's actions were not far short of an open challenge to the Council's – and therefore Lee's – authority, and that was something he could never tolerate. All in all, he felt his decision to put Deng under surveillance was the right one.

Deng lived in a house opposite the Buddhist Temple on Bayard Street, only a few minutes' walk from Lee's home. Oblivious of the man shadowing him, he spent those minutes wondering how Lee could have learned of the kidnapping. He didn't think it could have been through Ferrandini or the butler himself – even assuming they'd guessed any Chinese were behind it – because Lee hadn't contradicted him when he'd said, '*Only if they find out.*' Eventually Deng decided the leak must have come through one of the men that Lin Teng had used in the abduction.

When Deng reached home, he found Lin waiting for him. Thinking it better not to worry him by telling him that Lee knew about the kidnapping, Deng did not mention the matter.

'Any news?'

'Moreno's back. He's already been asking Violi about the microphone detector, though he didn't search for very long.'

Deng sucked his teeth in annoyance. 'You'd better tell Violi to remove all the bugs.' He considered a moment. 'On second thoughts, Moreno will probably be tired, and won't start searching until tomorrow morning. Tell Violi to remove them tonight, when everyone's asleep. Where has he put the detector?'

'In the youngest boy's room. Everyone will assume he was playing around with it.'

'Good. When Moreno starts to hunt for it, Violi can join in. If he retrieves it after a few minutes, nobody will suspect anything. Then once Moreno has done a sweep, Violi can reinstall the bugs. Okay?'

'Okay. But I have another piece of news. There's a big meeting tonight at a place called Burnham. It was called by Patellini. But we won't be able to follow Ferrandini. The security will be too tight.'

'Do you know the purpose of this meeting?'

'That's why I've come here. I thought you ought to listen to this.' He switched on the tape recorder: a conversation between Ferrandini himself and Ned Moreno. It lasted less than three minutes, and when it was over Deng looked at the younger man in puzzlement.

'What should I deduce from that?'

'It means Drew hasn't yet got in touch with Ferrandini.'

'So?'

'A lot of time has gone by. Maybe he's already been in touch with one of the other Families.'

'Then why hasn't Ferrandini been informed?'

'Suppose somebody's worried about security.'

'What do you mean?'

'The information about Drew came from someone in the administration. If Drew knows the government is involved, he's likely to think that Ferrandini is under observation and his phone is tapped. If so, he might think it safer to approach one of the other Families. The same would apply, if the Families themselves know the government is involved. So maybe this meeting hasn't been called for the reasons stated. Maybe they'll produce Drew, and Ferrandini doesn't know it.'

Deng nodded slowly. 'It's possible. More than possible, in fact.' He was thoughtful for several seconds. 'But you'd better carry on with your surveillance anyway, in case Drew has simply been delayed and still intends to contact Ferrandini directly.'

Lin nodded obediently and departed.

Deng spent a few minutes pondering the points which the man had made. Then he phoned his two outsiders and asked them to come round. Deng had converted the ground floor of his house into a Chinese restaurant. It offered six private rooms, ideal for discreet assignations or confidential meetings. He told the two men to ask for one of these.

They arrived twenty minutes later.

Björn Jensen and Ingmar Andersen were both from Stockholm originally, but were now naturalised Americans. Jensen, the senior partner, had worked as a mercenary in Burundi before teaming up with Andersen as problem solvers for one of the big Colombian families. They were both blond and in their late twenties, though Jensen's hair was already thinning. He was wiry and tense, whereas Andersen looked more muscular and relaxed.

On closed-circuit television Deng watched the two men enter his restaurant, then went downstairs. He gestured to his maître d'. 'Those two men who just came in – where did you put them?'

'Room six.'

'Okay, I'll take care of them. They're friends of a friend of mine. Make sure we're not disturbed.'

Deng joined the Swedes, sat down opposite them and pulled a map of New Jersey from his inside jacket pocket. He told them about the imminent meeting, pointing out the location of Burnham Manor on the map. 'There's just a possibility that Drew will be there. And there's also a chance he'll have certain documents on him. It's the documents that are important. If it comes to a choice between him or the documents, choose the latter.'

'Who's going to be attending the meeting, besides Ferrandini?' asked Jensen suspiciously.

Deng had not bargained for either the question or the suspicion that came with it, but he made his response as smooth as possible in order to appear innocent of any desire to withhold information. He left the room and went upstairs, reappearing a few seconds later with a sheet of paper, which he handed to Jensen.

'That's a list of the men I think will be there.'

Björn perused the names, noting that the list was headed '*The Friends of Salvatore*'. He looked up into Deng's eyes. 'To take out a single Englishman *before* he reaches Ferrandini is one thing; but this is something else. We'd have to act while he was approaching the manor, and these guys are going to be around. Besides that, I've heard of nearly all of them. Their pictures come out regularly in the big money magazines. They're some of the most powerful men in this country. If they're not members of CN themselves, then they've got a lot of friends who are. I told you at the beginning, Mr Deng, we only take on an assignment when we know *all* the facts.'

326

'And I *gave* you all the facts,' lied Deng, sounding indignant. 'At least, as I knew them at the time. I only just learned about this meeting – which was why I rang you.'

Jensen studied his face, then looked down again at the list of names, pursing his lips thoughtfully. 'You know, when I was in Colombia, I once heard a rumour about a ruling body governing the international Cosa Nostra. I was told it was called the Curia.' He looked up at Deng once more. 'That's what this is, isn't it?'

Deng decided the Swede showed too much certainty for him to risk a denial. He nodded. 'But I didn't know they were involved until a short while ago.'

Jensen spoke to Andersen in Swedish. 'What do you think?'

Ingmar shrugged. He didn't like having to think. It usually meant he then had to make some decision – an activity he much preferred Björn to handle.

'Up to you.'

'It's bloody dangerous.'

Andersen gave another shrug. 'Then ask for more money.'

But before Björn could relay this suggestion, Deng said, 'I'll triple your fee.'

'You mean quadruple,' replied Jensen at once.

Deng nodded. 'Okay.'

Out in the street again, Ingmar asked, 'What do you think?'

Björn pursed his lips. 'That he agreed a bit too quickly.'

'The Chinese Council must want these documents badly.'

'If it *is* the Chinese Council we're working for, and not just Deng on his tod.'

'What do you mean?'

'I mean, why are they using outsiders, anyway?'

'Deng already told us why: because if anybody catches a glimpse of us when we're knocking off Drew, *no one's* going to think we're Chinese.'

'And why is that important? Because the Council doesn't want anybody to suspect *they* had anything to do with it? Or because Deng doesn't want the Council to suspect *he* had anything to do with it?'

Ingmar shrugged. 'What's wrong with the first? Why do you always have to complicate everything? I bet you can't even look in a mirror without thinking your reflection's deceiving you.'

'How come Deng agreed to quadruple our fee so quickly? If the Council was in on it, don't you think he'd have checked back with Lee Kwan first?'

'Maybe they decided the limit beforehand,' suggested Ingmar. 'Anyway, we said we'd do it – now, *are* we going to or not?'

Jensen sighed. 'I suppose so. We've got to eat – even when we're surrounded by rattlesnakes.'

Behind them, Mao Chang watched the two men turn the corner and disappear from view. He had witnessed their arrival, noting both their purposefulness and caution, but no sign of that tourist curiosity usually displayed by Caucasians in Chinatown. So when they had entered the restaurant belonging to the same man Lee had told him to shadow, he had followed them inside – then observed Deng join them in a private room. From a phone in the cloakroom, Mao had immediately rung Lee for instructions, only to learn that his boss would be unavailable for at least another hour.

Now witnessing the departure of the two Europeans, Mao dearly wanted to follow them, to find out exactly who they were. But Lee's instructions had been precise: he was to keep Deng under surveillance. So, with a sigh of frustration, that's what he did.

Diana approached the New York Public Library feeling vaguely apprehensive. She wasn't sure how to straighten things about herself with Adam. Years ago her father had insisted she use the cover 'Jones' as a way of protecting her from golddiggers. To have not told Adam the whole truth, even after going to bed with him, made her feel devious and obscurely guilty. And now her father wanted to meet him, she had no choice but to come clean. Yet if he'd heard dark rumours about her family origins, he might not want anything more to do with her.

As soon as she reached the library entrance, he stepped out of the building and embraced her.

'What shall we do?' he asked.

'Watch TV in your apartment?'

Fifteen minutes later they were in bed making love. It was a tender encounter, free from the unbridled passion of the night before, because both had things weighing on their minds.

Adam eventually got out of bed and padded into the kitchen to fetch a bottle of champagne. As he twisted the wire, he pondered on his own dilemma. He could not continue much longer without making an approach to Ferrandini, because they would soon be running out of time if they were going to put their heads together. But first he would have to tell Diana who he really was, and she would most probably consider herself deceived. He eased off the cork and carried the bottle into the bedroom.

Diana was waiting with a serious expression. 'Richard, there's something I have to tell you,' she said in a rush. 'My surname isn't Jones.' She paused. 'It's Ferrandini.'

Adam took a deep breath. 'I know.'

She blinked at him. 'Since when?'

328

He reached for the pocket of his trousers, lying on the chair, to extract something, then climbed back into bed beside her. He pulled her onto her side so that they directly faced each other, only a few inches apart.

'Diana, every moment I spend with you is marvellous. I also know I want to spend a lot more time with you – to get to know you properly. I'm talking about what I feel *now*. But when I first met you a few days ago, that wasn't just a casual encounter. I *had* to get to know you. Look, I have something here to show you.'

He unpalmed the ring and passed it to her. She stared at it for a moment, then examined the inside of it behind the monogram. 'This belonged to my grandfather,' she murmured in puzzlement.

'How are you so sure?'

'Because of this little scratch cut on the back. There used to be three rings, all identical. One of them was lost, my father has the second, and my grandfather gave the third away. He told Dad he'd given it to a special friend, and that if ever someone approached us wearing it, we were to help that person in whatever way we could. No one outside the family knows about the rings, so how did you get hold of it?'

'Your grandfather commissioned me to help you – your whole family. You're supposed to be in some trouble. Yet you're clearly not – at least not for the moment.'

She stared at him, beginning to doubt the sanity of the man she was in bed with. 'My *grandfather* commissioned you?'

'Sort of. He left instructions with people in London, who commissioned me on his behalf. It's part of a plan he set up fifty years ago to protect you all in case anything happened to endanger you. As far as I can make out, you're not in any danger, but the scheme's gone operational anyway.'

'Did all this start two weeks ago?' When he nodded, she told him briefly about her family's surprise flight to the safety of the Catskills mansion.

'And your father never explained what was happening?'

'Not to me, and I've been trained not to ask questions. But what's this danger supposed to be?'

Adam scrutinised her before replying. 'My personal loyalty is to you, Diana, because of what I feel for you. But I owe something to your grandfather too, and through him to your father. Since I can't be the judge of what he wouldn't want you to know, you can ask me any question and I'll answer it if I'm able, but you must play fair with both me *and* your father. Don't pit us against each other. If you think he wouldn't want me to divulge something, then I don't think you should ask me about it.'

'I'm not a child. I know all about my family's origins. I know what

329

the bottom line of power is. And I know that my father is one of the most powerful men in this country. Do you understand what I'm saying?'

He sighed and nodded. In his mind's eye he saw a wine glass break and Diana lose a new virginity. Somehow he had hoped she was out of it all. Not just uninvolved, but ignorant – and therefore untarnished.

'Do you approve?' he asked quietly.

She stared at him. 'What do you expect me to say to that? How am I supposed to answer?' Her tone suggested a dam holding back a rapidly rising anger that threatened to break all over him.

Practically anything he said now might sound bad, so he decided to say nothing, but kept his unwavering gaze upon her.

That worked, for it was Diana who retreated from their confrontation. In a voice of earnest appeal, anger now absent, she said, 'You can't tell me to keep myself in the dark when it's a question of my own family being in danger. I know what's right and wrong, too, but when it comes to my family, then for me they are right and everyone else is wrong.'

'I respect that, Diana. I think most people feel that way.'

With heavy sarcasm, she replied, 'And I suppose the people *they* fuck with ask them what they think about their daddies.'

'I used the wrong question. I didn't want you to pass judgement on your father, Diana. I was trying to ask you to define your own position – so I could know how far it is from mine.'

'Where's yours?'

He sighed heavily. 'Let's just say that I don't think your father's part of the problem, but I don't think he's part of the solution either.'

She was silent for a while, considering this. Then she murmured. 'You're very diplomatic.'

'It's what I really think, Diana.'

'Is it? But you suspect he deals in drugs, don't you?'

He shook his head. 'He's too wealthy to need to.'

Adam then decided to tell her what he knew about the Belvedere Accords.

At the end she said, 'You suggested we're not in trouble for the moment. What do you mean?'

'Once the Accords are published, the Families won't have any hold over the government. You'll have no further protection.'

'From what exactly?' she asked uneasily.

'Prosecution, maybe.'

She fell silent. At length she said, 'If there's no need to negotiate anything, why don't you just stop the Accords from being published?'

'That's just the point: I don't know how to. Salvatore doesn't say where they are. And his final letter really *is* final. Somehow or other he expects me to deduce where he's hidden them.'

330

'Then I think you ought to talk to Dad as soon as possible.'

'So do I. But first I want to be absolutely sure there's no one close to him who might be behind all this.'

'What do you mean?'

'I mean, Diana, that we don't know *why* your grandfather's system was set off. The culprit might be someone who enjoys your father's trust, but who has hidden motives of his own.'

'Money, you mean?'

'Not necessarily, Diana. Power, perhaps. Or maybe someone wants to destroy the Families for the sake of some vengeance. It might even be someone fundamentally loyal who's being forced to cooperate with outsiders through some kind of blackmail.'

'So what do you want me to do?'

'I want you to arrange for me to see your father, without anyone else knowing about it. Call him and say you need his advice on a very personal matter. Don't make it sound too urgent, but make him think it's important to *you*.'

'Okay. But now tell me: is Richard your real name?'

'No, it's Adam. Adam Drew.' She frowned. 'What's the matter? Don't you like it?'

'I was just thinking that I found out the name of the first man I ever went to bed with *after* I went to bed with him.'

'Slut.'

She rolled over on top of him, and soon they both had good reason for postponing that call to her father.

It was not until early evening that Lee Kwan finally learned of the two tall blond occidentals who had called on Deng that afternoon. He found the news disturbing. What's that lunatic up to *now*? he wondered. But he strongly suspected that he knew the answer already. And if he was right, then Deng was defying the Council – a capital crime. The difficulty lay in proving that.

This was a delicate situation. Under normal circumstances, Lee would simply have let Deng carry out his act of defiance, then try to find proof of it to present to the Council and rid himself for ever of this thorn in his side. But these were not normal circumstances, and such a course might prove disastrous.

No, Deng had to be stopped, but how could Lee do this when he had only a hunch to go by? Deng would laugh in his face, and then get half the Council to join in. Though, at least by then, he would have cancelled his contract with the two blond Europeans.

After several minutes' thought, Lee plucked five grapes from the bowl on the table, picked up the telephone and dialled Deng's brother Kim. As soon as he could hear the ringing tone, he put all the grapes in his mouth. Then, when Kim answered, he said in English, 'You better tell your brother he got a tail who saw a couple of blond guys pay him a visit this afternoon. I overheard the tail phone somebody about them.' Then he hung up.

Kim heard the line go dead, and stood in shock for a few seconds. Then he rang his brother to tell him about this anonymous phone call.

Deng crossed to the window and scrutinised the crowds milling around below. Almost at once he spotted Mao in a bookshop across the street. Deng had seen him around before, but he didn't know who he was. Not that it mattered. Whether the man was working for Lee directly or indirectly, it all amounted to the same thing: Lee now knew of the existence of the Swedes.

No need to worry just yet. Nothing had happened so far, so they couldn't accuse him of any disobedience. But he felt an overwhelming claustrophobia. Wherever he turned, there was Lee – and the Council behind him – breathing down his neck. It caused a frustration the size of the Empire State Building.

But they'd all be singing a different tune if he could knock the Italians off their pedestal. He'd be a hero! And that would give him power! Power which he would use to smash Lee Kwan's face into the back of his head!

Abruptly Deng made up his mind. He took a pistol from a drawer and pocketed it. Then he hurried up the stairs to the top of the house, climbed out onto the roof and followed the escape route which he had devised for himself years before. Soon afterwards, he emerged on the Bowery and hailed a cab.

Twenty minutes later, he climbed into the surveillance van near Ferrandini's apartment.

36

'Wish me luck,' said Barbara Ferrandini.

Robert was putting on a tie in front of the wardrobe mirror. He glanced around at his wife, who was setting off to play duplicate bridge with one of the top players in the country. He came forward and kissed her lightly on the forehead.

'Yes, good luck,' he said gently, then added, smiling, 'Don't revoke, whatever you do. Alan will never forgive you.'

When Robert finished dressing, he looked in on his son Robin, who was lounging on his bed, reading. 'Where are Tom and Matt tonight?'

'Matt's gone bowling with friends. Tom's gone out with some girl called Karen. She's not bad at all. The last one he went out with looked like the before version of something thorough.'

Robert smiled. 'Are you in or out tonight?'

Robin glided off the bed. 'I've got a date with Laura at eleven. She wants to see some late movie. A pseudo-intellectual Italian thing off-off-off-Broadway.'

'Enjoy yourselves.'

'Where're you off to?'

'I've got a meeting.'

Robin grimaced. 'Have fun.'

As his son went back to his reading, Robert proceeded along to Moreno's apartment. The door was open and Ned was working at his desk with a computer spreadsheet. 'Any problems?'

Ned looked up. 'No. Everything's set.'

'Okay, I'm off. I'll see you later.'

'Bye.' Ned returned to his work.

A minute later, Fredo slipped into Ferrandini's study, picked up the phone and whispered a message into the receiver. It was not actually necessary to touch the phone, because the microphone was sensitive enough to pick up sounds anywhere in the room, but then he would have had to use a normal speaking voice, and he was concerned lest someone should overhear him.

On the multi-line telephone beside Ned, a light flashed on. It corresponded to the extension in Ferrandini's study. Ned glanced at it without much thought. He assumed it was Robin making a call.

333

But then, a second later, Robin himself poked his head around the door and said, 'Wanna beer?'

Ned glanced up at him, then down at the telephone – just as the light went off. The only other person in the apartment now was the butler, but Fredo never used the family's phones, since he had one in his own rooms. Besides, the call had lasted only seconds, so Ned decided Fredo must have happened to be in Robert's study and dialled the weather service or something. He turned back to Robin. 'Yeah, thanks.'

A short while later Robin returned with two cans. He set one down on the desk, peered over Ned's shoulder at the computer monitor and, in mock puzzlement, inquired, 'What's the object of the game?'

'The object is to finish the damn thing. So bug off.'

Robin grinned, and departed. But a quarter of an hour later he returned, peering at a newspaper. 'There's a Hitchcock movie on in ten minutes. *The Lady Vanishes*. Wanna watch it?'

'Yeah, I wouldn't mind seeing it again.'

'Okay.' Robin made a move towards Ned's television set.

'No, let's watch it in your room. That way, if I change my mind, I won't have to boot you out. Go on in. I'll be with you in a minute.'

A well-built man, dressed in paramilitary uniform and carrying a machine-pistol, glanced at his stop watch, then spoke into his hand radio – 'Ferrandini. Check.' – as a dark-windowed Lincoln Continental slowed to take the sharp curve off the road. It swept past him and through the wrought-iron gates of the walled estate, accelerated up the steep half-mile drive bordered by a fairway set in narrowing woodland, and glided to a gentle stop before the elegant if squat mock-Georgian mansion called Burnham Manor. It was built on the northern slope of a shallow New Jersey valley, fifty miles from New York City. In the forecourt two similarly equipped men studied the slope opposite, bared of its trees more than forty years previously by a security-conscious estate manager, and which therefore still received light from a sun hidden from their eyes by the immediately surrounding trees.

The chauffeur stepped out and hurried around to open the Lincoln's rear door. Ferrandini emerged and glanced around, as Stelio trotted down the steps to greet him. He wasn't smiling.

'Bad news, Robert. Don Vincenzo suffered a heart attack this afternoon as he was boarding his plane. He's now in hospital and the doctors say it doesn't look good.'

Robert froze for a moment, then his arms fell helplessly to his sides. He swung around to face the nearby trees. 'Dear God, no. Please, not Vincenzo. Not *now*!' He turned and climbed the dozen steps with downcast eyes, and Stelio followed a pace behind.

Overhead a patrolling gunship flew a wide circuit across the valley, watched by eyes on the crest of the opposite slope. Björn Jensen lay between two groundsheets, the top one covered with divots of artificial turf, sewn onto it. Two sticks propped it up in the front, providing him with a window over the dale below. As the helicopter came closer he turned these props on their sides, closing the 'window', and reached a hand for the comforting feel of his M16 beside him. The gunship flew in an arc which passed directly over him, but in his grass envelope it would need a sharp-eyed observer only yards away to spot him. As the sound of the helicopter faded, he reopened the window. Some of Stelio's men would undoubtedly have infrared scopes, but through the protection of the groundsheet and turf they would not detect him. Suddenly came a soft chirrup from his hand radio. He put it to his mouth.

'Yes?'

His assistant Ingmar Andersen reported, 'I'm in the woods a mile due east of the house. I've found the telephone lines and tapped them. I just heard that Cattagna won't be coming. He's had a heart attack.'

'Okay. Inform Deng.'

Another car was approaching the gates, and Jensen quickly raised a small pair of binoculars to his eyes. This was a Rolls Royce, and when it reached the carpark four men got out, but none of them was Drew. Patellini was accompanied by his assistant, a bodyguard and the chauffeur.

A distant cloud moved over the face of the sun, now low on the horizon. The valley turned grey.

Ned Moreno finished what he was doing and switched off the computer. Suddenly he realised he'd forgotten to ask Robert about his microphone detector. He entered Robin's room just as the film was starting. Sitting down in an armchair, he kicked off his shoes and put his feet up on a corner of the boy's bed. Robin pulled a couple of cigarettes from the packet on his bedside table, tossed one to Ned and switched off the light. Ned settled himself comfortably in his chair. Of all the family the member he felt most at ease with was Robin, who was closest to him in age and interests.

During the second commercial break he went off to ask Fredo to rustle them up a light dinner. Left on his own, Robin was reaching again for his packet of cigarettes, when the phone rang. He dropped the pack and picked up the receiver.

'Rob? It's Di. Is Dad there?'

'No, he's gone out to a meeting somewhere.'

'Did Ned go with him?'

'No, he's here with me.'

'Ask him where Dad went, will you?'

'Sure. Hang on.' He went towards the kitchen and called out. 'Hey, Ned, where's Dad gone?'

'To a meet. Didn't he tell you?' asked Ned in slight surprise, thinking Robert must really be distraught, because he doted on Robin and always informed him of his doings.

'Yes, but where?'

'Who wants to know?'

'Only Di.'

'Burnham.'

Robin went back to the phone and passed on the information. As he hung up, Ned returned and announced, 'Salad and tortellini *al pesto*. Fredo must have been thinking about you.'

'Ooh, we *are* witty tonight, aren't we?' replied Robin sarcastically.

The meal was ready in half an hour. They moved into the main sitting room, where Fredo served it up on trays, so that they could continue watching the movie.

Dinner was also being served at Burnham. At this convocation there were only twenty-three men present, since the rules of the Curia required that an heir could not represent a Codeholder whose incapacity might prove only temporary. Robert was deeply upset about Cattagna's absence – especially at a time like this. On the plus side, both Gabrielli and Lovegni had shared in those decisions recently made in Europe on behalf of the Curia, and had naturally drawn closer to Ferrandini in order to present a united front.

The presentation of their report on the European matter had taken place before dinner, and the trio had managed to persuade everyone else to put their objections on record before the meal began. Only Brunetti had bothered to say anything critical. It was clear to everyone else that the decisions they had made were the correct ones in the light of the information then available.

At the dinner table, the men had broken into groups of twos and threes for rather desultory small talk. Ferrandini tried to concentrate on what his neighbour was saying.

Beyond the window, night was falling over the valley.

Ned Moreno reached across for another of Robin's cigarettes. 'Did Diana say why she wanted to talk to your father?' he asked idly.

'No. I thought she'd gone out with her new boyfriend.'

'Didn't you tell her he was at a meet?'

'Sure, but she seemed keen to know exactly where he'd gone.'

Ned shook his head. 'She wouldn't bother him there unless it was important.' Robin gave a small grunt of uninterested agreement. The television distracted Ned for a moment. Then he asked, 'Who's her new boyfriend?'

'I think she said his name was Richard something-or-other. From Connecticut. He's a business consultant.'

Ned turned his attention back to the television as Fredo took their trays away. Distracted by the movie, neither Ned nor Robin had realised the implications of their exchange, but Fredo had. And he headed for Ferrandini's study at once. A moment later Robin noticed a light on the telephone flash on.

'Hey, Dad's back already.'

Ned got up quickly and went straight to Robert's study. Just as he got there, Fredo emerged and offered him a sheepish expression. Ned barely noticed it and went on in. Finding his boss was not there, he passed on through to the outer office. Puzzled, he returned to the sitting room.

'Which telephone light came on?' he asked Robin.

'The study.'

As Ned headed towards Robert's private suite, it occurred to him that maybe Fredo had been using the study phone again, so he doubled back.

Björn Jensen picked up his hand radio and heard Ingmar say, 'Deng's just told me he suspects Drew is with Ferrandini's daughter, and she's on her way to see her father now.'

And at that very moment a McLaren F1 was fast approaching the gates of Burnham Manor. Through his binoculars, Jensen watched in fascination as it slowed to a stop beside the two armed men guarding the entrance. From the way they checked the rear and boot of the vehicle, however, Björn could tell it had only one occupant. He saw one of the guards speak into a radio, and a moment later gesture for the girl to proceed. The car sped up the drive towards the house.

Jensen spoke into his radio. 'Ferrandini's daughter's just arrived. She's alone.'

Andersen at once relayed the news to Deng, who exclaimed to Hua, 'She's come to fetch her father. To take him to Drew!'

Moreno found the butler in the kitchen, washing up. 'Did Mr Ferrandini come in just now?'

'Not so far as I know, Ned.'

'You didn't use the phone in his study a moment ago, did you?'

'Just to check the time.'

'Oh, I see. Thanks.'

Ned went back to the sitting room and settled down to watch the rest of his interrupted film, but with a vague feeling now that something was not quite right. After a while he found himself staring unseeingly at the television screen.

'Is anything the matter with Fredo?'

Robin looked up. 'Maybe so. He's been sort of distant the last few days. I get the feeling there's something on his mind.'

'Perhaps he's got trouble with his son. Did you play squash with him this afternoon?'

'Michael's gone away somewhere for a few days.'

Ned received this information in silence, but now felt distinctly uneasy. After a moment he asked, 'How do you know?'

'Fredo told me,' replied Robin, glancing up in surprise.

Suddenly the missing debugger came into Ned's mind, and an alarm began to ring in his head. He got up and walked from the room.

'Hey, what's up with you?' called Robin after him.

Ignoring him, Ned went back into Robert's study, unscrewed the earpiece of the telephone receiver – and found the microphone immediately.

In a van in the street below, Hua had been listening closely to the disjointed conversation between Ned and Robin, and detected Moreno's growing suspicion, followed by an ominously abrupt departure from the room. Now Hua, straining to listen, picked up tiny but unmistakable sounds in his headphones. He swung around to Deng. 'Moreno's rumbled us.'

The prospect of catching Drew abruptly faded in Deng's mind. And, in its place, came the thought of Lee closing in on him.

'Do you know the frequency of his portable phone?'

'Sure.'

'Then block it.' Deng grabbed the radio and called Andersen. 'Cut the Burnham phone lines at once!'

'Okay,' replied Ingmar, calmly obedient.

'What good will that do?' asked Hua. 'Moreno can raise Stelio by radio.'

'Only if he knows which frequencies Stelio's using.'

'He can find them out easily. All he's got to do is phone Stelio's home base.'

'Seconds count, man!' exclaimed Deng, beginning to sweat.

'Deng just told me to cut the phone lines.'

'What for?'

'Moreno has found the bugs.'

The news made Jensen uneasy. Microphones were anonymous. Their discovery wouldn't have told Moreno anything beyond the fact they were there. But Ned would try to inform Ferrandini at once, and the cut phone lines would indicate that there were enemy agents in the immediate vicinity of Burnham Manor – a fact which he could easily relay to Stelio by radio.

Björn pursed his lips. He and Ingmar could be in serious trouble. Deng had compromised both of them for a gain of a few minutes.

The man was desperate, Jensen realised.

Ned scribbled a few words on a piece of paper, holstered his gun and returned to Robin's room. He gestured for the boy to follow him in silence. Together they slipped along to the butler's room. Ned tried the door handle, and found it open. Inside they saw Fredo kneeling in prayer before a crucifix nailed to the wall. The man looked up sharply, and Ned handed him the note: *Are there bugs in here too?*

Fredo shook his head sadly. There was no sign of fear on his face – just resignation and perhaps some relief that he no longer needed to betray the family he had served for twenty-six years.

When Ned had the full story, he learned that Fredo had made just three whispered reports into the microphone that day. The first informed the kidnappers that Drew had not yet made contact, but that Ferrandini was attending a special meeting in the evening. The second told them that Ferrandini had just set off for it. The third message said that Robert's daughter had gone out to meet a new boyfriend and, for some reason, had subsequently insisted on knowing where the big meeting was being held.

Ned took out his mobile phone to ring Robert, but heard only a very unfamiliar noise. Worried, he crossed to the butler's private phone and tried to ring Burnham Manor, but with no reply.

'That's impossible,' he murmured, feeling something squeeze in his stomach. 'Stelio always keeps a man close to the phones.' There were three lines to Burnham and he dialled a second one. After drawing a blank with the third, he muttered, 'My God, it's an all-out hit!'

He quickly called Stelio's office in the Lower East Side. The switchboard was manned around the clock. 'This is Moreno. The phone lines to Burnham have been cut. I think there's going to be a hit. Try and raise Stelio on the radio, to warn him.'

He hung up, then immediately dialled Ferrandini's helicopter charter company. 'This is Ned Moreno. I want a chopper over here right now. It can land on the roof.'

'We can't do that, Mr Moreno. Your building isn't licensed by the FAA as a heliport.'

'You can *hover*, can't you? We'll fix any fine with the police *and* the FAA. Now move it!'

'Yes, sir.'

Next he guided the butler into the bedroom, made him lie down and cuffed one hand to the bedpost. 'Sorry, Fredo, but I'm not taking any chances. We'll do what we can to save Michael.'

As Ned hurried out, Robin was at his heels.

'Where do you think *you're* going?'

'Ned, if Dad's in danger I'm going with you, and that's flat.'

'Stay behind to look after your brothers when they come home.'

'I'll leave a note for them.'

Ned turned to him. 'You're staying here, and that's final.'

'If I don't go with *you*, I charter another chopper and go on my own. And *that's* final.'

Ned glared at him. 'Fuck you Ferrandinis!' he hissed angrily. 'Not one of you can ever do as you're told!'

'Get me a gun, Ned,' replied Robin coldly.

A few minutes later they stood on the roof, watching the Bell Jet Lone Ranger manoeuvre to approach, its lights winking against the blackness of the sky above. The pilot decided it was safer to land than hover and, as soon as the helicopter touched down, Moreno climbed aboard. Robin made to get in behind him, but Ned gave him a sharp shove backwards, knocking him to the ground. Moreno signalled to the pilot with an upward jerk of his thumb. The machine whirled into the air and out over the immense abyss of Park Avenue, its miniature traffic bathed in a river of light thirty-six floors below.

Ned glanced down to see Robin get to his feet and shake his fist in impotent fury at the disappearing craft. He turned to the pilot. 'Full speed ahead, then call your base and tell them they lose the Ferrandini account if they answer any call from his kids without checking first with me.'

The pilot nodded. He angled the chopper steeply forward and the rotors bit savagely into the air.

37

The waiters left coffee and brandy on the sideboard and withdrew. As soon as the door closed, Patellini began.

'I think we ought to consider liaising with the government about all this. Maybe between us we can think of a way to contain the damage.'

Lovegni grunted, 'There *is* no way to contain the damage. Salvatore knew people might claim the document was all a fraud. That's why he had Roosevelt himself write that letter. The paper'll be fifty years old and they'll prove it with some sort of carbon dating. Everything's signed and countersigned: Roosevelt, his inner cabinet, and two popes. Who the hell is going to believe *that's* a fraud. No, Don Antonio, we may as well accept the fact now that it will all be confirmed and believed, and the following day they'll be setting fire to American embassies all over the world.'

'Maybe the Italians at least will be grateful their country didn't turn communist,' murmured someone.

Gabrielli was re-reading a copy of the Belvedere Accords, to refresh his memory on the details. Tossing the four sheets of paper onto the table, he replied, 'What happened in Italy isn't important. Not now – fifty years later. It's what's happened over here since that's going to make the shit hit the fan.'

There was silence then, till somebody knocked at the door. Ferrandini got up to open it.

Stelio stood there. 'I'm sorry, Robert. Your daughter's here. She insists on talking to you. Says it's very important.'

Robert frowned in surprise and irritation. He turned to the room to make his apologies, then followed Stelio out.

'Where is she?' he demanded.

'Waiting outside in the car.'

'Okay. I'll take care of it,' Robert said, gesturing Stelio to stay behind. He walked down the front steps to the stationary car. A few yards away a man with a machine gun was watching the night. Robert climbed in alongside his daughter and said crossly. 'This had better be important, young lady.'

'It is, Dad. I have Adam Drew waiting nearby. He needs to talk to you.'

Robert stared at her, then gave a huge sigh of relief. 'Thank God! Take me to him at once. No, wait, I'll just tell Stelio.'

'No, Dad. I promised Adam no one but you. I gave him my word.'

Ferrandini nodded. 'Okay. But I'll need to tell the others how long I'll be away. Where is he?'

'About a mile from here.'

He wound down the window and called up to Stelio, 'Tell the others I'll be back in half an hour.' Then he gestured for Diana to proceed. She let out the clutch and the car sped down the drive. 'How did he contact you?'

'He got to know me at the dance school.'

His head swung around to study her profile. 'Richard Andrews?' She nodded. 'When?'

'Friday.'

'And you've slept with him already?'

'He was the first, Dad, I swear. I held out till yesterday. Maybe the Pope ought to give me a medal,' she murmured to herself.

He stared at her for a moment longer – trying to come to terms with the fact that his little girl had grown into womanhood so soon – then turned unfocused eyes towards the drive ahead.

Björn Jensen's eyes were far from unfocused as he watched the McLaren emerge through the gate and turn eastwards. Only something vitally urgent would take Ferrandini away from a meeting of the Curia. And Björn knew exactly what it was.

Diana continued driving for a mile along the narrow road, heavily wooded on her left, to reach a crossroads. Here she turned left, and a hundred yards further along they came to a derelict cottage. From his vantage point, Jensen's binoculars followed her progress all the way. She was now almost at the limit of his view, as the forest subsequently concealed the road. From his prior study of the area he already knew about the derelict cottage. He would bet everything that was their rendezvous. After radioing a few hurried instructions to Ingmar, he slipped out of his hiding place, and crested the hill, his rifle at the ready, then went loping along the far side of the ridge, out of sight of the guards patrolling the mansion.

As soon as Diana coasted to a halt, Adam Drew emerged from some nearby trees, the Ruger P91 in his hand, but it was pointing unthreateningly towards the ground. He opened the passenger door for Ferrandini, who then climbed out. Together the two men stood in the pool of light thrown from the interior of the car, and examined each other. Then Ferrandini offered his hand and Adam accepted it, having to transfer the pistol to his left grip first.

'Do you think you need that?' inquired Ferrandini.

Adam shook his head and dropped the gun into the side pocket of the door. Instinctively they moved away from the vehicle, and out of Diana's earshot.

'Mr Drew, I'm afraid I've been responsible for making your life very difficult. I'm also ultimately responsible for the deaths of two of your companions, although I didn't specifically order that. I hope you can understand that I had grounds for believing then that you were going to cause my family very great damage. I'm not sure to what extent my words can ever compensate, but I'd like you to know that I deeply regret the misfortunes that have happened.'

Adam nodded slowly. The apology had sounded sincere.

'And Miro? What's happened to him?'

'The smuggler? I ordered his release the next day.'

'Thank heaven for that.' He gave an audible sigh. 'But now, Mr Ferrandini, I must ask you some questions.'

'And I must answer them. Unless you know everything about the Accords, you won't be able to assess the situation properly.'

'I have a fairly good idea already of what they're about.'

'Did my father disclose any of the terms?'

'No, he didn't. But once I knew there'd been some agreement between the US government and the Mafia in 1943 concerning Italy, I guessed it must have had something to do with the invasion, so I read up on the history of that period. The way it looks to me, the Allies deliberately messed up their negotiations for Italy's surrender, so that the Germans would have time to invade. By then, a lot of communists had come out of the closet. The Gestapo executed a lot of them; the Mafia took care of the ones that got away. They continued to do so after the war, too. Portella della Ginestra was one of the more famous massacres.'

'My congratulations, Mr Drew. You're very astute. But I'm afraid there's a bit more to it than that.' Ferrandini was about to continue, but just then the helicopter gunship whirled into the air above Burnham Manor and hurtled along the road eastwards, passing two hundred yards to the south. No longer circling, its motion seemed purposeful, and it crossed Robert's mind that Stelio had sent it after him for some reason. *What now?* he wondered.

He turned back to the Englishman. 'Mr Drew, I think we should return to the house and continue this conversation there.'

'I'm afraid I can't agree to that. I'd then be completely at the mercy of your friends, and I'm not sure I can trust them all.'

'You'd be under my personal protection. I give you my word that nothing will happen to you.'

'Mr Ferrandini, it's not that simple. The reason I wanted to speak to you in private is that I don't know how to stop the Accords from being published.'

343

Robert blinked. 'You what?'

'Your father says that I, and only I, have the power to stop it, but he doesn't say *how*.' Ferrandini could only stare at him in astonishment and dismay. 'That's one of the reasons I've taken so long to get in touch with you. I didn't think you'd believe me, or that your friends would either. Frankly, I don't fancy having the shit beaten out of me before I can convince them.'

'What matters is that you've convinced *me*. I repeat: you have my personal guarantee.'

Adam nodded resignedly. If Ferrandini's word wasn't solid, he'd be finished anyway.

They turned back towards Diana's car – and came face to face with Björn Jensen, holding a levelled M16 rifle.

'Your hands above your heads. Now!'

Diana jerked around in astonishment. She had not detected Jensen's silent approach. Drew's gun, in the side pocket of the passenger door, was impossible for her to reach without being noticed by this rifleman, but in the side pocket of the driver's door she kept a CS gas spray.

Out of the corner of his eye, Jensen glimpsed the move he had been expecting, as Diana's hand slid from her lap towards the pocket. 'That would be very unwise, Miss Ferrandini,' he said calmly, his Scandinavian accent now detectable.

'Keep still, Diana,' her father warned sharply. Her hand sprang back to her lap.

Jensen opened the driver's door, indicating for Diana to get out of the car. Keeping an alert eye on all three captives, he reached down and felt around in the side pocket. He withdrew the gas spray, gave a grunt of derision, and threw the little canister into the woods. Rapidly he passed behind Adam and frisked him expertly. He subjected Ferrandini to the same professional routine, though guessing that he would not come armed to a meeting of the Curia.

Hearing the sound of an approaching car, Drew tensed, ready to take advantage of the Swede's distraction. But Jensen's next words dashed that hope. 'Mr Ferrandini, turn around. If I think you can give a description of our car, your daughter will not survive. Now remove your tie. Quickly, please. Mr Drew will use it to blindfold you.'

As Drew was tying the knot, Ingmar Andersen's Volvo pulled up beside them. 'Okay, into the car,' commanded Jensen. 'You, Mr Drew, into the front. You and Mr Ferrandini will put your hands in your trouser pockets.' To Ingmar he said, 'Give me your gun. I can't cover them with a rifle at close quarters.'

The two Swedes exchanged weapons, then Jensen slid in alongside the Ferrandinis. Seconds later, the Volvo was speeding away up the hill. Just two miles further, the country lane met a more important road – one with a little traffic. Now that there were other vehicles around, Jensen felt less exposed and breathed a quiet sigh of relief.

On the southern horizon, two helicopters were circling.

Björn spoke a few words in Swedish to Ingmar, who gave a nod in agreement and passed the carphone over his shoulder to him. Jensen turned to Ferrandini.

'In a few minutes, we'll drop you. Your daughter will be our guarantee of safe passage. Tell the Curia to call off the helicopters, or she dies.'

'How much do you want?' asked Ferrandini.

'Five million dollars.'

'I can get that as soon as the banks open tomorrow.'

'Make the call. What's Stelio's number?'

Adam was puzzled. The Swede's actions had shown him to be a highly alert and intelligent man, and he'd obviously heard of the Curia, yet apparently he wasn't afraid of them. He was asking for a mere five million. Didn't he realise that was just a drop in a bucket to the man he was going to blackmail, and Ferrandini would spend fifty times as much afterwards in hunting down the men who had dared to threaten his daughter's life? He would promise them anything, while they had her in their possession, but once she was free, then so was he. Even if he swore not to pursue them, what intelligent man could risk believing him. True, in the darkness before the Volvo had driven up, the Swede's features had not been discernible; and, since Ferrandini had then been blindfolded, he could not have seen them at all. But the same did not hold for either Diana or himself. They would now be able to recognise their abductors. Identification could be only a matter of time, then the entire international Mafia would be hunting for them. The two Swedes could not possibly survive!

Suddenly, an ugly suspicion came over Adam, funnelled rapidly – by the abductors' own dreadful logic of survival – into a dire certainty. They could not simply park and hide somewhere nearby, because the patrolling helicopters would rapidly augment, and soon be supplemented by ground patrols, forming an inescapable dragnet. But if the Volvo tried to get through before the dragnet was in place, the existing helicopter patrols, who had only the scanty traffic of the mid-evening to scrutinise, would take a very close look at a vehicle with five occupants.

The Swedes' options were clear. The only thing they wanted from Ferrandini was for him to call off the helicopters. Then they would kill him and Diana, delaying with Adam only until he had told them where the Accords were hidden – assuming they didn't kill all three captives immediately.

The Swede was tapping out the number that Ferrandini had given him, when Drew remarked casually, 'You're going to need a lot more

345

than five million to hide from Ferrandini afterwards.'

Robert gasped, but Adam continued calmly, 'It's just as well for you that he and I have something which will force the Curia to cough up at least a thousand times as much – *and* give you protection for life, into the bargain.'

Jensen paused. 'What do you mean?'

Adam gave a little shrug, as if the answer was obvious. 'I mean you can't afford to kill Ferrandini – not if you want to stop working for peanuts and earn some *real* money.'

'How?'

'Simple. If we control the Curia, we control the worldwide drug-distribution network. I wonder what's the annual rake-off from *that.*'

Jensen blinked at him in the semi-darkness of the car. 'How do we control the Curia?'

'Through the Belvedere Accords, of course. I thought that was why you'd been sent to capture me.'

Jensen hesitated a moment. Then, remembering the helicopters, he redialled Stelio's number.

Now that the dangers had been signposted for him, Robert had no difficulty in duplicating Drew's thought processes. He didn't know how they were all going to get out of their predicament, but there would be *no* chance unless he himself cooperated now. So he ordered Stelio to cancel the search. Moments later, the helicopters ahead of them broke off and returned to their base. Ferrandini hoped Drew knew what he was doing.

But Adam didn't. Despite his outward calm and sureness, he'd been improvising furiously all the way.

For nearly a minute there was silence inside the speeding Volvo.

Jensen's original doubts about trusting Deng had been greatly increased by the man's decision to cut the phone lines. True, that decision had granted them a few precious minutes in which to capture Drew, but what if it had not? Björn did not expect the men who hired his services to care much what happened to him, but nor did he expect them to put his life so obviously at risk for the sake of a long shot. So he was far from happy with the way this assignment had been developing, and had pressed on with it only because an opportunity had arisen not only to complete the job, but also to escape.

But this was not all. Everything suggested that Deng himself was in serious trouble, and was grasping at straws to get himself out of it. What trouble could that be, if not some disobedience of the Council? So there was a distinct possibility that Deng might soon decide he could not afford the luxury of two freelancers wandering around who knew what he had done. And what if the Council was to find out, anyway? Björn and Ingmar would only get paid if Deng was still around to do the paying.

The situation now seemed both dangerous and treacherous.

But here was an unexpected and intriguing offer. Putting Drew's statements alongside Deng's actions, half-truths and lies, Jensen found they fitted like the fragments of a broken cup. He had not yet decided to rescind his contract with Deng, but he certainly wanted to hear more of Drew's proposals.

Finally he said, 'Explain.'

'The Accords are due to be published within a few weeks. If that happens, the Curia will lose its protection from the US government. But I can stop that publication.'

'How?'

'Because I know where they are.'

Drew's skill as a negotiator was at last required, though in circumstances that could scarcely be worse.

The first task of a professional negotiator, he told himself, was to gauge accurately the other party's wants, needs and aspirations, and, as far as was consonant with his own purpose, to fulfil them. These Scandinavians wanted money, needed protection and aspired to survive, so Adam's offer must have sounded very tempting, because the Accords would give them the lot.

There was only one problem: he hadn't the faintest idea where they were hidden. He was bullshitting to save their lives.

I'm on their territory, he thought. Unarmed, while they're armed. I've got to equalise things and get them on *my* territory. But what's my territory? The Matterhorn and the Northeast Wall of the Königsspitze and . . . And the North Face of the Eiger.

38

Ahead the skyscrapers of Manhattan could be seen low on the horizon.

'What are these Belvedere Accords?' demanded Jensen.

'A top-secret agreement involving the US government. The ultimate form of guarantee. Whoever possesses them has the government by the balls.'

'You said you know where they are. So you don't actually have them in your possession?'

This was Drew's moment. Every word had to sound relaxed, probable, convincing, even obvious: all to sell an idea – and buy a little time. 'No. I've got a copy. It wouldn't count as proof. Mr Ferrandini's father Salvatore set up a secret system to protect the original documents and I'm part of it. I was briefed by a merchant bank in London. My assignment is to make sure the members of the Curia and their families are safe. If so, I stop publication of the Accords; if not, I don't. In theory, all the members of the Curia are equal, but naturally Salvatore gave preference to his own family. I can't stop publication on my own; I must act jointly with Mr Ferrandini.'

Jensen fell silent for a moment. Then he asked, 'Where's this copy?'

'In an apartment on Fifth Avenue.'

Björn considered. If Drew's story was false, then why was everyone making such a fuss about him? He murmured a few words of Swedish to his companion, who nodded. To Drew he said, 'Okay, take us there. Miss Ferrandini, you can remove your father's blindfold.'

Twenty minutes later they drove into the carpark underneath Turner's building and pulled up close to the express elevators. Within seconds they were rising rapidly towards the penthouse. Under Björn's minute scrutiny, Adam unlocked the apartment door. His actions seemed natural and casual – belying the furious activity of his brain. All the while he was conscious of the gun in Jensen's hands, the rifle in Andersen's.

When the door opened, Björn made a gesture, and Ingmar entered first, alone. He moved rapidly from room to room to check that the place was deserted. Then he returned to give the all clear.

By now, Drew had something of the measure of the two Scandinavians. Andersen was obviously something close to an automaton, though no less dangerous for all that. Content to let the other do the thinking for the pair of them, he would have little imagination to appeal to. Jensen was a different proposition, both intelligent and imaginative. That was a strength, but could also be a weakness . . .

Drew led them into the sitting room as if he owned the place. 'The bar's over there,' he said airily.

'Let's get on with it,' growled Björn. 'Where are those papers?'

'Hidden in a storeroom up on the roof.'

'Show me.' Björn glanced at Andersen. 'You stay here and keep them covered.'

Perfect, thought Adam; they're separating. He glanced at Diana and Ferrandini, who were watching him tensely, then went back out to the lobby. That storeroom was the only place in Lawrence's apartment where he knew of a weapon. But the Swede would be watching like a hawk, while expecting him to produce the promised document – which did not exist. Drew's bluff had less than five minutes of life before being exposed. In that time he had to disable Jensen. If not, he and the Ferrandinis would die this very night. Adam had gambled everything on something he had remembered about Lawrence's apartment.

He climbed up the stairs. Taking both keys off their hooks, he fiddled with the dials of the time switch. 'It's the burglar alarm,' he explained, then opened the door and stepped outside, counting the seconds rigorously. 'The storeroom is over there,' he pointed. 'The best place to hide something valuable is in a trash can.' As he reached it, he pretended to have difficulty with the lock, so it took more than fifteen seconds to open the door. Reaching inside, he switched on the dim interior light and waited for Jensen to survey the room. Then he crossed over to a chest standing among all the mountaineering equipment. The Very pistol lay close by.

Just as he started to open the box, the roof lights came on outside, flooding the storeroom with a blue and white glare. The man would need to be inhuman not to glance backwards to see what had happened.

The moment was Drew's.

It had to be, because there would never be another.

The Very pistol swung up and around – Jensen's head was already turning back towards him – and fired at almost point-blank range. The magnesium based flare slammed into the man's forehead, melting his flesh, and he reeled backwards with arms flying, his mouth registering shocked surprise. Strontium nitrate flooded the room with an evil red light. As his right arm struck the doorpost, the gun flew

349

out and arced through the air, then vanished into the void beyond the roof railing.

Oh, shit! screamed a voice in Adam's mind.

Jensen's corpse slid down the wall and slumped on the floor.

Adam raced to the railing and searched the abyss of forty floors. The gun was gone. He swung around, his eyes searching desperately for a solution. There was no phone up here on the roof, and Andersen had the stairs in his sight.

Drew ran back to the storeroom, where his gaze reconnoitred the equipment mechanically. Suddenly his eyes focused on climbing ropes. Ingmar would be covering his two hostages and the lobby outside, but not the window, and Adam could reach it in a single rappel. But what good would that do? The glass was bound to be reinforced – not even a hammer would break it. It would need a bullet, and maybe not even then . . .

Abruptly he remembered that Andersen was armed with a high-velocity rifle. His eyes narrowed. Maybe, just maybe . . .

Desperately Adam hunted through the chest, but could find no more cartridges for the Very pistol. *Jesus, Lawrence! Couldn't you keep something practical instead of all this crap?*

Then his eyes alighted on the grappling hook with its launcher. Hurriedly he began his preparations.

Within six minutes, everything was ready, and the nylon ropes were dangling from the railing. As he climbed over it, he looked down at the street forty floors below.

Tell me to cut the rope!

Sweat burst from his pores – and he was back on the Eiger eight months ago. The best months for climbing any cliff-face were in autumn or winter, because the danger from falling stones – easily dislodged during thaws – was lessened. Most of the stones that dropped down the North Face were tiny, but in falling more than five thousand feet they became deadly missiles. On the Eiger the most perilous section was the third icefield – a sixty-five-degree exposed slope two-thirds of the way up the mountain.

The three of them had been just underneath this. Adam was in the lead at that point, then James, and lastly Adrian. The föhn had come from the southwest, so they hadn't been able to spot its approach. The rain precipitation at the top of the mountain was tremendous, and caused a thaw. Adam had just hammered a piton into a crack, and was in the process of setting up the belay, when the first stones arrived. Though he shouted a warning, one of them, pebble-sized, struck his brother on the top of his helmet and knocked him out cold. He merely slumped against the rockface, momentarily safe. But then came a second stone, hitting Adrian and leaving him dizzy,

350

so he lost his balance and fell, dragging James's unconscious body with him. The two men dangled over abysmal space, held by the rope attached to Adam's waist, then anchoring itself at the piton just next to him.

Standing on a narrow ledge, Adam pulled on the rope with all his strength, to take the strain off the piton, which he knew could not hold the weight of all three of them. If he relaxed his grip on the rope, the piton would spring free and all three would go. Adrian was now trying to climb up the rope towards James. Adam's arm and back muscles screamed at him for relief. A cold mist scudded along the mountain face, rising at the same time – ghostly fingers of a white terror reaching up for him. He *knew* he could not hold out till Adrian reached the ledge.

Wake up, James! Tell me to cut the rope! Give me permission to kill you!
The pressure brought knotted veins to his head and neck.
Tell me to cut the rope!
His body racked by agony he could bear no longer, he transferred the strain momentarily to a single arm, then whipped out his knife . . . and cut. Horrified, he watched his brother and Adrian, still retaining their relative positions, slowly fall away . . . diminish in size . . . become tiny . . .

And then they were gone.
Adam was alone.
Unmoving and alone.
Night fell and the scudding mist turned grey.
He woke to the sound of rotors. Above the icefield hovered a helicopter – the men aboard risking their lives to reach him. The sun had been up for several hours.

A rope was lowered, and all Adam had to do was put his boot in the foothold and survive. He did so because that was the way back to warmth.

The Swiss Army Rescue officer later told him they'd found the bodies. James had lost an arm. It was never recovered.

Adam gaped down at forty floors and wondered, for the thousandth time, what it would feel like to fall so far.

An image of Diana came into his mind.

He swallowed, and began to feed out the rope.

39

Ingmar's eyes switched uneasily from his captives, sitting on the edge of the sofa, to the stairs out in the lobby. Where the hell was Björn? What was taking him so long? Was it possible the bloody Englishman had got the better of him? If so, Drew would now be armed, so Ingmar's options were few. He would have to kill the Ferrandinis at once, then go hunting for him.

Diana glanced apprehensively at her father's ashen face. And she could guess the reason for it. During their private talk outside her car earlier, Drew must have explained to him that he didn't know how to stop publication of the Accords. So everything Adam had said to the Swedes was pure bluff. But he must have had some reason for bringing them here – some plan to put Jensen off his guard and disarm him. And this long delay was a hopeful sign.

But even if Adam had been successful, what could he do against that rifle pointing straight towards the stairs? Maybe Adam had called the police, but they would take far too long to arrive. Long before then, this man would have taken some drastic action.

She studied his face and saw a nervous tension hitherto absent. Clearly, he was used to Jensen doing the thinking for them, and now was having to do a little for himself. The man was on a short fuse. What was Adam planning?

But the attack, when it happened, came from a completely unexpected direction.

Her father caught a movement from the corner of his eye, glanced at the window, and started. Diana's eyes widened. The gunman swung around.

A darkly-silhouetted figure was climbing down outside the window, just beyond the roof overhang.

The Englishman!

Andersen did not hesitate. He raised the M16 and fired, and the window exploded into a thousand shards of flying glass – the figure beyond, falling out of sight. He ran over to see the body plummeting into the darkness, a rope streaming behind it.

A second rope – looping back upwards – dangled four feet in front of him, at knee height. If Ingmar had been granted time to think, he might have wondered why there were two ropes. If Drew had been climbing down the rope still dangling, then what was the purpose of the second one?

In fact, it had just emerged from two pulleys attached to the roof railing. Standing on the roof ledge Adam had merely been holding the end of the rope, letting go as soon as the window shattered.

No longer wearing his jacket – which was on its way down to the sidewalk with Björn Jensen inside it – Drew suddenly rappelled into view down the dangling double rope, passing through a figure-of-eight descender attached to a harness, his gloved left hand and legs controlling his descent, his right arm supporting the launcher, from which protruded the three curved hooks of the grappling iron. The single rope connected to the other end of this was looped into coils hanging loosely on his wrist, though he was also gripping it a third of the way along its length, in order to use it later to get back into Turner's apartment.

Startled, Andersen jerked back into the room. The rocket-powered grappling hook was cartridge-fired. Adam pulled the trigger. Abruptly the grapnel shot out of the launcher, the single rope spiralling off his wrist. The projectile grazed Ingmar's arm, thudded against the wall behind, then dropped to the floor, the rope snaking across the carpet away from it. The forward motion of the rocket had caused Adam to rotate slightly, which he countered with a backward jerk of his left elbow.

For a frozen moment no one moved.

Had all gone well, the grapnel would have injured Andersen sufficiently for Robert or Diana to seize the rifle and, by pulling the grapnel rope, bring Drew close enough to the window for him to swing himself into the room.

But all had not gone well.

Adam had missed.

Thunderstruck, Diana and Robert Ferrandini stared with wide-eyed horror.

And now Ingmar's rifle began to swing up.

Drew was clinging to a double rope which came to an end only two feet below him. There was nowhere for him to go. Death was only a second away.

He had failed!

The barrel of the M16 was now levelled at Drew's chest.

And that was when Adam did something unbelievable.

He let go the double rope – his body at once yanking the karabiner down off the end of it – and fell!

Ingmar fired. The bullet shot through the space occupied by Drew's body a millisecond before, clipping the dangling rope, then smashed an office window across the street, while Adam, now clutching an unanchored rope, was dropping towards the street forty floors below.

In the apartment, three metres above, Ingmar stared at that same rope as it suddenly grew taut. He was starting to turn when the grapnel abruptly leapt away from the wall and arced through the air towards him. Two of its claws slammed into the back of his thigh, jerking him towards the open window.

Six metres below, Adam was now falling inwards to the wall.

Even in his blind agony, Ingmar had wits enough to raise the rifle to act as a bar across the window struts. But he only managed to connect with one, then his forward momentum plunged him through the gap.

Adam's feet – aided by the Swede's struggle to survive – sought and found the narrow window ledge two floors below Lawrence Turner's apartment.

Andersen's left hand tried to seize the double rope, swinging unpredictably. He momentarily caught its very end between his thumb and index finger, but it slipped from his grip, and now there was nothing to save him.

Adam flattened himself against the glass.

Andersen hurtled past him, screaming, into the void. The grappling hook was still embedded in his leg, the single rope streaming out behind.

Just in time, Adam remembered to release it.

Diana Ferrandini ran to the window, Robert a fraction behind her.

Far below, Andersen was still falling. In the deeper background, two ant-like passers-by were hurrying towards the prone figure of Jensen. When they spotted the newcomer, they quickly changed direction to get out of his way.

Adam stood on a six-inch-wide window ledge, his outstretched arms clinging to the glass. Andersen hit the sidewalk in the same instant that Robert recovered from his shock. If he could get upstairs to untie that double rope still oscillating in front of the window . . . But as he reached the roof, he noticed the storeroom and several coiled ropes hanging on hooks. Seizing two of them, he hurried back downstairs.

Moments later a rope dropped down beside Adam, balanced precariously on his ledge. He caught hold of it.

'What have you anchored it to?' he shouted.

'To a window strut,' replied Ferrandini.

'What knot have you used?'

'A great-great-granny knot.'

Have to do, I suppose, thought Adam, unless I want to wait for the fire brigade. And he began to jumar up the wall.

A minute later, Ferrandini and Diana hauled him into safety and all three collapsed on the sofas.

Drew was hardly able to believe what had happened. He owed his survival to the fact that the Swede had braked Adam's fall trying to prevent his own.

He was alive because *his* interests had coincided with Ingmar's.

But this set Drew on an intriguing track of thought. The Accords had lain for half a century in a *safe* place. Yet *now*, whoever was looking after them would be *in favour* of publication.

A guardian who concealed them and revealed them on demand, yet who could be trusted not to make his own decisions about them? No such automaton existed.

Salvatore's whole scheme depended on people whose interests coincided with his own. When he wanted to be a Capper, he could rely on other Cappers; when he wanted to be a Blower, he could rely on other Blowers. But who could possibly have interests which turned him from Capper into Blower at the same time as Salvatore?

Again, the answer was no one.

In that case, the custodian had to be unaware he possessed them, which could only mean he thought it was something else he was looking after!

40

'What a godawful mess *this* all is,' said Robert, after he had caught
his breath. He looked across at Adam. 'How many phone lines in this
apartment?'

'Two.'

'Okay. Diana, use one of them to phone home and make sure
everyone's all right. Then call for a helicopter. Tell them they'll be
hearing from the police to authorise a landing on the roof here.'

Robert, meantime, had two calls of his own to make. The first
involved a friend in the NYPD, to arrange a little cooperation so that
they wouldn't waste time answering a lot of awkward questions. The
very last thing he wanted now was to be detained while the police
tried to sort out paperwork. Next, he rang Ned Moreno at Burnham
to say they would soon be on their way there.

Taking advantage of their distraction, Adam slipped off to his own
room. There he took Salvatore's third letter from its hiding place and
re-read a part of it. After a moment's thought, he took out his lighter
and set fire to the letter, then threw the ashes into the lavatory and
flushed them away.

The helicopter landed in the Burnham Manor carpark. Stelio's men
were no longer patrolling, but were now in combat-ready positions.
Stelio and his platoon of men at once formed a protective wall around
their three charges, to escort them up the steps and into the house.

Peter Gabrielli and Philip Lovegni, relief writ large on their faces,
came up to greet Ferrandini at once. Other members of the Curia,
all now armed, were standing about the hall in groups of twos and
threes.

Ned Moreno was talking into a phone, and gestured his boss to
come over. Covering the mouthpiece, he murmured, 'It's Lee Kwan.'

Ferrandini paused to collect his thoughts, then took the receiver.
'Yes, Mr Lee.'

'Good evening, Mr Ferrandini. I understand that a member of
our community has been causing you some problems. First I would
like to say that his actions in no way reflect any policy of the Chinese
Council. Second I must assure you that he has already ceased to be
a thorn in your side and ours. The Council ordered his detention

shortly after ten o'clock – some two and a half hours ago – and he was apprehended an hour later, together with his misguided assistants. I tried earlier to warn you that he had hired two professional assassins as part of his unsanctioned campaign against you, but your assistant has already informed me of the happy outcome of that episode. I feel it would not be out of place to offer you my congratulations on your successful handling of the matter. Perhaps you would be so kind as to inform your butler that I have made arrangements for his son's release and safe conduct home.'

'Thank you, Mr Lee. Your consideration is much appreciated.'

'Not at all. Youth must have its day, as they say – and some young men have quite definitely had theirs. There's just one last thing I must tell you. This whole affair resulted from a sale of information concerning your affairs by Mr David Ewing, operational head of the CIA.'

'I understand. I'll see the matter is taken care of. Ten thousand years to you, Mr Lee.'

'And to you too, Mr Ferrandini.'

Hanging up, Robert turned to Ned Moreno, who handed him a handwritten message. He scanned it briefly, pursing his lips.

'You can inform Fredo that his son will be free within a few hours. Also tell him to leave my home tonight. I do not want to see him ever again. Give him a year's salary and a reference, but he leaves tonight.'

By now the other Curia members were drifting back into the great dining room. Beckoning Drew along, Ferrandini followed them inside. Adam first gave Diana's hand a surreptitious squeeze, then joined her father.

Robert walked to his chair and gripped the back of it while he waited for all to retake their seats. Drew came to hover a yard behind him.

Ferrandini announced, 'I apologise for my prolonged absence, gentlemen. As you may have learned, it was entirely beyond my control. But a full explanation must be postponed for more urgent news: good and bad. One problem at least is over. The Chinese had a renegade, and they've sorted out that difficulty on their own.'

He surveyed their faces for a moment, then glanced down at Ned's handwritten message. 'And now for some very sad news. Vincenzo suffered a second coronary. He died just twenty minutes ago.'

Wordlessly the members of the Curia rose to their feet, bowed their heads, and for two minutes prayed silently.

As the men sat down once more, Ferrandini went on, 'Gentlemen, I am at last able to present to you Mr Adam Drew. He is here under my personal protection, and in your name, I have given him our word on that. Under Rule Eleven, I demand a show of hands to indicate that you will honour it.' These last seven words were primarily for Adam's benefit, and all twenty-two men raised their hands at once.

Ferrandini continued, 'Vincenzo was the last of the original signatories of the Articles of Association of the Curia, and the last of the direct participants in the Belvedere agreement. It's a strange coincidence that he should leave us at the same time that we are joined here by Mr Drew, to whom my father, in his own way, entrusted control of that agreement. Perhaps this is the mysterious hand of Fate.' He shrugged. 'However, we are not out of the woods yet. Although my father has *somehow* given him control over publication of the Accords, he hasn't explained either how it can be stopped or where the originals are hidden.'

Ferrandini's listeners gave vent to a variety of oaths and gasps of dismay. He waited for them to quieten, then went on, 'Mr Drew is nevertheless the key to our restoration of the status quo ante, so we must obviously try to make him our ally. In the circumstances, I propose that we explain to him exactly what happened in 1943. All those in favour?' Twenty-three hands went up. He turned to Adam. 'It seems we can now tell you everything.'

Then there was silence. All eyes focused on Ferrandini, but he seemed to be having difficulty in finding a way to begin.

Philip Lovegni broke in, 'Robert, perhaps it would be better if you spoke to Mr Drew in private. I propose we adjourn our meeting for one hour.'

Gabrielli stood up immediately, and everyone else followed suit.

After walking along the table to retrieve the copy of the Belvedere Accords, Ferrandini folded the sheets, then put them into his inside jacket pocket. He took Adam gently by the elbow and led him into the adjoining library, but did not turn on the light. Instead he crossed to the window, and Adam went to join him there. They lit up cigarettes and looked out at the starry sky visible above the ridge on the far side of the valley.

'So where do we begin?'

'Perhaps we could start with an explanation of what the Curia actually is,' suggested Drew.

'It's the ruling body for Cosa Nostra international, which it governs directly. Through this, it also exercises behind-the-scenes influence on a large number of other organisations engaging in criminal activities.'

'But why would a man as wealthy as you want to involve himself at all?'

Ferrandini shrugged. 'Things are already pretty bad, but if we weren't around they'd be a lot worse. The world can't control its deprived any more. We're a lot closer than most people realise to the society that existed five thousand years ago, when the difference

358

between "to want" and "to take" barely existed. For the last five millennia, whether by accident or design, the rich have used religion – the threat of hellfire and the promise of a great big granary in the sky – to keep the poor satisfied with their lot. Or perhaps I should say with their little. In recent decades the system has been breaking down. More and more of the deprived see crime as the only solution to their poverty.

'There are now only two ways to curb the crime explosion: one to set up a police state – which the Curia thinks would be a cure worse than the disease; the other to keep an eye on things from the inside. So that's what we do. If the various groups and Families keep themselves within tolerable limits of behaviour and size, we usually take no action, but if their development threatens the existing order, either through excessive systematic violence or by becoming too big and powerful, then we intervene.'

'How do you monitor them?'

'Through Cosa Nostra and its various allies.'

'And how can you exercise control while remaining so secret?'

'Again through Cosa Nostra. If we can, we use our contacts to infiltrate the group in question, and thus acquire proof of criminal activity – such as the time and place of a drug shipment – which we arrange to be handed over to the police. If infiltration proves too difficult, we fall back on direct action.'

'Hired killers?'

'Yes. Commandos usually.'

Drew was thoughtful. 'So, you control other groups through the Mafia. And, presumably, you control the Mafia itself, because there are *two* Mafias – the American and the Sicilian – you can control them by playing one off against the other.'

Ferrandini shook his head. 'No, it doesn't need to be so Macchiavellian. Our power derives from the Belvedere Accords. Although we didn't have the documents in our possession, we could issue a code to have them made public at any time, and that gave us a hold over the US government.'

'Yes, but you couldn't use that without damaging *yourselves*.'

Ferrandini shook his head. 'The H-bomb couldn't be used during the Cold War either, but it still gave both sides every reason to try to get along. What do you do with an enemy you can't obliterate? You try and keep him contented. That's the smart thing to do. That's what the government does.'

'You mean the President?'

'No. Only two departments within the permanent administration know about us – the Attorney General's Office and the State Department. The politicians aren't usually told about us, because the civil servants rightly don't trust them.

'Well, as the government can't destroy us, it makes an effort to keep us happy, which means following our recommendations to apply pressure on other organisations. That power, in effect, makes the Curia the licensing authority for organised crime.

'The Sicilian Cosa Nostra has a motive to cooperate with us because, in return for its obedience in keeping its own house in order, we license it to distribute drugs worldwide, and we stop its competitors from becoming too rich and powerful. That's why it can compete successfully with the Triads, or with the Japanese Yakuza which is five times the size of the Mafia.

'The American Cosa Nostra obeys us, firstly, because we can use the US government to bring pressure on them and make life difficult, and, secondly, because we can license the Sicilians to operate in other fields of activity whenever we want. We keep the Sicilians tough and the Americans are afraid of them, so if the US Cosa Nostra doesn't toe the line, we can bring over Sicilians in force to put them out of business. In return for our keeping the Sicilians in check, the Americans inform us about what's going on in South America and Asia. They're well placed to do so, because they set up the deals. The Sicilians also use them as agents. You see, not many people speak Italian, but nearly everybody speaks English.

'So, far from having to play off one group against another, the situation is quite harmonious. Everybody cooperates because they're doing very nicely with the existing arrangements.'

Adam nodded. 'I'm beginning to get the picture.' He stubbed out his cigarette. 'And you members of the Curia are so rich, you don't need to get your hands dirty by participating in criminal activities yourselves.'

'Exactly. That was a very important objective for my father – to get his own family out of direct involvement.'

'But you still license the distribution of drugs. Have you ever visited an addicts' rehabilitation centre?'

'Yes. My father took me to one near West Point when I was a boy. He made me promise to do the same with my own children.'

'So you know how people can end up?'

Ferrandini sighed heavily. 'Mr Drew, there is one very unpleasant fact of life: if there's a need for something, someone will fill it. I didn't create human nature, nor did my father. God did that, for reasons best known to Himself. The essential point, Mr Drew, is that what's happening is going to happen anyway, whether *we* control it or someone else does.'

Adam nodded, as if he was dismissing the point. 'So it was your father who arranged all this?'

'Yes. He also set up the protection system, though that was supposed to have been settled by secret lottery. But my father knew his own scheme would be better than anybody else's, so he decided to trick the Curia. He needed an accomplice, however, so he brought another member of the group in on his plans – Vincenzo Cattagna, the man who died tonight. It was he who put us on the right track.'

Drew replied gently, 'I would have got to you anyway – as your father intended. Cattagna put you, ultimately, on the *wrong* track, because three innocent men died.'

Ferrandini blinked at him, now seeing for the first time the unintended disservice Vincenzo had performed. Salvatore's scheme would have become perfect, if those two Sicilian layabouts had waited until tonight before killing Adriano Lupillo.

Adam went on. 'From what you've said, the Curia seems to be the next best thing to an unofficial department of the FBI. If it helps to control international crime, it's practically *part* of the US government. So what I don't understand is why you were afraid they would make a move against you.'

'Because it's *our* decision to run things this way, Mr Drew – not the US government's. It naturally doesn't like the arrangement, because the Belvedere Accords encroach upon its sovereignty. Which is another way of saying that the government thinks it should have the *right* to make mistakes. Please note, Mr Drew, that it could change the arrangements at any time, simply by defying us and to hell with the consequences. But we believe that the alternatives would be worse, and up till now the government has lacked the guts to challenge us. But suppose it changes its mind – what then?' He smiled thinly. 'It's the old dilemma, isn't it? While you hold a tiger by its tail, you're safe; but what do you do when you want to let go? That's the position we have been in since 1943.'

From his inside jacket pocket, he took out the copy of the Belvedere Accords. There were four folded sheets of paper. He passed three of them to Drew. 'Those are copies of the three pages notarised by Pope Pius XII.'

Adam scanned the contents and found almost nothing he did not already know. Only the last clause was a surprise. He frowned in puzzlement. 'I don't understand the reason for this last part.'

Ferrandini handed over the fourth sheet. 'That's a letter signed by President Roosevelt and his advisers, confirming the US government's adherence to the terms of the agreement, and explaining the rationale behind that last clause. This letter was not shown to the Pope, because he would never have agreed to sign such a document, even as a witness.'

Drew read the letter through, slowly nodding his now complete understanding of Salvatore's need for the system of protection called Belvedere.

41

Adam Drew opened his eyes and saw wallpaper. Bluebells alternated restfully with daisies.

Four days had gone by since the Burnham Manor meeting. He had spent them as Ferrandini's guest in the Manhattan apartment and by now felt almost part of the family. He played squash with Ned Moreno and Robert's sons, and spent most of the rest of the time with his daughter. Adam and Diana scrupulously observed all the forms when they were actually under her father's roof, but occasionally they would slip away to Turner's apartment. Everybody knew this; but no one had made any comment, apart from a few sniggering remarks from the two younger boys, which their father had sharply silenced.

For Adam, life had become surreal. Yet his pleasant daily routine was painted against a backdrop of suffering and murder.

He got up to open the curtains and let in the new day. It was sunny again – like yesterday.

After showering and dressing, he went along to the dining room. Ferrandini was breakfasting there alone. Looking up from his newspaper, he greeted Adam cheerfully.

'You seem in a good mood,' said Drew.

'Within narrow limits of nervous tension, I suppose I am.'

'What's in the papers?'

'Some CIA chief's car blew up when he switched on the ignition.'

'Who was it?'

'David Ewing. Apparently an Iranian terrorist group was responsible,' he added gravely.

Just then, the new butler entered with a plate of ham and eggs, which he placed in front of his employer. Ferrandini eyed the food with suspicion. 'I certainly miss Fredo,' he said, after the man had gone. 'The whole family does. They've been imploring me to bring him back.'

'Then why don't you? You can't really blame the man for what he did. You'd have done the same. Besides, they told him it was *me* they were after, not any of your family.'

'I agree. But is there any point in asking him back? If we can't figure out where my father hid the Accords, I'm going to take the whole family away to an island in the South Pacific.'

Adam grunted. 'Swiss Family Ferrandini. You'll still need a butler.'

Robert tasted the ham and eggs, then threw down his fork in disgust. 'I'll call him this morning.'

After breakfast, Adam slipped out of the apartment unobserved and went to Tiffany's to pick up the identical copy of Salvatore's ring which he had asked them to make.

The copy was necessary because there could be only one reason that Salvatore had not explained how to stop publication of the Accords: he wanted his agent dependent on his own family itself. Adam was an insurance policy, yes, but Salvatore could not trust a total stranger, however many precautions he had taken to select the right man for the job – not with the future of his family at stake. True, if this present crisis had arisen not through the meddling of a pair of Sicilian ne'er-do-wells, but because the US government really had decided to destroy the Belvedere structure, then Salvatore would have had nothing to lose. But Adam knew the man had been too intelligent to think he had a plaster suitable for every sore. Only idiots thought they could foresee the unforeseeable. To ensure that his agent would not leave the Ferrandinis in the lurch, Salvatore must have arranged matters, so that Drew would only be able to locate the Accords with the assistance of the Ferrandinis themselves.

Adam had used this very reason to persuade Jensen and Andersen of the value of Ferrandini's life, but at that time he only *suspected* that it was true. A short while later, after his exploit with the grapnel, he had followed a train of thought which had led him to *know* it was true, and also to guess where the Accords were hidden.

Drew's escape had been almost miraculous. There had been too much slack in the rope. If the grappling hook had found a clear passage, it would either have sailed straight through the window, and Adam would have fallen to his death, or it would have caught against a strut, and his own inertia would have tripled his weight. His *one* chance was what had actually happened. The Swede had braked his fall, by trying to stop himself from falling.

What had struck Adam particularly was how he had used someone whose interests were, for the moment, the same as his own. *A man, wanting to kill him, had tried to save his life, in order to save his own.* It had made him think then about how Salvatore had set up his whole scheme; how it relied on different people knowing different things, yet carrying out their various functions because it was in their interests to do so.

So then Drew had asked himself: in whose interests would it be to publish the Accords?

Adam hired a car and drove out of the city, taking the Palisades Interstate Parkway northwards to West Point. He soon found the drug

363

addiction rehabilitation centre run by Protestant nuns. It was a mock-Regency mansion set in some twenty acres of parkland and overlooking the Hudson River. A sign announced that it was run by the Daughters of Charity, an order founded in 1869 to the rule of St Vincent de Paul. The centre was called the Belle Vue Rehabilitation Centre. The name was not lost on Adam – one last little joke of Salvatore's, he supposed.

If Ferrandini or any of his children had read Salvatore's final letter, they would at once have spotted the reference to the rehabilitation centre, because Salvatore had taken Robert there as a teenager, and made him promise to do the same with his own children. Ostensibly, the motive had been a lesson in the danger of drugs, but the real reason was simply that they should know the place existed.

Yet, as clever a device as this had been, Salvatore had not quite dared to leave his agent with absolutely no clue at all, so Salvatore had included a failsafe device – a clue which *anyone* could interpret, although it was buried deep. If Adam had been unable to contact the Ferrandinis, he would have been forced to rely on the tools which Salvatore himself had given him, and before long would begin to wonder why he had been specifically instructed to destroy the first two letters, but not the third. In fact Salvatore had forcefully interrupted Adam's reading of it – '*Go now!*' – to make him use the Barrow Street escape route. The reason given was: ' . . . *it is now essential that you become a truly free agent . . .*' But why? What was so important about that particular moment?

It was important because Drew was in the process of reading a letter which he wanted Drew to preserve at all costs. Clearly, this apparently threadbare text concealed a clue of importance. And it contained one very odd line: '*By the way, all that stuff about Barton & Willis moving somewhere else was hogwash in case the Russians should read the Moscow letter*'. That was odd, because it could not matter at all if the Russians read it. So Salvatore could only have written it to signpost the importance of the setup which sustained the nuns.

At the reception desk, he produced the Davis & Associates documentation before asking to speak to the mother superior. A minute later he was shown into an oak-panelled office. Behind a large desk sat a plump, jolly woman in her late fifties. She waved him to a chair and introduced herself as Mother Josephine.

'I understand you're from Davis's,' she said pleasantly.

'I think these are what you need as proof of my bona fides.'

He handed over the two rings. Mother Josephine examined the inside of one of them, then she pulled a drawer fully out from the desk. On a hook screwed into its back, hung a third ring – obviously the one Salvatore claimed to have lost. She took it off and compared it with one of the others.

She looked up. 'Everything's in order. What can I do for you?'

'I need to examine all the material belonging to Davis & Associates.'

The Mother Superior's head ducked backwards in a gesture of incredulity. '*All* of it? You'll need a month of Sundays.' She picked up a bunch of keys from her desk, then escorted him down to the basement and along a corridor. Unlocking the end door, she showed him into a large room full of filing cabinets. There were more than sixty, all unlabelled.

'Which of these date back to 1943?'

'They all do. They contain the records of a firm which Davis's had bought out the year before. The records are kept in case some legal action should arise from previous transactions.'

Drew hid his dismay. 'May I have the keys to them?'

'There's only one key. It opens them all.' She removed it from her keyring and handed it over.

He opened the first cabinet to find ancient folders full of yellowed papers – legal letters between long-dead correspondents, concerning transactions dating back to the early 1920s. Some folders were tagged, but most were not. Adam was perplexed. There had to be some simple way of identifying the cabinet which contained the Accords.

His thoughts were interrupted by Mother Josephine. 'I'll leave you to it. I'll be in my office, if you should need me.'

'Just one moment. I noticed you examined only one of the rings I handed you. Would *one* have been enough?'

'Oh, yes. In fact, it wasn't necessary to produce a ring at all, but in that case you would have had to make a rough sketch of the scratch mark on the inside.'

'I see. Tell me, were you expecting me?'

Mother Josephine blinked. 'Should I have been?'

Drew wondered about that blink. He watched her eyes turn inwards. She was obviously wondering about something. And it was not at all difficult for Adam to guess what. 'Am I right in thinking Davis & Associates owns this building and you pay them a nominal rental through a firm of lawyers called Barton, Willis, Lord & Hooper?'

'Yes. In return, we look after these records for Davis's.'

'But there's another legal firm you deal with, isn't there? One that manages a company on behalf of a Protestant sect in the Midwest, which makes substantial contributions to your upkeep, in return for your carrying out a simple task?'

The Mother Superior hesitated.

'And you're also required to send an auditor periodically to check the law firm's accounts for that company?'

Mother Josephine gave a wary nod. 'Yes. It's called Harkness Ball Bearings, Incorporated.'

Adam smiled. 'It might interest you to know that Harkness Ball Bearings actually belongs to Davis & Associates.'

Mother Josephine studied his face, then nodded. 'Once a month, one of us has to go to the New York Public Library to check the classified ads in all the top British newspapers. Once a certain announcement appeared, we're supposed to count sixty days from the date of that newspaper, then open a sealed envelope and follow the instructions found inside.'

Drew waited for her to continue, then realised she was waiting for *him*. And almost at once he saw the reason. She was simply expecting him to give her the text of the advert.

He gave it and she turned on her heel, gesturing for him to follow.

Back in her office, she moved some books aside on a shelf, to expose an ancient safe with a combination lock. From this she extracted an envelope, and a moment later, she was reading the contents.

'This is a letter from Davis & Associates,' she remarked, obviously surprised that two tasks from two different firms, which she previously thought entirely independent, had now suddenly coalesced. 'On the sixtieth day after the appearance of the advertisement we are supposed to destroy all the papers in the files downstairs, except those marked with an *X* on the back, whose contents are to be published in the local newspapers, and by any other newspaper which subsequently asks to see them. But it confirms that these same instructions can be cancelled by anyone producing a ring or able to describe the scratch mark.'

Salvatore had stumped Adam again. It looked as if he would have to work his way through all sixty-odd filing cabinets.

He went back down into the basement and, guessing that Salvatore would have made the Accords as inaccessible as possible, started with the cabinets furthest from the door. In the bottom drawer of the third that he came to, there was a file tagged '*Williamson & Sons*'. In this he found a sealed foolscap envelope, labelled '*Company Prospectus*'. It was marked with an *X* on the back. He opened it and extracted seven pages: the originals of the Belvedere Accords, together with a list of access codes to the various funds held, in the name of S. Davis, by Hamblyn's Merchant Bank and the Bessmer Schweizerische Handelsbank, and a signed letter to each bank, instructing them to relinquish control over the funds to the bearer. The seventh page was a final message from Salvatore.

Well done, my friend. You have got here, and I add to my congratulations my deepest gratitude.

Is there anything more to say? There wasn't in 1943. I mean that this is not the letter I left for you then, but now I am more than thirty-three years older, and my doctors have diagnosed cancer. They say I shall be dead within three months and I have decided to write you a new letter. Exactly why, I'm not sure, for it can change nothing.

The world has become immensely more unpredictable since 1943 and, without having any specific motive for my unease, I think it is this which makes me suspect that one day your services will be called upon.

Was Belvedere a chimera? A manifestation of that same need for absolute and eternal security that made men devise the concept of Heaven, and still makes some of them strive to reach it?

And what do you, my champion, think of the world order Belvedere has helped to maintain?

In 1943 – as I'm sure you will have deduced from the questions I put to you in New York – I believed that much of life which is ugly is also necessary, e.g. excrement. I also believed that the weak, who must exist as long as there are non-weak, could in sufficient numbers swamp the strong. Nearly thirty-four years have gone by since then, and thus far I have been vindicated thoroughly. What might be the solution to the problem of the weak, I have no idea. But I now think I was wrong in not examining with you the other side of the coin: what to do about the strong.

This problem is more threatening still. For if the weak are the addicts of this world, then the strong are merely those who evolve to feed – in order to feed on – the weak: i.e. the pushers.

But they too must eat. And if deprived of one source of income, they will obviously turn to others. Such as theft, extortion, kidnapping, and murder. The most dangerous of them will be the most organised, as many pushers already are.

The logic seems ineluctable: if we make life easier for the hopeless, it will be the hopeful who will pay the price; whereas, if we leave the already condemned to be sucked dry, then their leeches, having an easy source of food, will leave the rest of us alone.

I don't have the answer. I only know that to me Belvedere was the least terrible solution.

For the moment at least, it seems the government still agrees. So I have some cause to hope . . .

. . . That you will never exist.
Your friend,
Salvatore.

Roosevelt's letter expounded the same argument in more explicit language. The key sentence read: '*The high price of narcotics derives from their being decreed illegal substances and the monopolistic nature of the sales networks, hence making their distribution an attractive proposition*

367

for the criminally minded, thus diverting them from other activities, likely to be more injurious to the wellbeing of the healthy majority'. The rest of the letter explained the decisions of the Roosevelt administration concerning the prosecution of the war in 1943.

The last clause of the Belvedere Accords was an undertaking by the United States government to maintain narcotics as prohibited substances, but to vigorously pursue those persons and organisations engaging in their distribution and sale, and also to use its influence in the world to persuade other governments to adopt the same policies. To this clause, in ignorance of its true purpose, Pope Pius XII and the future Pope Paul VI had been able to put their names as witnesses.

Drew returned to Mother Josephine's office, to take his leave. She eyed the foolscap envelope with interest, obviously dying to know what was in it. But the opportunity which these Protestant nuns had unknowingly had for more than half a century, to damage the Catholic Church and change the world, was now gone forever.

Adam thanked her and departed.

Cornwall and West Point became New York City without his even realising it. He returned the car to the rental agency, then strolled thoughtfully along the streets, wondering whether to change the world, or leave it as Salvatore had fashioned it.

An awesome responsibility.

Adam now saw that, from the very beginning, Salvatore had been forced along the only route open to him. Every fork in the road had offered a choice between a dead-end and, eventually, Belvedere. Consequently, he had lived the rest of his life fearful of having miscalculated. Afraid that, one day, up would stand some other arrogant meddler, who would arrest the leaders of the Families, legalise drugs, and usher in a new world order of harmony and peace.

And *that* was why Adam existed. Salvatore had needed not only an insurance poliby to guard against the unforeseeable – like the meddling of those two Sicilian reprobates – but also an agent able to reason with a man who could not be reasoned with. That was why so much money had been set aside for that day when Salvatore would need to find an Adam and equip him with enormous resources to save his family from the naive fanaticism of some new incompetent messiah.

Drew looked around and found himself in Park Avenue, near the Pan Am Building. He headed for Ferrandini's apartment. It was six o'clock when he walked in. He found Robert in the kitchen, making himself a snack.

'I think Diana's looking for you. Want some toast and pâté?'

Ferrandini's three sons came herding boisterously into the kitchen, following the smell of the toast, and arguing vociferously about a football game they had just been watching on television. They greeted Adam with goodnatured familiarity.

'Where've you been all day?' Robin wanted to know.

'Just sorting out something for your father,' replied Adam, smiling. He handed Robert the envelope, then went out to ask Diana if she would like some toast.

Epilogue

Diana Ferrandini and Adam Drew were married in St Patrick's Cathedral three months afterwards. Their first child, a son, was born eight months later. The Ferrandinis all wanted the boy to be given a typical Italian-American name, but Adam put his foot down. Already he felt that Salvatore had come to own him body and soul, sucking him into his family, into its life and its laws and traditions. Salvatore would not own Adam's son. The child was baptised Edmund Christian, after two mountaineers that Drew admired – Sir Edmund Hillary and Chris Bonington. The baptism, however, was Roman Catholic. Adam did not much mind, since he intended bringing up his son agnostic, anyway.

Their second child, a daughter, was named Sofia Barbara, after Diana's grandmother and mother respectively. The girl was born within a year of her brother, but by that time the parents were divorced. Diana remarried. Her new husband was a champion tennis player called Vincent Antonioni, originally from Rome, though his ancestry was Sicilian.

Adam, still haunted by his brother's death, was deeply affected by this new failure, and his resultant chronic depression obliged him to return to psychiatric treatment. He was concerned too about the future of his children. Edmund – known as Eddie – was spending time separately with each parent, but Drew found it increasingly hard to counter the influence of the Ferrandinis. His son was being brought up too much in a Sicilian-American environment, and being groomed as one of Robert Ferrandini's eventual heirs.

Two years after the divorce, Adam attempted a solo scaling of the North Face.

He did not return.

The Eiger had at last claimed Drew's debt – and his life.

Salvatore now claimed what remained of him.

Author's Note

Towards 2.00 pm on 20 July 1943, three American tanks arrived at Villalba. The crowds shouted: '*Viva l'America! Viva la Mafia! Viva Don Calò!*' Calogero Vizzini was rapidly elected mayor of Villalba and then made an honorary colonel by the US Military Governor of Sicily, Colonel Alfonso La Ponto. Vizzini was present at important meetings of the Allied High Command, concerning the future of Sicily. He apparently favoured the moderates, who sought a secession from Italy and a political union with either Britain or the United States.

On 16 September 1944, the left-wing Popular Front staged a public meeting in the town square of Villalba. Vizzini had granted permission beforehand to the socialist politician Girolamo Li Causi to address the meeting, but he had forbidden the subject of agrarian reform to be mentioned. When Li Causi disobeyed him, Vizzini's men began firing into the crowd. Li Causi and thirteen other people were wounded. The gunmen remained at liberty for fourteen years. They were then tried and found guilty, but all were subsequently released under a general amnesty.

Vizzini supported a bandit by the name of Salvatore Giuliano, who shared his patron's apparent political aims and even wrote letters to President Truman, urging him to annex Sicily as the forty-ninth state. On 1 May 1947, Giuliano and his men ambushed a communist parade near Portella della Ginestra, near Palermo. Eleven people, including women and children, were killed. Later realising that he could not control Giuliano, Vizzini arranged with the Italian Minister of the Interior, Mario Scelba, to have the bandit shot in his sleep.

In 1949, Don Calò and Lucky Luciano started a candy factory together. The candy was exported to many European countries, as well as to Canada and the US. In 1954, the socialist newspaper *Avanti!* published an article implying that the candy was laced with heroin. The factory closed down overnight. This was the only time that Vizzini and Luciano were ever linked in the press, though they were once photographed together at the Albergo del Sole in Palermo. The photographer was beaten up and his camera was smashed. After receiving a new camera and a cash sum, he withdrew charges.

Don Calò died on 10 July 1954, fourteen days before his seventy-seventh birthday. Ten thousand people attended his funeral. Vizzini's youngest brother Monsignor Giovanni, a bishop, had passed away in August 1952. The middle brother Salvatore, a priest, outlived Calogero by five years, expiring in November 1959. The remains of all three men now lie in the family vault in Villalba cemetery. On the side of Calogero's sarcophagus are the words: A Man and a Gentleman.

Today, the townsfolk of Villalba show decidedly mixed feelings when discussing Don Calogero Vizzini, but there is undoubtedly respect, probably admiration and possibly affection. It is generally accepted that, owing to his influence, western Sicily was spared most of the devastation suffered by the Italian mainland.

The voting system employed by the Italians has given Italy half a century of revolving-door governments, but the communists have never ruled there.

I would like to thank those who read the manuscript and made invaluable suggestions: my brother Russell, Ana Sánchez Rué, Jonathan Crown, Henry Sire, Paul Barber and his wife Alejandra, and especially Jacqueline Minett of the Universidad Autónoma de Barcelona (EUTI), who for many years encouraged me to continue writing. Thanks also to Claudia Fantl and my secretary Montse Forés who, between them, kept my life and business more or less under control while I wrote this book.

Special thanks are also due to my agent Sarah Molloy of AM Heath, for her wise counsel and astute representation, and to my editor Peter Lavery of Hodder Headline, for helping to polish every page of this book and vigilantly shepherding every stray participle back to its fold.

Thanks finally to those who helped me in my research for this novel: Mr S. Skrekas in New York; Bohumil Švarc, Managing Director of the Tschechische Elbe-Schiffahrts-A.G. in Děčín, Czechia; Marian Fabuš and Attile Marosi in Košice, Slovakia; Daniel Ruhier of the Federal Office for Civil Aviation in Bern, Switzerland; Professor Bernard Knight of the Wales Institute of Forensic Medicine, Cardiff Royal Infirmary; Mrs G. Williams of Radyr School, Cardiff; Mark Berrisford and Norman Carter, both mountaineers, of Up & Under, Cardiff; Keith Bradford of Pains-Wessex Ltd, Salisbury. And in Sicily: 'Davide' of Enna Bassa; Rosario Immordino and Rosario Alessi of Villalba; Signor Dentici of Palermo. I am also grateful to two other gentlemen, one from New York and the other from Palermo, who have asked not to be named.